DRAGON'S HEIR

Book 2 of the Blood of the Covenants Series

Leah E. Welker

LIGHTBOUND MEDIA

Library of Congress Control Number: 2024940469

Print ISBN: 9781964174044

Ebook ISBN: 9781964174037

First Edition

CONTENTS

Key Terms & Translations	IX
The Six Realms	XI
Prologue	1
1. Talk	7
2. Thinking	23
3. Secrets	37
4. Weapon	51
5. Power	76
6. Stars	101
7. Darkness	114
8. Angel	125
9. Niceties	136
10. Even	153
11. Queen	177
12. Duty	192
13. Date	207
14. Gone	210
15. Shots	213

16. Senses   216

17. Reach   221

18. Mad   231

19. Idiots   235

20. Sleep   252

21. Awake   258

22. Buzz   267

23. Monster   274

24. Pull   286

25. RSVP   298

26. Won   312

27. Push   332

28. Questions   348

29. Look   358

30. Plans   373

31. Parting   385

32. Dream   403

33. Star   426

34. Trust   435

35. Steam   447

36. Appearances   454

37. Want   464

38. Jinx   471

39. Moondaughter   478

Epilogue   490

About the Author   493

To my siblings—Tia, Mark, and Jenessa—for a lifetime of love, laughter, adventure, and friendship. You will always have a place in my dreams.

Had I the heavens' embroidered cloths,

Enwrought with golden and silver light,

The blue and the dim and the dark cloths

Of night and light and the half light,

I would spread the cloths under your feet:

But I, being poor, have only my dreams;

I have spread my dreams under your feet;

Tread softly because you tread on my dreams.

William Butler Yeats

KEY TERMS & TRANSLATIONS

Races

draká ("druh-KAH"): the original "dragons."

amá ("ah-MAH"): human(s); the sentient inhabitants of Earth.

dramá ("druh-MAH"): the race that emerged from the combination of draká and humans.

Blood Manifestations

drakón ("drah-KOHN"): dramá chosen to have far greater magic and gain a drakáform.

amón ("ah-MOHN"): dramá who are not chosen, yet still have the Blood of the Covenants and cannot accurately be called "human."

Distances

Rough equivalents

ild: inch.

foot: literal translation.

erd: yard (only a couple dramá feet).

ald: 100 dramá feet.

eld: half an English Imperial mile.

elden: an English Imperial mile.

Time

dek: Roughly 1 minute, made of 56 moments.

deken: Roughly 1 hour, made of 56 dek.

day: 28 deken.

THE SIX REALMS

Sun	Planet	Capital	Clan	Color	Specialty
Kaldrir	Ythra	Crownhold	Sunfilled	Gold	Central governance, priesthood, guarding Tree, maintaining sungates
Kyalid	Ekrel	Krevenyir	Battleblood	Violet	Battle, smithing, exploring, peacekeeping
Ashga	Oshal	Rosin	Starkissed	Sapphire	Magic, scholarship, diplomacy, artistry
Olmen	Romskal	Palla	Strongshield	Scarlet	Civil service, law, administration
Winalken	Yonvey	Remik	Brightflare	Orange	Tinkering, financing, mining, farming
Yedrik	Ykran	Danyeth	Peacegrowth	Emerald	Healing, farming, conserving

PROLOGUE

IN THE BEGINNING WERE the Creators.

Most all we know about Them, those highest of all beings, are encapsulated in that very title: *Creator*. They are the omnipotent, immortal beings that form the stars and worlds of the cosmos, and when They are done forming the suns and planets of a system, They create life itself.

The first life They create in each world is that world's Tree. For it is the Tree that protects a world from the darker powers that prowl around the outskirts of the light, ever searching for a way to defy the Creators' purposes. A Tree forms an invisible, intangible barrier around Her world that almost entirely shuts the dark ones out.

Once the Tree is planted and grows powerful enough to form that shield, the Creators make all the other forms of life, from the kind too small to see to the kind too vast to comprehend. Once the world is flooded with such life, and all is set into balance, then, and only then, do the Creators form the Tree's children.

Each Tree is given one sapient race to tend and guard from the dark ones that would destroy them. Thus, She is the race's Mother in spirit, even if not in flesh.

Like any mother, however, She can only guide. She cannot coerce—for choice, by the Creators' decree, is sacred. Her children are free to choose to ignore, abandon, or even weaken Her...and Her protections around their world. The greater heed Her children pay to Her wisdom, the more power She has to protect them, the more they prosper; the less heed they pay to Her, the less power She has, the more Her children suffer from their own foolishness, and the more the dark ones slip in and take hold.

Sadly, this happened to the race that first inhabited Ythra, the mother world of our Six Realms. The draká, whom you would know as *dragons*, were the Tree of Flame's first children, and from the scant records they left, we believe they lasted for millennia, waxing and waning in their faithfulness to the Tree, as all civilizations do.

Finally, a thousand years ago, their greed and pride became so severe that they nearly annihilated themselves through famine and war. Then, as their Tree's power to protect them flagged, a dark one struck.

The Devourer of that time was an immense, dark spirit of terrible power with a never-ending hunger for all that lives. By then, it had amassed a mighty army from the dregs of its other conquests, for if the Devourer managed to at least partially consume the spirit of a living being, that life became its slave, what we call a "consumed."

Long had the Devourer slavered after a race so large and full of power as the draká were, with whom it could conquer worlds without number and on whom it could gorge for eons. Long had it watched and waited for its opportunity, and long had the Tree of Flame warned Her children of its plans, but to no avail. The Devourer launched the First Invasion at the draká's greatest moment of self-inflicted weakness, easily tearing its darkrifts through the Tree's thinned barrier across Ythra.

It is a miracle the draká even survived. Even then, it was only at great cost. To belatedly bolster the Tree's waned power brought on by their own neglect, many draká had to give their blood and very lives to the Tree. With that freely offered sacrifice, the Tree strengthened enough to close the Devourer's gates and allow the draká to disperse the Devourer's forces now trapped in their world.

Once a dark one invades, however, it is no simple thing to keep it out. In this case, the Devourer's consumed armies scattered and hid themselves. Some broke free of its control, but some generations still slavishly serve it to this day and do its bidding to erode our safety and prosperity.

The draká of that time were in especially perilous straits. Famine, war, and then invasion had brought them nearly to extinction. Battered, bloodied, and starving, the draká finally turned as one to the Tree of Flame and asked Her how they were to survive.

She told them: they would have to change, and to change, they would need the help of another Tree's children. To reach those children, they would need gates of their own—gates of the Creators' original design, fueled by the Tree Herself.

To be worthy of such gates, the draká swore the First Covenant. The terms:

1. To guard the gates as they guard the Tree.

2. To only use the gates to go where the Tree permits.

3. To never claim a world with another Tree's children as their own.

4. To never take whatever belongs to another Tree's children by force, only by trade or gift.

When all draká who remained swore the First Covenant, the Tree revealed to them how to construct a sungate. So, at great sacrifice, they did.

One thing you must understand about the draká is that they were magical by nature—there would have been no other way for such large and remarkable creatures to exist except if magic were in their very blood. However, their magic could go no further than that; all the power they had went into maintaining their very lives. So it is with our drakón when they enter their drakáforms to this very day; even our King, the most powerful drakón among us, can barely light a candle while he is in his drakáform.

The Tree could give some of the power to the blaze that first sungate required, but the draká still had to give the first spark, and that spark required the sacrifice of yet more lives, even if it was to power the gate for only a few seconds. The moment the gate was alight, the Tree's chosen Seven rushed through...and set foot on Earth.

Yes, Earthren, this was when dragons first came to your world. For your people were the ones the draká needed—the children of Ice.

Tragically, your people had long since abandoned and entirely forgotten your Tree, the Tree of Ice. Even when the Seven found a clan of humans willing to listen to and then help them, the group had to follow the visions of their wisewoman and rely on the dogged determination and ingenuity of their chief to find the Tree in the frozen wastes of the place you call Greenland.

Yet find Her they did, and before Her, seven humans and the Seven draká swore the Second Covenant. The exact terms and wording, we do not know. Only that all fourteen of them became new creatures, a new race entirely—the dramá. The word itself reflects the merging of two races into one, combining *draká* with the Drona word for human, *amá*.

Moreover, all fourteen were granted the Blood manifestation of drakón, and thus were able to be in amá- or drakáform at will, so long as they had enough power to maintain the latter form. But now, in amáform ("humanform," if you will), all the magic of a draká's body condensed into a smaller, more efficient form, leaving an unprecedented excess. For the very first time for both races, they were capable of *wielding* power.

No lives had to be sacrificed to power the gate to return to Ythra. The Fourteen were able to light it with no harm to any of them, and they and the rest of the human tribe who had agreed to come to the new world went through.

When they arrived, a new order began on Ythra, with the Covenants as their foundation and the Tree as their guide. The original Seven draká and the seven humans who changed with them became the founders of our seven clans, and the formerly human chief was appointed the first Sunfilled Monarch, with the draká who swore with him as his Heir. Thus both races were represented within the Golden Crown, and a new era of hope and increasing prosperity dawned.

Not all ran smoothly with the two races' integration, however. Only a few generations later, amón—dramá with only an amáform (whom you might consider "human," though they have the Blood of the Covenants, even as latent as it is)—outnumbered drakón. Yet drakón, being more physically and magically powerful, did not equally share their power and privileges with the amón as the

Tree commanded, beginning to think themselves inherently superior, destined to not just be their people's protectors but also rulers.

The dramá became divided, and the drakón increasingly arrogant and abusive toward the amón, ignoring the Tree's warnings and commands. Finally, the Tree declared that the Moontouched—the clan with the most amón and thus considered the least of the clans—would be the next clan to receive a Realm of their own. When the Brightflare Clan hotly protested, the Queen sided with the Brightflare, citing the need for peace.

Then, at that delicate juncture, the Lord of the Moontouched Clan died and the other clans rejected his amón Heir. When she came to Crownhold to contest her claim, she was assassinated by an unknown hand.

Enraged and afraid, the Moontouched Clan as one petitioned the Tree of Flame to allow them to leave the other six clans and return to Earth, the only remaining place where they thought they could belong. Before the other clans could react, the Tree granted their request, and the Moontouched left.

Then, at their second, secret request, the Tree shattered the sungate that connected Ythra to Earth, allowing the Moontouched to fully sever themselves from the other six and shattering the bedrock order established by the First and Second Covenants.

Mournful and repentant, the dramá changed their ways once more, putting in safeguards to protect and elevate amón to their equitable place. Even so, their actions were too late to reclaim the Moontouched, whom they thought lost to them forever. Thus the Seven Clans became the Six Clans, and what should have been the Seven Realms became the Six Realms, and appeared as if they would always be so.

Little did the common dramá realize that the Covenants, the very foundation of their magic and thus existence, had been torn asunder and unraveled more with every passing century. Only the people's and Monarchs' increasing faithfulness to the Tree shored up that magical reserve enough to prevent an entire collapse.

Then the day of our redemption dawned, in the most seemingly unremarkable of ways: a young Earthren woman, Sarah Lind, an unknowing descendant of the Moontouched Clan, fell through a frozen creek near her home on Earth and into the "least" and "last" of the Six Realms: Ykran, Realm of the Peace-growth Clan.

There, the Golden Heir, Koriben Sunfilled, found her. Together, along with Koriben's rightwing bodyguard, Yvera Battleblood, and leftwing adviser, Ko-rinth Starkissed, they began their urgent quest of finding Sarah's way home and restoring the Covenants.

Near where Sarah first emerged, they discovered a new kind of gate, a moon-gate, and went through it to find an abandoned mountain hold—not on Earth, nor any of the Six Realms, but on a new world entirely.

There, Sarah and Koriben received a message from the Tree of Ice that the new world was to be given to the Moontouched Clan as the Seventh Realm, and Sarah was the Tree's chosen leader to restore that very clan. Sarah and Koriben were instructed to find the five other moongates hidden in the five other Realms, and then the Trees of Ice and Flame would reveal the final gate that would lead to Earth, where the Tree of Ice waited to invest Sarah with the power Sarah would need to help the dramá in their darkest hour. For the Tree of Ice warned them that on the Winter Solstice, the Devourer would invade again, this time striking straight at the heart of the Realms: the Tree of Flame.

Which meant Sarah and Koriben had only ten days to find the gates, restore the Covenants, and save us all.

In my opinion, it is then that their story *truly* begins.

Chapter One

TALK

Sarah

As I sat in my newly gifted kitchen and faced the two drakón who were glaring at me, I did my best to stave off a headache.

It had long ago begun pounding in between my eyes and didn't feel like it would let up soon; at least the warm mug of tea in one hand had taken off the worst of it, the steam and the tea's mildly spiced flavor helping clear my sinuses. The healing Ben had given me earlier that day to drive off my previous headache felt like a lifetime ago.

I glanced at Kor, thinking to address the more reasonable of the pair. Surely he understood I was only the messenger in this tense situation.

Ben's leftwing (meaning his primary adviser, diplomat, and spy) was sitting across from me, his brown, aristocratic face twisted with a scowl. His dark sapphire eyes—the color of which perfectly matched his short, luxurious, perfectly styled curls—were unusually hard, their normal charismatic, mischievous glint gone to reveal the cunning core I was coming to learn always rested just below the surface.

"I told you," I said to him, scowling in return. A few days ago, I would have never been so bold. Now, I was simply too darn *tired* to be shy. "I've told you every *single* word the Tree told me. In order. Do you know how ridiculous it is that I can even *remember* every single word?"

"Of course you do," Yvera snapped.

As a proper rightwing and bodyguard to Ben, she was perhaps the most fearsome young woman I'd ever met. She must have been over six and a half feet tall, with a warrior's body, high cheekbones, perfect eyebrows marred only by a single scar, olive skin, and violet eyes and hair, the kinky strands currently tightly bound in her usual long, thick braid.

Yvera wasn't the most patient of souls normally, but ever since I'd said the word "Devourer," she hadn't been able to stay still, and she was currently doing her best to wear a track into the stone floor of my kitchen.

My floor, I thought with wry amusement. *My kitchen.*

Would wonders never cease. But then, this one had already done wonders for my heart. I hadn't realized how soul weary I'd become from the constant moving on Earth. How listless, how powerless I'd felt, like driftwood at the mercy of the sea. I loved my parents and knew they loved me; yet the work that they had chosen had taken a toll I hadn't yet been able to put into words to them. Not until I'd been given a home, all my own. One that no one was going to take from me—not if it had been made for me a thousand years ago and then declared to be mine today by the closest thing to a deity that I would probably ever encounter.

No matter what I chose. Whether or not I took up the mantle of Moon-touched leader in the end, this would be my home.

That unconditional gift...meant everything; it gave me a surge of something that I was only just beginning to put a name to. I'd been flexing that new muscle a lot since Yvera and Kor began badgering me with questions as soon as Ben left to go warn his father, the King, of everything the Tree of Ice had just told us.

Since I'd been weak from opening the moongate for Ben, Kor had held me in his arms as Ben went through. But as soon as the doors were closed, I'd ordered Kor to put me down without taking no for an answer, had marched into the kitchen—*my* kitchen—and had flatly refused to start talking until I was done fumbling around trying to figure out how to make myself tea—or tsha, or whatever they called it here. Only when I'd sat down with my mug and the wings had sat down with me like civilized people did I tell them everything.

Of course, as I'd said, the sitting part didn't last very long for Yvera, but I understood, so I didn't make her stay still after that.

When I looked at Kor for an explanation for her latest outburst, Kor said, "The Tree's words leave an impression. Or so I'm told."

"You've heard Her speak, Kor," Yvera growled. "Same as everybody else."

"Yet it's supposedly different for Heirs." Kor looked back at me and smirked. "And Monarchs."

As usual, having no clue what his subtext meant, I ignored it. "Anyway. Like I said, I have told you absolutely everything. There's no point in interrogating me when I'm pretty sure both of you know far more about what's going on right now than I do."

"We shouldn't just be sitting here," Yvera shot at Kor. "Only ten days.... Hellfrost, we shouldn't even be *here*. I need to be with my wings, part of the planning, the preparations—"

"Whoa, whoa," I said, holding up my hands. "Hold up. You have wings? I thought you *were*—"

"As we are wings to Ben, to aid him in whatever he requires, we have wings to aid us," Kor said, drumming his fingers on the table. Other than his rapid-fire questions, that was the main indicator he might be just as agitated as Yvera right now. "Who do you think has been handling our stewardships at Crownhold while we've been tearing across the outskirts of the Six Realms with Ben?"

I gave him a look. "I honestly have barely even had a moment to breathe since I got to your Six Realms, let alone to ponder the complexities of how it all runs."

"Shame, that," Kor said with a sigh. "If only *I'd* been left in charge of your introduction to society."

"Torch it, Kor," Yvera said, marching over to him to brace her hands on the table and shove her face in his. "I need—"

"Ben's orders were clear, Yv," Kor snapped, eyes taking on a literal glow. "There's a sequence to these things that you should well know. First the King must be informed, and that's precisely what Ben has gone to do. Since we have the luxury of waiting for the King's command on how to proceed, wait we must. We do the Realms no favors by throwing them into chaos."

That's why Ben left Kor in charge, I thought wryly. Because even though Kor hated this period of inaction as much as Yvera did, he could think about the big picture.

For a moment, I thought Yvera was going to strangle him, and the dangerous light in Kor's eyes dared her to try.

"Kor, Yv," I began uneasily.

Yvera stilled, hardness fading from her expression as she cocked her head, as if hearing something. She shoved away from the table with a brusque, "It's Ben," before striding out of the kitchen and into the bedroom area.

I was baffled at the direction she was heading and rose.

"Sit," Kor ordered wearily. "She's going to want him all to herself for a bit. Blessed Flame, at least Ben kept some of his sense and didn't call *me.*"

He put his head in his hands and bunched his fingers in his hair.

"Oh," I realized, feeling rather stupid. "He's calling her."

My heart sunk in disappointment, for more than just the fact that Ben wasn't on his way yet.

To distract myself, I asked, "How does that work, exactly? The calling."

Kor glanced up at me in surprise. "Ben didn't show you? When you talked to Svyer?"

"The call was already going when I came in. I still don't even know what he was using."

Absently, Kor pulled a roundish, sapphire blue object out of thin air with a flick of his wrist and set it between us. It wasn't precisely the same shape as the golden one Ben had had, having a bit more of a flattish edge on one side, and it was smaller. "Something like that. That's my call scale. Or...one of them, anyway."

I looked down at the smooth, convex tear-drop shape about the size of my hand. "That's a *scale*? One of *your* scales?"

Kor smirked as he propped his chin on his fist. "I *am* drakón, after all."

Somehow, I kept forgetting that fact. They were obviously different from me in size, coloring, and power, but somehow my mind kept skipping over the reality that at any moment, these drakón could turn into creatures with a size and lethality that could give the megalodon nightmares.

Especially Ben.

"But how...?"

"If you're thinking we just tear one of them off whenever we have need of one—no, absolutely not." He shuddered. "That would be painful and needless. Because we naturally shed scales, like skin. The trickier part is figuring out what to *do* with all of them. It's a terrible risk to leave them lying around; if a consumed—or, Flame forbid, one of *us* with ill intent—got ahold of one of them, and had enough power and knowledge, there are nasty things they could do to or through that drakón."

That reminded me of some things he and the others had said. "Like you said the consumed could do if they had my blood."

"Like, but not as bad. On the list of bits of a person that have the most potential for magical use—good *or* ill—blood ranks the highest." He gave me a look. "If I get into why right now, we'll be here a few deken more."

"That's fine," I said quickly. "Where do scales rank?"

"For a drakón, high, but still not as high as blood and claws." Kor shuddered again. "We don't shed claws like scales. They don't even grow out like fingernails do. They're more like teeth in that respect. Losing one is...not a good thing."

"Do they grow back?" I asked tentatively.

Kor looked down, lips pressed into a thin line. "Not...easily."

Figuring we had better leave it at that, I touched his scale. In the back of my mind, I marveled at its smoothness and richness of color, like beautifully polished and glazed pottery. "So you try to make sure no one gets your scales. Then what *do* you do with them?"

Kor waved dismissively. "Throw them in our hoard, usually."

Misunderstanding my stare, Kor explained quickly, "'Hoard' is a casual term we use for our ether stores—that nowhere-place unique to each drakón where we keep our things. By now, I probably have a stack of my unaltered scales as big as my drakáform is."

Dragon hoard—check, I thought in wry amusement. *Full of piles of valuables, castoffs, and junk—check.*

In Ben's case (assuming he had a similar stash), the pile of scales would even be gold. In color, at least.

And to his enemies, perhaps just as valuable as the metal. I shuddered a bit at that thought.

"But clearly you use them for other things sometimes." I tapped the scale. "You said this was your 'call' scale."

"One of them," Kor reminded me, holding up a finger. "One of the best uses we've discovered for our shed scales is for calling. First, we magically pair two scales from the same draká together. Second, we enchant them with the calling spell—which, conveniently, makes them useless for any other magical purpose. Scales, blood, and whatnot can only take one spell, then they're done, so if you want to do another spell, you need more scales or blood."

"That's one protection against misuse, I guess," I mused.

Kor nodded. "Especially since the third step is to give a person one scale and keep the other for yourself. When someone activates a scale that's paired with one in your possession, you feel something inside letting you know."

"What's that like?" I asked, fascinated.

Kor pursed his lips in thought. "It's...a bit like hearing their voice calling your name, except without words."

"Oh!" I felt a bit relieved, my petty jealousy swept away. "That's what Ben did just now. He had one of Yvera's scales, and when he used his of the pair...."

"Yvera 'heard' him calling her and went somewhere to speak with him on her scale of the pair," Kor finished, nodding.

"You need a new set of scales for *each* person you want to be able to contact you?"

"Precisely," Kor said with a wry smile. He tapped the scale. "As I said, this is just *one* of my call scales. Mine of the set that Ben shares, actually. Technically, though, I can either use my own scale of the set to call Ben, or I can use the scale Ben has given me of his own. So only one set of scales is necessary for the two of us to call each other. We wouldn't even have to use *our* scales; as long as each of us had one of a paired set that came from a single drakón...."

I grimaced. "That still would make for carrying around...a lot of scales."

I imagined carrying around a cellphone for each person in my contacts. That...simply would not work.

As if echoing my thoughts, Kor said, "Yes, it sounds cumbersome, doesn't it? The only reason it works is because we drakón can 'carry' whatever we like with us, and because in feeling the call, most of us can instinctively follow the feeling to pull out the scale we need."

He paused, musing. "It's like...standing in the middle of dozens of threads, all tied to you and going out of sight into the ether. Even if you can't remember which tie goes where, when you feel the tug of one, you know—because of the tug—which one to tug back. If *we* need to do the tugging, it's usually enough to just think of the person we wish to speak to in order to pull out their scale."

The complexity puzzled me a bit, but clearly the system worked well enough for them, so I had to admire it. The fact that it could work across the galaxy was a feat humanity was nowhere close to matching; I imagined there were quite a few scientists who would put up with greater complexity and inconvenience than that to be able to do the same.

"So, Ben *couldn't* have called...me, for example," I said as casually as I could. "Since I don't have one of his scales."

Kor's eyes met mine again, and they sparkled in a way that told me he suspected more than I wanted him to. "Indeed. Even if he wished to. Trust me, he'd much rather be speaking to *you* right now than hammering discretion into his rightwing's head."

I glanced down at the table, tracing the smooth stone with my finger. "Only because I'd be easier to deal with."

"True, but that wouldn't be the only reason," Kor said enigmatically. Perhaps having mercy on me, his tone changed to dry. "As I said, it's all for the better that Ben called Yvera. That way, she doesn't feel miffed *and* can yell at Ben instead of me."

He gave a long-suffering sigh. I noticed, though, that he seemed more relaxed than before. Perhaps I had distracted him just as well as he had distracted me.

"You're a good teacher," I said, before I could think better of it.

His startled blink made the risk of inflating his ego worth it. "Excuse me?"

I kept my tone level. "I mean, you're brilliant, and that's a simple fact. You know more than I'll ever know about…anything related to the dramá and the Six Realms. And yet, as long as you're focused on making sure I understand, you don't make things complicated. You didn't go over my head with the detail or jargon that I know is in yours. You broke it all down for me very well."

I'd expected him to smirk, make some droll comment asking me to go on. I'd expected the usual: vanity, ego, flirtation.

Instead, his face became serious, and his eyes were sad as he looked away. I tried not to stare as I wondered if I had ever seen that combination on him. For a moment, one fleeting moment, he seemed like a different person.

"Kor, I don't know what I said—"

"No harm done," he said with a wave. But still he wouldn't look back at me, and instead kept his gaze on some distant corner of the kitchen. "You just reminded me…I used to enjoy teaching. Not dealing with hatchlings, of course. Never had the patience for littles."

He snorted, and I laughed.

He sobered and poured himself some of my tea, even though it must have been cool by now. "But thinking, intelligent adults, the kind who could appreciate the thrill of discovery at the edge of the unknown, as I did…. I was intending to become a professor, you know. When Ben asked me to be his leftwing."

"I didn't know," I said quietly.

"Well, now you do," Kor said brusquely, and drank what must have been half his cup in one go. Then held it up to eye level with a grimace. Then looked at me. "Don't suppose you'd let me get into…."

I smiled apologetically. "I don't think it's the time for wine, Kor."

"It's always the time for wine," he muttered, but he threw back the rest of the tea and slammed the cup back on the table with a quiet gag. "Don't know how Ben stands the stuff. It's his mother's influence, obviously, but still…."

"Of course it is," I said with a sigh.

Kor raised an eyebrow. "Ben's spoken to you about his mother?"

"Just a little, here and there."

"About what?" Kor demanded, leaning in.

Surprised into telling him, especially since I thought nothing of it, I said honestly, "About how she prepared him to be the Heir by teaching him to make his own bed. About cooking, singing. He sang one of the songs she taught him. He has a nice voice—"

At Kor's stare, I felt heat rising to my cheeks. "What?"

"Ben never talks about his mother," Kor said flatly. "Ever. Her death is one of the most defining aspects of his adulthood; really, it's the moment he stopped being a child, even at fourteen. And he torched well won't talk about it with *anyone*. It's just festered like a disease inside him that I can't rid him of, as much as it's holding him back. And here, after not even three days of knowing you, he's not only bringing her up, he's...*singing*."

He rose and started pacing. But unlike Yvera's impatient movement, his pacing seemed excited, his eyes bright and expression intense.

"Kor?" I said uneasily.

"Sarah, you have no idea how happy you've made me today," Kor said with fierce satisfaction. I was almost surprised he wasn't rubbing his hands together with melodramatic glee.

I narrowed my eyes at him. "You said that to me once before. After you tricked me into touching the doorgem."

He waved a hand. "Yes, yes, that's related, but also different. That was about your potential, your suitability, independent of anything else. *This* is directly about Ben."

"Directly?" I demanded. "So the other was indirect—"

"Sarah!" Yvera's voice echoed out from the bedroom...area. Sounding none too pleased about having to say my name.

Making a mental note to come up with a name for my hold's sleeping area (*Dormitory? But that makes it sound like a school.*), I pushed up from the table.

"Better go see what she wants," Kor agreed, since he'd paused in his pacing to look warily in that direction as well. "Judging from her tone, I'd guess Ben wants to talk to you next."

My heart jumped, giving me the bit of courage I needed to face Yvera. I tried to play casual, though, by giving a reluctant sigh. "I suppose."

I paused at the exit from the kitchen and looked back.

"Kor?"

"Yes?" he said absently. He hadn't resumed pacing, but his eyes were bright and distant at the same time—full of enigmatic plotting, no doubt.

"What did you want to teach? If you don't mind me asking?"

He was startled out of his reverie into looking at me. That same sadness flitted through his eyes for a moment before he closed it off and shrugged, as if it hardly mattered now. Which made me certain that it did.

"Magical history, with an emphasis on the origin of the Covenants, believe it or not. Perhaps it was one of the reasons Ben chose me. He could have had no idea at the time, of course, but...the Tree is patient in how She plants Her seeds, not caring if it takes years before they come to fruition. It's one of the things I admire—and distrust—most about Her."

"Both?"

His eyes met mine directly and burned for a moment. "Both, with Her. Always both."

He smirked, some of the Kor I knew coming back. "It may surprise you, but I have difficulty trusting in anything but my own brilliance."

I rolled my eyes, and he laughed.

"SARAH LIND!"

I'm surprised she even remembers the last name, I thought dryly—and was contrarily touched. Yvera paid more attention than she let on.

"That's your final warning," Kor said, nodding his head toward her voice. "You won't like what comes next, trust me."

"I'm going! Just...." I bit my lip, then took the plunge. I seemed to be doing that a lot more lately. "I don't think you should give up the hope of teaching just yet. Who knows? If we survive the next ten days, you might just have the time."

Then, before he could react, I darted out of the kitchen and went to face down a purple dragon to talk to a prince.

I was so intent on my quest, it didn't occur to me to wonder how Kor had known his area of focus was of use to Ben now—when he wasn't supposed to know about the broken Covenants at all.

THE DRAGON ORDEAL WASN'T as bad as I'd feared. All I had to do was walk up to Yvera's room, where she stood in the doorway, still speaking with Ben.

"Yes, yes," she was saying impatiently. "Same to you. Keep some of the elites with you tonight. No, Ben, I'm serious about this. I'm going to call and send some of them over if you don't swear to me now. And it won't be the ones you like."

My heart sunk at the sign that Ben wouldn't be returning immediately, but I immediately scolded myself. I had no idea how exhausting interstellar travel was, especially the way he'd done it, being far from any of these sungates they kept fussing about.

It was a good thing that he was taking some time to rest before coming back. It was a good thing.

I was repeating that to myself when Yvera caught sight of me. She only glanced briefly and then looked back down at the scale she held in her hand. "The girl's here. Time to swear."

"Gah, fine." I faintly heard Ben's voice from this distance. "I'll ask Ordran to stay over. Will that satisfy you?"

"Good choice," Yvera said, and her lips pulled into something approaching a smile. "You haven't caught up with him in a while."

Oh, good. A male, I thought. Then tried very hard to pretend I hadn't thought it.

"We still won't, since I'll probably be asleep by the time he arrives," Ben said wearily. "Just hand me to Sarah, will you?"

"Fine," Yvera snapped, her temper abruptly souring again as she shoved the scale at me. "I've got other calls to make now, anyway."

Though she didn't quite *slam* her door in my face, she closed it as quickly as was possible without making a sound.

"Well...." I said awkwardly, looking down at the image of Ben sitting in my hands.

Ben sighed. His elbows were propped on whatever desk he was sitting at, making it convenient for him to run his hands over his face and hair just then. I tried not to ogle at how attractive that made his tussled, shoulder-length golden hair look. I focused on the exhaustion written as plain as day on his face.

"Ben," I said gently as I walked to my room. "You should be getting that rest, not talking to me."

He laughed tiredly. "I wanted to tell you myself that I wasn't coming back tonight, but apparently you've gathered that already."

"I have," I said, and paused in my doorway. Though it pained me more than it had any right to, I said, "Message delivered, and I understand why. You need rest. So, end this call to get it."

"I can't, not yet," Ben moaned, closing his golden eyes for a moment as he leaned back in his chair. "After you is Kor, and he's sure to have his own questions."

"Keep it short with him, then," I said sternly. "He can wait until morning for details."

Ben laughed again, shaking his head.

"What?"

"Nothing. It's just, you sounded so much like Avva. He said the same thing."

"Well, your father is obviously a wise person. You should listen to him."

"I will, don't worry. I'll satisfy Kor with the essentials—which are passing along Avva's orders for how he's to proceed—and then I'll end the call. Probably by simply falling asleep at my desk."

"Is that your room? In your home?" I asked curiously, looking to the side of him.

His pale skin went red, and he plucked his scale off the wall to ruin the perspective before I could get a good look. "What? Oh. Yes. Er. It's a bit messy now, so...nothing to see here."

I burst out laughing. "You're acting like it's a crime scene."

"A what?" he asked, his face scrunching in confusion.

"The place where a crime has taken place. You know, like a robbery or a murder."

"Oh, I see." Ben smiled wryly. "Well, I haven't killed anyone...today."

We both sobered at the poor joke. For the first time, I felt the chill realization that he must have, at some point. How could he have avoided it? It would have been someone bad, or some consumed monster, but his people were at war against the consumed for their very survival, and it was his job to protect them.

So, yes, Ben must have killed before.

That should have frightened me, even more than the fact that he could turn into a behemoth at will. Yet...it didn't. Because this was still Ben.

"Anyway," he said quickly, "you're just going to have to take my word for it that there is *no* body lying on my floor, because there is no way I am showing anyone my bedroom in this state, much less you."

My heart fluttered at that seemingly unconscious emphasis on me, but I didn't follow up on it. Not tonight, when he was so tired. "I honestly wouldn't judge, Ben."

"Nope," he said stubbornly, sticking out his jaw. He had such a good one; not even his short beard hid that....

I rolled my eyes to hide my real thoughts. "Your friend is going to see it anyway, isn't he?"

Ben winced, looking behind his shoulder. "Oh, that's right...."

I wagged a finger at him. "Don't you dare start cleaning before he arrives."

He looked guiltily back at me. "How did you know.... Never mind."

He just laughed, shaking his head. "Anyway, I didn't mean to talk about my room, or Kor, or the dozens of things I have going on right now. This was supposed to be about you."

"Me?" I asked in surprise.

"Yes, you," Ben said, shaking his head. His expression softened. "How are you doing, Sarah? You just.... Well, you just talked to your Tree for the first time. And, on top of all the things She told you and asked you to do, you saw your world swallowed by shadow."

I sat down at my desk abruptly as it all hit. I hid the sting in my eyes and the tremble in my fingers by fiddling around to hang Yvera's scale in the brackets on the wall. When I finally had that set, I sat back, folding my hands to hopefully still the trembling.

I swallowed the hard lump in my throat and said quietly, "You saw yours do it too."

His golden eyes were too piercing. "That's how I know some of what you must feel."

That mattered. Dang it, but that mattered. So much.

I put my head in my hands, the tears spilling over.

"Agh, Sarah," Ben groaned. "See, this is exactly why I argued with Avva that I should come straight back."

How I wanted those strong, warm arms of his around me right then. At least my heart warmed to hear he'd argued with his father, whom he seemed to deeply respect, for my sake. Even though he was wrong in this case.

"No, Ben," I said, looking up and taking a deep breath. "I'm fine, really. The full shock of it only just hit, I think. Even now, it still feels too...unreal to really sink in. You know far better than I do what...all of this means. I just have the barest idea. For tonight...it can stay that way. Right?"

I hadn't meant to end on a plea, but I did.

"Of course it can," Ben said firmly. "For tonight, that's enough."

I let out a breath. "Then...then I'm fine, for tonight. Just exhausted, mostly. Which I know you can relate to as well."

He chuckled. "That I can."

"Besides, all the bad stuff we saw? It's not going to happen. It simply won't. That was just to warn us. We're going to do this, Ben. We're going to stop it from ever happening."

He smiled slightly, but his eyes were pained. "You're right. It *won't* happen, to any of our worlds. I swear it."

"Thank you," I whispered.

I didn't like the heaviness that lingered in his eyes, so I thought of something that might cheer him up. "Oh! I made tea—I mean, tsha."

"You didn't!" he said with a startled laugh.

I grinned. "I did. Aren't you proud of me? It took me a bit to figure the teapot out—had to have Kor tell me you were supposed to put the leaves in, that the spout had a filter to keep the leaves from pouring into the cup. I'm used to tea coming in bags, you know? You heat the hot water—just the water—and put the hot water and the bag in the mug, and the…juices or whatever filter through the bag that way. It occurred to me I never got to try that tsha that you gave me in the clearing, so I haven't had any until just now, but you know what? I liked it. It's stronger than I'm used to. Kind of spicy, too, in a way I can't quite put my finger on.... Aha! It's…warm, aside from just the heat of the water. Like spicy sunshine in a plant. I liked it."

That was the truth. Though I might have tried it with the determination to like it, there was no need to tell him that.

Ben didn't seem to notice when I stopped babbling. He just looked at me, head tilted, a kind of dazed look in his eyes, an unconscious smile on his face.

Heat rose in my cheeks. "Uh, Earth to Ben?"

Just as I realized that phrase wouldn't quite make sense to him (even with magic translation), he started, as if suddenly woken. "What? Oh, sorry!"

He leaned back with a groan, putting his hand to his forehead. "Clearly, I need sleep."

"Then hang up—that means end the call—" I explained at his confusion. "—and call Kor to give him his orders so you can get it. That's an order. From me."

Boy, was I flexing my new *something* tonight.

Ben chuckled tiredly. "Yes, ma'am. If…you're *sure* you'll be alright for tonight."

I smiled and met his gaze full on to show him I was telling the truth. "I will be. Like you, I don't have energy for anything else except sleep. Unlike you, I have nothing to do but just that."

"Lucky," he said with a crooked smile. "I'll let you get to it, then. Warm dreams, Sarah."

I liked that. Especially since the word *warm* in his language, *kahlay*, had a nuance that conveyed more than just heat: light, safety, family.

I smiled. "Warm dreams, Ben."

Ben reached toward his pair of the scales, then the image of him faded, leaving only the purple surface of Yvera's scale.

Now that he couldn't see or hear, I allowed my smile to fade.

"And come back soon," I whispered, shivering.

I'd told him the truth: I would be fine. For tonight. But until his crushing warmth drove off the chill in my bones, my dreams would not be *kahlay*.

Chapter Two

THINKING

Koriben

EARLY THE NEXT MORNING (about midday for this part of the Athalin Jungle), I had a few dek of pacing on the mesa before Sarah got around to opening the gate, and that was fine by me.

Alright—it wasn't fine. It felt like I was walking on a bedrock of needles, with all my senses poised for the sign of my relief, but I needed those few dek to get myself under some semblance of control.

In that moment, I wanted to see no one more than Sarah in all the Six Realms. That was precisely the problem. Being the dimtorch I was, the truth had to hit me like a warhammer to the head last night, leaving me nearly as dazed.

I wasn't just attracted to Sarah. I was a good halfway to being madly in love with her.

Mad was exactly what I'd be to let myself get any further carried away. I must have lost some of my senses to come this far.

There were as many reasons why I shouldn't pursue any sort of relationship with Sarah as there were cavities in this mesa, beginning with the Realms-shattering revelation we received from her Tree last night, the urgency of the task we had been given, and the fate of all our worlds hanging in the balance. Now was *not* the time to be distracted with thoughts of asking her....

STOP! I inwardly shouted, shaking myself.

Besides, that was assuming she found me the least bit appealing in that way, and she'd made no sign I could discern. By pressing a suit on her now, I would be betraying her trust, her friendship. I was already asking almost everything from her. Would I ask this too?

On top of all those reasons was the oath I'd silently taken after Avvi's death: I would not perpetuate the cycle that had led to my existence. So frayed was the power of the Covenants now that my parents had offered portions of their very lives to the Tree to give me mine. Avvi's flameheart gave out six years ago, perhaps years before it otherwise would have, and now Avva was fading too. His only hope now rested with Sarah, little did she know it—because the Trees had promised that if the breach in the Covenants was mended, They would provide a cure through her.

After so many years of despair, when I'd found Sarah, I'd nearly collapsed from the jittery hope that I might not be the death of my father after all. My mother's death alone had been more than I could bear.

No more, I'd sworn to myself six years ago. *Not again.*

That was the one thing the Tree could not ask of me, the one thing I would refuse Her, point-blank. She would have to find another Heir, because She would not get one from me. No matter how noble Her intentions, no matter the willingness of the sacrificed, I would not give Her another chance to take the life of someone I loved.

I would never become my father—for many reasons, most of them being my insurmountable shortcomings, but though this might be my greatest failing of all, this was the one I chose.

Yet now, a little voice in my mind whispered, *But you didn't know when you took that oath that there might be no need for it.*

If the Covenants were restored to full strength...would sacrifice for future Heirs be necessary? If not....

My flameheart stirred with the first embers of that sort that I had felt in six years. Dangerous flickers, beginning to heat the bedrock of my soul and eat at the dusty kindling that had filtered down there to spread.

No! I shouted again, but I knew the refusal was weaker this time. I put my head in my hands, not even caring that I continued to pace blindly because my feet had memorized the path. I had to get a grip, *now*. Sarah could be opening the gate at any moment, and I needed to have myself firmly in hand by then or risk giving myself away from sheer discomfiture.

I made myself think. Not hope—*think*. Surely there were enough sobering implications of the Covenants' restoration to bury the hope.

For one thing, one enormous thing: If Sarah took her rightful place to restore the Covenants, a relationship between us would not just be politically complicated—our Trees might forbid it.

When my cousin, Svyer, had told me that Sarah's destined role would not block her from me, she assumed Sarah was to become the next Lady Moon-touched, in which case, Svyer would have been right. Hellwinds, in that scenario, Sarah and I might have been hard pressed on all sides *to* marry. Golden Royals married Nobles, the heads of our clans, all the time. Avvi had been the Heir of hers.

That kind of match *was* encouraged by all: by the Warflight and the Temple because the heads of clans were the most powerful of their clans, as the Golden Monarch and Heir were of all, and by the politicians, particularly if the clan in question hadn't had a consort chosen from their ranks in a while. By that calculus, I would have been nearly forced to propose to Sarah after all the dust had settled. Even though she had no clan yet to be up in arms about having their turn sharing the Crown, anyone smart enough to give up their own clan's chance would agree that the most symbolically and magically important thing to bring the Moontouched back into the fold would be offering a Royal marriage to Sarah.

Even if—gah, Flame forbid—it was to Avva. That would make for the grandest gesture, after all. A Monarch had failed the Moontouched, and a Monarch should make amends. Even I could agree with the logic...even if I was adamantly against the method.

Fortunately, Avva had firmly entrenched himself as a sworn widower, and the common people were rather taken by his century-long devotion to his wife.

Besides, our kind, particularly drakón, did not remarry often; something about our draká natures bound us too closely to our mates to let them go, even long after they were dead.

No, that burden of societal expectation would no doubt have fallen to me.... Hence Svyer's well-meaning encouragement.

All that was moot, because the Tree of Flame and now the Tree of Ice had implied They did not intend Sarah to become a lady, but something more, and that meant she couldn't be the Heir of Flame's or even the *King* of Flame's mere *consort*. The Trees weren't just giving the Moontouched their own world, nor were They rebalancing the scales. They were changing the status quo altogether. How, I still wasn't entirely sure, but I knew the Trees torched well wouldn't let me mess it up just because of...whatever this was I was struggling with inside.

Once Sarah—*if* Sarah fully embraced her birthright, which I should pray to the Trees and Creators she would, then the Trees might prohibit not just a marriage between us but...anything. Beyond friendship, that was.

But, the tiny, crackling voice in the embers whispered, no matter how hard I tried to stamp it out, *if she passes the mantle to another....*

Sarah would still be Moontouched—one of the choice few, perhaps even the equivalent to a lady, if there would be such a thing for them. Then all the political, martial, and religious reasoning would apply to the two of us after all, but twofold again, if the highest Moontouched leader was unavailable....

No, I said one last time, lowering my hands to look at Yedrik, Ykran's sun, in a desperate plea for both strength and sanity. But it was only a moan this time.

I could simply be...*open* to the idea of marrying Sarah. That's all it could be for now, couldn't it? Just an openness. For six years, I had expected to have to keep my oath to not marry at all—or at least to no one I could care about, which amounted to more misery than bachelorhood in my mind. I was just feeling jittery at the possibility of being presented with a palatable option.

Alright, that was pushing it too far. From now on, I had to be more honest with myself, because glossing over what I felt was perhaps the reason I'd fallen so far. I had to name it to fight it.

Fight with what? I growled, running a hand through my hair. This wasn't like any fight I'd ever been through, trained for. I wasn't more than halfway in, and already I'd run out of ways to smother the hope. Other than Sarah's lack of interest, of course. But that could change, too. That was what courtship was about, wasn't it? Encouraging interest? I could just go about it more subtly than simply asking her outright....

I winced. Even if I had experience with this sort of thing...I wasn't subtle. As Kor repeatedly reminded me, I was only marginally better than Yvera, and that was a low bar.

Then what? What was my weapon?

I looked up at the sun...and found my answer. Not a way to stamp out the hope...but at least a way to bank the coals for later, to bury them so that hopefully they didn't impede what was most important.

Time. We had ten days—twelve or thirteen, if we were lucky—before the dust settled and the political volpin descended, and the topic would be forced on both of us, whether or not we willed it. Assuming we even survived.

First things first: find the five gates scattered across the remaining realms, get Sarah to Earth and the Tree of Ice, get back to Ythra with her and whatever the Tree of Flame had promised would help Avva, save him, protect my Tree from the boldest and most devastating of the Devourer's attacks since the Covenantal Age, protect Sarah, survive.

If Sarah's very role did not bar a relationship, if after all that Sarah found *me* desirable...then I could talk to her.

But only then. Any sooner would only be distracting and selfish, as I'd already realized. It was only after we survived and found out what was left for me to give that I could offer her anything.

That seemed to satisfy the embers, which then allowed me to bury them with deep breaths, slowing steps, and steadying pulses from my flameheart. Their quieting came because my resolution to wait was tantamount to surrender...and I knew that.

But an Heir had to know when to be pragmatic about their battles, and this one, it seemed, had been doomed from nearly the start, and not just because of my treacherous feelings. No matter what way I thought about it, it seemed fate would deal the hand, and my only choice was to wait to see how the cards fell.

If fate decreed I marry Sarah, then I was....

No, honestly. In that moment, the hope flared dangerously under the bank of ash, and I had to name the emotion to silence it: desire, and more than just the physical. I wanted her more than I had wanted anything since Avva's healing—and, torch it, this was only supposed to be halfway.

Even halfway, I knew. I was the Heir; I was trained to think too strategically to not know. It was just as Kor said from the very beginning, what I had dangerously blinded myself to for too long: he could have searched through all the Realms for me and not found one I would want more.

If fate decreed I could never....

My footsteps finally stilled. My flameheart dimmed dangerously, despite the sun beating down on me. I couldn't feel it through the chill that went through my blood and, most painfully, through my chest.

You would think that if fate dealt me that hand, I would still be better off than where I was three days ago, thinking that if I didn't find the Moontouched Heir, I could lose my father and would never be able to marry at all...but you would be wrong.

Especially if the Tree of Ice had a different consort in mind for Sarah.

That thought brought a mixture of bile to my throat and a suffocating rage to my chest that I had never before felt and which took precious second after second to tame.

Well, I thought, when I could at last put together a somewhat sensible thought. *Then that is even more reason to wait.*

The embers flared, and I couldn't call them hope any longer. Hope didn't have that kind of...edge.

Or, they whispered, *even more reason to begin now.*

This time, I silenced that whisper with a firm finality. I wasn't the most submissive of Heirs since Avvi's death, particularly in my thoughts, and her death had been the catalyst for the one vow I would keep in defiance of even a direct order from my Tree. But I still believed, loved, and trusted my Tree, and by extension, Her Sister. Even in my most agonizing moments, somehow I still knew deep down that She only did and asked for what was right, what was best for all.

In those times, I didn't know why I still believed, but I did. Kor would call that naivety. Avva would call that wisdom.

Avvi would have called that faith.

Perhaps I believed...because she had. Even though she gave her life because of that belief. Perhaps...*because* she gave her life for it. Because if I gave it all up.... If I turned my back on my Tree, rescinded my oath as Heir, left my people to fend for themselves with no one to replace me....

Then what was it for?

No. I would *not* tolerate thoughts of undermining either my Tree or Sarah's. If fate dealt me the second hand.... Well, I would have to rely on the Tree to give me the strength to bear it.

I CAME TO THAT place of stillness not a second too soon, because just then the white outlines of the moongate began rising from the ground, as if the two-dimensional tree were truly sprouting from the stone. Even as my flameheart flared with renewed anticipation and anxiety, I let out a breath of relief. I'd wondered in the back of my mind if I would have to wait here until night, and we didn't have that kind of time to waste. Not to mention I might just run into our old "friend" the lish again.

The lish.... Ah, torch it, that was going to make the Devourer's assault hit harder. No doubt that thought had already occurred to Avva. Thank the Flame he was in charge of all of that. Though part of me was as anxious as my wings to be in the middle of the discreet whirl of preparations that had begun almost the moment my conference with Avva had ended last night, another part of me was grateful to be insulated from it. Despite the urgency, it would no doubt require an endless amount of tedious administrivia that I simply didn't have the patience for now. The Tree of Ice had given us a formidable task, but it at least gave me something to do that felt like it directly mattered.

And gave me a lot more time with Sarah....

Focus, I told myself sternly as the doors solidified. *Wait, remember. Now is not the time. Wait.*

I took a deep, steadying breath, and hoped my face looked at least somewhat...settled.

The doors swung outward, revealing the same frozen curtain as before, but standing on the other side of it....

Sarah. Despite how the plane of ice distorted and fragmented my view of her, the sight of her slight figure, long brown hair, lighter brown skin, and soulful eyes was still unmistakable and enough to make my flameheart pound again.

"Ben!" she gasped. Despite how her voice sounded through the ice, almost as if I were under water and she up above, her delight was unmistakable.

Then she burst through the ice curtain and jumped at me, arms raised. As if we had rehearsed this (and perhaps I had, in my deepest dreams last night), I instantly raised my arms and caught her, then took her up on the standing offer she'd made me last night and crushed her to me with as much force as I dared.

Everything fell into place again, as if nothing about this morning had ever been wrong or painful or uncertain. Those feelings were already a distant memory with the even stronger one of having her in my arms.

"Well, that's something new!" I said with as easy a laugh as I could manage, even though my flameheart blazed hotter than the sun at my back.

"What?" Sarah asked, lifting her head from my shoulder and leaning back to meet my eyes. I shifted one of my hands lower on her back to support her better.

I grinned at her. "I've never had someone so happy to see me they threw themselves at me."

She blushed and squirmed a bit, but when I loosened my hold, thinking she wanted down, she tightened her own around my neck. I liked her just where she was, so I tightened my grip again in turn.

Still blushing, her long eyelashes veiling her warm brown eyes as they avoided mine, she said, "Well, you know, Kor and Yvera aren't much company, and it's a big, empty place."

Ah, of course. I tried to keep my smile in place, hoping she didn't see evidence of the pang of disappointment that shot through me. What else could I have expected? Friendship was what she wanted, what she *needed*, and so friendship was what I would give her. For as long as I could.

I can do this, I realized with sudden conviction, born from the strength I felt now that I was with her again that was completely independent from what I felt from the sun. Because it came from her.

For ten days, I can be whatever she needs.

For ten days.

Still, I had better set her down, before the proximity of our faces started tempting me more than I could handle. I did so, saying as lightly as I could, "It's actually quite small for a hold, but I understand what you mean. It's not meant to be as empty as it is, but it won't stay that way, I promise."

"Really?" Sarah asked in puzzlement.

"Really," I said easily, putting an arm around her shoulders to guide her casually back through the ice. Just before we passed through, I darted surreptitious glances left and right to make sure no one had been in sight to see me, her, or the gate. She really shouldn't have risked coming through to greet me, but I was still too full of the warmth of her greeting to worry her about that now.

Although...once we were through the ice, I turned back to look at the doors on the other side with a frown.

"What do you mean by that?" Sarah prompted.

"What?" I looked at her. "Oh, sorry. I mean, we're bringing your family here, right?"

Uncertainty flickered across her face. "Er.... Are we? I know the Tree made this hold for me, and it's not like I wouldn't be happy to have them here too, to share this with me, but...."

"Hold that thought," I said, then pointed to the doors on the other side of the ice. "How are we supposed to close those? To make sure no one finds this gate?"

"Oh." Sarah scrunched her face for a moment. "Wait. Didn't the ones on that side close on their own before? When the lish was coming after us?"

I blinked. "Oh, yeah. I guess they must have. I closed them myself yesterday before I surged, but...maybe I didn't have to."

"Still, I get your point. Just in case...." Then her jaw set, and she raised her hands. "Hang on, I think I can feel something there, something I can *pull*."

That's what it looked like she did: pull at the doors as if there were ropes attached to each one that she drew to herself, hand over hand. I watched in fascination, which turned quickly to awe as her hands and eyes began to glow.

The hands: ours did that sometimes, in a way, but it was mostly swirls of power around them. Hers seem to spread on the surface of her skin in swirls like snow flurries. Simply beautiful. Perhaps most miraculous of all was to watch the confident set of her shoulders, the smile of satisfaction tugging at her lips—such a contrast with her denial and even fear of what she was just the morning before. The combined effect was breathtaking.

Blessed Flame...I was in deep. How could I not have seen that before?

"There," Sarah said, panting slightly as the doors on the other side finally closed and she lowered her hands.

She pointed at the inner set of doors with a sheepish look at me. "I...think we can just push these shut the old-fashioned way. Do you mind?"

I laughed. "Of course not. You did the hard part, now let me do the easy."

"I can push one of them myself," she insisted, and before I could stop her, she rushed to one door. I shrugged and took the other, and we pushed them closed together. When the stone met, the glow in all the outlines faded and became only decorative stone.

"Did the glow fade, when you closed them before?" I asked as I traced the middle line in fascination.

"No, but I think that's because it was night, and now it's maybe morning?"

"It is," I confirmed, cocking my head. "Just about dawn, actually."

"Figures," she said with a yawn. Before I could ask how well she'd slept, she asked, "Did the door disappear, on the other side, when I closed it?"

"It did indeed. Not just invisible—as if it had never even been there. I walked through the same space and everything."

"Really?" she asked with wide eyes. "I...know I'm new at this whole magic and gates thing, but that sounds like powerful stuff."

"As far as I can tell, it is," I agreed, feeling a flicker of unease. Only in the sense of not knowing what all this meant for her, but that was quite enough. "Sungates don't disappear. Ever. They may close at night, or when needed—"

Or if they didn't have enough power, which was a danger we had thus far avoided in all but a few isolated instances, but the threat of a widespread outage grew by the day.

I shook my head to dispel the anxiousness and hoped she would interpret it as accompanying my following words. "—but that's it: they stay there."

"Sometime you're going to have to take me through one of these sungates, if only so I know what the differences are that you guys keep talking about."

"Oh, you couldn't avoid that even if you wanted to," I said with a grim smile. "We'll be taking one today, in fact, to get to the next realm."

"To search for the next gate," Sarah said with a firm nod. My flameheart grew from pride and shrunk from pain at the determined set to her shoulders. "Right. When do we need to leave?"

She hesitated one beat, then added sheepishly, "Uh, you might have to wake Kor and Yvera. Kor went straight back to bed after waking me to tell me you were at the gate."

Hopefully he was civil. It had been a gamble between which of my wings would be the least troublesome messenger at this deken.

"I figured that would be the case," I said with a chuckle. "That's fine. We can afford to give them a deken or two more to get going after the night they had."

"That *we* had, too," Sarah pointed out firmly, scrutinizing me. "Speaking of which, did you even sleep? You're here early."

"I slept," I said. Which was the truth. Though my head had still been spinning so much from my epiphany that I'd had to drug myself with dreamhaze to get any. Even so, it wore off in about four deken, and as soon as I was awake, my mind and emotions were whirling like a hurricane again, so I decided I might as well set off and think along the way.

In hindsight, I probably shouldn't be making major life decisions on four deken of sleep, but I had a feeling that was the way my life was going to go for the next ten days.

"And you?" I turned the scrutiny back on her, holding her shoulders as I really looked at her for the first time that morning. I mean, I'd done hardly anything *but* look at her, but this was the first time I noticed the little details, such as her disheveled hair, her loose-fitting clothing, her bare feet....

"Sarah," I demanded before she could answer my first question. "Did you rush straight out of bed to let me in?"

She bit her lip. "Ummm...."

"Sarah," I groaned, heading for the kitchen. "Come on."

"Kor said you were waiting!" Sarah protested as she hurried to catch up, and I slowed my pace.

"I told *him* to tell you to take your time. Did he do that?"

"Er...I'm sure he meant to. He kind of...mumbled his way through the message."

I sighed. That had been the risk in picking Kor.

"He does that. It's incredible how brilliant he is most of the time. What people often don't know is that he is pretty much incoherent for the first quarter deken or so after waking up. I have to plan around that."

"Oh. He seemed clear enough yesterday morning."

That gave me pause. Yesterday morning...we woke up in the entrance hall of this hold. Sarah was right: Kor was alert and coherent from the first moment he opened his eyes. Strange, that. He *was* asleep right before. After all, he sleep-pushed me right into Sarah....

I inwardly groaned at my stupidity and made a mental note to give Kor some stern words in private about respecting Sarah's boundaries. And *mine*. Yes, I had...sort of changed my mind about Sarah, but he didn't know that—and I wasn't about to tell him.

For Sarah's sake, I muttered, "Must have been adrenaline."

"Right," Sarah agreed quickly, but I noticed out of the corner of my eye that her cheeks were darker.

We entered the kitchen. Sarah looked up at me, cheeks cooling. "You'll be OK for a bit? I'd like to take a few minutes to, you know...."

She ran a hand through her disheveled hair self-consciously.

"Of course, you do that," I said. "Take all the time you need. While you do, I'll make breakfast."

She stopped in the arch that led to the water-rooms and turned. "Oh, Ben, you don't have to do that! You just got back, and you made dinner last night...."

"You helped," I pointed out as I began getting out the pans I'd need. "The least I can do for dragging you out of bed after a night like the last one is give you a warm meal."

When she looked ready to protest again, I added, "It's for the others, too. Kor and Yvera are going to be more cheerful when I wake them up if I tell them there's cooked food—even if it's cold by then."

Sarah sighed but nodded reluctantly. "Alright. I'll hurry back so I can help."

"Take your time," I repeated sternly.

She just smiled and turned away.

"Oh, and Sarah?"

She stopped and looked over her shoulder curiously. "What?"

I hesitated. "I know you prefer dressing in the clothes from your world, and I understand that. I would too. But you should probably wear only the things Svyer got you. You're going to attract enough attention as it is...."

To my surprise, she just nodded. "Right. I understand." She wrinkled her nose. "I was planning on wearing some other shoes, anyway. Mine are...fragrant."

I hadn't noticed...which was odd, but every time I was around her, all I smelled was her normal, enigmatic scent, getting stronger and more intoxicating by the day as her power awoke.

"If you have any questions...." I hesitated, then taking my turn to go red, I looked down and fussed with the ingredients in the strange, cold box Sarah had called a "fridge." I needed the cold right now. "Ask Yvera?"

Even thinking about the logistics of her changing had been a terrible idea.

She just laughed easily and called over her shoulder as she went on her way, "I think I can figure it out."

Thank the Flame for that. Only after a good solid five dek of busying myself with the task of making breakfast for three drakón and one Earthren did the heat in me cool to an acceptable, *friendly* level.

Sarah clearly was not used to being taken care of, but by the Flame, she was going to have to get used to it. No matter what fate decreed, that was something I didn't think I was ever going to be able to stop trying to do.

CHAPTER THREE
SECRETS

SARAH

I HADN'T INTENDED ON taking a shower, but once I got to the bathroom and smelled myself again, I sighed and decided it was worth it. Maybe that's what Ben had been kindly implying when he told me to take my time. Belatedly, I remembered how sensitive drakón noses were and winced.

Fortunately, Yvera must have requisitioned some of my towels already, because one of the formerly empty stone shelves was stuffed full of them. I grabbed one and then entered one of the stalls. At least these showers had *stalls*, unlike the ones Svyer had shown me how to use.

To my surprise, the controls were a blend of the new and the familiar. I ran my finger over the crystals I wanted, but this time they were set in a circle, in a gradient from blue to red. They glowed at my touch, the color becoming more vibrant, and all I had to do to turn the heat up or down was touch a crystal again to light or dim it. Dimming them all turned the water off, just as activating one had turned it on.

Then came the final decision: put my "pajamas" (the loosest clothing I'd found in my bags) back on or make a dash for my room wrapped in a towel.

I sighed. Though the pajamas weren't that smelly, I *had* slept in them, and the whole point was to start out fresh and nice smelling, for me as much as for Ben. The divinely herbal scent of the soap dispensed in the water lingered on my skin, and I didn't want to lose a bit. I was going to need all the confidence I could get today as we started off on our search for the next gate.

I compromised by using two towels, one around my torso and one over my shoulders. That would keep my wet hair off my back, anyway. Still, I was glad that Kor and Yvera were still asleep.

By the time I approached the kitchen and peered cautiously inside, Ben was softly singing to himself, an unconscious smile on his face as he worked. Maybe I had been wrong to try dissuading him from making breakfast. The sight of his simple peace as he cooked warmed my own heart and made me think that today just might be OK after all.

I hated to disturb that peace by crossing the room in only a couple of towels. He had been so adorably awkward in offering to help answer questions about *clothes* that I was sure he would go red again the moment he saw me. But what else could I do? I wasn't aware of any way into the dorm area except through the kitchen.

If only there was a way for me to sneak through...while holding the towels around my body and my pajamas in a ball against my chest.

Hang on a sec. I had *magic* now, didn't I? Surely it could help somehow in this situation. Was that how Kor seemed to sometimes appear out of nowhere? Did he make himself invisible?

I had no idea how to go about doing what I wanted. This was the first time I'd considered doing magic, with no item to interact with or pull it out of me.

Even as I thought about the possibility, I took on a soft white glow, and my hands glistened with their swirling patterns. As if attracted like moths to a flame, or perhaps summoned by my desire, a few of this hold's mysterious helping lights floated out from the glowing stones on the wall and down to me.

"Why, hello there," I whispered in delight. "Is that where you guys go during the day? Do you have cozy little nests in there?"

They bobbed, and I felt a confirming feeling, but both movement and feeling were less energetic than they had been last night.

"Sorry to wake you," I told them regretfully. "You can go back now. This isn't *that* important."

They just continued to hover around me, as if to say, *It was important enough that we came, so get on with it so we can go back to sleep.*

I sighed, figuring that arguing with them wasn't worth it. Then considered. Even if *they* could make me invisible, that sounded like a lot of magic to my inexperienced mind, and I didn't want to ask that of them now.

Did I really need invisibility? What did I *need*? Articulated in a way to allow them maximum flexibility in how to bring it about?

After a few moments, I thought I had it. "Do you know how I can get back to my bedroom without Ben seeing me?"

As if all they'd been waiting for was the specific request, they slowly flew in unison to the center of the outer wall in the small antechamber I was standing in between the bathrooms and kitchen. As if they were white crayons, when they brushed themselves over the walls, wherever they touched, a glow lingered. They traced a miniature version of the many arched doors all over the hold, complete with the white tree in the center. The only difference other than the size was that this appeared to be a single door instead of a double.

I inhaled in excitement. "A secret passage! Perfect!"

And, because none of the drakón were with me in that moment, it could *remain* a secret for at least a bit. A little part of my home for just me to savor for a time, even if it was only a morning.

Take that, Kor, I thought smugly as I pressed my free hand to the door. It swung inward silently, and the empty doorway was just right for my five-foot-six-inch height—truly meant for me. I chuckled to myself as I thought of Ben, who must have been over seven feet tall, trying to fit through.

One light floated into the dark passageway ahead of me, and the others drew back.

"Thank you!" I whispered to them as they drifted back to their glowing nests. They hummed quietly in reply and disappeared inside.

When I stepped inside the passage, I saw it was wide enough for one drakón abreast and tall enough for Kor, though Ben and Yvera would have to stoop. It appeared, as much of the hold did, to be carved straight from the mountain rock, with no seams for blocks in the walls or tiles in the floor and the only variations being that of the natural veins in the stone. The passage itself formed a continuous arch, going straight left and right for as far as I could see in the light of my hovering guide.

Feeling a mix of thrill and trepidation, I slowly pushed the stone door closed, and Ben's voice and cooking clatter faded to complete silence.

"Alright," I whispered to the light. The low volume wasn't necessary anymore, but...you know, secret passage. Besides, the echoes in this long, small, stone space were formidable. "Let's go find my room. Do you know which one that is?"

Either it did, or it didn't understand me, because it simply floated down the passage to the left (south) with no other reply. I shrugged and followed.

Strange that, even though I walked barefoot and barelegged through the cold stone passage, with wet hair still dampening the towel on my shoulders, I didn't feel discomfort. I knew it was cold—cold enough that my breath steamed just a little in the light of my guide; I simply didn't mind. In fact, the cold and even the darkness felt good...energizing. Nothing compared to the shot of energy I'd felt when the sun went down last night, but it was a tiny boost, like a cup of coffee on a sleepy morning. With the adrenaline I'd felt ever since Kor had told me Ben was back, I hadn't realized how weary I was feeling until I felt the weariness eased.

Was this what it was like for the drakón in the nighttime, the weariness? And was this boost what they felt with a bit of heat? If so, *why* was I so completely reversed? Despite my relief from the physical fog, I felt anxiety about the difference creeping back in, especially when I remembered Ben's look of worry from last sunset. Was there something wrong with me? Had the Tree made a mistake?

We passed a door to the left, which dimly illuminated itself once it came in range of the floating light, like glow-in-the-dark plastic given just a few seconds of sunlight, and it faded away soon after it fell back into shadow. It was set into the wall I'd come through, which made sense to me given the rough map of the hold in my head. As did the gentle curve of the passage to the left, as part of the outer edge of the oval coming to the southern end. It occurred to me that if this passage went around the entire hold, then the hold would have *two* rims:

the inner one that was the enormous balcony ringing the garden, and this outer one.

Like an eye, I realized. The Inner Rim would be the edge of the white, with the garden the iris and the waterfall the pupil, and the Outer Rim being the eyelid.

Though after we kept walking for a while, I became confused. Surely the first door had been to the kitchen, so that made sense why we didn't go through it, but surely we should have encountered a door to the bedroom area by now....

Then we came to another door. Which was set into the wall to the right.

"What's this?" I murmured to myself, heartbeat picking up in excitement.

Something new, since it didn't fit anywhere in my mental map, but the light was hovering in front of it, clearly intending me to go in.

I placed my hand on the door. The glow brightened for a moment, and I felt a sudden sharp drain of energy and the popping sensation I'd had when I'd broken the seals on the storage rooms. My anticipation rose further, and I pushed.

The door swung inward slightly, and I and the light went through.

My jaw dropped.

Well.... I thought faintly. *I did ask them to get me to my room.*

I just hadn't realized that they would have assumed this would be it.

It was clearly a bedroom, but one fit for a queen. Unlike all the other bedrooms, which had been reasonably sized and unfurnished, this one was large enough for a family, in my opinion, and fully stocked with everything I could have wanted or imagined.

It was like a miniature version of the hold itself, with a grand central seating space, plumply cushioned and illuminated by another ice-rose skylight, with a peacefully gurgling fountain and ring of mossy and hardy-looking plants, all sunken down a couple steps below the rest.

A rim of a stone walkway went around the center area and led to various themed nooks. My eyes were immediately drawn to a cozy reading nook lined with shelves stuffed with vibrantly colored leather spines, a nest of cushions and pillows, and even curtains (currently pulled back) for an extra bit of privacy. There was another area with a desk, complete with a writing easel and appearing stocked with stationery and odds and ends I didn't bother to identify. Another area appeared to be a workstation of some sort, with things I faintly recognized as being magical tools, including one of the rods Kor had tried to swipe.

Perhaps most disturbing of all, a giant loom occupied the final nook, almost teasing me into coming over to touch it, to run my hand through the baskets of yarn, to run it over the beautifully carved and polished spindle....

Of course whoever had built this place would have known what I had never told a single soul: that I'd inexplicably yearned to learn spinning and weaving ever since visiting a historical immersion village that had reenacted old crafts and ways of life. If they were trying to tempt me into accepting a role as their long-lost leader...dang it, it was working.

Although I found a bit of fortification against their wiles in the largest area, the one directly across from me. It was the grandest as well as being the biggest, lined with curved dressers and an enormous vanity, hung with blue tapestries with white trees, covered in a plush blue rug that looked like it could swallow me up to the ankles, and with a gigantic oval bed—draped with thick, velvety blue curtains that went around a matching ring suspended straight from the ceiling—as its centerpiece.

I shook my head at the folly. How they could have predicted me so well in every other instance and then create *that* was beyond me. What would I ever do with a bed that big? It added a whole other definition to the term "king sized." I would drown in that sea of sumptuous white comforters and pillows.

There was something nagging at me about the wall behind the bed, though. The bed was set in the center of the area, and beyond was a gentle curve of a wall covered from floor to ceiling with matching velvet drapes. What were the drapes covering?

My curiosity got the better of me, and I rounded the rim to find out. Interestingly, the temperature rose noticeably the moment I crossed the boundary of the "bedroom," and I realized how (if not why) when I reached down and felt the stone floor: it radiated a soft heat. Interesting, that. If there *wasn't* something wrong with me, and if I truly was meant to gain energy from the cold, then why heat the sleeping area?

Then I laughed a little at myself as I realized it was the same reason you wouldn't want to drink coffee before bed. Hadn't I worried just last night how I was ever going to sleep at night? The exhaustion of all that had come in the hours after sunset had let me finally sink into sleep, but I had still mildly worried I would have to become nocturnal.

The heated floor, the plushness of the carpet and tapestries, the curtains, the sumptuous comforter could all be designed to help me—or rather, the Moontouched leader, whoever that would be—to *rest*. For that leader, heat might be that signal to the body that it was the time to lay their burdens down to do so.

If cold and dark was the Moontouched's lot in life, perhaps there were ways for them—for us—to be able to function as normal people, after all. That thought gave me hope.

Though the size of the bed was still ridiculous. I mean, really. You could have fit a couple drakón in there, with room to spare. Even *Ben* could....

I stopped myself right there.

For further distraction, I continued straight to the back curtains and waded through the rug for good measure. Sure enough, though the rug didn't quite sink me up to my ankles, it was still the deepest I'd ever walked on. I was serious when I said that I *waded*.

I had to search a bit to find the center split in the heavy velvet curtains, and as soon as I came across it, I let the curtain fall back with a yelp as a spear of light shot through. I laughed again at myself and moved the curtain aside as I realized what the thickness and tingle of magic inside the curtains had so thoroughly concealed: an enormous, floor-to-ceiling window.

The curtain was so heavy, I opted to slip behind it, since the slant of the window left a comfortable space to stand in between the curtain and the glass. Just as with the window in the hall, the glass was set seamlessly into the stone, except this time it took up the entire wall, giving me a breathtaking view of the icy, mountainous landscape, resplendent in morning sunlight. For a moment, I just stood there in awe.

Then the thought came to me, arising so separately it hardly felt like my own. *All this was made for you.*

It wasn't a selfish, possessive thought. Rather, the reverse: it was a longing to be a part of something. To have something worth caring for, worth protecting. To pass down with pride to the ones who came after.

I offer it to you, the other-voice continued, and now I recognized a different Presence inside me, of something bigger than myself.

It filled me with a heaviness that was both energizing and exhausting at the same time. I would have been frightened, except I recognized something of the same feeling from when I'd stood in the darkness with Ben last night and heard the Tree of Ice speak. The words didn't come in the same voice. They still felt more like my voice than Hers, even though they weren't my words; but perhaps that was simply the heavy filter of distance and method.

It was made for you, to give you the strength and protection to do what you must for the sake of all worlds. Though We are not mortal, though We ask much, We are not heartless. We do what We can to help ease the burdens We place on Our children.

It was everything I hadn't realized I'd ever wanted and offered so freely and with such love. What was stopping me from reaching out to take it?

Are you unworthy, Sarah?

I winced at the familiar question.

I'm no ruler, I told the voice, just as I had answered the King. If anything, the bed area just behind me proved that. It was the one piece of the puzzle that didn't fit into place.

Yet, the voice whispered back. I didn't know whether it was answering my words or my thoughts.

She said no more, and the unsettling feeling of Presence left me not a moment later.

In its sudden absence, I sagged, and I had to throw out one hand against the glass to keep myself from toppling into it. Even so, I slid down its surface and shivered. My guide hovered around me, buzzing and pulsing in anxiety.

"I'll be alright," I breathed, and leaned my head against the glass and closed my eyes. "Just give me a minute."

I took comfort from remembering Ben had said that communing with a Tree did this to a person. Hopefully he was also right that it would get easier with time. Now I appreciated—and regretted—to an even greater degree what Ben had done so willingly for me to get the answer I needed on the mesa. If it had felt like this....

Yet, exhaustion aside, the Presence had left me with a sense of peace and strength I couldn't quite describe—one that had been worth the cost. It was like the satisfied high after a good run, the kind that left me trembling but triumphant, every part of my body tingling and alive.

I found myself thinking the strangest and perhaps craziest thought I'd ever had: *I could get used to this.*

Even crazier...I wanted to.

AFTER A FEW MINUTES, my legs no longer felt like jelly, and I pushed myself to my feet. I sighed at the loss of time. I didn't know how long my detour had taken, but I didn't want to leave Ben by himself much longer, much less worry him if he started to wonder where I was. Plus, it really was time I put some clothes on. Even though I wasn't ready to accept this bedroom—this suite, basically—as mine, I made a decision.

I slipped out of the curtain, and as I held one edge aside for the light to float through after me, I said, "Are there clothes in here? That would fit me?"

I figured I could always return them later.

The light flew over to a dresser and, by some means I couldn't discern, pulled a drawer open. Then another. Then another.

In each, I found a different type of clothing, and I grabbed the first thing my hands touched from each. In short order I had on the comfiest, most formfitting and yet breathable underwear I'd ever had, a pair of black pants that hugged my hips and thighs just right while being breathable, and a V-neck sweater the color and softness of a cloud that draped and clung in all the right places and had me pleasantly warm in seconds.

While I was busy dressing, two lights came to me, hefting a knee-high leather boot each. "Oh, thank you," I crooned to them. While I sat down on the vanity stool and bent over to put them on, I felt a tugging on my hair and shot straight up again. In the mirror, I saw the two lights had been joined by a third, and they were buzzing around the back of my head in annoyance.

"Are you trying...to do my hair?" I asked in bafflement.

They hummed in unified confirmation.

"Alright," I said, dragging out the word, but since they were sacrificing sleep...or recharging time...or whatever they normally did during the day, and seemed so determined, I decided it wasn't worth arguing.

As soon as I had given my tacit approval, they set to work again, radiating a gentle heat as they quickly weaved in and out of my hair until it was dry within seconds. Then I watched in fascination as they somehow lifted one part of my hair at a time and danced around each other, weaving, weaving, weaving, until in no time at all I had a crown braid around my head like the one Svyer had done for me, yet even Svyer hadn't inserted clear gemstones or small, white, jewellike flowers at artistic intervals. I had to admit, my self-confidence was bolstered to see myself done up as well as a princess could hope, but my practicality was screaming too loudly for me to ignore.

"Um.... It's beautiful," I said as I turned my head this way and that. "Absolutely beautiful. But don't you think it's a bit...."

The three buzzed warningly—the equivalent of a glare.

"OK, OK," I said in surrender, throwing up my hands. "If you think it's what's best for traveling to another realm to find another gate and facing who-knows-what along the way."

One of the lights rubbed against my cheek and hummed in confirmation, and my heart melted just a bit.

"Thank you, then," I said sincerely. Even though I silently promised myself I'd remove every pin and flower as soon as we left the hold. After all, some of those could be valuable, and I didn't want to lose them. Especially if I was going to be handing this room and its contents over to someone else.

"Now," I said briskly as I rose. "I thank you, all of you, for your help, especially during the day, but I really have to get back to Ben as soon as possible. How do I do that? Um...without going through the secret kitchen door, if there is one."

One light bobbed on ahead while the other two retreated. I waved them goodbye over my shoulder and blew them a kiss as I followed my new...or old...guide. Sometime, I was going to have to learn how to distinguish which light was which. Assuming there was a meaningful difference, which I would until told otherwise.

The light led me through the still-open bedroom door and back into the secret passage, but instead of leading me right or left, it floated straight to a door that illuminated itself directly across from my bedroom one. I was positive it hadn't been there before, but then, it hadn't needed to be.

When I pushed that door open, I entered another narrow passage that went straight out before me, at a perpendicular angle to the Outer Rim. After closing the door to the Outer Rim, I followed the light to the end and another identical door. Once I emerged from that one, it took me a second to get my bearings, and then I recognized where I was. I looked back at the still-open door for confirmation and saw that the connecting passage I'd just emerged from went straight through the space in between Ben's and Kor's rooms in the dormitory. Yvera's and mine were directly across the way, and I could hear Ben's voice floating through the kitchen beyond the in-between chamber to the left.

Thank you, I mouthed to the light. It bobbed and hummed in confirmation and floated to a lightstone, disappearing inside. I pushed the door closed, and not just the glowing lines but every trace vanished. Curious, I pressed my hand to the center of where I remembered the door to be. The pattern of the tree illuminated itself just under my hand but nowhere else; I felt what I could only describe as *potential* there, waiting for my call. When I removed my hand, the sense of potential faded, as did the handprint outline of the tree, leaving the stone as blank as it had been when we first walked into this area.

I fixed the door's location in my mind, and then satisfied that I could both find and activate it again if I needed to, I hurried toward the kitchen and the voices there. My heart sank when I recognized Yvera's; not only was she not the easiest person to be around (at least if you were me), I felt the loss of the alone time I'd been hoping to have with Ben.

"I'm here!" I said with a cheer that was a tad forced as I hurried in, rolling up my sleeves. "Sorry that took longer than I expected. Is there anything left for me to help...."

I trailed off as I came to a stop, finally reading the room. Ben and Yvera faced off across the counter. Ben's hands gripped the countertop with telling force; it was a good thing the surface was solid stone, or he might have done some damage, and then what would my ancestors think? His jaw was clenched, and his gold eyes glowed slightly—not a good sign.

For once, Yvera was the calm one, staring him down with folded arms and a cocked hip. Neither of them so much as turned to look at me, though from the pause in their exchange, I assumed they knew I was there.

My heart clenched and my breath caught. "What's wrong?"

"Nothing," Ben said curtly, his eyes not leaving Yvera's. "Nothing *whatsoever.*"

"Think about it," she said simply, and with a toss of her braid, she turned to stride back to the dorm area. As she passed me, she sniffed in disdain.

"Are you dressed for work or a feast, Earthren?"

"Yv," Ben said dangerously.

Strangely, having Yvera bring it up so baldly made me feel better. First off, if she was throwing out casual insults, we were safe for the moment. Second, it gave me a chance to explain and laugh at myself.

I chuckled and turned as I spoke to keep addressing her, since she didn't stop. "I'm ready to go to work, don't worry. My...helpers decided I needed their assistance getting ready this morning."

In case they were listening, I left it at that.

She huffed, and even with her back to me, I could feel her roll her eyes, but I was a female too, and if she thought I wouldn't notice that her own braid down her back was more elaborate than usual, that her leather clothes were on the sexy end of rugged, she was wrong. Instead of putting me down, her comment made me rather more...smug.

I'd never had another woman think I was a genuine threat before. I rather liked it.

Even though it was all for naught, of course, because as far as I could tell, Ben hadn't noticed either of our efforts. Speaking of whom....

"Ignore her," Ben groaned.

I turned around and resumed my walk to him. He was bowing his head, but as I approached, he straightened and gave me a strained smile.

"How much of that did you hear?"

"None of it," I said honestly. Kor would have been so disappointed with my total lack of spy skills.

I didn't regret it, though, when Ben let out a breath of relief and relaxed his shoulders somewhat. "Good."

"Do you want to talk about it?" I said quietly.

"Not really," he said with a sigh. He ran a hand through his hair. "Yvera's just...out of sorts, that's all. This situation is hard on all of us, but...defense is her job. Her life, really. All her friends except me, and everyone in the flight she's supposed to lead, are getting ready to defend our home right now from the biggest threat our generation has faced, and she's...."

"Here," I said, leaning back against the counter. "That would be tough."

I felt a little guilty for my smugness a bit ago.

"Yeah," Ben muttered, turning away as he set a frying pan back on the hot disk. Something was telling about how fixed his gaze was on the pan. "Mind, I'm not making excuses for her. She said some things I'm not going to repeat. It's just.... It's making her see threats that aren't there."

Like me, I thought. That was why Ben was so furious, and why he was being so vague now.

I took back my guilt. Still, I wasn't mad at her. Again...I understood. Right now, her world as she knew it was unraveling, and no one embodied that fraying more than I did. It would be so easy to make me into more than just a threat to her chances with Ben.

That didn't mean I was going to roll over for her. If anything, she was teaching me I had more of a competitive drive than I'd realized. At the beginning, I'd intended to make peace, to show her I made no claim, but though I knew she'd understood my message, she didn't seem to care. If she was going to keep making this a thing between us....

Well, it might as well be a thing.

Just like that, while watching Ben cool his temper by frying sausages in a pan, I decided I was going to reach for what I wanted.

At least...this one thing.

Ben cleared his throat awkwardly, and his cheeks flushed a bit as he darted glances my way. "Er...you look very nice, by the way. Your hair is very...pretty."

I turned to grab the stack of plates at the end of the counter so he wouldn't see my expression. He was probably just saying that to make up for Yvera's slight, but still....

She'd made him notice. The irony would have killed her. I would bet my last (albeit measly) waitressing paycheck that he hadn't said the same to Yvera, or she wouldn't have been so sour.

"Thanks," I said casually as I carried the plates to the table.

With my back to him, I smirked in the direction of the dorms.

Earthren, 1. Drakón, 0.

Chapter Four

WEAPON

KORIBEN

As Sarah and I finished up and set out breakfast, I tried as little as mortally possible to think about Yvera and what she'd said.

The accusations she'd made, really: that Sarah was a burden at best, and hinting at her being far worse. Just before Sarah had interrupted, Yvera had been implying that something or *someone* was obviously giving the Devourer the confidence to strike so boldly. If Yvera had been any more direct, with anyone but me in absolute privacy, that level of accusation could have triggered a hearing before the Tree.

The Tree of Flame didn't take false accusations of collusion with the Devourer lightly. Our survival was too dependent on our unity for Her to allow us to turn on each other with suspicion or greed, so every case was brought directly to Her for examination and judgment. Not only could She discern the truth of the matter, She could detect any taint of consumption. If the accused was innocent in intent but unknowingly influenced, She could burn away the taint and free the victim. If the accused was guilty in deed and in heart, judgment was left to Her. If the accused was innocent and clean, the Tree's judgment fell on the accuser, and Her punishments for knowingly false accusations were severe.

With all of this being common knowledge, serious accusations were rare, and anyone with sense and good intent would know to be as certain as possible before making them. Yvera should have known better than to even hint at such a thing.

Underneath my simmering anger, though, I was baffled. My rightwing and best friend wasn't normally this blind. True, she didn't trust easily, but she had good instincts and could recognize a genuine person when she saw one. She and Sarah had wildly different personalities and skill sets, but couldn't she see what value Sarah brought to the table?

She'd called Sarah a *burden*, just because she was smaller and less experienced. Perhaps part of that was my fault: all my personal focus and all my guidance to my wings regarding Sarah had been to protect and care for her. I was the one who always emphasized her vulnerabilities. It took a metaphorical knuckle-wrap on my head from Avva, as usual, to remind me that my focus had been too narrow—doing as much harm as good when it came to her wellbeing and development as a leader.

Hopefully this morning would help change everyone else's view, too. Including Sarah's.

Once I'd sat down and started digging in, telling Sarah to do the same, she asked if Yvera was coming. She didn't seem the least bit bothered speaking of her, which probably meant she was telling the truth when she said she hadn't heard anything. Which was good.

Like I'd said to Sarah, I wasn't excusing my friend, but I didn't want Sarah's self-esteem to take a hit just because Yvera was under a lot of strain right now and saying things she wasn't really thinking through. Plus, with one thing right after the other, I was sure Yvera hadn't made a great impression on Sarah these past few days, and since I hoped to keep both of them in my life for some time to come, I was invested in trying to get them to get along. Somehow.

One miracle at a time, I thought to myself with a sigh. That was yet another project for after we all survived the invasion.

"Probably not," I said in answer to Sarah's question. "She said she ate before her practice this morning."

If she gets hungry, she knows she can eat the cold leftovers after we leave, I thought angrily. She knew me better than almost anyone, meaning she'd know to steer clear of me for at least a deken or two while I cooled off from her "message." What she was counting on was my reason then kicking in, allowing doubt about Sarah to enter my thoughts.

I snorted. Sarah looked up questioningly, but I just shook my head.

If Sarah was an agent of the Devourer, I'd eat my tail, and that wasn't just my emotions doing the thinking for me. Of all people, I knew the voice of a Tree, and I'd heard one speak to Sarah and declare Her intention to make Sarah Her Heir. If we couldn't trust Trees to be able to pick out who was trustworthy and untainted among us, well—we might as well surrender to the Devourer now.

Really, what was Yvera thinking?

Kor stumbled, bleary-eyed, into the kitchen, mumbling something about food. I ignored him, since there wasn't much point in trying to converse with him at this stage, but I gestured absently to the free plate next to me.

"Morning, Kor," Sarah said politely.

He gave her a baleful look and muttered something that sounded impolite enough I elbowed him.

"Wha'?" he said, blinking at me with slightly more focus.

"Eat," I said simply, pointing to the food I was piling on his plate.

Kor scowled as he picked up his fork. "Whatchu think 'm herefer? The thimulashing covosashion?"

Sarah just blinked at him. "That didn't even translate for me."

Don't bother, I told her silently. *Incoherent, remember?*

She mouthed an "Oh," then refocused on her food. But I caught a grin tugging at her lips, and I knew why. After being put down intellectually by Kor all day, I often found comfort in knowing that in the morning, the tables would be turned.

After a few dek of digesting food, Kor looked up and blinked at Sarah as if noticing her for the first time. "Yo hair. Iz shiny."

I choked on a bit of tsha I'd been swallowing, but it was worth it. Oooh, yes. I lived for these mornings, in which Kor could make even my bumbling compliment sound graceful by comparison.

Sarah visibly struggled to keep a straight face. "Yes, thank you. The lights did it this morning."

"They dith? Inthasting…" Kor said thoughtfully—with his mouth full of mashed ukka. He swallowed, blinked, and declared, "I'd like to observe."

"Next time, I'll see if you're…available."

"Good," Kor said solemnly, and returned his focus to his plate.

Sarah's chest was shaking with suppressed laughter, so I decided to get her out before Kor became fully conscious. He *hated* being laughed at, and he could hold a grudge like nobody else.

"Alright, Sarah," I said, standing up. "If you're done, then follow me. We'd better get started before we lose too much daylight."

"Are we leaving already?" she asked, standing quickly.

"What?" Kor asked, looking up with his most alert blink yet. I estimated he was now at seventy-percent capacity, and thus entering the danger zone.

"Not just yet," I assured them both. "We'll give Kor a bit more time to wake up while you and I work on something."

"Good," Kor grunted again, shoving more food in his face.

"WHAT ARE WE WORKING ON?" Sarah asked curiously as she followed me out.

I took a deep, steadying breath. "Do you remember what the Tree said to you last night about…Her Heir needing to return with me to help Avva drive off the Devourer?"

"Yes," she answered quietly. Which told me she understood some of the implications, and their seriousness.

Still, to make sure we were on the same page, I elaborated out loud. "That means that, if you accept what She offers you, you'll be going straight into danger. Even *if* I'm able to keep you perfectly safe over these next ten days, we know we can't spare you from that much. Again, even then, Avva and I will keep you as safe as we can, but I'll be torched before I bring you into a battle without preparing you as best as I can to defend yourself."

She was quiet for a few moments, and I let her process. "I agree," she finally said with a sigh. "But Ben...what can I *do*?"

She gestured to herself, then to me. "Compared to you, I'm...."

"Stop right there," I said sternly, holding up a finger. "This is partially my fault. I've been so focused on making up for your vulnerabilities that I haven't tried to pull out your strengths, but from now on, that's what I'll try to do. Keep me accountable: if I slip up, call me out."

When I met her gaze to show her I was serious, her lips twitched. "Alright. *What* strengths, though? Other than the fact that I seem to be able to charge up at night."

"Don't underestimate how realms-shaking that is by itself," I pointed out. "It could be the very reason you'll be needed at the battle. The Devourer is attacking on literally the darkest day possible: a winter solstice and a solar eclipse."

"Really? Ugh, that's...." Sarah trailed off in horror.

"Exactly," I agreed. "We can send warriors through sungates to other places to regain their strength during the eclipse, but that tactic has problems of its own."

"The gates," Sarah whispered, glancing fearfully at me. "If they fail...."

She understood so much already. Smart, and with a good memory, she was putting the pieces together faster than I'd wished her to for her own sake.

"Yes," I said simply, throat tight.

"But I'm just one person," Sarah protested. "Sure, *maybe* I could have more power than you would at night, but what good could I do in the grand scheme of things? How am *I* supposed to tip the scales?"

I would a thousand times have rather told her that she shouldn't worry, that she could stay back, somewhere safe, while others risked their lives to defend all worlds from the Devourer's hunger. Not her.

But I couldn't.

Instead, I said grimly, "That's what we're going to figure out."

"We're going to the armory," Sarah realized as we passed through the arch that led to the meeting hall on the left and on the right....

"I suppose with all the steel it has on display, that's as good a name as any," I mused as we walked into the room to the right. "But its main purpose isn't to store weapons."

"Then what?" Sarah asked.

I stepped into one of the inlaid metal rings on the floor, crouched, and brushed my fingers along the rim, giving it some of my energy to activate it. Sarah yelped and jumped back as a magical field of the same silver color shot up around me, encasing me in a translucent dome about forty feet in diameter. At least *this* worked like it was supposed to. This circle, this training floor, was as familiar to me as my own bedroom.

Even if I was used to gold.

With one flex of my fingers, I summoned a ball of fire to my palm, wound back, and hurled it with shattering force at the far edge of the dome. The ball exploded against the surface, sending sparks and tongues of flame everywhere. My lips twitched as I watched the remnants fall, and I wondered what the Moontouched who had made this room would have thought of the Heir of Flame making the first scorch marks on their spotless floor. But the dome had held perfectly, and that had been the point of my demonstration.

I pointed at the unscathed magical surface. "To train, holding nothing back. *Without* bringing the mountain down on top of us."

Sarah's eyes were wide, her fists clenched. Since I hadn't strengthened the shield to the point at which it blocked sound or smell, I caught a whiff of salty sweat mingling with her cool scent.

My hand fell back to my side, and my flameheart chilled. I took one step forward, then realized that might be the opposite of reassuring, and froze.

"Sarah...." I said helplessly, not knowing what else to say or do.

At the sound of my voice, she blinked, then shook herself. She laughed shakily as she rubbed her arms. "Sorry, I'm fine. You just...startled me. I don't know how, but I keep forgetting you're...."

"A torched idiot?" I supplied ruefully.

"No," she said with surprising calm. "Dangerous."

I blinked. "How in the Six Realms could you forget that?"

No one else I'd ever met could. I was the Heir, *and* the son of Kavarian Sunfilled, for Flame's sake. To everyone else, that meant something.

She laughed, the sound normal and relaxed now. "I dunno. Most of the time, you're just...you."

Flame above, I was doomed—and what was worse, I was in deep enough that I no longer cared.

To hide how her simple explanation had made me feel, I said gruffly, "Well, try to remember. Because I'm not always going to be able to give you a warning before I have to throw a fireball—or worse."

"Point taken," she said firmly. "All the points. I have a lot to learn, this is a training ground where you can teach me, and you're dangerous—because you have to be."

"You are too," I said. "Don't forget that, either."

"I don't *feel* dangerous." She looked to where the fireball had hit, at the scorch marks on the floor. "I can't be you, Ben."

I dismissed the dome with a gentle tap and approached her slowly, but she showed no sign of trepidation. She looked up at me with complete trust—such a stark difference from her fear from before. Or had it been fear? Something of it lingered in her eyes, but trust couldn't mingle with fear. Unless it wasn't fear at all, but...awe.

Shoving aside my own torrent of self-centered feelings, hope burning hot among them, I focused firmly on her. I kneeled on one knee in front of her, making her head higher than mine.

I gave her a crooked smile. "Sarah, do you really think the Seven Realms need two of me?"

Her lips tugged into an answering smile. "Personally, I think you're pretty great."

It's not about you right now, I chanted to myself. *It's not about you.*

Still, I couldn't help widening my smile. "Let me put it this way, then: do you think the Tree of Ice needs an Heir like me?"

That gave her pause. Her smile faded. "I guess...not."

"Why would that be?" I prompted patiently.

Flame, I was sounding like my father.

She huffed at being forced to state the obvious, as I had done many times before. "Because she didn't choose someone like you."

When I simply waited with a small smile, she finally finished the statement, her voice quiet. "She chose...me."

"Exactly. Which means that *you*—" I tapped her gently on the forehead. "—are what we need. I feel that to the core of my flameheart. There's something special about you—many somethings, probably—that I don't have, that I can't offer the Seven Realms. You are what we need, Sarah. Today. Tomorrow. In ten days. In fourteen, forty, eighty years. You might not be right now what you need to be then, but you have the seeds inside you, and you have until then to grow them, with Her help. For what it's worth, you have all of mine."

Her eyes glistened. To my surprise, she threw her arms around me, nearly making me lose my balance.

"Thank you," she said thickly, resting her head on my shoulder.

"Er...you're welcome?" I tentatively put my own arms around her. "Flame, Sarah, I didn't mean to make you cry."

"Yeah, you did," she said with a laugh, pulling away slowly. Though I regretted the distance, I warmed at how her hands lingered on my shoulders, and how she seemed content with mine on her hips.

Teasingly, she said, "You can't just say things like that to a girl and not expect her to cry."

"Uh...sorry?" Was that what I was supposed to say?

All I knew for certain was that I was *not* supposed to be thinking about how close her lips were to mine.

She wiped her eyes, sniffed, and smiled. "They're good tears, don't worry. I needed that."

"Well, good, then, I guess," I mumbled. Then, because I *had* to put some distance between us or I would do something that would ruin the gift I'd somehow given—*Friend, friend, friend, not about you, you're her friend*—I pulled back and rose to my feet.

"So," I said, clearing my throat. "Time to brainstorm."

She blinked. "About what?"

I smiled crookedly. "How you can be dangerous."

She followed me to the wall of weaponry. "Ben...."

"Step one," I said, ignoring her. "Finding some weapons that work for *you*, so we can train you on them. I don't expect you to be good at it from day one, but the sooner we start, the sooner you can have *something* that is more likely to do harm to your enemies than to you."

"Very comforting," Sarah muttered.

"Except for that pep talk to start you out, it's not my job to be comforting."

She sighed. "It's your job to keep me alive, I get it."

I grinned at her. "So glad we're on the same page."

I lifted a large battleax down from the wall with both hands. She eyed it sidelong. "You gotta be kidding."

I chuckled. "In a way, I am. See, something like this—not for you. But just because it's one of the biggest and meanest-looking things on this wall doesn't mean it's the deadliest."

That got her thinking. She pursed her lips and scanned the wall. "What is, then?"

I had already done my scan for this lesson, so, after putting the ax back, I went straight to a bit of leather, picked it up, and handed it to her.

"What's this?" she said in puzzlement.

"It's a sling. You put some pebbles in here, swing it around—"

"Oh, I see. I've heard of a sling before. I've never held one in my hands, I guess."

She examined it for a few moments longer and then raised an eyebrow at me. "*This* is the deadliest weapon?"

"Think of it this way: sometimes, you don't need to take out broad swaths of monsters, as that battleax is meant to do. Sometimes you just need to kill the one who's the brains directing the rest, with something small, quick, fast, and ordinary, something that lets you keep your distance, something that's light, something that's harmless looking. If a *sling* is what you need and can use, then yes, it's the deadliest thing here."

"But you could apply that logic to practically anything here," Sarah said impatiently.

I just gave her a look and waited.

It didn't take her long. She huffed and handed the sling back to me. "Which means there's no right answer here. I get it. Except I'm fairly limited when it comes to things I *can* use."

"Probably not as much as you think," I corrected. "Let me be the judge of that. Go on. Look everything over. Point at whatever speaks to you, whether or not you think it's practical, and I'll let you know if it is."

"Whatever 'speaks' to me," she grumbled. She half-heartedly paced a bit in front of the display.

I had to admit the variety was overwhelming. Maybe that's why it was all out like this, instead of being stored more sensibly in an armory, as Sarah had assumed this was. Maybe it was for this very moment: for Sarah to see all the options at once and discover which was for her...and which was not.

She stopped pacing and looked back at me, troubled.

"What's wrong?" I asked, already breaking my promise to not be comforting by gentling my voice.

She sighed. "They're all...weapons. Meant to kill, I mean, or hurt, at the very least. I can't look at them all without feeling sick."

Ah, yes. I thought this might be an issue. Being half Peacegrowth, I'd had to work past this as well.

I took down a broadsword, the one Yvera had admired earlier, and I brought it to Sarah and kneeled in front of her again, holding the sword out on the flat of my palms so she could study it.

"This is a *beautiful* blade. I don't know if you know anything about smithing...."

She shook her head.

"Then just trust me when I say it's among the finest craftsmanship I've seen. The balance, the edge...." I shook my head as I stood up and stepped back so that I could move with it, giving it a few swings, some passes through a few stances. It could have been made for me, like an extension of my arm. I straightened, holding the hilt with both hands and the blade upright, almost touching my nose.

"Magnificent," I said simply. "But...."

I set it gently back in its holders on the wall. "Worthless, all the same, if you just look at the blade."

"What do you mean?"

"It has no soul," I said firmly. "In the end, it is just a lump of metal with a bit of rocks, resin, wood. It simply *is*. And what it is, is of no worth if we forget its intended purpose: to protect souls. To guard our greatest treasures...."

I met her eyes, and she gazed back soberly. "Each other."

Could she hear in my words, see in my face, what I would give to keep her safe?

I looked away before she could see too much. "The Battlebloods are our greatest defenders and warriors, and we rely on them dearly, yet any culture that revolves around bloodshed is in danger of loving it for its own sake. So, they have a strict code that each of the ones who decides to take up the call must solemnly swear to, and their Lady judges infractions severely. Yvera took the oath, and when I became Heir, I also became an honorary member of the clan, so I did too."

"What is it?" Sarah asked quietly.

I shrugged. "It has many more nuances that I'll not bore you with right now, but the essence is in the first few lines: I will spill blood only to save it from being spilled. I will not kill unless those I protect will be killed. I will put my feet on the path to battle only if it is the way to peace. I will be strength for the weak, fire for the flameless, a shield to the scaleless."

Perhaps it was time I reminded Yvera of that part of her oath.

I finished quietly. "I will give my life willingly, if my Tree asks it of me, for the good of all the Realms."

It had never occurred to me, until that moment, that Avva made that oath, when he became Heir. As did Avvi when she married him. The Tree could have simply called on their oaths. Instead, She gave them a choice.

Sarah came up to me and, to my surprise, twined her fingers with mine. When I looked down at her, her brown eyes gazed up at me with surprising fierceness. Now *there* was a bit of the fire I had been hoping to awake, and somehow I'd done it without even trying.

I realized how when she spoke. "You're going to be fine. We are *all* going to be fine."

I smiled with more force than I felt. "Of course we are. All of us. We're here to make sure of that. Starting with...."

Sarah groaned. "Step one."

But when she pulled away, there was a more determined set to her jaw, and that gave me relief.

Still, she stood a bit helplessly, looking at the overwhelming variety.

"Try closing your eyes for a moment," I suggested.

When she raised an eyebrow at me, I grinned. "Just trust me."

She sighed, but she did as I asked.

"Now, take a few deep breaths."

She did, and slowly, her shoulders relaxed, her chin came to neutral, the line between her eyes smoothed.

"The greatest warriors are the ones who make certain they use their strengths rather than compensate for their weaknesses. What are your strengths, Sarah?"

"I don't know!" she said in frustration.

"Then let me help a bit, to get you started," I said calmly. "You're fast. I've seen you run, remember?"

Her unexpected burst of speed that first time, when she'd run from me, had nearly given me a heart attack. So had her brave run over the dark mesa to an invisible gate, though fear had mixed with pride in my flameheart that time.

"Not as fast as you," she muttered, clearly remembering as well. "Or Yvera."

"So you won't be able to outrun the two of us," I said with a shrug. "But I bet you my month's stipend that you can outsprint Kor."

That brought a small smile to her lips.

"Fortunately for you, Yvera and I are unusually long-legged. You won't often be facing a person or creature that can outrun you: and if you can run, *do*. That's the second secret: a fight avoided is a fight won."

She nodded, eyes still closed.

"So you're fast," I repeated. "And agile. You could one day maneuver like I could only dream. But I'd prefer that until you have more stamina and experience in combat that you keep your distance."

Was that right? Was I letting my fears hold her back?

But she nodded in relief. "That feels right to me, too."

Praying I wasn't leading her in the wrong direction, I said, "Good. Follow that feeling, then. A long-range weapon of some kind. If the Moontouched who made this training room for you knew what you would need, what would they put there for you that you could use from a distance? Something you're maybe already familiar with? Something that wouldn't require too much training before you could use it to defend yourself?"

I was eyeing the lightweight crossbow as I spoke, but I followed my own gut and kept my prompts vague. This had to come from her, after all. Besides, even that crossbow might take her a bit of strength training to be able to draw by herself, and it wasn't so useful when the enemy was closing range....

Her face scrunched in thought. "Well, that would be.... But surely there isn't...."

Her eyes opened, searching without expectation. Then her eyes suddenly widened, falling on something in the corner of the room. Far from the crossbow.

"What?" I asked.

Without answering, she walked to that corner, and I followed. I saw many options in that area, including some throwing knives that maybe I could get her started on, but she reached for something that escaped my notice until that very moment. Which was odd, considering I had never seen its like before, and I thought I had been meticulously trained in every weapon known in the Six Realms.

It was made of silver metal burnished matte, perhaps for better grip or to not be as reflective. It had a handle that Sarah grasped to take it down, then another, perpendicular portion above the grip that protruded inches beyond her knuckles. For the life of me, I couldn't figure out what it was supposed to do. Was it some kind of bludgeon?

"What *is* it?" I asked, baffled.

"So, you *haven't* seen something like this?" Sarah asked, seeming unsurprised.

"No," I said in consternation. "Have you?"

"Yes," she said quietly. "It's called a gun."

"An Earthren weapon?" That made me feel better and worse at the same time. If I didn't know what it did, how was I supposed to train her on it? Or keep her from harming herself?

Her lips twitched. "I guess you could call it that. One of the deadliest inventions of man."

Since she'd said that her kind made weapons that could level cities, that didn't make me feel better.

"You know how to use it?" I asked in a level tone, trying hard to hide my unease.

"More than I would like," she said with a frown. "Mom and Dad don't like guns. They wouldn't allow any in our home, but when Michael moved out, he got one. He took me to a range a few times, taught me how to shoot it. He said Mom and Dad had good intentions, but that times were changing, getting more dangerous. He said he wanted me to be able to defend myself."

She met my gaze and shrugged. "He took his older-brother protective duties seriously even before he became a cop."

Well, he had earned himself many points in my ledger for that. One would hope, then, that this protective brother would know what he was about in handing her one and showing her how to use it.

"What does it do?"

"Well, it's meant to shoot ammunition...." At my raised eyebrow, she clarified. "Er, think hard metal objects, like stones for the sling. It shoots them so fast that, depending on the gun and the distance involved, the bullet can go clear through someone."

I stared at her, but unfortunately, I could imagine such a wound all too well. Drakón skilled in magic could do such a thing: take a pebble and thrust it with power so fast and with such force...but that took finesse, and usually more control and power than it was worth. Especially since, if the intended victim was prepared and was wearing the right armor, they could defend against it easily enough.

"What about shields, armor?" I asked. "Can something stop it?"

"Some things can, but the armor is expensive, heavy, and bulky, so usually only soldiers and police use it. I think it is mostly just for the torso, to protect the most vital organs, but I'm not sure about that. Most times, there's really nothing you can do against a gun, except get it away from the shooter or take them out first. We don't have magic, like you do."

"I see," I said grimly. No wonder it would be such a devastating weapon.

Perhaps it was just the sort of edge someone like her needed in my worlds. Why else would it have been there? Why else would she have been drawn to it? I took one deep breath, asking the Tree for one simple answer.

A question so simple—just a *yes* or a *no*—had a low enough cost that I only felt a mild drain on my strength to open the connection for just a single moment. When my flameheart warmed and surety filled me, I sent Her a silent thanks and straightened.

I expected that to be all, but the Tree added something more in farewell. *Trust. You are right to be wary of such a thing, but trust in Us. Trust in her.*

Then Her presence faded.

"Well," I said calmly, hopefully showing no sign I had doubted. "Want to try it out?"

"Really?" Sarah said in apprehension. "You really think this is it?"

"Oh, I'll get you trying some other things, don't worry," I said with a crooked smile, putting a hand on her shoulder. "But this is the only thing you've already used, right?"

"Yeees," Sarah said, drawing out the word as she examined the smooth metal device in her hands, turning it this way and that. "Sort of? It's a gun, but I've never seen one quite like it. For one thing, they don't normally have *this*."

She ran a finger down the clear crystalline strip inlaid in each side of the barrel.

"For another...." She pulled at it from a few angles, brow furrowed. "I can't get the magazine to come out—the part where you load the ammunition."

She looked all around where the gun had hung and down on the shelves below. "For that matter, I don't see any ammunition."

"What if it doesn't need ammunition?"

"Of course it needs...." Sarah straightened suddenly, looking up at me with widening eyes. She looked back down at the gun, then back at me.

"What?" I asked, spreading my hands.

"Everything in this place," she said slowly. "It's been recognizable to you as being from your worlds, your magic, your technology. Or it's been a blend of both our worlds, like the fridge, or the showers, or the automatic lights. *Or* it's been something completely other, something only the Moontouched could have created, by themselves—like the helping lights, or the moongates. But it's never been entirely *mine*. Or...Earthren, however you want to put it. If this had been what I thought it was, in its entirety, that would have broken the pattern. But you know what? I don't think it is. I think you're right: I don't think it shoots ammunition."

She looked down at the thing in her hands as if seeing it for the first time. "But then...what *does* it shoot?"

I shrugged helplessly. "Your guess is as good as mine—probably better."

Sarah bit her lip. When she spoke, she seemed like she could hardly believe she was saying the words. "I guess the only way to find out is...to try it out."

"Let's do it," I agreed.

I strode to the west wall, where there were metal rings inlaid just as they were on the floor, except in sizes ranging from a few feet to ten across. I brushed one of the ten-foot ones, and the silver field of energy snapped into existence, filling the circle.

"That's my target?" Sarah asked uneasily.

"What's wrong?" I asked as I walked back to her.

"Ben...gun ammunition is made of metal. If they bullet off that stone wall...."

"First," I said pointedly as I reached her. "I thought you said it didn't shoot ammunition. Second, nothing is going to bullet. That field entraps anything that hits it: stones, arrows, bolts, spears—all of it. They'll just stick like womasps in aldew."

"I have no idea what either of those things are."

I chuckled. "Whatever hits it will stick, alright? But, just in case...."

I led her to the hundred-foot marker in front of the target. Then I crouched a moment to touch the barrier line. The faintest field yet sprung up as a straight, floor-to-ceiling wall that stretched across the whole room. It was so translucent, you had to focus to even tell it was there, but it was, shimmering like a soap bubble.

"Don't be fooled by how delicate it looks," I said. I summoned an arcball to my hand with a slight shift to scales and back. "It's flexible enough on this side to let things through..."

I threw the rubber ball, just as I had the fire one. It flew straight through the barrier without the slightest resistance, but when it bounced off the far wall and careened at an angle back toward the barrier, it bounced off as if the barrier had been just as hard as the stone wall it first hit.

While the ball lost momentum by pinging around the space on the other side, I grinned at Sarah, whose jaw had dropped, and finished my sentence. "...but strong enough on the other side to not let anything come back."

Sarah's eyes followed the ball's trajectory and shook her head. "When we get to Earth, remind me to introduce you to a sport we call baseball. I think you'd like it."

"If you say so." My gut said we wouldn't have time to play games. "My point is, we've taken all the precautions we can take."

"All except the hearing protection, I guess," Sarah said with a sigh.

"Hearing?" I asked curiously.

"Guns are loud," she explained, holding out the weapon. "At least the ones I'm used to. It's like setting off a tiny explosion in your hand, and that would echo in this room like a thunderclap. I don't know what this one is going to do, but...."

I shrugged. "Better safe than sorry, I guess. May I?"

I reached out tentatively, remembering the last time I'd had to convince her to let me do magic on her ears.

I needn't have worried. She immediately stepped toward me. "Sure. What are you doing, though? I mean, how is it going to work?"

"I'm going to create another barrier, sort of like all of these, but this one will block out sound, and because it doesn't have any sort of anchor, I'm going to have to focus constantly to maintain it. It's a quick fix just for this experiment. I'll pull out some stuff I have if it looks like we're going to need it."

She frowned. "Why not just use it now, and save your power?"

I grinned. "Because it's a bit of a goopy mess. I assumed you'd want to skip on risking your hair if you could."

She laughed. "Yeah, I guess I do. I don't care personally, but I'm not sure my helpers would forgive me if I messed it up."

Nor would I. She was beautiful normally, but when I'd first seen her rush into the kitchen, wearing that clinging sweater, with her dark brown hair in a crown shining like the stars...my stomach had dropped, and it had been surprisingly hard to keep my eyes on Yvera.

Yvera had a bit of a point about the practicality of it, but I was also having a hard time caring.

"So...." I lifted my hands again.

"Go ahead," she said, looking at me with perfect trust. The contrast from before warmed my flameheart.

I cupped both her ears in my hands and brought a sheen of power to the surface of my skin. I shaped it to her ears, focusing on what I wanted it to do: block sound, protect her delicate membranes. Then I hardened it in place and pulled away. Even after I let go, I felt a constant invisible pull from each of the gold casings around her ears, to which I gave a constant trickle of energy, and would for as long as the experiment lasted.

I hadn't mentioned to Sarah that I could create an anchor for my power, much like the metal lines in the floors and walls were, but that would involve my blood again, and though she might trust me now, if she disliked my expenditure of power for her sake, she would dislike my bleeding for her even less—even though the amount of power spent would be about the same, if you counted what I'd need to heal. With the blood, I would just have to concentrate less—one payment of power and done—which made it the better choice in my mind, but I wasn't going to bother trying to convince her of that.

"Are they working?" I asked.

Sarah watched my lips move, but she just blinked. Louder than necessary, she said, "If you just asked if they're working, then that's a definite yes. Geez, I can't hear *anything*. Except a ringing."

That's your mind compensating for the silence, I told her with my inner voice.

"I figured."

Well, I said, gesturing to the target. *Have at it.*

She frowned at me. "Aren't you going to do your ears, too?"

No. Before she could protest, I said firmly, *My ears are a bit...tougher, and any damage to them will heal within moments at this time of day. Besides, if neither of us can hear, how are we supposed to know how loud the gun is? That's kind of an important detail for us to be aware of.*

She scowled, but she turned toward the target. She paused for a moment, brow furrowed, and then walked beyond the hundred-foot mark and took a few more steps to come right up against the barrier. Then she tentatively probed the end of the barrel through the barrier so that the tip, where I presumed something would shoot forth, was beyond it.

"Just in case," she told me, looking over her shoulder. "And...just in case, stay behind me."

I nodded. What I didn't say was that I had power tingling at the surface of my skin, ready at a second's notice to throw up an additional shield around her.

She settled into a stable stance, bringing both hands to the handle of the gun.

Wait, I said quickly as something occurred to me. *Just give me a second to alert Kor and Yv.*

Sarah nodded and relaxed.

Normally, communicating with an inner voice was a bit like directing an arrow of thought to your target, as I had just done with Sarah, but private communication required knowing your target's location. I could see Sarah, so that made it easy to use my inner voice with just her. Had anyone else been in the room, they wouldn't have heard a thing. However, not knowing exactly where my wings were, I instead had to cast a wide net, projecting my inner voice far and wide, akin to indiscriminately shouting—except with my power carrying the silent message, it went much further than a shout could.

Kor, Yv. Don't be alarmed if you hear a loud noise coming from the training court. Sarah and I are experimenting with something.

Their replies were immediate and typical.

With what? Yvera demanded.

Without *me?* Kor said in consternation.

I tuned them out and nodded to Sarah. She looked back at the target, raised the gun again, resettled, and took a deep breath. Then pulled the crossbow-like trigger.

The inlaid crystal strips flared white, I saw the faintest and quickest of blurs, and I heard a soft *thwap.* But that was all. Sarah slowly lowered the gun, keeping both hands on it, and stared at the target, as did I.

A slightly misting shard of *something* stuck out from somewhere near the outer ring of the target.

"What is *that?*" Sarah asked.

"It's cold, whatever it is," I said, straining all my senses, including tapping into the map of heat I could feel through my flameheart. I felt a void of warmth right where the shard was.

Sarah looked back at me. "What? Did you say something?"

I waved the shields on her ears away. "You won't be needing those. That's quieter than even a bow. As I said, whatever it is, it's cold. Freezing. My guess is ice."

Sarah stared at the gun in her hands as if it were about to come alive and bite her. "I am holding...an ice dart gun."

I wasn't sure what a dart gun was specifically, but *dart* seemed as good a description as any for the tiny ice shard.

"Did you feel a drain when you shot it?" I asked, eyeing the now steadily glowing white strips on the gun.

"Yeah," Sarah said wearily. "A big one. Seems a lot of effort for just one shot."

"Maybe not. Try taking another and see if it drains as much."

"OK," Sarah said slowly. She raised the gun again, sighted, and pulled the trigger.

This time, because I was waiting for it, I felt the tiny flare of power, the temperature drop around the gun and even Sarah, the cold rush of energy rocketing from the tip. This time, the shard appeared a few feet closer to the center of the circle.

"That wasn't so bad," Sarah said in relief. "And the kickback is almost nothing—nothing compared to what I'm used to."

My hunch was right. "The drain wouldn't have been as much because—"

"What in the hellwinds is going on?" Yvera cried, rushing into the court. Her sharp violet eyes took stock of the situation in an instant. If the setup of a training court was as familiar to me as my bedroom, to Yvera, it was her mother's womb.

"Ben, what is *that*?" Yvera demanded as she strode over to me, pointing at the weapon in Sarah's hands.

"Sarah says it's called a gun," I said calmly, folding my arms and giving her a look that was a wordless command to *cool the torch down*. "We think it's a magic-class precision stealth shooter with a short-to-medium range and—for now—ice projectiles."

"We do?" Sarah said in confusion. "And...for *now*?"

I inwardly sighed. I'd been *trying* to win Sarah some points in Yvera's ledger.

Kor burst into the room, hair wet and mussed, shirt untucked, gasping. "What...did I...miss?"

"Let me see that," Yvera snapped, going to Sarah.

"Yv," I said quietly. She would know from my tone that would be her only warning.

She paused. Then she held out her hand, and, from between clenched teeth, she said, "Please?"

Oh, this is going to be good, Kor silently said to me as he came to my side. A smirk was on his lips, and his eyes were bright. Yvera may know weapons, but Kor knew *magic*—and this was perhaps more of the latter than the former.

I knew them both, especially in combination. But, still feeling some of the embers from my temper this morning and thinking Yvera needed the lesson, I stayed silent.

"Sure, I guess," Sarah said with a shrug. She showed the gun to Yvera, pointing to the parts as she mentioned them. "You point this end at the target, and you pull this—"

"I think I can figure it out," Yvera said irritably, snatching the gun. "I've been shooting crossbows since before you knew your letters."

With one hand, she pointed at the target, sighted, and pulled the trigger.

Nothing happened. Nothing...except the gun flaring white hot and Yvera dropping it with a hiss and a string of colorful curses. It hit the stone floor with a loud clatter, and Sarah winced. Kor shook with suppressed laughter, but since he valued his life, he kept it in.

"Are you OK?" Sarah gasped, tiptoeing to peer as closely as she dared at Yvera's hand.

"Fine," Yvera hissed, stepping away from her, but I knew from the way she held her pink hand that it would be stinging with a shallow burn.

She glared at Sarah as I felt her send a surge of energy to her hand to heal it. "You knew it was imprinted, didn't you?"

"Imprinted?" Sarah said in bafflement.

"No, she didn't," I told Yvera coolly, arms still folded. "I was just explaining that to her before you so rudely interrupted us."

She turned her gaze to mine, a wounded look entering her eyes, but chagrin was also there, and she looked away when I only raised an eyebrow. She knew she was the one at fault here.

Sarah, apparently, disagreed. "Ben!" she snapped, pointing at the gun on the floor. "You knew that would happen?"

"I guessed it would."

"You should have warned her," Sarah scolded as she crouched cautiously over the gun.

"She shouldn't have needed the warning."

Even if she couldn't have guessed at a distance that the weapon was imprinted, as Kor and I did, she should have felt it as soon as she touched the gun. But for her own stubborn, blind reasons, she'd ignored the warning signs and tried to use it anyway. That was the arrogant idiocy that got a rightwing and her leader killed. Hence why I wasn't feeling guilty, and why Yvera was so furious—with no one right now more than herself.

"You can pick that up," I continued quickly, since I saw Kor looking as if he wished to elaborate, and Yvera was already suffering enough without him rubbing it in. "It should be cool to the touch for you."

Sarah prodded the gun with a finger, and finding it just as I said, picked it up gingerly and rose with it to her feet. "What do you mean, imprinted?"

"Meaning just what you saw and felt. That gun was probably always meant for you, but the first time you used it, you sealed it as your own. That's why the first shot took so much out of you, on top of giving it a full charge. From now on, only you'll be able to use it."

Which gave me a great deal of comfort. A powerful weapon was only good if you could make sure it didn't fall into the wrong hands.

Sarah ran her hand along the barrel, over the white glow. "These strips...." She glanced at me. "They weren't white before, were they?"

"No, they weren't. That's what made me suspect it had imprinted on you. Think of them as like the doorgems at the last hold, except that gun will have to be melted down before it will answer to anyone else."

Sarah's eyes widened. "You mean it won't shoot—at all? For anyone else?"

I shook my head. "It's a common feature of magic-based weaponry. You give it its power, you focus its purpose, so it bonds to you—like molding itself to your unique shape."

"What do you mean, focus its purpose?"

"It shot two ice shards, probably because that was the simplest thing it could do with what you gave it, but another property of magic-class weapons is that their greatest limitations are usually how much imagination and power you put into them. At the very least, you could give the ice specific properties. Sharpness, hardness, or accuracy, for example. Perhaps even light."

Sarah cocked her head as she listened intently to me. At the last suggestion, she blinked. "Why would I want my darts to glow?"

Yvera snorted at that lack of tactical imagination, but I ignored her.

"Say you were separated from us momentarily." Flame forbid, but both she and I needed to plan for that contingency. "If it wouldn't attract unwelcome attention, you could use the lights to guide us back to you."

Her face cleared. "Oh! Like a signal flare."

"Or perhaps you wish to track your target in the dark," Yvera muttered.

Sarah grimaced, and I sighed. I had been trying to start her thinking along the nonlethal lines for a reason.

"Yes, yes," Kor said with slight impatience. "That's all wonderful. Give it another shot, will you? So I can observe this time."

Sarah rolled her eyes, but her lips twitched as she met my gaze, and I wondered if she were remembering Kor's less articulate request from not too long ago, which Kor had probably already forgotten. He tended not to remember his mumble state. Or so he claimed.

"Alright, Kor. For you," Sarah said dryly, and she aimed and fired.

And hit just a foot shy of center.

With a weapon like that in her hands, that she already was looking confident using and rapidly improving in, that no one could use against her if they got it out of her hands...I was feeling better already.

"Next time," I murmured. "Think *accuracy*. Imagine it hitting center with all your might."

Sarah nodded grimly without looking away from the target, sighted, and pulled the trigger.

With a soft hiss and *thwip*...the shard hit dead center.

Kor and even Yvera stared at the slightly steaming shard, which they would know full well had traveled with enough speed and force to pierce through a heart.

Oh, yes. Much better.

CHAPTER FIVE

POWER

SARAH

IT TOOK ANOTHER HOUR for us to leave. Since packing was simplicity itself for drakón, about ten minutes of that was Ben going through my things to handpick what went into my backpack to best ensure my survival and comfort (in that order), and the rest of it was debating in my kitchen where we were going to go next.

To no one's surprise, Kor had already thought on and researched the matter, and equally unsurprising, he thought we should go to his home world, Oshal, first. Yvera flatly disagreed, thinking we should go to hers, Ekrel. The only thing the drakón appeared to agree on without having to discuss was that we were not going to Ythra.

I had been the one to suggest it, thinking wistfully of seeing Ben's home and meeting the King in person. So far, I'd only heard about him or talked with him once over scale, but I had a feeling that being in the same room as him would be another experience entirely, one I was looking forward to with surprising fervor.

I also thought Ythra was the choice that would make everyone happy. After all, the part of Yvera's angst that wasn't about me was about not being in the center of the action, and Kor had seemed to feel some of the same. I also hadn't forgotten that note of longing in Ben's voice when he had gazed at the image of his home world.

"No," Ben said simply, while Kor shook his head grimly and Yvera snorted.

"No," Kor agreed. "Better do that one last."

"Because of the symbolism?" I asked, baffled.

"Because Crownhold is in torched chaos right now," Yvera said. "If we aren't going to ride the whirlwind, we'd better stay clear of it."

"A bit of an overstatement," Kor corrected. "It's very calm, purposeful chaos. This is Kavarian, Alyish, and Eskala, after all."

"Avva and his wings," Ben explained at my blank look. "Alyish is his rightwing—a legendary general who has proved himself an exceptional strategist and warrior over his decades of leading the Warflight."

"My great-grandfather," Yvera said with a proud smirk.

Figures, I thought.

"And the leftwing, Eskala," Kor said with a dreamy look that had me staring. "Perhaps the most brilliant mind to have ever graced the Six Realms."

Yvera elbowed him in the chest, making him squawk in protest. "What was that for?"

"I've told you—stop this mooning over Eskala. It's wrong."

"She's single!"

"And three times your age," Yvera said with a gagging sound.

"And remarkably well-aged," Kor said, dreaminess undeterred.

"She's not a wine, you dimtorch!"

"In any case," Ben said loudly, addressing me. When the others fell silent, he lowered his voice to a normal level. "Rumor is now fully circulating across the Six Realms that I and my wings have found a Moontouched Earthren. Avva hasn't acknowledged the rumor or announced you yet, since he's waiting for your final decision. Even so, you set one foot in Crownhold, or even Ythra, and that's tantamount to open acknowledgement, and then the political games begin. Not only would that be unfair to you, we can't afford to be distracted right now—or *be* distracting. No, we'll do Ythra last, when hopefully everyone is fully focused on the Tree's defense."

"I see," I said slowly, gut twisting. Most of my interest in seeing Ben's home withered, leaving a dread for when I'd have no choice.

Could I really do this? Enter this world of power and politics as one of its major players? Every time I thought that just maybe I had what was in me to take the Tree's offer....

I'd tried to control my expression, but unfortunately, Ben must still have seen something of my doubt and dread.

He gripped my shoulder, face softening. "It will be alright, I promise. I'll be there, we'll all be there, to help."

I heard Yvera's quiet snort, but I only nodded to Ben, hoping he'd just drop it. "So...where do *you* think we should go, then?"

Ben gazed back at me and said seriously, "I think that's up to you."

Yvera groaned. "*Ben*, why are you asking the ignorant Earthren to make all the important decisions?"

"I don't know," Ben told her flatly. "Maybe because last time she did, we discovered this hold."

"Last time, we nearly died," Yvera snapped back.

"The Tree told us to stay, and the Tree told us to listen to her," Ben said, eyes flashing. "You have a problem with that, take it up with Her."

Yvera flinched as if he'd slapped her and stepped back, falling silent. I wondered if Ben's words held a double meaning for her.

Ben let that silence sink in as he put both hands on the table and met both his wings' gazes by turns, because even Kor had looked skeptical.

"When are you two going to get it?" he said finally. "Who was the one who felt like there was some reason to linger on that mesa?"

Neither of them answered. Yvera wouldn't meet his gaze, Kor met it coolly.

"Who was the one who even *saw* that first moongate? Who was the one who opened it? Who commands *all* the moongates we're looking for?"

Still silence.

"Ben—" I murmured.

"No, Sarah. You need to hear this, too." Without taking his eyes off his wings, Ben pushed off the table and straightened. "We have ten days to search five worlds for invisible, insubstantial gates powered by a magic that we can't detect or understand that have remained undiscovered for a thousand years. *Ten days.*

To do that, we're going to need more than knowledge, more than skill. We're going to need Sarah. Because without her instincts telling us where to go and what to do, we might as well give up now."

The silence hung long and heavy this time. I had a difficult time swallowing, and my stomach now felt twisted into knots with dread. If that speech was supposed to make me feel better, it had failed.

"Here's a thought," Kor said quietly. "If it's so important to the Trees that we get to Earth, and if They control our access to the gates, why are They sending us on this mad rush of a hunt for all the others before they'll give up Earth's? Why the search at all?"

"Kor," Yvera snapped, looking livid.

"You've thought it," Kor snapped back. "As much as you try to convince me otherwise, I know you have a brain in that head of yours, so you've thought it. Don't put on self-righteous airs just because I'm the only one who dares to say it out loud. Don't give me some ashes about 'there must need to be an order to things.' The Trees have always had complete control of the gates, from the swearing of the First Covenant. They could open the gate to Earth, but They haven't. Instead, They give us this ridiculous task, with a deadline that we can only meet with Their help. Why?"

Yvera looked so furious she was white. Ben didn't seem shaken; he only gazed back, arms folded, face expressionless.

"The Trees have been in perfect control of all of this for the entire past torched year of our lives—and beyond," Kor cried. "We searched and searched for Sarah, when the Tree of Flame could have told us exactly when and where she would appear—and neither of you ever asked why. You just did what the Tree told you, like usual. Well, I'm fed up and asking why. Why send Sarah *now*? Why try to restore the Moontouched when it's almost too late for them to do us any good? Why, when time is apparently so precious, send us on this torched hunt when our duties should lie elsewhere? Why? So They can watch us and laugh as we race around through Their hoops, then pat us on the heads as if we were good little hatchlings and give us our treat? *Why*?"

Kor let that sink in. Then he pointed at the archway out into the Rim. "If all the Trees cared about was our survival, we would have been standing here a year ago—*at least*—and the gate to Earth would already be out there. We would be walking straight through it, presenting Sarah to the Tree of Ice, getting her invested, and getting her right back here to be trained and educated *properly*, and outfitted with wings and a clan of her own, so that by the time the Devourer came—on the day the Trees knew it would be coming *all along*—she would be even somewhat prepared to help us meet it. But in Their infinite wisdom, that's not the way They wanted it to be. They have the answers. They have the power. Yet this is how They chose to use it, all supposedly in the name of *saving* us. So, I ask the question that is on all our minds, but I am the only one who will say it: *why?*"

I looked at Ben, as did Yvera. My heart was thumping, wondering what answer he would give. I certainly didn't expect the one that came.

"Kor," Ben said quietly, almost gently. "If you wish to take a leave of absence to go ask the Tree your questions, it's granted."

Kor snorted, folding his arms. "As if She would answer me."

"She tends to not reward a confrontational attitude," Ben agreed mildly. "I've learned that from personal experience."

I blinked. Ben? Confrontational with his Tree? I'd never heard him talk about Her with anything but reverence. I had a hard time imagining what would make him mulish with Her. I must not have been the only one, because Yvera was visibly startled.

"I don't have an answer for you, Kor," Ben continued, spreading his hands. "All I can say is that, even though everything you said has merit, I still trust Her—I still trust Them. I'll still do what They say, even as needless as it seems to us now. Call that stupidity if you want, but I don't exactly see another solution. Do you?"

"No," Kor said darkly.

Ben rounded the table between them and offered his hand to Kor. "So where does that leave you, Korinth Starkissed? Once again following your naive Heir on another seemingly dimtorch quest, or...not?"

Ben's words had been mild, but from Yvera's inhale and the flash in Kor's eyes, I guessed something more significant was going on than I could see on the surface.

Kor clenched his jaw for a long, tense moment, and his fingers dug into his folded arms. Finally, he huffed and broke Ben's gaze, scowling at a distant corner of the kitchen. "Of course I'm coming. Your chances are dim already, but they'd be abysmal without me."

"They would indeed," Ben said with a thin smile.

When Kor finally took his hand, they just gripped, without shaking, eyes locked.

"Thank you, Kor," Ben said with relief when they let go. "I was *not* looking forward to finding another leftwing. There's not a one that could have replaced you."

I had to suppress a gasp as I finally realized just what had been at stake.

Kor sniffed. "True."

Sobering, he said grimly, "You realize I'm still going to ask 'why' when the Tree is concerned—in private. I'll present a unified front, like a good leftwing, but when we're alone...."

"I wouldn't ask for anything less from you. Honestly, I'm surprised it's taken this long to come to this."

"I don't trust the Tree," Kor said, rolling his eyes. "But, Flame only knows why...I trust you."

"You realize that makes no logical sense?" Ben teased lightly. "Since I just do what the Tree tells me to...."

"I *know*," Kor growled. "So, if you want to keep me as a leftwing, I advise you to not put it in so many words like that again. It is one of the very few things I put excruciating effort into *not* thinking about."

Ben smiled. "Noted."

He turned back to me. "Now that's resolved, let's figure out where we're going."

My mind froze with stage fright. "Er...what are my options again?"

Kor sighed in resignation, but when he came over to the table where I was sitting, he placed a hemisphere of dark crystal on the surface and tapped it.

A hologram of each of the Six Realms and their suns appeared, stacked one on top of the other. Each sun was in the center and stayed still, forming a perfect vertical line, and their planets hovered around them in their various orbits. They even showed the illuminated and dark sides, the tilts of the axis....

"Oh!" I exclaimed, looking at the six stacked solar systems. "It's like an interstellar clock!"

Yvera rolled her eyes, but Kor nodded in approval. "Exactly. *And* a calendar. See, if I turn on the overlay...."

He tapped the hemisphere again, and this time the paths of the orbits appeared, each differently colored, with hundreds of notches, some longer than others.

"These show the days," Kor said, running his finger through the notches. His finger paused at one of the longer ones. "And these show the start of the months."

He tapped one of the runes that hovered between two long notches; I presumed the rune would give me the name of the month if I could read their script.

"Traditionally, each realm has its own calendar." Kor pointed to several orbits. "But for simplicity's sake, the standard across the realms is that of Kaldrir."

He pointed to the topmost sun, one of the largest. I dimly recognized the broad desert swaths of its orbiting Ythra.

"That's why the Tree of Ice gave us the days by Kaldrir," I murmured, fascinated. At some point—I didn't even know when—I'd pushed to my feet and kneeled on the stone bench for a better look, so my eyes were nearly level with that highest sun.

"Correct," Kor said in a carefully neutral tone. "We would have assumed that without further information, but it's good She made that clear."

Trying to change the topic for his sake, I pointed to the lines that had appeared through each planet when he'd turned on the calendar overlay. Different runes hovered at the end of each. "What do these mean?"

Kor gladly continued the lesson. "Those help you discern the season in each hemisphere—"

"Yes, yes," Yvera said impatiently. She jabbed her finger at Ythra. "But as you can see, day one is burning away, and we haven't even left this torched hold. Save the lectures for when we've saved the Realms, will you?"

"Yv," Ben warned, putting a hand on her shoulder. He grimaced apologetically at me and Kor. "Sorry to cut this short, but though she didn't have to be so rude about it, Yvera has a point. Thank you for getting out the solarus, Kor. It's a good visual aid for this."

He dropped his hand from Yvera's shoulder and, catching my gaze, named each planet below Ythra as he pointed to it. "Ekrel of the Battleblood. Oshal of the Starkissed. Romskal of the Strongshield. Yonvey of the Brightflare. Ykran of the Peacegrowth."

Ben's finger lingered over Ykran. "That's where we found the first gate."

At the last planet, I thought. *Interesting.*

Tuned in carefully to my budding instincts, I followed that latest unfurling. "I promise this question is relevant to my decision: what's behind the order of these?"

I gestured from top to bottom.

"Ythra was the first planet," Ben said carefully. "The birthplace of draká. Traditionally, the realms are arranged thereafter in the order in which we discovered and settled them."

"That's the simple answer," Kor said with a smirk. "Following my Heir's orders, I won't get into the controversy behind it."

I could well imagine there was contention about the order. Such struggles may seem petty to some people (usually the people at the top), but as the third child of eight, I was all too aware that order *mattered.*

"Remind me," I said quietly. "The original controversy around the Moontouched was about the order in which they were to receive their own realm, correct?"

I took the silence from the drakón ringed about me as confirmation and the encouragement I needed to keep following this feeling to its conclusion.

"I was brought to this planet." My finger hovered over Ykran. "The one belonging to the clan too peaceful to fuss that they were left until last. I'm guessing it's even one of the last places you guys looked for me."

More silence. Ben was going red from sheepishness, Yvera had folded her arms and looked away, and Kor was watching me with that intent look of his that made his eyes almost seem to glitter.

As a distracting aside, I got an inkling where his clan had gotten their name.

Reining in my focus—because I was on to something, I knew it—I continued. "It seems to me that means something. Say the Trees aren't cruel or crazy. Say there is some reason for all this running, or, well, flying around. I still have no idea what that might be, but I think we have our first hint here. If you insist on going with my gut, then I say that next we go to..."

My finger hovered over the next planet up.

Yonvey, Ben supplied silently, saving me from my embarrassment at having already forgotten the name.

"...Yonvey," I said with conviction, hoping Kor and Yvera didn't notice the slight heat rising to my cheeks.

Then the last will be first.... Kor murmured silently to me.

"What?" I asked, nonplused.

"Nothing," Kor said, a bit too casually. "As good a reasoning as any, I suppose. Just wish I'd known that in advance so I could have done better research on potential moongate locations."

"Well, Kor, I think we've found a general order you can predict from now on," Ben said quietly. When I glanced at him, his eyes were on the display, his expression heavy.

I felt a twinge of regret. I hadn't meant my explanation to be directly condemning, but I knew Ben well enough by now to know that he would take on needless guilt anyway.

"Great," Yvera grumbled. "*Brightflare.*"

"What's so bad about the Brightflare?" I asked.

Don't get her started, Kor said urgently.

Nearly at the same time, Ben forced some vigor into his voice to forestall Yvera. "Well, now that we know where we're going, it's time to fly out."

I COULD GET USED to this, I thought with some surprise.

After wrapping up in my kitchen, we went back through the moongate (the only active one we had unlocked and thus our only way back into the Six Realms) and onto the mesa in the Peacegrowth world of Ykran, and now we were in the air once again, soaring over the jungle where I'd first appeared.

It was only my fourth time flying on Ben's back, and only the second with a saddle, but already I felt surprisingly at home as I gazed out into the cloudless blue, as I watched the dragons' giant shadows skim over that undulating green carpet of the jungle canopy below. As long as Ben's wing-beats remained steady and his flight path level, I found something oddly meditative—almost trancelike—about flying. Even my contemplation of the height I would fall if the saddle somehow failed me was almost dreamily fatalistic.

I idly wondered how difficult it would be for Ben to catch me.

It was also getting easier to think of the giant, gold-scaled behemoth just underneath me as *Ben.* Seeing another transformation on the mesa had added a layer of solidity to the connection, and so did hearing his inner voice check in with me occasionally, coinciding with the golden dragon's enormous head turning as far as he dared to glance at me. I didn't understand how there could be something so familiar about his eyes, even with them changed to black reptilian slits set in golden orbs, but there was.

Speaking of which....

Ben's head swiveled, eyeing me. *Still doing alright?*

I took out the blue flag and waved it to indicate *yes.*

Good. We're almost there, don't worry. You should be able to see Kergin Hold in a few dek.

I still didn't know what dek were, but if we were almost there, then I assumed it wouldn't be long, so I turned my focus to the horizon.

Sure enough, in about five minutes or so, I saw a mountain range rise in the distance, with specks of varying colors flying in and out of it like bees around a hive. Those "bees" formed into dragons, of course, and a small group of them broke off in their circling loop and began flying in our direction, a scarlet one letting out a trumpeting bellow that Ben answered. It clearly was a greeting of some kind, not aggressive—I recalled *those* kinds of roars with piercing clarity—but the sound, on top of startling me, was loud enough that I felt the vibrations even through the saddle, and my ears rang a bit afterward. Finally, his warm, spicy scent enveloped me in a dizzying cloud as the wind blew his breath back to me.

Well, I thought faintly. *At least it doesn't stink.*

Far from it, actually; something about that scent made *me* hot inside, and longing curled itself like a new and voracious kind of hunger in my stomach.

Sorry about that, Ben said sheepishly, perhaps belatedly realizing in part what effect his answering bellow would have on me. He must have simply guessed, because he didn't spare a glance backward as he and his wings approached the other group.

The rest of their communication, if any, must have been mind to mind, because the others didn't make any other sound I could discern other than the thunderclaps of their wings as they circled and merged with our group, ringing around us from all sides like airstrip workers guiding us in. Or perhaps they were an honor guard; surely they had recognized Ben, from their silent conversation if not by sight or the bellow.

I studied the rapidly approaching mountains in fascination.

Now I saw why everyone had dismissed Elspeth Hold, the first hold I'd seen and the one where I'd met Svyer, as being a backwater outpost. For example, it had had only one landing pad, whereas this one seemed to have ones dotting the range—more than I could easily count. The number of dragons on them and flying about was dizzying to me, not to mention the drakón and amón scurrying about on the pads, moving around cargo, talking in groups, making repairs, and shimmying up and down the mounting platforms.

We angled for one of the highest and yet largest pads, taking up the widest available peak; even then, it was shored up on many sides with giant blocks of stone so that it formed a perfect oval, and at its center...

...could only be a sungate.

The enormous arch made of smooth stone blocks towered at least hundreds of feet tall and several hundred feet wide. Inside it...was fire. An enormous wall of fire, waving, flickering tongues licking beyond the arch but never spreading beyond—filling the arch in its entirety but confined to it perfectly. I could see now why it was called a *sun*gate; it even burned nearly as bright to my eyes, making it hard to even look at closely. Insofar as I was able to, I eyed the fire nervously.

We were really going to go through *that*?

We had come at the gate from the side, so we circled around. I assumed that was because we were aiming for the long strip of the oval to land, and I organized all the anxious questions I had for Ben, readying them for the moment he changed back and could hear me normally. Even when we came around to face the gate and the honor guard suddenly veered off, I still didn't realize what was coming next.

Get ready, Ben said.

I assumed he meant for the landing, but then he drew in his wings more closely than I'd expected, and we fell into a sharp dive.

Going *far* too quickly to land.

"Beeeeee—" I screamed.

Before I could even finish, before I even could fully comprehend what was happening, I was surrounded by fire. Heat overwhelmed me; it didn't burn, but it sure stung and crackled, going up even my nostrils and into my open mouth. It was gone in an instant, however, and in the next instant, I wished it was back, because it was preferable to the sensation of being compressed and stretched and shot through a cannon of light through a dark void—the most extreme rollercoaster ever, with G-forces that no being should ever be able to withstand. I might have gone momentarily insane trying to comprehend what was happening to me.

Then the void spat us back out through another roaring mouth of flame, and we were flying through the open air once more, shooting over a grassy plain and slowly climbing with each mighty wingbeat.

"—erg," I choked as a late, incoherent end to my scream.

Ben, I am going to kill you, I thought in a daze.

Oblivious to his impending doom, Ben said, *And that's that. Not too bad, right?*

I took in a deep lungful of air, slowly forcing myself to loosen my death grip on the saddle and forgo thoughts of murder in favor of examining our new surroundings.

More dragons flew and circled around us, more walked or sat on the ground below, with an even greater hubbub than there had been on the other side. For once, the hold didn't appear to be in a mountain. When I glanced behind, I saw the sungate had been on the highest rise around, but rolling plains stretched as far as I could see. The plains immediately below were dotted with orderly mounds, and drakón and amón descended or came up from them, so I presumed the main settlement was still underground.

An enormous wall made of off-white stone ringed the settlement, and on top of it rested a dome as translucent as a soap bubble; as we flew through, I only felt the slightest of tingles. Beyond lay fields upon fields of farmland, forming a quilt of greens, tans, and browns. I observed placid-looking beasts like giant, hairy rhinos pulling plows through the dirt and carts down the neat grid-roads.

Sarah? Ben asked, anxious this time. As soon as he leveled out, he glanced back at me.

Since I didn't know how to make death threats using flag signals, I did the next best thing: I ignored him.

Sarah, are you alright? Ben demanded urgently.

I met his reptilian eye, glaring hot daggers at him.

Alright, I can see you're mad, he said cautiously. *You can yell at me later. Just let me know now if you are physically sound or if I need to land now to heal you. Blue for fine, red for healing.*

I grumbled to myself, but I got out the blue flag and waved it sharply. He swiveled his head back to face front.

Thank you, and sorry. Like I said, you can yell at me all you want when we land, but remember that might be a deken or so.

We had discussed this. Guessing that the Moontouched might once again have built the moongate somewhere remote for the sake of secrecy, we had emerged from the most rural sungate on Yonvey. We would fly around the countryside until we got hungry and the drakón tired, then we would stop for a midday meal. Then we would get back in the air until we had to seek some place to spend the night. All of this was to give me as much exposure to as much of Yonvey as possible, hoping I would simply *feel* if a moongate was nearby.

It wasn't much of a plan, but...even Kor had to admit that it was our only option. Especially after we all saw the gate on Ykran vanish completely as soon as I closed it behind us, just as Ben had described it had done before for him. There was a reason the gates had not been discovered yet; the Moontouched had made them to be undetectable to anyone but—presumably—other Moontouched. We could only hope that we wouldn't have to spend another dangerous night in the open to find the next one.

I had a bright candle of hope that it wouldn't be necessary again. I now had something of a feel for the moongates, like another sense entirely. The closest comparison I could come up with was a sense of magnetism, a pull for something deep inside of me. I could feel something of that magnetic field even after the Ykran gate had vanished, something that lingered there....

My main worry now was about how close I had to be to feel it again.

The drakón flew as low to the ground as they dared whenever they could, but they had to balance my potential need for proximity with the perhaps equally urgent need for discretion. I realized now why Ben hadn't even shifted into humanform before going through the gate. He had warned me they would try to go through quickly to avoid as much scrutiny as possible—particularly questions about where we were going from people who didn't need to know. Even so, Ben and his wings were too recognizable, especially together, for us to have gotten out of the Brightflare settlement we had emerged into without being noticed, and word would quickly spread as to where in the Six Realms the Heir was now. Avoiding settled areas from then on as much as we could and flying high as possible when we couldn't were our only ways to keep our exact location from being tracked.

So, temper cooling, and twisted stomach settling, I got into the rhythm of the search, straining with all my might to feel what might be out there to feel.

To my sharp disappointment, I hadn't felt a thing by the time we landed near a small stream. I eyed the shade underneath the trees lining the banks longingly; the clear blue sky had seemed lovely at first, but eventually the glare in my eyes and UV rays on my skin became too much. Fortunately, I had light brown Latina skin from my mom; if I'd been as pale as my British-Norwegian dad, I might have been as pink as a strawberry by then.

Kor helped me down as he had before, with no slips this time, while Yvera remained in drakáform to pace up and down the bank, eyeing the placid herd of large, fat animals that looked something like a cross between a hippo and a hairy cow. They had to have been domesticated or stupid to not spook at three dragons landing within eyeshot; they just kept chewing right along.

I didn't know why Yvera was watching them. Were they dangerous? Did she think they could hide assassins somewhere in their herd? She couldn't possibly be thinking of eating....

My stomach churned, and I lost a bit of my appetite.

Ben approached me warily in humanform, hands in his pockets, shoulders hunched slightly. "Still mad?" he asked.

"What?" I asked absently, shifting my attention to him. Then I remembered and scowled. "Not really, but you know you deserve a slap or something for that, right?"

"For what?" he asked sheepishly.

"For not preparing me better! Ben, that wasn't just intense, that was...*insane*, and I don't mean that in a good way. I think I lost my mind for a moment back there. You just—just—dove right in—"

"I warned you we'd go through quickly," he protested.

"You didn't say you weren't even going to *land*," I cried, gesturing at the ground with both hands. "That dive alone gave me a heart attack."

At his flash of concern, I rolled my eyes and held up a hand. "No, not *literally*. And *then* I didn't know if the fire was going to burn me—"

"I wouldn't have brought you through if it would have," Ben snapped, his own temper flaring.

"What if it *could* have, Ben?" I said grimly. "I don't know if you've noticed this by now, but *I am not like you.*"

That gave him pause. He hesitated before speaking again, just looking at me.

I took a deep breath. "I don't know how any of this works. I know this sounds ignorant and silly right now, but...I'm not just human—I'm of ice. What if...."

Ben inhaled sharply. "I...."

I sighed. "It was all just very intense, very sudden, and without explanation. Consequently, I felt like I might just be about to die in three different ways in as many seconds. Can you understand why I was just a little mad?"

"Yes," he groaned, putting a hand to his forehead. "Flame, Sarah...I'm sorry."

He didn't make it easy to stay mad at him. I took another deep breath and then stepped up to him, putting my arms around him. "Don't do it again," I muttered, but I felt the last of the tension melt away as Ben put his own arms around me and held me close.

"I can't promise not to be so idiotic again," he said ruefully, "since it seems to be ingrained in me. But I *am* sorry, and I promise to try harder to explain things like that in the future, and to think more about how things could be...different for you."

"Thanks," I said with a sigh.

"Mind if I check?" Ben asked awkwardly as he took a step back. His hands lingered on my shoulders. "Now that you've got me thinking...."

"I'm pretty sure I'm OK, but go ahead," I said, shrugging. He had already done a healing check today, but secretly, I was all for another round.

When his warm power sunk into me, I had to bite my tongue to hold back a sigh of pleasure. You'd think after all the sun exposure I'd had that his heat wouldn't feel so good, but you'd be wrong. Speaking of, though....

Ben's power lingered on the surface of my exposed skin, sending pleasant tingles everywhere, and he sighed. "You're sunburnt. Of course."

"Am I?" I said, struggling to keep my voice from sounding dreamy. "It's harder to tell, with my skin tone."

"You'd be feeling it in a deken or two," he said with a frown of concentration. Presumably to aid in the healing, he moved one hand to my throat and brushed the fingers of the other down the side of my face. The intentness of his expression kept me from thinking his touch was a caress, but it felt enough like one that my treacherous heart picked up the pace anyway.

"Does that hurt?" Ben asked in concern, eyes flicking down toward my heart. I sincerely hoped his sense of my heartbeat came only from the healing connection and that he couldn't detect it normally.

"No," I said tightly. Which wasn't very convincing.

"Hold on, I almost have the sun damage healed," he soothed.

Goodness, I could *smell* him now—that warm, enticing aroma I'd caught on his dragon breath, like sand and salty surf on a tropical breeze, like sunbaked desert stone with a hint of juniper and creosote. Was it stronger right now because of his use of magic? Whatever the cause, it was making my head swim dangerously. I found myself caught between a fervent wish that he'd never stop and an urgent need for him to finish before I did something a lot more forward than I should at this stage of trying to win him. Especially in front of Yvera.

"There," he said, pulling away.

As his power faded, I was left feeling colder than I had any right to, standing on that plain, with the warm sun beating down.

"I should have thought to put sunbalm in your pack," Ben sighed, rubbing the back of his neck as he eyed the bag I was wearing. "I think I have some...."

"If not, I do," Kor called.

Ben and I turned. Kor, showing surprising initiative, had already spread a blanket and begun setting out a lunch. Yvera, now human, stood nearby, looking pointedly away.

Kor paused in laying out the food and, with the next shapeshift of his hand, produced a small round tin and held it out.

Ben strode over and took it. "Thank you," he said gratefully, then passed the tin to me. "This should help. You smear it on—"

"I understand," I said, popping open the tin. "We have something similar."

Similar, but not exactly like. I did indeed find a balm inside the tin—clearish, hard, and waxy. It warmed and melted easily enough at the touch of my finger to allow me to scratch out a thin layer. The herbal smell was pungent but still pleasant, almost minty, an improvement over the usual chemical smell. When I rubbed it on my arm, it spread surprisingly well, warming to a gel that absorbed into my skin without a trace.

"Nice," I said appreciatively as I approached the blanket.

Yvera, I noted, had meanwhile made good use of her long legs by nonchalantly crossing the distance to position herself on the only free side of Ben, since Kor was on the other. That was fine by me. Sitting *across* from someone is sometimes just as good as sitting by them. I was certain Yvera's scowl as I sat down came from her realizing that now Ben was looking directly at me.

It was so petty I almost rolled my eyes. Yvera must not have gone to high school.

"You took the gems out," Ben noted, looking at my hair.

"Yup," I said, picking up a roll. "As soon as I could once we were in the air. I only left them in while we were in the hold to avoid hurting the lights' feelings."

"Shame," Kor said with a frown.

My lips twitched as I briefly met Ben's gaze. "Why? Because they were...shiny?"

Ben choked on a bite of purple-and-red fruit. Yvera looked at him in concern, but he just waved to show he was fine.

"No." Kor's frown deepened, and he didn't appear to realize what I was referencing. "They formed a complex spell weave that I was looking forward to further dissecting."

We all stared at him.

"What?" he protested. "*None* of you saw it? The weave was quite advanced and delicate, true, but it was obviously not just for show."

"They were part of a *spell*?" I said, gaping.

"What was its purpose?" Ben demanded. For some reason, his cheeks were slightly red.

"Like I said, it was complex, advanced, and delicate, and I was hoping to study it further," Kor retorted. "All I caught were the uppermost layers. Something about protection and strength, I think. Seemed appropriate to me for sending off their Heir into the dangerous unknown."

Guilt twisted inside my stomach even as my heart warmed. I dug the pins out of the pocket of my pants and showed them to Kor.

"Can you tell anything from these?"

"May I?" Kor said, holding out his hand.

I spilled the pins into his hand. He poked them around, his gaze intent for the next several minutes, occasionally picking one up to hold it to the light. Meanwhile, I ate, not even needing Ben's encouragement now; I was ravenous, and that was even after snacking a couple of times during the flight.

Kor finally sighed in frustration and handed the pins back to me. "I couldn't glean much. The diamonds were the anchors, but the spell was in the *weave*, the net of magic the lights cast as they put them in, and that was so delicate that it's long gone by now. It might not have been disrupted with one or two pins coming loose, but *all* of them...."

My fingers froze in their grip around the pins. "Wait...these are...*diamonds*?"

"Of course," Kor snorted after taking a swig from his canteen. "What did you think they were?"

"Something much less valuable!" I spluttered. "I can't just wear these in my hair!"

Kor and Ben stared at me.

"Why?" Kor said. "They seem suited to the purpose."

Yvera snorted and climbed to her feet. "I'm going to look around," she told Ben, jerking her thumb over her shoulder. She tossed her braid and strode off, calling, "*Try* not to get yourself killed while I'm gone."

"Oh no," Ben called back dryly, rolling his eyes. "That's exactly what I was planning on doing."

"Yeah, well, find another hobby."

With that, Yvera leaped forward and shifted into her dragonform. After causing a small windstorm with her flapping wings, she launched into the air.

"It's been tough on her," Ben sighed as he looked over his shoulder to watch her rise into the sky. "Being cooped up in that hold for so long."

So that was another reason her temper had been short lately. I felt sorry for her. I didn't excuse her, since she really should work on her anger management, but I could feel sympathy.

"I honestly thought she might murder us, one by one," Kor said placidly, popping a grape-like blue fruit into his mouth. "And you *know* she'd start with me."

Are you so sure of that? I thought dryly.

I held out the pins. "Can we get back to the fact that my lights put a bunch of priceless gems into my hair as *ornaments*?"

"Not just ornaments," Kor said impatiently. "And hardly priceless. They're one of the lowest gem denominations for a reason, after all."

"Wait, hold up," I said, throwing up both hands. "You use *gems* as *money*?"

"Of course. They're hard, useful, small—"

"—and darn rare!"

"Hardly," Kor said in surprise. "Any halftorch alchemist can turn *pebbles* into quartz, and so on. Diamonds aren't the absolute easiest to make, but they aren't the hardest."

"Not to mention all the natural ones we find in our digging underground," Ben added. "Natural ones are the best for magical purposes, so *those* we generally don't use as money, unless it's at a much higher value, but mortal-made ones are fair game."

I gaped. Blinked. And closed my mouth. I supposed...that all made sense. If you could *make* gems....

"But what keeps some good alchemist from literally making their own money?"

"Why shouldn't they?" Ben asked in surprise. "They're providing a useful service. Same as any trade. Especially if they charge them up first."

"But...inflation...fraud...." I trailed off as I realized I didn't know nearly enough about economics to know just *why* people making their own money was a bad idea.

The drakón just stared at me.

"Fraud?" Ben frowned. "You mean producing flawed gems? That could be a problem, I suppose...."

"It most certainly is, Ben," Kor said with a snort. "Just because cases of knowingly selling flawed gems don't fall under *your* jurisdiction doesn't mean they aren't a bite on the tail."

Ben sighed. "I get it. The point right now is that gemmakers generally charge them up before selling them—it's one of their greatest values added, after all—but even if they didn't, anyone, even amón, can test if the gems are any good by giving them a bit of spark."

"By what?" I asked.

Ben reached over and tapped one of the gemstone—*diamond*—ends of the pins in my hand. The moment he did, the diamond flared with golden light and then dimmed to about the brightness of a candle.

"Even amón have that much power to give," Ben explained. "How do you think they would have lit the doorgems in the guest wing?"

I hadn't thought about that—but for crying out loud, I'd only been in the Six Realms for *four days*.

Ben seemed to realize that at the same time, or read it from my expression, because he smiled sheepishly and continued. "If there had been any internal flaw in that gem, it wouldn't have lit, making it useless and worth nothing more than a bauble. We trade gems and crystals because they're *useful*."

"What are they used *for*?" I asked in fascination, holding the now-golden diamond up to inspect it.

"Everything," Ben said with a shrug. "You've seen plenty of examples already. Everything is powered by gems or crystals, one way or another. For drakón, they provide an energy-saving anchor—uh...a way to *root* the power we give so that it keeps going without us needing to concentrate or give it more energy, at least for a long while. For amón, gems are the only way they'd save up enough spark to work magic-based devices at all. That's why *charged* gems have the best value to amón. Because gems are a way of carrying and storing power. See, even if you have all the gems you need, or if the device you want to run has the gems built into it already, you can take a fresh, charged stone...."

Ben took the golden-diamond pin from me and touched it to another, normal diamond. Like one candle lighting another, some of the light from the golden diamond ran into the second. When Ben pulled the golden diamond away, both pins glowed, if only just enough to discern in broad daylight.

"You can even give it all," Ben said, tipping the first diamond to touch the second again. This time, *all* the light from the first spilled into the second; the first became as dull as the others, and the second as bright as the first had been. Or...nearly....

"A bit of energy is lost from the transfer," Ben said, confirming my suspicion. "So it's not a perfect system, but it works well enough for us. It's often not worth making the gems interchangeable, so the power loss is expected."

I thought that all through...and realized something that suddenly made it all make much more sense to me.

"Oh! So you're not really trading *gems* at all. Your real currency is...power." Wasn't it the same everywhere?

Ben blinked at me, as if he had never quite thought of it that way before—even though this was *his* world. Worlds.

Kor chuckled and elbowed Ben. "I told you this one was smart."

I ignored Kor in favor of thinking through another realization, and this one was more disturbing. "If power is the most important thing...what's keeping drakón from always being richer than the amón?"

They were already at such an advantage physically, let alone defensively.... Then add essentially an infinite source of income?

Kor clapped slowly. "Got it in one," he said with a grin.

Ben sighed. This, at least, was a problem he was familiar with. "For one thing, drakón are strictly forbidden from exacting a price for charging an amón's gems; the *only* thing they may ask for is a rough equivalent in food, which is fair, considering the drakón is going to need to replenish themselves somehow for the energy they give. They're also forbidden from directly selling charged gems. Gem*makers* and gem*chargers*—who have to be drakón because of the amount of power involved—legally have to work with a gem*bank* and a gem*seller*, both of whom must be amón-run, and the gembanks and sellers can only compensate the drakón beyond food and other necessities in a certain percentage of sales."

"It gets complicated," Kor said with a smirk. "Just trust me on that. There's a reason he normally leaves that sort of thing to me."

Ben grimaced. "I have to admit, monetary policy is not my favorite subject."

"I can see why," I said with a wry chuckle.

"Point being," Ben said, rubbing his forehead, "we know it's a potential problem. That it...*was* a problem, centuries ago—"

His eyes flicked to mine, then looked away.

"—but that we've tried everything we can think of to give amón a fair chance, ever since," he finished grimly. "Probably half the oaths I've taken as Heir tie back somehow to making sure amón are treated equitably. Every drakón who becomes one takes at least the standard three, and...we think it's been working."

"Drakón are also distributed more evenly in the population than they used to be," Kor pointed out to Ben. "That, my dear Heir, has made a difference just as much as any well-meaning Crown efforts have."

"They are?" Ben asked in surprise.

Kor sighed. "When are you going to pay better attention to my papers?"

"Maybe when they stop being so...." Ben chose his next word carefully under Kor's glare. "Long?"

Kor grunted. "Well, here's the summary of the last one: drakón used to emerge solely in family lines—direct descendants of the swearers of the Covenants, in fact."

"I know that," Ben said impatiently.

"That formed the common perception that drakón can only come from lines that have had a drakón. But if you account for all the current drakón and study a statistically significant sampling of their bloodlines, as I have, then an interesting trend emerges. True, there's a drakón in every single line at this point, but there is for everyone in the Six Realms by now, and more and more drakón are emerging from bloodlines that haven't had a drakón in *generations*, some as far back as four or five, and traditionally strong drakón lines are having fewer drakón emerge."

"The 'weakening of the Blood,'" Ben said distastefully.

"That's just it: it's not a weakening. We have the same number of drakón we always have. It's a *distributing*."

Ben was quiet for a long moment, thoughtful. "Does Avva know about this?"

"Yes, since he was one of the advance readers, and it came out with his seal," Kor said, rolling his eyes. "*And* I co-authored it with Eskala."

"How did *I* not know about this?" Ben groaned, covering his eyes with one hand.

"Well," Kor said grudgingly. "To be fair, it's my *latest* published paper, and it's taken nearly an entire year to clear the review chain. It was published only last month. Though I tried to bring it up, you were preoccupied with that aldak infestation on Romskal."

"Now I think I remember," Ben said with a sigh. "And I think I remember you talking about it before, around the time all this...started, a year ago."

"Like I said," Kor repeated grudgingly. "You've been preoccupied."

"But this is blasted important," Ben said in exasperation. "Kor, this is huge. It's a shove right back at the elitists, right where we needed it most."

"Hmm, yes. I wonder why I wrote it." Kor's words were dry, but then puzzlement and a scowl came over his face.

He muttered to himself, "It took nearly a year to publish, just before...."

His hard, sparkling sapphire eyes met mine, and I felt a shiver of understanding.

Oblivious, Ben got up and paced a bit. "Not weakened, not diluted. *Distributed.* Blessed Flame, Kor. You're a torched genius."

Kor answered through clenched teeth. "Perhaps less of one than I had thought."

Ben still didn't seem to hear. "Tell me Avva has made good use of this."

"Oh, he has—through Eskala, mostly, to maintain some semblance of neutrality. She's been very busy with the elitists this past month."

"Hence why she's a co-author," Ben said absently. "Even though you probably did most of the work."

"Yes, well, Eskala also helped me—*ahem*—shorten the paper a bit. Among other things."

A purple dragon circled overhead. *Are you two done yet? Or are we going to be here until nightfall?*

"I'm done," I said quickly, rising. Even though I was pretty sure Yvera didn't care and hadn't included me as one of the "two," Ben wouldn't leave until he knew I'd had my fill, and I was *not* going to be responsible for our near deaths again...

...for as long as I could help it.

Chapter Six

STARS

Koriben

SARAH FELT NOTHING DURING the remaining deken, so when the sun began lowering, we turned to the settlement where we'd planned to spend the night: a farming settlement on the outskirts of the Great Plains.

Yonvey was one of the safest of the realms. Partly because it was one of the newest, with some of the most open terrain, which led to incursions being fewer and more manageable when they occurred. That relative safety combined with Brightflare's industrious ingenuity made Yonvey the greatest farming and artificing hub of the Six Realms.

Still, Brightflares were also prudent by nature, so they didn't let their currently peaceable circumstances lull them into carelessness. Hence, even in this flat, bucolic farmland, they built tall, carefully reinforced and spelled walls large enough to contain their herds during the night, with powerful domes—their permashields were unrivaled in the clans—above and intricate warrens below, with the upper levels for residency and the lower depths for storage of all their hard-earned produce and goods. Which, of course, only they knew the extent and layout of.

"As lost as a Battleblood in a Brightflare's warren" was a common saying for being aggravatingly out of your element. As cliché as it was...there was a good reason Yvera wasn't looking forward to returning to Yonvey, especially not so soon after being cooped up in the Moontouched hold.

Though that hold was about to feel spacious by comparison.

As we approached the settlement of Kipeth, an orange Brightflare in draká-form trumpeted a welcome to me as she circled the watch above, and I replied at the lowest volume I dared, mindful this time of Sarah on my back.

Welcome, Heir Koriben, a voice said a moment later. *I am Altha of the Kipeth Watch.*

I greet you, Altha, I said, trying my best to not let my weariness enter my inner voice. *I am with my wings and a rider, requesting nightshelter.*

Technically, protocol dictated that I name anyone who wouldn't be known by title alone, but I hoped I wouldn't be called out on it.

No such luck.

Ah, yes, I'd heard you'd taken on a "rider" of late, Altha said, but fortunately she seemed more amused than anything by my evasiveness. *Land permission granted. I will notify the elder of your request.*

All standard protocol, of course. I didn't expect my request to be denied—nightshelter never was, not for anyone. Now, your accommodations for the night could *vary*. If you were an enemy of the hold, it might even be a prison cell. But your request still wouldn't be denied, and even a cell and the mercy of your dramá enemies were often preferable to what ruled the night.

By the time we'd circled lower to a sufficient height, flown through the permashield, and touched down on the crude rings of dirt that served as landing circles, the elder had come out to greet us.

The elder was amón, which was nice to see. Of course, Brightflares were the least concerned of the clans with what the rest of them thought of as the superior advantages of drakón. The leaders the Brightflares sought after were those who could get results, and amón ingenuity and nimbleness were as good as drakón brawn in bringing those about.

Her dark brown, gray-flecked hair was in a tight bun, but wisps that had loosened over the workday blew in the wind from our landings. She wore the typical Brightflare work uniform: a loose, breathable shirt; durable trousers; practical boots; and a multi-pocketed apron stuffed full of the odds and ends of her craft. Only the medallion she wore on her chest with the Brightflare topaz in the center definitively identified her as the elder among the crowd of others who had gathered to see us, but the hard, authoritative look in her eyes might have given me a hint.

Since she was amón, I waited to greet her until I could change, which meant waiting for Kor to get Sarah off my back, but the elder stood patiently—if with folded arms.

As soon as Kor silently told me Sarah was off, I changed back and walked to the elder, hoping to keep the focus on me as much as possible. Unfortunately for me, I was usually good at that.

When I reached her, I gave her a deep nod of respect. She nodded back to me, and we clasped arms.

"Heir Koriben," she greeted simply. "I am Elder Monith. You and those with you are welcome to nightshelter at Kipeth."

"I thank you, Elder Monith."

The nice thing about Brightflares was that they kept the formalities to a minimum. The bad thing was...

"And who is this rider you have with you? She doesn't indicate trouble, I hope."

...they got straight to the point.

Monith eyed something behind me, but I didn't glance to check what it was. I could only trust that Kor was keeping the crowd away from Sarah.

"Not trouble," I assured her. "Her name is Sarah, and she's traveling with us for the time being."

Monith raised an eyebrow, but she seemed to sense that this wasn't the kind of thing I wanted to discuss in the open air. Besides, she was running out of questions a leader of her standing could ask me before I could simply smile politely and say, "Crown business."

The minor interrogation I'd undergone at Elspeth Hold a few days back had been a different matter, since I'd been out long past sunset, when they had expected me, and danger, a wildgate, and rogue ahglen had been involved. This time, we had encountered no dangers and had done things by the book.

"What brings you to our corner of Yonvey?"

I smiled politely. "Crown business."

"Very well," she said impatiently. "Flame watch and warm you. My grandson Wikal will show you to the guest wing. I have work to do."

She waved me aside and strode away. Far from being offended, I only grinned after her.

Like I said, there were advantages to dealing with Brightflares.

"Follow me, please, Koriben, sir," a boy of about eight or nine summers said. No doubt the awe in his eyes as he gazed up at me had something to do with his unusual politeness—at least in comparison with his grandmother.

Out of the corner of my eye, I saw my wings approaching, Sarah in between them. Yvera had argued long and hard with me about staying aboveground tonight, but I had insisted that she stay below to help Sarah, and she looked none too happy about the prospect.

"We'll follow," I assured Wikal with a friendly smile. "And you can call me Ben."

He grew red and flustered at that. As if not knowing what else to do, he pointed and began jogging ahead.

We followed, as I'd promised, and soon we were descending a gradual sloping path that led us through a mouth of earth only just tall enough for me to not have to duck.

"Brightflare are...efficient," I heard Kor murmur to Sarah.

"You mean downright stingy," Yvera muttered.

Kor continued in a louder voice. "Most of the ground above is used as night pasture for their herds, which you saw they're still gathering in, and they live just below."

"Efficient," Sarah agreed politely.

Fortunately, Brightflares generally kept their guest quarters on the uppermost level, so only after a dek of descending the "efficiently lit" stone corridor, we turned off and the boy presented us with the branch of guest rooms.

"There's a set of water-rooms down there," he said eagerly, pointing to the end of the hall. "Do you need anything? Food? I can bring you something from dinner...maybe."

"We'll eat our own food tonight, thank you," I told him with a smile.

As I thought it might, that statement made Wikal sigh with relief. He clearly wanted to be helpful, but I was sure he wasn't looking forward to handling the complexities of advance payment that the Brightflare would insist on for any benefits they offered beyond the bare minimum requirements of nightshelter.

"That's so thoughtful of you, though," Sarah added kindly, lingering behind with me as Kor and Yvera began scanning the options with varyingly concealed dubiousness.

Wikal looked at her in surprise, as if noticing her for the first time.

"You're amón!" he gaped as he stared at her eyes and hair. Then reddened again. "Oh, sorry. I just mean...you're amón, and you're traveling with the Heir. *And* his wings. On Crown business. That's so awesome!"

Sarah laughed. "It is, in fact."

Funny, I thought with surprise. *She seems to mean that.*

"So, what are you doing?" he asked eagerly.

I expected Sarah to be uncertain. Instead, she darted glances to each side and then leaned forward. In a conspiratorial whisper, she said, "Can you keep a secret?"

I felt a flicker of alarm, but Sarah brushed the back of my hand with her fingers, a gesture that seemed a request for trust.

The boy's eyes grew huge. "Yes!" he exclaimed breathlessly.

"I'm helping him with a secret mission," Sarah whispered. "A mission so secret that I can't say anything more at the moment, but it's something that only someone like me can help him with."

"That's so flaming!" Wikal exclaimed with shining eyes. Then blushed at his language and stammered to me, "Er, sorry, Heir, sir."

"Ben," I reminded him, having a hard time keeping my face serious.

"Sorry, er, Ben, sir." He looked back at Sarah, his eyes somehow even more worshipful than they had been when looking at me. "Wait until I tell—"

He paused, crestfallen. "Wait. I can't tell. Anyone."

"No, I'm afraid not," Sarah said with a sad shake of her head. "But don't worry. I don't think you'll have to keep the secret forever. Everyone is going to hear about it, sooner or later. Then you can tell all your friends what I told you. And you can tell them how much you helped us do it."

All enthusiasm magically restored, the boy threw his arms around her in a hug so sudden and tight that Sarah gave a soft, "Oof!"

"Thank you!" he said as he backed up, then went red again and bolted.

Sarah held a hand over her mouth until Wikal was out of hearing, but when she met my eyes, we both broke into chuckles.

"You were incredible," I said, putting a hand on her shoulder.

She shrugged modestly. "I just told him essentially the same thing you were going to tell him, just in a way that made him feel special. I have little brothers, after all."

Brothers. In plural. Would that ever cease to amaze me?

"Yes, well," I said, nudging her toward the rooms. "I doubt that your little brothers are half in love with you right now, but that boy most certainly is."

I thought, *And I might be slightly more than half.*

You'd think that since I was able to go to bed early for the first time in days that my exhausted body would sink off immediately, but in this case, you'd be wrong.

As I'd told Sarah, I wasn't typically one to toss and turn, but toss and turn I did, trying to find a position that would allow me to relax into oblivion. It wasn't just the spartan mattress and thin pillow. I'd slept soundly on far worse in all my travels and hunts. Eventually, you just learned to shut down, no matter the circumstances, to get the rest you needed for survival...or that was how it normally worked for me.

Yet that shutdown wouldn't come. As much as I wanted to deny the reason, I knew exactly why: my thoughts and memories kept spinning relentlessly in my head...and all of them were about Sarah.

I groaned and flopped onto my stomach, shoving my face into my pillow. My nose touched the mattress—the pillow was that thin. I debated the merits of getting out my own pillow, but even that wasn't a good enough distraction.

Friend, friend, friend, I told myself—not sure at this point whether it was a mantra or a curse.

Then I heard a soft knock on my door.

I pushed myself up immediately. There were only a few people who would knock on my door right now, in this remote warren on Yonvey, and none of them would have been so timid about it except....

"What is it?" I asked urgently as I threw open the door.

Sarah stood slack-jawed, cheeks warming. She seemed completely frozen aside from her eyes, and the only hint I got as to why was the way her eyes kept darting up to my face and then drifting downward.

To my bare chest.

Belatedly, I remembered her discomfort with Kor's shirtlessness. Male modesty must have been more stringent for Earthren than for us. Kor's method of getting a bit more sunshine wasn't uncommon, and men—especially drakón—on Ythra went about bare-chested all the time. It wasn't my usual style, since shirtlessness meant something a bit more significant when the Heir or Monarch did it in public, but that didn't mean it made me uncomfortable, and, as was evident, I preferred sleeping without a shirt.

I always wore trousers, though. Again, I'd had too many rough, dangerous nights to not at least wear *those.*

"Oh, sorry," I said. I ducked back into my room to grab the shirt I'd tossed aside, since apparently I'd broken Sarah with the severity of my infraction and might not be able to get her to say what was wrong until I fixed it.

"What's wrong?" I asked as I came back, pulling on my shirt.

"S—sorry," Sarah stammered, but I waved her apology aside.

"Don't mention it. Now, *what's wrong?*"

"Nothing's wrong...exactly," Sarah said. Her face was very warm now, as if the thaw of her brain had finally let the rest of her discomfort through. "I am just...having a Moontouched moment. I think if I have to stay in that room any longer, I'll be bouncing off the walls, and since Yvera only just fell asleep, she would kill me."

To avoid the doorgem problem we'd encountered at Elspeth, we had put Sarah in Yvera's room. Since Yvera had already been miffed about having to guard Sarah in the water-room, I'd had to give her a direct order to let Sarah bunk with her. But if we were going to avoid Sarah having to touch a doorgem and reveal her painfully unique white soulcolor *again,* she had to stay with Yvera, Kor, or me, and I was *not* going to let it be Kor.

"Oh," I said dumbly, relaxing my grip on the doorframe as adrenaline faded and shame kicked in. "Er. Sorry. I didn't think about that."

Although I should have. She was coming into her power, and her strength would be increasing day by day—er, or rather, night by night—and last night she had been able to drain off the excess by speaking with her Tree and opening the gate for me. She would get even more excess tonight, with no way for her to spend any of it.

"Um...." I said lamely. "Is there anything I can do...?"

Sarah's voice came out in nearly a squeak. "Want to...go for a walk...? With me?"

A walk in the dark, practically alone with her aside from the occasional herd or wall watcher, with Kor and Yvera asleep and none the wiser. It was a terrible idea.

"Of course," I said immediately, ducking back into my room. "Just let me...."

I didn't even pause long enough to sit. I simply grabbed my boots and hopped them on while Sarah stood in the illuminated doorway and peered into the dark.

"No need to rush," Sarah blurted. "I know I woke you up.... I'm sorry for that too, by the way."

"No problem," I reassured her, getting the second boot firmly on. "I wasn't asleep yet. Maybe a walk is just what I need too."

Or maybe what I needed was a solid knock to the head. I shouldn't be doing this. At the very least, I should wake up Yvera...no, make that Kor, to come with us. At the very, very least, I should wake one of them to tell them what we were doing. I should....

Instead of doing any of those things, I stepped out and closed my door softly so that neither of my wings would hear. Then, unconsciously, with my head so distracted from the raging debate inside, I took Sarah's hand and led us away.

By the time Sarah's cold skin registered in my brain, it was too late to pull away without drawing undue attention to the fact. Especially with her grip tight in mine.

"Flame," I sighed, looking down at her. "You're freezing again."

"Oh, sorry," she said, trying to pull away, but by then, I wasn't having it. Out of friendly concern, of course.

"No, it's fine. But...are *you* fine?" I asked earnestly, pausing. I eyed her torso, covered only by her clingy cloud of a sweater. Even then, her sleeves were pushed up to her elbows. "Should we go back for your coat?"

That would risk Yvera waking...and then insisting on coming along.

"No!" Sarah said, a bit too quickly, which made me think she was afraid of the same thing. If, no doubt, for different reasons, since all she was worried about was Yvera's temper.

A bit more calmly, she said, "Besides, I don't *feel* cold. In fact, I feel warm. Stifling, actually. I have to get out of here. I need air...."

"Alright, alright," I soothed, resuming our walk up the inclined road to the surface. "If you're *sure....* "

"Positive," she said, and for once, she surged ahead and began pulling me forward. "I can almost feel it...."

"A gate?" I asked, with both hope and alarm. I *knew* I should have woken my wings.

"No," she said, shaking her head. Her hair spilled freely with the motion; she must have pulled the braid out for sleep. Though the crown had been lovely, I found something mesmerizing about watching the warm, dark waves move freely. Something that made my fingers burn to wind through them....

"I don't know *what* I feel," she continued in frustration. "Just that I need it, and now."

When we emerged, the cool, open air was a welcome change to the mustiness of below, even with the various livestock odors of dung, hairy hides, and feed.

Sarah let out a deep breath of relief and paused both of us to turn her head upward and close her eyes. I was familiar with the look—that sweet relief, that surge of *something* as vital to living as food or sleep. But for myself and everyone else I'd known...that something was the sun.

I looked upward, and all I saw was the faint shimmer of the permashield, and beyond that...darkness.

"It's a pity you can't see the stars," I said quietly. The lights on the wall, the permashield, and the thin cloud cover had entirely concealed them.

"But I can feel them," Sarah whispered.

I quickly returned my gaze to her. Her eyes were still closed, but the faintest of white shimmers were churning, like illuminated rivulets of water, across her skin. Watching that dance...I found it hard to breathe.

I forced out, "The stars?"

Were *they* the source of her power?

Eyes still closed, Sarah furrowed her brow. "Not...*them* exactly. More like...I can feel...the holes of them."

As I stared, her eyes blinked open and looked at me bashfully. The shimmering dance of light over her skin faded at the same time. "That doesn't make any sense, does it?"

"No," I admitted with a tight smile. I clenched her hand. "But I believe you."

"Thank you," she said with a self-conscious laugh, tucking her hair behind her ear.

Unable to resist the impulse any longer, I reached out and untucked that hair again, feeling the silkiness spill through my fingers as I set it free. Her breath caught, but when our eyes met, she didn't seem upset. Her eyes were simply wide, full of questions.

Before I could find the answers, we heard voices coming up from below, and we both took a sudden step apart. I decided I had pushed my luck too far and pulled my hand out of hers.

I tried to clear my throat without sounding like that was what I was doing and said, "Er, would you like to see the view from the top of the wall? I know you said you wanted a walk, and that seems as good a destination as any...."

And the walls had lots of bright lights and patrolling watchers. Unlike the many dark paths on the grounds, or the herd pens full of unbothered, bulky livestock....

Many a raunchy ballad had been written about young couples using the placid Brightflare bolloth as cover for romantic rendezvous. Written by non-Brightflares, of course. Not that every teenage Brightflare was as serious as their parents, just that Brightflares wouldn't admit to one of their own publicizing such a thing.

"Sure," Sarah said, but something about her cheer sounded a tad...forced.

She couldn't be...disappointed. Could she? As I led the way through the darkness, the embers of hope flickered under the ash I'd buried them in, and I wondered.

Fortunately, Sarah broke the silence soon after, her tone conversational. "Have you been here before?"

"To Kipeth?" I paused. "I don't think so. I didn't recognize that elder, anyway, but Brightflares, once they figure out a system that works, do little to change it, so one Great Plains settlement is much like the next."

"Have you been over a lot of Yonvey?"

"Most of it. Most of every other Realm, too. Even before...this past year, I'd been to most every major hold and settlement in the Six Realms, and a fair share of the smaller ones. Just the nature of the job."

"That much travel must have been hard."

I hesitated to share this bit, then sighed and decided she needed to know. "The work was harder. Between sungates and flying, I could be dealing with a nasty incursion of krathen in Ykran in the morning, hunting for a rogue polyan in Romskal in the afternoon, and returning to Ythra to sleep in my own bed by nightfall. Travel was...the easy part."

Silence fell for a bit. When I glanced back at Sarah, she seemed thoughtful. "Was that a typical day for you?"

"That was a bit of an extreme example, but I had those days occasionally. The role of the Heir of Flame is to be a more mobile, more...expendable version of the Monarch. Of course, no one puts it that way, especially Avva, but there's a reason everyone calls on me to do the most dangerous and grueling tasks that require Crown attention, and it's not just because I'm younger. If he died...."

I took a deep, steadying breath. "Losing his wisdom, his experience, his steadiness and strength, all the good efforts he is leading...well, the Realms might just fall apart. Whereas if I were killed or incapacitated...that's different."

"That's not true!" Sarah said. The sudden vehemence in her voice made me glance at her in surprise.

"I don't mean that in the way you probably thought," I said peaceably, holding up a hand. "It's just facts. I know my worth compared to his—"

Sarah grabbed my forearm and pulled me to a stop. Her eyes burned icy fires for a moment, flashing silver in the night, making me stare. "Koriben Sunfilled, don't you dare talk that way about yourself ever again."

I hadn't ever seen her this mad. Not even earlier today when she said I'd deserved a slap. "You've met him," I said cautiously. "Just look at it logically: I could never match up—"

"'Never' is quite a long time," Sarah snapped. "Especially coming from a twenty-year-old. You have the seeds of him inside of you, Ben. I've seen *that*. If I deserve the time to grow into what I have to be, don't you think you do, too?"

"Of course...." I began automatically. Then realized how she had turned my own words—my own fervent belief—back on me. I just stood there, stupefied. I felt as if she'd given me more than just a slap.

"Stop comparing yourself to him," Sarah said more quietly. "Just...stop. Sure, you might never be just like him...but maybe you're not meant to be."

"I...." I couldn't think. Let alone string together a counterargument. I had never had someone put it just the way she had, in a way that had seemed to pierce straight to my flameheart and turn it into a bonfire.

Maybe you're not meant to be just like him.

It's what Avva had tried to tell me in a hundred different ways over the years, but I had never listened. Partly because it had been *Avva* saying it. He was my father, and it was easy for him to have faith that I had what it took to keep the Realms together after he was gone. He wouldn't be there to see me let things fall apart when I couldn't do everything the way he had always done them.

"I've said this once before, but I guess you need to hear it again," Sarah continued, her voice so soft it was almost a whisper now. "I wouldn't have *anyone* else in the Six Realms with me right here, right now. Not even your father."

Torch it. Had anyone ever seen *me* the way she had? Had anyone ever cared to? Especially once they had met both of us. To everyone else, I was just the shadow cast by my father's sun. Even Yvera, who knew me perhaps better than anyone but Avva, saw me in his light. She was the one always telling me if Avva would disapprove of this or that. Of how Avva would have done it this way or that way.

Everyone else seemed to fervently believe I *had* to be him, or all was lost. Or so I'd thought.

Sarah smiled. "I think...you are going to be an *incredible* King one day. Your own kind of incredible. If I do nothing else, I want to stick around long enough to see it happen."

She paused, then added quickly, "Er—a long, *long* time from now."

I chuckled weakly—mostly to hide how close she'd come to hitting a raw nerve. At least that little prod was enough to snap me out of my stupor. And resist the urge to crush her lips to mine.

"Yes," I said fervently. "I'll drink to that—a long, *long* time from now."

CHAPTER SEVEN

DARKNESS

SARAH

WE WERE SILENT FOR most of the rest of our walk to the wall. Part of me still fumed a bit about Ben's perception of himself, making me want to go on, but I'd said what I'd felt needed to be said, and *something* seemed to have gotten through to him, judging from his startled reactions and his quiet thoughtfulness now. Better to let him mull it over than stir the waters again with words that wouldn't have the same power.

Another part of me cursed my insistence on killing the mood...or shifting it, anyway. Goodness gracious, hadn't I coached and badgered myself to nigh insanity for nearly an hour before I'd finally got the courage to go forward with my plan and ask him on a walk? Of course, half the reason I finally did it was because I was almost certain he wouldn't even hear the knock, because no doubt he would have fallen asleep by then.

Just to be clear, I really *did* need a walk. As I had huddled in the bedroll on the floor, trying to stay still so that Yvera could drift into sleep, I'd nearly exploded from the energy that was filling me. If Ben hadn't answered—as I'd half-hoped he wouldn't—I'd intended to go on my own, confident that the way to and from the surface was simple enough for even me to remember.

Then he'd answered, immediately, and....

Heavens. I had not been prepared to see Koriben Sunfilled, the drakón Heir of Flame, without a shirt. Probably one of the few reasons I was brave enough to squeak out my offer was that those rehearsed words were the only ones left in my head after my brain rebooted.

What must he be thinking of me? I groaned to myself as we walked in silence. He'd said not to mention it when I tried to apologize, but surely he had been at least a bit disapproving of how I'd stared, obviously unable to keep my eyes off his impossible perfection....

But then...he took my hand.

He had done that at least once before, I thought. In fact, he touched me quite a lot: platonic touches of support and reassurance, little nudges of guidance and protectiveness. He did it so unconsciously, though, I always assumed that dramá were simply a touchy bunch, or that Ben at least was.

That's what I assumed when he had taken my hand back there, even though it startled me that he would do something like that after my blunder. Still, his mind seemed to be on something else for a moment...until he noticed the temperature of my skin. Then, fully present, he had refused to let me pull away—instead, tightening his grip and laying his other over the back of mine for a moment for good measure.

When we reached the surface, and he brushed his fingers through my hair.... Surely that look in his eyes hadn't been platonic. Right? *Right?*

But then *why* had he pulled away? Sure, someone was coming. But why not lead me down one of those nice, shadowy paths? Why remove his hand *then* and casually suggest we go to the currently brightest and most populated place in this sleepy farm town?

He's probably being kind, I thought miserably as I followed him; my steps were slowing, but Ben, even lost in his own thoughts, was unconsciously slowing his to match. That was Ben: kind. After my ogling, he had finally realized my own interest, and for a moment, he thought, why not? He was male, after all. But the approaching voices snapped him out of it, reminded him of the things an Heir had to take into consideration, and he had concluded it would simply be cruel to give me hope.

And he was right, darn it. What was *I* thinking? I had no idea what he needed to consider in a permanent partner, but I wasn't it. I'd been so caught up in just trying to reach for something I wanted for once that I'd forgotten why I didn't make a habit of it: having Ben, even for a few seconds, would make losing him agony.

I'm really in that *deep now,* I realized in quiet horror. Too deep for casually making out in dark corners like I'd planned. I knew now with a chilling certainty that after getting a taste of him, of that warm scent coming straight from his lips, after being given permission to run my hand over his chest just once, of feeling his warm, kind arms cradle me in *that* way for once, even once....

That would ruin me.

I nearly hung my head in defeat. I had only just begun, and already I was finished. But competitiveness was no excuse to do that to myself. Surely I had at least that much self-love and self-preservation.

Right...?

Well...at the very least, I had that much respect for Ben's wishes. I had made my play, as clumsy as it had been, and he'd given me his answer—one kinder than I deserved.

At least I tried, I told myself. I felt a flicker of pride at that. I'd tried. Small comfort though it would be in the days ahead, at least I knew now. That was more than I'd ever had before, with any guy. It would have to be enough with Ben.

Still...it was a good thing we were in shadows right now, and that Ben wasn't entirely present, because I couldn't help a tear or two from escaping. Only the tip of the iceberg, of course; I'd cry my fill later, after Ben went back to bed and presumed I'd done the same. Then I'd come back up, find my dark corner, and have a good, cathartic sob.

I was glad to see us at last approaching a brightly illuminated door in the wall. The timing was perfect: my couple of tear trails were dry, and I was ready for a distraction to prevent any others. Although I considered telling Ben that I was ready to turn back....

"Ben!"

The purple-haired, purple-armored drakón standing guard at the gate waved at Ben enthusiastically. I felt a momentary spike of relief, as useless as I knew it was now, to see the guard was clearly male. The beard—which seemed customary on most of the men I'd seen—was a dead giveaway.

"Aldrek," Ben said, coming back to the present with a broad smile. The two young men clasped arms. "What mischief did you get yourself into to be assigned to *Kipeth*?"

Aldrek groaned as they let go. "It's a long story, which I'm sure you'll hear about from Master Kressa. The better question is, what are *you* doing here?"

Ben's smile faded a bit. "Crown—"

"—business, yes, I figured," he said with a laugh. "I was actually asking what you were doing wandering about in *my* direction after dark. Don't get me wrong, I'd heard you'd taken nightshelter here but didn't think I'd be relieved in time to talk to you, so this is a nice surprise. But don't let *me* get in the way of your pleasant evening."

He winked at me. I just blinked back at him. When I'd seen the purple hair, the shade nearly identical to Yvera's, I'd braced myself for him to get cold and stern the moment he noticed me. Probably silly of me to assume, but there it was.

Ben grew red for some reason. "Oh, er, this is Sarah, by the way. Sarah, this is Aldrek Battleblood, Yvera's younger brother."

"Please don't hold it against me," Aldrek said with a grin. "I'm nothing like her, trust me."

I had already seen that for myself, and I couldn't help but smile back. "I won't."

"Yes, you've seemed to have made it your life's mission to *not be Yvera*," Ben said with a chuckle.

"Torch right," Aldrek said. "She's enough of an iceheart for both of us."

"She's not really," Ben protested loyally.

Aldrek rolled his eyes. "Around *you*, maybe."

He gave me a significant look that made it clear he, too, knew what everyone else but Ben did, and he fully expected me to have realized the same. I nodded slightly.

Smart, he told me silently and swiftly. *But don't let that make you lose heart.*

Before Ben could catch on to the silent exchange, Aldrek said smoothly, "Well, if you've come my way, that must mean you want on the wall, right?"

"If we may," Ben said with a crooked smile.

"You're clearly not the kind of troublemakers I'm set here to block, so of course," Aldrek said with a shrug.

He put his hand on the door, which had a gem like our guest rooms did, except when this one flashed purple, the color faded as soon as the door swung open.

"Although, if you'd like something with a bit more *privacy*—"

"I thought she'd like the view," Ben said quickly, putting his hand briefly on Aldrek's shoulder in farewell and passing his friend to enter. "Thanks, Aldrek!"

"Thank you," I said with a wan smile as I followed more slowly. I intended that for the encouragement, too. As useless as it was, it had been well meant, and coming from Yvera's brother, meant something more to me besides. I wished I had the inner voice to tell him that directly.

Aldrek's smile faded for the first time. *Don't lose heart,* he repeated. *He's smart in a lot of ways, and a torched good Heir, but he's a bit of a dimtorch in this one.*

I just kept my smile and shook my head slightly, then followed Ben inside.

We passed through a short corridor before entering the main interior, which seemed to be a much longer corridor stretching as far as I could see, with at least several rooms leading off. I could see what Aldrek had meant about a lack of privacy; even at this time of night, the inside of the wall was surprisingly bright and bustling in comparison with the sedate darkness of the pastures outside. I saw at least four amón—immediately recognizable by their normal heights, builds, and hair colors—and two drakón going about their business at a brisk pace. One of the drakón waved and greeted Ben briefly as she passed, but even she didn't pause.

As we ascended the stairs, Ben explained the difference. "The Brightflare know they have to keep things dark and peaceful out there so that the herds can rest, but the need for defense never ends, so in here, they can have as much light and make as much noise as they need to in order to make sure all is safe within."

"Efficient," I said, repeating Kor's diplomatic word from before.

Ben's lips twitched. "That's Brightflare in an agshell."

I soon stopped paying attention to my surroundings and spent all my focus on trying not to humiliate myself with my inability to keep up with Ben's natural pace on the seemingly never-ending flights of stairs.

"Sorry," Ben said sheepishly during one of my many pauses to breathe and let the fire in my legs die down. "I didn't think.... We can turn back if you'd like."

My common sense screamed at me to take the easy out. I'd had enough pride bruising tonight, hadn't I? I should just take what dignity I had left and go have my cry. But that thought only made me more stubborn.

Plus, there was my much less practical side, which told me I might not have much more time with Ben once things were over, even as a friend. Greedy for punishment, I didn't want to relinquish a single moment.

"No," I panted. "I wanted...something to burn off the energy...and this is doing a good job of that."

That was the truth. Plus, the exhaustion might just help me finally fall asleep tonight *without* the cry. After all, a bruised heart was no excuse for being so dull and tired tomorrow that I wasted more of our precious time searching. Too much was riding on my being alert and attentive for me to keep pushing back sleep for self-centered reasons.

But man...I had found the sure way to make the rest of my time with Ben feel like an eternity.

Finally, we came to the last landing. Ben patiently gave me all the time I needed to find where my breath had gone, and when I'd finally stopped wheezing, I waved at him to lead the way.

He put his hand on the door. The gem flared gold, presumably recognizing him as an authorized person, because it swung open and allowed us to pass through into the night.

I breathed the cooler air in—deeply, deeply grateful to feel the wind, even as warm as it was, drying the sweat I was drenched in. Although something inside of me still didn't release. When I examined the strange feeling, all I could think was, *I wish they would turn out these lights.*

So odd.

The bright strips running along each side of the rampart and crystals glowing at intervals in the parapet cast a helpful illumination on this otherwise dark, cloudy night. And yet, even though they weren't any brighter than the ones inside had been, my eyes stung slightly, and I found my gaze casting about for the restful-looking darkness that lay beyond the wall.

My own strange words to Ben came back to me. *I can feel the holes of them.*

Not the stars themselves...but the punches that their light made through the void. Did I actually have a sense for...darkness?

Ben's voice interrupted my existential crisis as he came to my side. "Pretty, isn't it? What you can see of it, I guess."

What? I thought, snapping my attention back to the moment. I realized I had come to the edge of the wall, right up to the waist-high parapet that was there to presumably keep absent-minded dark-seekers like me from tumbling to their deaths. My hands rested on the stone top—still warm from the sun—as if prepared to push me up so I could do just that.

I removed my hands as casually as I could. Besides, I didn't need the heat. It was different from Ben's warmth, somehow. More stifling.

I forced myself to focus on what I could see in front of me so that I could answer him.

Fortunately, at that moment, the clouds parted enough to allow a bit of moonlight to illuminate the scene.

It *was* pretty: the broad plains stretching on for miles, the rolling fields of grain and pasture, and, in the distance, a faint glitter. The sea, maybe. Hadn't Ben said we were near it now?

My attention was drawn a second later to the highest point in my field of vision—a hill a mile or two away and about forty-five degrees to the right from us, either left to fallow or for pasture.

On the hill's peak....

"Ben," I gasped, grabbing his arm.

"What is it?" he asked urgently.

"Do you see that?" I asked, pointing with my other hand. "There, on that hill?"

He followed my finger and shook his head sharply. "No, I don't."

He shouldn't have been able to miss it. Unless it was invisible again...or I was hallucinating. That last possibility had my stomach clenching in dread.

"Sarah," Ben said intently, annunciating each word precisely. "Is it a gate?"

I stared at the arched doors, the white tree emblazoned on its surface, and I swallowed. "That...is what it looks like."

I looked up at him, eyes wide, heart pounding. Only he would know what this meant—and what we risked by going after it.

"What should we do?" I whispered.

Ben hesitated, glancing at the sky. "Did it only appear when the moon came out?"

"Yes."

Now that I was paying attention, I could feel that *pull*, that magnetism reaching for me.

Ben kept looking at the sky, and he groaned. "It's supposed to rain for the rest of the night...."

One of his friends had warned him of the incoming bad weather during one of my breath breaks. Now the warning didn't just mean we might get wet on our way back to our rooms. It meant there would be no more moonlight.

Ben glanced back at the other side of the wall, down at the settlement inside. I knew where he was looking, and what that look meant. Kor and Yvera were sound asleep, perhaps too far to reach in time.

Ben looked back at me. "Did you feel anything before? Was it *there* before, just hidden?"

"I...I don't know," I stammered.

Ben put his hands on my shoulders, eyes burning. "I am so sorry to ask this, Sarah, but we have to be sure. Was it there?"

I took a deep breath. Then I scanned through my memories, comparing it to what I felt now. While I came to the answer, I felt something else, something that frosted my heart entirely over.

"No," I said with finality. "It wasn't there, Ben. At all. But now it's fading."

The reason for the fading magnetism, the waning glow, was obvious: the patch in the clouds was moving.

Ben followed my gaze to the sky and cursed sharply. He let go of me and put his head in his hands.

"Rothen are circling the walls," Ben said. His flat tone was obvious even through the muffling of his hands. He lowered his hands and glared down at the darkness outside. "I can smell them. They can't fly, and these walls are spelled against their climbing, so they're not a threat right now, but they're torched fast runners. The moment we cross the permashield...."

By that, I assumed he meant the magical shimmer that capped the entire wall. He glanced at the sky again.

I swallowed. "We know where it is now. We can go during the day...."

His eyes met mine, golden and hard. The eyes of an Heir. "Do you think it will be there during the day?"

My heart pounded, but I felt a coolness wash over me, as if a breath of ice were whispering the sad answer in my ear. "No," I said with eerie calm. "It won't be."

"I was afraid of that," Ben said grimly.

"We can try tomorrow night—" I began.

"You heard her," Ben said, referring to his weather friend. "Rain until dawn the next day. Even if we knew it would be clear...it would be another day."

A day of just sitting around and waiting. When we only had nine left. Eight, after that one.

I nodded slowly. "You know the situation better. Your call. But I'll follow you."

He gazed at me, eyes blazing with agony as the Ben I knew mixed with the Heir.

Finally, his face hardened. "Where is it? Exactly?"

My heart rate sped up, but I pointed. "There. At the very top of that highest hill."

Ben followed my finger and nodded sharply, returning his gaze to mine.

"Sarah, what I'm about to do may disturb you, but there's no time to explain. Do you trust me?"

I nodded immediately.

"Good. Remember that."

Then he stepped back and, crossing his arms in front of him, pulled off his shirt.

It was a good thing I'd already gotten my cognitive failure over with for the night, but my cheeks still immediately increased in temperature. "Uh...Ben...."

"No time," he snapped, spinning gracefully on his heel to kneel on one knee with his back to me. "Get on my back. Now."

His dead serious tone and my memory of the krathen snapped me out of it and I rushed forward, throwing my arms around his neck. Though there was a heck of a difference—in temperature alone—between climbing on then and now, I kept focused. At least mostly.

"Legs too," he said sharply, bringing my legs around his waist as he stood. "Hold tight."

Is he really going to change now? *On the wall?* I thought the question but didn't dare distract him by asking it out loud. I just focused on gripping as hard as I could with both arms and legs—and tried to ignore the building heat in the pit of my stomach.

Though he really put my trust to the test when he stepped on top of the parapet.

As if reading my thoughts, he repeated, "Trust me."

Then he dove.

I was too frozen from fear to even scream. I just clenched my eyes shut and tucked my head against him....

I felt a sudden shove from both sides that pushed me into the very center of Ben's back, then a mighty snap from either side, and our fall abruptly leveled off.

But Ben hadn't changed.

At least...not much. I felt scales roughening into being under my hands where there had been skin, but Ben kept the same human shape.

Unable to comprehend what was happening by feel alone, I dared opening my eyes. Because my cheek had been pressed against his shoulder, the first thing

I saw other than the night sky was a large, outstretched wing. Not as large as a dragon's wing, but the same shape...and color...as Ben's.

Suddenly, I got a glimmer of understanding about what was pinching me from both sides.

I gasped, shifting to get a better look.

Hold still! Ben cried. *This is hard enough without you throwing me off balance!*

I froze in place. "You're.... You're...." I babbled, but fortunately, my nonsense words were probably lost on the wind of our gliding passage.

We're coming in fast, Ben said grimly. *But the rothen are faster, and they've spotted us. Can you get the doors to open from a distance?*

I still didn't know what rothen were, but I thought I heard an insect-like chittering from below, and I really didn't want to find the source.

After a moment, he added, *Without moving your head much?*

Without moving another muscle in my body, I turned my head up and got a sideways view of the moongate. The perspective and speed were dizzying, but with the focus and instincts born only from adrenaline, I reached forward with that *something* that connected me to those doors and *pushed* with all my might.

It felt like trying to move a mountain with nothing more than my eighteen-year-old, untrained muscles. Somehow, miraculously...that mountain moved. The doors began slowly swinging inward.

It wasn't enough. We were still going too fast, and the growing crack wasn't wide enough. I felt new tears stinging my eyes in the wind. My strength was draining from me dangerously fast. I could see black at the edges of my vision.

Just as we were about to smack into the doors like bugs on a windshield—or so I thought—Ben flexed his wings to turn them, and us, perpendicular to the ground, so we soared straight through the crack.

Flashes of light, so much light as my little helpers swarmed us in a bright cocoon....

Then I finally found darkness.

Chapter Eight

ANGEL

KORIBEN

SARAH'S LIGHTS SURROUNDED US in a swarm as soon as we flew through the doors. At first, I thought they were attacking, but then I understood why they were there when Sarah's grip suddenly went slack, and she fell limply from me.

"No!" I cried, flameheart sputtering, but I couldn't do anything to help her right then. I just had to hope the lights would be enough to cushion her fall.

I leveled myself and spread my wings wide. The sudden press of air ballooning against them *hurt*, but they held, and I slowed to a safer speed, one that allowed my legs to lower and then hit the ground running.

It was a good thing my hunch had been right, and we'd come through the welcome gate, with its eternally long corridor.

I finally was able to skid to a halt. Then I whirled right around and began running straight back with all my might, changing fully back into amáform as I did so.

I thanked the Flame that my second hunch was also correct: this was a "welcoming" gate in the euphemistic sense, in being prepared to intimidate guests...or defend against enemies.

Rothen already pressed at the doors, but the icy film over the arch seemed to cause the giant, wingless insects pain, since they hissed and retreated each time they stuck a limb or antennae through. I could only assume Sarah was in the solid cocoon of light on the ground, because I couldn't see her anywhere else, but that cocoon was far closer to the open doors than I liked.

Close enough to tempt one of the rothen all the way through.

With a savage cry, I sent a ball of fire racing ahead of me—one far larger and deadlier than the small one I'd tossed in demonstration for Sarah this morning.

The rothen screamed and writhed—again, still too close to Sarah. It accidentally kicked the light cocoon in its convulsions, momentarily knocking one of her arms free. The lights snatched the arm back inside in seconds, but the momentary sight seemed enough to encourage a couple of the dying rothen's fellows through.

But by then, I was there.

I'd chosen my warhammer for this, summoning it when I was nearly on them so it wouldn't slow me down before. This wasn't the time for a sword's finesse or even an ax's blows.

I swung with all my might, feeling insect bodies crack, snap, and fly under each blow. Then they were back behind the ice, and I had a few seconds to slam one door shut with one arm. A rothen recklessly tried to press through the remaining opening, but I'd expected that and crushed its head against the wall with a one-handed swing. Then I kicked its body back, dropped the hammer, and slammed the second door shut.

Silence, as complete as the last time, when we'd fled from the lish. I heard not a single insectile chitter of rage from the other side—only my panting breaths. The glowing line between the doors faded, and then the crack disappeared to almost nothing again.

And all was still.

I pushed back to stand somewhat straight, casting one dizzied glance at the insect parts and goo scattered around me. A few of the lights separated themselves from Sarah to drift over the wreckage. Something about their movements struck me as irritated, especially as they examined the chips I'd made in the floor and walls.

"Sorry about the mess," I mumbled to them.

I stumbled my way over to Sarah and collapsed to my knees. The lights parted, flowing away far enough so that I could see her. Her eyes were closed, her body still, her skin too pale.

Praying with all my remaining willpower to the Flame, I reached forward and cupped her face in one of my hands, sending a reckless amount of power into her.

I felt her pulse at once—relatively steady. I let out a breath, then focused on the other details. Breathing, fine. Some bruises, so the lights hadn't been able to save her from everything, but at least they'd cushioned the most critical part: her head. No concussion there, not even a bruise. The only reason she was unconscious was the same as last time: a sudden energy drain beyond her capacity. At least this time, it shouldn't take her as long to recover. I could already feel her power resurging. In fact....

Her eyes moved under her lids, and then her nose wrinkled, and she cracked her eyes open. "Ben?" she rasped.

"Here," I murmured, heaving another breath of relief. My thumb traced her cheek, and my eyes stung treacherously. "Here. We're safe. We're fine. You did it, Sarah."

"But you're a mess," she said, eyes widening. Her nose wrinkled again. "And, *gah*, you *stink*."

She pushed herself up slowly and stared at the mess of parts, goo, and stone chips. "What on Earth...did you do to my hold?"

I couldn't help it. I fell back onto my rear and laughed—laughed until I cried.

I FIGURED THAT *SOMEONE* from the wall watch had to have seen my dramatic dive and disappearance, so though I felt as if I were going to my execution, I closed myself in my bedroom as soon as I was sure Sarah was fine and settled in her own, and I called my rightwing.

Contacting her had been a good idea, since I'd clearly woken her up, which meant I'd caught her before anyone else got to her. Although, to say that she was furious with me...would be like saying Kaldrir was merely warm. I knew it was bad because after my quick explanation, she couldn't even speak, not even to swear, for a full dek. Then she said one filthy word and ended the call.

I groaned and put my head in my hands. Then felt some of the ick from the fight. Well, if I was going to face execution in the morning...I might as well be clean and well rested for it. I got up with a moan as I felt strained muscles pull and went to the water-room.

When I came back, Sarah was standing outside my door. "I still can't sleep," she explained with a grimace. "I just keep thinking about...everything. Is now 'later'?"

She was referring to my promise that I would explain "later," putting her off by telling her how urgent it was for me to contact at least one of my wings to inform them we were alright. Though I hadn't said it out loud, I thought what she needed most was rest, but apparently that wasn't going to happen just yet.

I sighed. Well, the explanation was simple enough, especially since she'd seen some of it, even though she didn't know what it meant. I waved her inside. "Go on."

She relaxed in relief and went immediately to the chair at my desk, the one I had brought for her.... Had it really been *last* night? Flame, that felt like forever.

I sank down on my bed, since the only other option was the floor. "What do you want to know first?"

She turned around to sit backward in the chair, with the back of it in front of her and said immediately, "What the heck did you *do*? You were.... You were human, but...not. You had *wings*."

I felt it again: that dread that first came when I realized she grew up thinking drakón were monsters. She'd made that clear in the first moments after we'd met from her frantic need to know *where* the "dragon" had gone, from the horror that had dawned on her face when she finally believed it was me.

I felt it even stronger each time I had to reveal some aspect of that nature to her, each time with more to lose if she recoiled from me.

Something about my reluctance must have shown, because her face softened. "It's alright, Ben. I won't judge. Promise. Whatever you became, I know it was still *you*."

That meant more to me than she would ever know.

I took a deep breath. "It's called the half-form. Technically, many drakón can manage it for at least a few seconds. In practice...only the Monarch and Heir are powerful enough to hold it for longer than that."

"Why is that?" she asked, only curious. She rested one arm on the back of the chair and used the other to prop up her chin.

Her calm gave me further relief.

I shrugged wearily. "I dunno. It's hard, for some reason, to hold ourselves in a state in between. It's...like holding onto something slippery; whatever magic that lets us change wants to keep the change going."

"Is that why you haven't done it before, in front of me? The difficulty?"

"That, and there was no reason to." And no reason to scare her off, either. "Contrary to what you might think after that last...experience...the half-form isn't that useful. Most times, it's just better to be fully one or the other."

"But you used it just now," Sarah mused. "Because...of the difficulty of changing fully on the wall?"

"No," I said, blinking. "Because I didn't have enough spark to change fully. Not at night."

"Oh," Sarah said. "Right...."

"There were other advantages," I admitted. "So, I might have tried the half-form even in the day. Such as maybe avoiding anyone on the wall from seeing us leave; there's no way we could have left without notice in my full form. And finally, getting us through the doors without me having to land and change to fit through. It was a gamble—quite a lot of gambles, actually."

"You didn't have much time to decide," she said kindly. She laid both her arms flat on the back of the chair and rested her cheek on them. "You made the right one, in the end."

"It came close," I rasped. "I asked you for too much, to open the doors from a distance—"

"I managed it, didn't I?" she said angrily, raising her head.

"Yes," I said, shaking my head. "And you were incredible, as always. But you fell off me in the hall. Sarah, if the lights hadn't been there to catch you, if you hit your head...."

"You would have healed me."

"Some things can't be healed in time," I snapped.

When she didn't answer, I put my head in my hands. "Agh, Sarah."

I took a deep breath and lowered them. "I'm sorry for that. I'm not mad at you, I promise. I'm mad at me, for how close it came. I shouldn't have taken all those risks with you. I should have just waited another torched day."

Sarah's chin jutted out stubbornly. "And I'm still saying that you made the right call."

"Really?" I said dryly. "How are your ribs feeling right now?"

She laid a hand over her upper abdomen.

"A rothen kicked you—on *accident*. But it got that close to you, Sarah. Like you saw, rothen got through the gate and into the hold, and one of them got that close to your unconscious body. If I hadn't reached you just seconds later, I can't imagine what...."

But I *could* imagine it, all too well. I had seen a rothen bite a helpless amón clean in two.

Some of the deadness I felt in that moment must have been visible, because Sarah rose from her chair and cautiously approached me. Then wordlessly held out her arms.

I crushed her to me. A terrible idea, to end all my terrible ideas of the night, with me still sitting on my bed, and her now standing between my legs. But I didn't care, because with my nose in her hair, inhaling her cool, clear scent with each breath, what had broken inside of me when she had fallen off my back slowly healed. My flameheart sputtered to life again, taking the fresh oxygen she fed it to build back up to a blaze.

"I could have lost you," I whispered. "And it would have been my torched fault."

"You didn't," she said firmly. "Because you *were* there.... And now I forgive you for smashing bug guts all over my entrance."

I laughed shakily. "Did you see the chips, too?"

"Yes," she said primly. "You might have to make that up to me a bit more before I'll forgive you for those."

"What if I heal those bruises of yours?" I said, pushing her away while my hands lingered on her waist. "I didn't have the energy when I was checking you over and noticed them, but now...."

"No, those can wait until morning," she said. When I was about to protest, she said firmly, "They're not bad, honest. Maybe it just brushed me.... Besides, I have a different idea for how you can make it up to me."

"And that is...?" I asked, clueless.

"Do you trust me?" she said innocently.

"Yeees," I said, dragging out the word. I was starting to feel uneasy.

"Then will you *promise* to do me this one, tiny favor?"

"But what *is*—"

"Nope. You have to promise first. You have to trust me, like I trusted you. And trust me when I say that there's no comparison between what you asked me to do and what I'm about to ask you to."

Knowing I would regret this, but unable to resist that look in her eyes any longer, I sighed and said, "Alright, fine. I promise. What is it?"

She stepped back, eyes surprisingly eager. "Could you...show me the half-form?"

"*Now*?" I asked, baffled.

"Yes, now. I wasn't able to get a good look before."

I knew that. I'd been *counting* on that.

"You *want* to?"

"Yes," she said, crossing her arms. "How else am I supposed to really comprehend what just happened? I keep trying to put the pieces together in my head, but they just won't fit. I think that's why I can't let myself sleep."

"I'm...tired," I said, unconvincingly. Because, to be honest, I'd been wide awake ever since she had stepped into my arms, and now that counted double as my flameheart beat nervously.

She raised an eyebrow, not buying it. "If you have enough energy to offer to heal me, surely you have enough to do this. Besides, I know I phrased that as a question in the beginning, but you *promised*."

And knew I'd regret it. I groaned, but I saw no way around it. I'd given my word.

"Fine," I said heavily, flapping my hand. "Give me more room. All the room, actually."

Sarah went all the way to the doorway. Probably better that way, in case it got too much for her and she needed to bolt.

Alright, maybe that was not giving her enough credit. She'd faced down greater dangers by now than me in my half-form, with astounding composure. But though I knew I had done the same...in that moment, I couldn't think of anything I had dreaded more than seeing her expression of perfect trust return to that first one of horror.

I took off the shirt I'd put on after my shower.

"Is that...part of it, the transformation? Does the cloth prevent it?" she asked in a carefully neutral tone.

I noticed she was keeping her eyes firmly on my face. Well, she'd asked for this, so if it made her uncomfortable, then she could call a stop to it.

"No." I shrugged. "I just don't want to ruin the shirt. I destroy enough things as it is."

"Oooh," she said, cheeks warming further. "Right."

Partly to delay the inevitable, I elaborated. "I could shift away the shirt into the ether as I change, which is what I do with my clothes in a full shift, but it's easier just taking it off for this. There's enough for me to concentrate on to keep the shift in a halfway state without dealing with my shirt, too."

"Got it." She nodded, gesturing for me to get on with it.

Groaning inside, I took a deep breath, stepped into the center of the room, and began. Good thing my flameheart was surging again. It was the reason I could do this at all.

I drew on that fire...and let it fill my blood, and from there, let it *change* me. Just a little, though. Once the fire began, it was hard to rein in. In fact, it had taken me a couple years after first becoming drakón to even manage the half-form for a moment, and a couple years more before I could hold it, as an Heir was supposed to be able to do. Then there had been a whole ceremony to celebrate, in which I'd had to hold it for half a deken.

As I'd said...it *meant* something when Avva and I went shirtless in public. It meant people were going to expect a display: the most flagrant sign they could receive of the strength of the Crown, and thus in their greatest defenders. People cheered when they were expecting it, when it was part of some ceremony or other. They cowered when they weren't, when we used it to intimidate some scum who didn't deserve to breathe the same air as the Tree's freedom-loving children. Taking my cue from Avva...I used the form seldom. Only when it was absolutely necessary, in fact.

Or...when I'd been gullible enough to make blind promises to beautiful girls with wide, pleading eyes.

It was different every time. Before, my wings had come in hard and fast, and thank the Flame for that. This time, I felt the scales come first, spreading out from my heart and over my chest. I took unusual care in controlling them, feeling a vanity I wasn't normally afflicted with. The self-consciousness was normal; the need to make this form look *appealing*, if such a thing was possible, was entirely new. This form was *meant* to inspire fear, after all—a kind of fear that couldn't be managed in quite the same way as a drakáform maw in your face.

There was nothing so terrifying as seeing something that looked like *you* become something that still looked like you...and yet looked just as much like a monster.

I hadn't ever intended to show Sarah this form, and for good reason. If there was anything that could bring back her fear of drakón, this was it.

The scales didn't normally cover my entire skin, but this time I was able to hold them in a kind of golden frond pattern on my chest and just brushing the tops and sides of my shoulders, a bit like a mantle. I could feel the scales crawl down my legs and up my spine as well, but since I had trousers on and was facing Sarah, I was less worried about those.

I also kept the horns short enough that hopefully they wouldn't peek through my hair. No need to worry her with those yet. Same with the eyes, which would probably be one of the most disturbing things to her. From the lack of change in my vision, I felt confident that I kept them mostly normal, but I couldn't help their glow.

Since what Sarah was really waiting for were the *wings*...I couldn't avoid those.

They emerged from my back last, and slowly. I rolled my shoulders, letting them take their time after the abuse I'd given them earlier. They didn't hurt now; the transformation had healed them, but I felt an extra bit of weariness as I slowly unfurled them. The wings were the most completely transformed part of me, aside from the size: they were perfect miniature versions of my drakáform ones.

Only when everything was fully in place and I felt like I had the change in a firm stasis did I risk jolting my concentration by glancing at Sarah.

Her jaw had dropped, and her eyes were wide, but my flameheart throbbed to see not fear there...but awe.

Before I could doubt what I saw, she took a step forward. Then another, then another. Then she hesitated. "Is it alright if I...."

"If you want to...." I said doubtfully. Then winced—I had forgotten about the voice. Even that was altered by the half-transformation, becoming far deeper. At least I'd somehow avoided the worst of the roughness.

Not risking speaking again, I told her silently, *It's safe, if that's what you're asking. I'm not about to turn feral and bite you. I just didn't want my wings hitting you when they came out.*

She slowly paced a half circle around me, looking at me from every angle she could. I shifted my feet nervously, risking my wings tipping over something to keep her from seeing behind me.

What? I asked nervously.

When she met my eyes, hers were shining—for a moment, literally, with a flash of silver. "Ben...I don't have words. You're *incredible*."

I stared back at her. No one had ever used that word—or its translation into Drona—to describe a half-form before. Then again, no one I knew of had ever tried so hard as I had to make it....

Incredible.

"You...like it?" I asked, startled into using my outer voice.

"Ben, you look like an angel," she murmured in awe. Then chuckled tightly. "That is, if angels had bat wings instead of feathered."

"Feathered?" I asked in confusion. Since my outer voice required less concentration than my inner, and it didn't seem to bother her, I continued using it. "Bat? And what the torch is an *angel*?"

She hesitated. "Well...the closest comparison I can think of in your theology is...a Tree."

I froze. "A *Tree*?" I choked.

Maybe I *shouldn't* have tried so hard. But I hadn't *meant* to commit blasphemy! Surely the Tree would understand that.

She threw up her hands. "OK, maybe that wasn't a good comparison. Forget I said that. Basically, what I meant was that you looked like something so awe-inspiring and—gosh, dang it, you're going to make me say it, aren't you?—*attractive* that you couldn't be real."

Attractive. I had somehow made a form that was meant to invoke primal terror not just incredible but...*attractive*. Too attractive to be real.

I was not sure how I felt about that at all. Alright, truth: I didn't know how I *should* feel about it. Because I was pretty sure I shouldn't be feeling this roaring pleasure in my flameheart right now.

Just to be absolutely clear....

"You think...I'm attractive right now," I said slowly.

"That's what I said," she retorted, hands on her hips. There was a strange sort of challenge in her eyes. "I would dare any straight female to stand in this room and not feel the same. So, take that as you will."

Flame above....

Why hadn't I tried this before?

CHAPTER NINE

NICETIES

SARAH

AFTER BEN DRAGGED THAT embarrassing admission out of me, I decided it was high time I fled, so I mumbled excuses and a goodnight and beat a hasty retreat to my bedroom. Even so, it was some time before I cooled down and stopped internally squirming enough for sleep.

Ben woke me early the next morning. According to the information he'd just gotten from his wings, the gate and our disappearance had strangely gone unnoticed by anyone in Kipeth.

Once I'd woken up enough to grasp the implications, Ben—still standing awkwardly in my doorway—said, "I can only think the Trees were involved, so we'd better take full advantage of the torched miracle They've given us."

Hence why he had woken me before dawn—by Kipeth's time—so that we could hopefully sneak back into the settlement before anyone noticed we were missing, thus minimizing questions and gossip and keeping the gate's existence and location secret.

Once Ben left, I stumbled through a quick wake-up routine. Every time my foggy mind grumbled that he was being paranoid, I remembered the bug guts plastered all over the entrance hall...and over Ben himself.

I didn't remain sleep-fogged for long.

Especially when I rejoined Ben, awake enough now to remember another image of him permanently seared into my mind. It didn't help that he was now wearing a set of golden armor so perfectly fitted to him and beautifully designed that it looked fit for a god.

Gracious, what had I been thinking, asking to see his half-form? As I trotted up to him, I could hardly look at him without feeling hot and cold all over.

It was so unfair. How could I have discovered something I wanted more than anything and learned I couldn't have it *in the same night*?

Ben, on the other hand, seemed remarkably undisturbed by memory or melancholy. In fact, his grin was unusually cheerful as I approached.

He's being kind, I reminded myself. *You did this to yourself, after all.*

He'd made his lack of interest politely clear when he stepped away from me in front of the entrance to the warren. With any luck, he just thought I was simply attracted to him—and surely he was used to that. As I'd snapped at him last night, I dared any straight female *not* to be. Hopefully he would leave it at that and not look any deeper.

"Ready?" he said brightly. "Got your gun?"

In answer to his second question, I patted the hip holster I was wearing underneath the boat cloak my lights had handed me as I was getting dressed in the bathroom. I had thought the heavy, oiled cloak a bit overkill at first until I remembered the forecast for Kipeth for today and the long walk ahead to the town. How the lights had known about *that*, I had no idea...but then, how did they ever anticipate my needs?

"As I'll ever be," I answered as evenly as I could.

Ben put his hand on my shoulder; fortunately, the inside of his gauntlets were leathery and padded.

"Sorry about this, again," he said. "About the lack of sleep and...everything to do with last night, really."

Kind as ever.

"Not your fault," I mumbled, shrugging him off and beginning to walk.

To change the subject, I asked, "So why didn't we come in through *that* last night?"

I pointed to the new gate that we were circling around the southern end of the Inner Rim to reach. The Yonvey gate had appeared next to the Ykran one, identical to the latter apart from the symbol in its center of a crossed shepherd's crook and hammer. The first thing we did after coming out of the entrance hall last night was check for it. Seeing it glowing there had made our efforts all seem worth it, at least at the time. Now...I wasn't so sure.

Would it have been better if I'd never asked Ben on a walk? Or if I had waited long enough to feel the gate come into being and woken them all?

"A cautionary measure," Ben explained easily, clearly unbothered by questions of *what if.* Which...was a strange contrast from last night, actually.

For Pete's sake, where was his good mood coming from?

He gestured to the two gates we had unlocked. "My guess is that either these moongates are set to always connect to the entrance gate the first time they are activated, or the gates have an override that reroutes to the entrance in times of danger."

"Why there?" I asked curiously, becoming interested in spite of myself.

"Think about it: even if you *want* someone else to be able to use your gates, do you always want them to be brought straight into the heart of your home? Or do you want them to arrive a nice, long way away and have to travel down a long, narrow passage that gives you plenty of time to decide whether to allow them in the rest of the way or to activate your defenses? And if *you're* using the gates, and you're in *danger....*"

I inhaled in understanding. "You keep enemies from following you into the heart. Just like last night."

"Just like last night," Ben agreed. "The Tree of Ice had hinted the gates had that feature, so I was counting on it. Contrary to what you might think, I was *trying* to not have to smash insects into anything...important."

"You *try* not to break things," I said, surprising myself with a grin as I quoted his words from last night.

"Yes," he said ruefully. "That now counts double when it comes to you."

My smile faded as he looked back at the door. He'd said it casually enough, *looked* natural as he turned his attention away, but....

How deep had he seen?

"Alright," Ben said, clapping his gauntleted hands together as we stopped in front of the door. "Now for the fun part.... The part I'm not so good at, either. Sneaking."

"You think the...bugs...are still out there?" I asked. I didn't hide my nervousness. In fact, I encouraged the feeling. It felt better—braver, even—than the cringing shame that made me want to run in the other direction.

"If the rothen aren't consumed, they should be bedded down by now, or out of sight of Kipeth, at least," Ben said grimly. "But if they are...they could be following orders that override their instincts."

"Which do you think it is?" I asked quietly, rubbing my arms as goosebumps crawled over them.

Ben hesitated, then met my eyes. "I'm not going to gild this for you. I think it's the latter. That's why I asked Yvera to scout ahead to meet us."

"Why do you think that?"

He clenched his jaw for a moment, then said, "It's how they kept trying to go for you. The ice barrier.... It caused them pain. Now that I think back, it even iced over their joints a bit when they crossed it, but they ignored that and went for you anyway, even after I torched the first one. Especially when they saw you were so vulnerable. Rothen are big, and their jaws can be deadly if they can get them around you, but they're easily scared off. They should have run."

"But they didn't," I concluded quietly, goosebumps reaching my spine.

"No," Ben said darkly, glaring at the doors in front of him as he folded his arms.

"Ben...." I asked hesitantly. I wasn't sure he would give me the answer, even if he knew it. I wasn't sure I even wanted to know. "What do they want with me?"

He was quiet for a moment, then sighed. I guessed that this was the question he had been hoping I wouldn't ask. "The Devourer is no fool, and unfortunately...it already seems to know what you are. It will know that the Trees sending you now of all times is no coincidence. It may not know *how* you are meant to stop it...but it won't take any chances."

"So, it's trying to kill me first," I whispered.

Ben didn't answer. His eyes remained fixed on the gate, but his fingers were digging into the plate over his arms, and his eyes took on a dangerous glow.

My heart pounded. "Ben?"

He blinked and shifted, as if hearing something. "Yvera is calling."

He pulled out a golden scale, and colors shone on its surface. I wasn't at the right angle to see the image, just mostly the glow on Ben's face as he held it up.

"I'm on this frosted hill," Yvera snapped. "Rothen were just here, alright, but they scattered when they smelled me coming."

"That's my Yv," Ben said with a smile.

"Yeah, yeah—get your torched rear out here before I think of *more* ways to kill you and dispose of your oversized body."

"Will do."

The glow faded and Ben put away the scale. He cast me a wary look. "Er...just fair warning...she is *furious* with me. I'd hoped she would have cooled off by now, but death threats toward me are never a good sign. As soon as she has me safe, she might rip into me."

"Just for getting her up this early?" I asked, raising an eyebrow. That seemed a little extreme, even for her.

"That...didn't help my case," Ben said with a wince. "But no. It's mainly about last night."

"Aaah," I said. I understood now—possibly more than Ben did.

When I'd originally made my silly little plan, I had *hoped* that Yvera wouldn't find out about it....

Well, maybe she'd spare my life if I told her about what came of it: worse than nothing.

And yet...part of me—the competitive, slightly suicidal part that apparently *still* hadn't completely died—wanted to let her come to her own conclusions about how we'd spent our time last night. Before *and* after our little adventure.

"Do you think you could just *crack* the gate open?" Ben asked. "Just enough for us to slip through? Visibility looked low out there, but just in case...."

"I can try," I said with a shrug.

I put my hands on either side of the doors, reached down into the depths within me, and brought up power.

It came sluggishly, since it was well past dawn here, but it came, rising from the nothingness inside...somewhere in the region of my abdomen, I realized. Sometime, I would have to ask Ben how doing magic *felt* to him. I had a hunch that it was very different.

I took what it gave me and coaxed it through my hands and into the doors.

They flashed with a glow and began creeping outward. I backed up for a moment—proud at how much less drained I felt than last time—but when the doors were far enough apart for even Ben to slip through sideways, I put my hands on them again and asked them nicely to stop.

So they did, grinding to a halt. As did the doors on the other side, which had mirrored the motion of the inner ones with perfect symmetry. Through the icy curtain, I could see the slightly blurred image of Yvera approaching in the dim light, fully armored, claymore drawn.

I gulped and wondered if it would have been better for us to face the rothen.

As if wondering the same thing, Ben put his hand on my shoulder to pull me gently back, and he slipped through first. If he and Yvera spoke, it was silently, because I heard nothing.

Then Ben stuck himself back through halfway. "It's clear. Come on."

To my surprise, he grabbed my hand and pulled me gently through. Once I was clear and standing, blinking, on top of the rainy hill of another world, he let go just long enough to push the doors closed and grabbed my hand again, oblivious to Yvera's intensified glare burning a hole through me.

Gracious. I thought Ben's behavior on our walk last night meant he was trying to let me down easy, but if that were the case, you'd think he would stop *touching* me unless it was absolutely necessary. However, being the glutton for punishment I was, I wasn't about to point that out to him.

In fact, I met Yvera's glare and—truly suicidal now—raised an eyebrow. As if daring her to do something about it.

She just looked away as the doors faded to nothingness. "Come on," she said icily, and turned and strode away into the rainy darkness.

I shivered, and not from the rain. It was relatively warm, and the boat cloak was surprisingly effective protection. Not only did the hood stay put astonishingly well when I pulled it up, but the rain slid off the cloth as if it were plastic.

Ben, no doubt assuming I was cold, grimaced. *I'm sorry,* he said silently, and set off after Yvera, gently pulling me with him. *We'll get inside as soon as we can, I promise.*

"And then we'll stay there?" I whispered in amusement.

Er...no, Ben admitted. *If I had to risk your life to save us time, then we had better make use of it.*

"Don't worry about it," I reassured him. "It's just rain."

Will you two focus on being quiet? Yvera snapped, her inner voice echoing in that way that told me she was speaking to both of us. *I didn't get up at this hellfrosted deken and run through this hellfrosted drench to have you torching bring the watch down on us now.*

Sorry, Ben said quickly, then let go of my hand to focus on his footsteps and balance.

Still, he gestured for me to go ahead and pleaded, *Stay near me.*

I spared him a nod before returning my own attention to the descent down the muddy, slippery grass.

Ben didn't give himself enough credit. At least when he was focused, he moved with unusual grace and stealth for his size; I hardly heard him behind me. Even his armor was remarkably quiet—not nearly as clanging as I would imagine metal plate to be. More like...a quiet clacking, when it made any sound at all, and that much didn't travel far through the drenching rain. Either the drakón were both *that* strong, or it was much lighter than plate, too, because both of them moved with nearly the same ease as they did in their normal clothing.

Then the obvious finally hit me: why his and Yvera's armor so perfectly matched their own colors...the colors of their *scales.*

Of course, I sighed.

Presumably yet another use they'd found for their endless supply of scales. As I kept an eye on Yvera ahead, I wondered how protective those scales were, before and after being molded into armor.

Still, even our best efforts at being quiet didn't seem like they would do much good. Visibility wasn't great, and the sky was still dark, but I could see the walls of Kipeth in the distance, which meant that anyone keeping any sort of watch should be able to spot movement at the least, and we were descending the highest hill in the area, bare of anything except overgrown grass.

Which we were doing a good job of trampling down further as we followed a path someone had already made before us. Someone...or something. As I looked around, I realized that the grass had a maze of paths, and with a chill, I understood what had made them. Perhaps our tracks would go unnoticed, after all. Ironic that the lingering and searching rothen had unintentionally done us a favor.

That still left how visible we were now. Didn't it?

Then I noticed something odd. Perhaps the rain had kept me from seeing it right away, but eventually a slight haze in the air caught my eye. I stopped in alarm, looking around. The haze—like waves of heat over a sunbaked road—surrounded us.

What is it? Ben asked sharply. I felt him place a hand on my shoulder; for what purpose, I didn't know, since the grip didn't feel comforting.

I pointed around us, then whispered, "Do you see it? The haze?"

I glanced back at him in time to see his shoulders relax, and he let go of me. *That's the mirage Kor is casting. It's not much, but in these conditions, it should be enough to keep us from being spotted.*

"Kor?" I whispered in surprise, looking around. "Is he here?"

Ben nodded in Kipeth's direction. *No, he's on the wall.*

I glanced, and I thought I could just make out one lone figure standing there. My eyes widened. I had just tried to perform magic from several hundred feet away, and that had knocked me out. I didn't know how to compare the magnitude of opening a gate to casting a mirage, but I had enough experience by now to know that distance mattered in magic, and that even the simplest task would probably be excruciating or even impossible for me across the mile or so that Kor was working with. Yet there he was, doing it. Before dawn. Standing in the pouring rain.

When I glanced at Ben, I said, "Surely that's not...easy?"

It's not, Ben said with serious simplicity.

Less talking, more walking, Yvera chided, glancing back.

Not wanting to prolong Kor's herculean feat of magic, I hurried on.

It was a long mile—probably more like a couple on foot once we reached the bottom and began following the dirt roads around the fields. Still, at least with the flat, hard-packed roads, we made quicker progress, covering three times the distance in the same time as our descent took. Even with the whole wide road—at least the equivalent of a four-lane freeway—to ourselves, we kept to the same formation, with Yvera leading, me following, and Ben taking the rear. When I would glance back at Ben, I would see him scanning our surroundings carefully, head cocked to listen and nostrils inhaling visibly, scenting the air.

His wariness was probably unnecessary...but better safe than sorry, especially given Ben's suspicions about the Devourer sending consumed after me. I also listened, for what it was worth, and rehearsed in my mind how I would reach through the folds of my cloak for my gun if necessary.

Still the haze surrounded us, if anything growing stronger the closer we came.

Finally, we reached the wall. We turned off the large road that led to a set of huge gates to walk on a smaller road that skirted the wall and eventually came to a smaller, single door—but still big enough that not even Ben would have to duck.

On some signal I couldn't hear—perhaps a silent communication—the door opened, and Aldrek peeked out.

"Sorry," he said with mock severity. "No drenched sakat allowed. Go scurry along back to the holes you came from."

"Shut it," Yvera said, shoving past him.

"Well, if you *insist,*" her brother said with a shrug, beginning to close the door.

"Not on *him,* you dimtorch!"

"Thanks, Aldrek," Ben said with a chuckle, nudging me forward when Aldrek grinned and pushed it open again.

"For you, Ben, anytime. Especially since your *left*wing asked so nicely."

I went inside. After a short passage, I emerged into a larger room. It was bare except for benches along the sides, a durable brown rug in the center, and crystals radiating warmth set on pedestals in the corners.

"Hey, *I'm* the one who asked you," Yvera said, wringing out her braid into a convenient mop bucket. I wondered why she bothered, since we would just get drenched again when we stepped inside the city.

"You didn't *ask*," Aldrek said, rolling his eyes as he followed Ben into the room. "You never ask. You ordered. *Kor* asked. Nicely."

"I'm the rightwing of the Heir, and you're a sworn member of the King's Warflight. I don't have to *ask*."

"Please drip on the rug," Aldrek asked me, then looked pointedly at his sister. "There, you see? It's called common courtesy, and a little of it wouldn't kill you, command structure or no, especially since I'm working a double shift for you."

"Have you been up the whole night?" I asked, distressed.

He waved off my concern. "Yes, but I was already scheduled for the night shift, so don't worry about it. Once you've stayed up twenty-eight deken, what's another two?"

"Then I don't see what the big deal is," Yvera said in frustration, folding her arms. She honestly didn't seem to. I didn't know whether to be amused or feel sorry for her. "You're doing your duty, one you are perfectly capable of, and aiding the Crown besides."

"The point, dear sister, is *asking nicely* when you can costs next to nothing but reaps great rewards."

"Don't bother, Aldrek," Kor said wearily as he came through the corridor on the other side of the room. "Surely you of all people know that if she could be taught manners, she would have learned them by now."

"Kor," I greeted in concern, taking a few steps forward. "How are you doing?"

Out of the corner of my eye, I thought I saw Aldrek gesturing demonstratively to me with both hands, while Yvera glared daggers at him.

"I have been better, and we still have further to go," Kor said with a groan, pinching the bridge of his nose with one hand and putting his hand on my shoulder with the other for support.

In that moment, something strange happened. Later on, I realized it must have started with my concern, my wish that I could do *something* to help, and my frustration that I wasn't strong or experienced enough with magic to take the burden of concealment off him.

Then my magic...rose up. Seemingly unbidden, or so I thought at the time. In the background, I heard Yvera and her brother bickering, but their voices became muffled as the rising magic pulled me into a trancelike state of focus. Instead of gathering in my hands as it had done most times before, it traveled up through my chest, through my shoulder...and into Kor.

Kor's eyes snapped open and met mine, sapphires flashing.

What...are you doing? he asked, inner voice flat.

I just stared back at him, as startled and confused as he was. Probably more.

"What is it?"

Ben's hard voice, just behind me, pierced through my trance. The moment my concentration broke, the magic snapped back inside me and into the nether it came from.

"Kor?" Ben said with folded arms. He was not asking nicely. I tried to think if I had ever seen him look so hard; his armor really took his naturally intimidating features to the next level.

That also gave me my first hint why he hadn't worn it before this morning.

I took a step to the side and looked between the two of them, not knowing what to say. Kor's piercing gaze never left me. I expected him to lie to Ben, say it was nothing, but he was smarter than that.

"Something...I need time to ponder," Kor said quietly, slowly taking his hand off my shoulder.

"And your preliminary assessment is?" Ben said with a raised eyebrow.

By now, even the two Battlebloods had fallen silent and were watching us, waiting for Kor's answer.

"Is that we had best be going, if we don't want all our efforts to be for naught," Kor said smoothly. He turned on his heel and strode down the corridor he had come through. "Dawn is nearly here."

Ah, I thought wearily. *That would be the reason I'm feeling so tired right now.*

Ben eyed Kor as he strode away, which made me look, too. Was it just me, or was Kor's step firmer than before?

I finished my thought in a daze. *One of the reasons.*

Ben's jaw set as he glanced at me, as if he had come to the same conclusion, but he followed Kor. "Come on."

I pondered as I followed Ben—thinking more about Ben than about what had just happened, which said something pathetic about me, but there it was.

Ben, and sometimes other people, seemed to not think highly of his intelligence. I wondered, though, if that was because he was usually around Kor. That seemed outrageously unfair to me. *Everyone* looked stupid next to Kor. (Except first thing in the morning.)

Many times by now, I had seen Ben become as observant, knowledgeable, laser-focused, and quick-thinking as a four-star general. Last night, he had made several hard calculations in a matter of pressure-filled seconds, and just now, he had felt nothing that Kor and I had felt, and yet he had somehow come to the same suspicion I had.

There were all kinds of intelligence. My gut told me Ben had certain kinds in bucketloads.

WE GOT BACK TO our rooms undetected, at least as far as we knew. Not a moment too soon, since the settlement was stirring like a sleepy beehive, and many times we had to duck behind herds, carts, or other objects, in addition to sneaking and relying on Kor's mirages. Getting through the main opening to the underground section and to our rooms was the hardest part, requiring us to wait for a blessed break in the foot traffic and dash to the guest hallway.

Then we had a few minutes to catch our breath and pack up whatever things we had left. Rather, I caught my breath, since none of the drakón were winded (of course), they packed, and by the time I was done, so were they—and Ben had grabbed *my* things, too.

Now we made no secret of our leaving, instead striding straight into and through the rapidly increasing crowds to the surface and across the settlement to the landing circles. People would frequently and shamelessly stop and stare, and the crowd parted deferentially and nudged or called to their neighbors to do the same, as if Ben were an ambulance on the way to the hospital. Though I thought with idle amusement that we could have caught and held a few more stares if Ben had kept his armor on. Alas, Ben had changed into his regular loose, comfortable gold clothing and brown leather belt and boots.

Probably reason number two he hadn't worn the armor until this morning: the curious stares could have easily turned to nervous ones.

He didn't appear as if he minded in any obvious way, and he nodded in thanks to the people who made way for him, but I thought I knew him well enough by now to see a certain tightness in his eyes and tension in his neck that wasn't normally there. His fingers would frequently twitch into momentary fists, before he would take a deep breath and consciously unflex them.

He doesn't like attention, I thought with surprise. I didn't know why that hadn't occurred to me before, when it fit in so well with what I knew of him. Of course, I hadn't seen him in a crowd this large since we'd left the first hold he had brought me to on Ykran, and I hadn't known how to read him back then.

But...Ben was the Heir, their future King. And he was *him*—all seven or so feet of golden masculine glory. Surely this was just a way of life for him.

That doesn't make it any less exhausting, I realized as I kept watching. *Perhaps...it makes it even worse.*

Take me, for example. I would have been scared stiff if all those eyes had been immediately drawn to me. The stares I *was* getting—once they slid off Ben and his flanking wings and caught sight of little ol' me trailing behind—were bad enough. But at least I knew that, if I chose, the stares could all go away, and I could just burrow in my hold or my home on Earth for the rest of my life. That possibility went a long way to helping me keep my head up and my shoulders down.

Ben didn't have that option. Or, at least, he didn't think he did. This really was his *life*...forever.

For a moment, I imagined it...and then immediately flinched away from the image.

Why did everyone keep thinking *I* was the Moontouched Heir?

Word that Ben was leaving must have gone around, because a crowd met us at the landing circle, gathering around its perimeter, and the stern woman from last night stood at the point where the stem of the dirt road we were on met the circle.

Everything and everyone were relatively dry, because, to my surprise, the permashield above kept off the worst of the rain. Some wetness still filtered down, but it felt more like a mist by the time it descended on us. I still wore my boat cloak, because I could tell from the thunderous taps on the shield above that the rain was still pouring down, and we were about to soar up into it.

Plus, the hood, which faithfully stayed in place—*had* to be by magic—was very handy in enduring all those looks.

"Heir Koriben," the woman said. She seemed slightly less stern this morning. Perhaps she'd slept well...or maybe she was relieved the Heir was leaving after only one night's stay, *without* causing any trouble.

"Elder Monith," Ben said politely. Since I was behind him, I couldn't see his expression, but nothing in his posture or tone now gave away that he would much rather be a mile high in the sky right now.

"I trust you slept peacefully?"

"Business kept me up late and woke me early, but what sleep I received was peaceful and comfortable," Ben said with a deferential nod. I was mildly impressed that he had somehow been both completely truthful and polite. "I, my wings, and my charge thank you for Kipeth's hospitality."

"Good. Flame go with you," Monith said with a nod in return. They both clasped arms, and when they separated, she stepped aside.

Ben, Kor, and Yvera strode into the circle, beginning to go their separate ways to shapeshift. I took a few steps forward, just to be inside the circle, and then held back.

I watched Ben's transformation in awe. The dramatic yet dizzying shifts in musculature were becoming less nauseating with exposure, but I was sure I'd never get used to the impossibility of it: that one moment he could be...well, *Ben*—for all his size and godlike coloring, perhaps one of the gentlest young men I'd met so far in my life....

Then in the next, be a creature of the size, glory, and might to give nightmares nightmares.

"Miss?"

I turned to see a friendly young woman come up to me.

"If you'll follow me...?" she said, pointing to a rolling set of stairs that a couple others were pushing into the circle.

"Oh, sure," I said, grateful that I wouldn't have to rely on Kor's dragon hand to get onto Ben's back this time. "Thank you."

By then, Ben had settled low on the ground and tucked his wings against his sides, and the young man and woman who were handling the stairs rushed them up to his side with practiced skill. I followed the first young woman at a more sedate pace, allowing the stair handlers to get settled and lock the wheels. For the first time, this felt a bit like I was at an airport, about to get on an airplane. A giant, golden, awe-inspiring airplane with folded wings that was watching me approach with reptilian eyes.

He turned his head to watch my progress up the stairs as well, perhaps for lack of anything better to do. After all, the steps seemed perfectly sturdy, as was the single railing. True, the steps were damp, but the soles of my boots (dramá sure seemed to know how to make *boots*) kept traction well.

I had only gotten up the first five steps, however, before a youthful voice cried urgently, "Wait!"

Surprised murmurs broke out. I turned, and from my vantage, I had no trouble seeing the young boy dashing through the crowd toward us.

The sweet brown-haired boy from last night. What was his name?

Ignoring the whispers, I carefully descended, since I was the only one of the four of us not currently an enormous, intimidating dragon that could swallow boys his size in one gulp. If he had been hoping to talk to Ben in his humanform, he was a bit out of luck, but perhaps I would do. But the boy made a beeline for me once he was in the clear, waving something small and metallic in his hand.

"Just...got...away...." he panted as soon as he got to me. He leaned over, bracing himself against a thigh with one hand. With the other, he proffered the thing he had been waving. "Had...to give...you this."

I took the thing he offered, my cheeks growing warm from both the gift and the attention; the crowd around the circle had only gotten larger, and now all eyes were fixed on me. It was a small, smooth, metal whistle with a leather cord through one end and an orange gem in the center.

"Do you...like it?" he said eagerly, straightening. "I made it...in Avva's shop."

"I love it," I said, and made the emotion both true and in the forefront of my mind, forcing myself with surprising strength to ignore the whispers, chuckles, and stares all around.

The boy beamed. "I got up *deken* ago to finish it for you. The Tree said it was important."

I became still.

"The...Tree?" I asked carefully. And quietly, but the stair attendants had heard his initial exclamation, and they were glancing at each other with rolled eyes and exasperated looks.

To which the boy was still, fortunately, oblivious.

"Yes," he said earnestly. "She was in my dreams last night. She said you would need that, that I had to get up, finish it, and give it to you. She said it was very important, that it was how I could help you. And I did!"

He beamed at his accomplishment, even though his hair was tousled and damp, his skin was pale, and his shoulders drooped from exhaustion.

My heart clenched and throat constricted. Tears stung my eyes. Whether or not the Tree had really appeared to him, I was touched more than I could say by his sacrifice. No one...had ever done something quite like that for me before.

Then, as if a little voice were whispering it in my mind, I remembered his name.

"You did help me," I said solemnly. "In a big way. Thank you, Wikal."

The boy gaped. "You—you remember my name?"

"Yes," I said with a smile. To cover up my guilt for forgetting it until the last minute, I impulsively leaned in and kissed his cheek. That brought on a round of chuckles all around, but I ignored them.

"Thank you," I repeated as I straightened and slipped the whistle over my neck.

I'd been expecting him to wipe his cheek and go "ick" like my little brothers would have done—that's why I did it to them, after all—but the boy just flushed and stared up at me with stars in his eyes.

"Er, you're welcome," he said, eyes darting away with sudden shyness.

Now you've done it, Ben said. *He's officially in love.*

I turned my back to the boy so I could give the dragon a skeptical look.

I'm serious, Ben insisted as I climbed the stairs. His voice sounded almost like a grumble. *He's probably praying to the Tree right this second that you'll wait for him to be old enough to court you.*

Perhaps he saw my quiet huff of a laugh, because he shifted, and the movement almost seemed...impatient, or irritated. A stark contrast to his normal rigid stillness when I was about to get on him.

It happens, with the depths of our connections and the lengths of our lives, Ben snapped, confirming that his irritation hadn't been in my imagination. *That's exactly what my father did, back when he was just a nobody Sunfilled boy from a small northern hold and he met my mother—the Peacegrowth Heir.*

That made me hesitate on a step.

Everyone knows the story, Ben muttered, turning his head to watch the boy be led away by a parent or relative. *I'll bet you my stipend that Wikal does, too.*

Oh dear, I thought numbly. What had I done?

Congratulations, Kor said with relish. *You've officially made Ben jealous, and with more panache than I might have been able to plan myself.*

Made Ben...*jealous?*

Both drakón were off their rockers, reading far too much into a simple gift and a sisterly peck on the cheek....

Right?

Chapter Ten

EVEN

Koriben

I FOUND MYSELF UNEXPECTEDLY grateful that we had a long flight through the drenching rain. Hopefully by the time we landed, the deluge would have quenched the hot embers inside that were eating their way through my chest.

Something must have tipped Kor off—perhaps the grueling pace I was setting—because a few dek after we had leveled and settled on our flight path, he said innocently, *My, someone seems a little short-tempered for some reason.*

No, I'm not, I said. But the smoke trailing from my nostrils gave me away.

You're a terrible liar, even as a draká, Kor said in amusement. *I know.... You're wondering why a little Brightflare boy gets a kiss from Sarah, and you don't.*

Nonsense, I snapped back.

Not quite a blatant lie that time. I was thinking it...but I *did* know it was utter nonsense. Wikal was just a boy, practically a hatchling, and that's exactly how Sarah saw him. That's why she felt she could act the way she did. End of story.

I had no reason to be thinking about how to get that whistle away from Sarah and send it back to him...with a kind note hinting at her impending unavailability.

You know that there's an easy way to fix that, don't you?

It took me a frantic moment to remember what Kor had said last, because surely he couldn't have been reading my mind...and then more smoke slipped through my nostrils.

I gritted my teeth. *You're assuming that I should kiss her.*

Notice how I avoided saying *want to*.

We can't afford to alienate Sarah, I reminded him sternly, falling back on the last argument he'd heard from me on the matter. The essence still held true, so hopefully Kor wouldn't discover how far my thinking had shifted.

Oh, come on, Kor said innocently. *Just a little peck on the cheek won't hurt, same as she gave him. Then you'd be even.*

That....

That was actually not a terrible idea. Brothers did that, right? Friends, sometimes? Right? Then I could gauge her reaction....

Blessed Flame.... The idea rooted in my head like a stubborn, spiky desert weed that I couldn't pull out, no matter how hard I tried, because its root went too deep. The worst bit of it all was the dimtorch impulse to, as Kor put it, *be even*. At a deeper level, I knew it was to prove to myself that I meant at least as much to Sarah as some...random, starry-eyed *boy* she'd only just met.

Surely more. Hopefully much more.

Kor wisely said nothing else, letting his weed grow.

Flame, I hated him sometimes.

THE SUN WAS SHINING blessedly warm over Romskal by the time we emerged from the sungate and soared over the red rock of the Korpeth Mountains. Between the warm currents and the sun, even though it was lowering, I was feeling dry and energized in moments.

About that same time, though, Kor told me, *Sarah is waving the red flag.*

What? I asked urgently. I risked my balance to glance back. Sure enough, she was waving the flag, if a bit sheepishly. Her hood was down and her heavy cloak flapped in the wind.

What is it? I asked her anxiously. *Is it urgent?*

She hesitated.

Wave the black if it's urgent—that one means danger. Wave the red again for no.

Relieved, she lifted and waved the red again.

My flameheart lost some of its chill. *Can you wait a few....*

Argh. We were really going to have to go over time-telling at some point. Soon.

Can you wait until we're out of sight of the sungate and its hold? I asked instead. *Blue for yes.*

She got out the blue and waved it in her other hand.

Alright, but we'll hurry, I promise.

I'd slackened our pace, luxuriating in the dry warmth, but now I redoubled it, and Kor and Yvera picked up theirs to match.

What's the rush? Yvera grumbled. *We're close enough to Kellig that we'll get there in a deken.*

Sarah needs something, I said absently, on the lookout for a good place to land with a bit of privacy.

Oh, Sarah *needs something now, does she?*

Yv, I said in a warning tone, allocating more of my focus for the conversation.

Don't "Yv," me, my rightwing snapped. *Don't forget all that* you *have to answer to me for right now—because of that girl. I waited this long, but I won't for much longer.*

Strange. She *had* waited. She could have mentally torn into me the entire flight here so far...but she hadn't. That kind of patience...much less holding a temper for this long...wasn't like her.

Then again...she could read me just as well as Kor could. Perhaps she had known that if she'd laid in while my own mood was that sour, it might have come to blows.

Well, you can wait just a bit longer, I said. *I'll give you your chance, I promise, but Sarah takes priority.*

Wrong thing to say, Yvera said in a dangerously quiet tone.

I felt a chill. Signs of Yvera's true temper coming out: First, making death threats toward me. Second...quiet. The calm before the storm.

Maybe...this would have to be more than just a quick stop.

There's the shelter, Kor suggested soberly, as if reading my mind again.

I hesitated.

Ben, I don't relish the thought of spending a night outdoors again any more than you do, but you have to admit...there's a pattern here. It might just be necessary.

We had been over this, briefly, last night and this morning, when discussing over scale where we would go next. We had discussed the night element, in fact. That's why we had chosen this gate, deliberately emerging somewhere on Romskal that was toward the end of its day. But we had planned on making for Kellig Hold, which had some good views and enough privacy that Kor might have been able to conceal our flight out in the dark, if Sarah spotted something soon enough after sunset for me to manage flight.

However, Kor had also mentioned a shelter wasn't far from Goldek Gate. With the memory of rothen rushing for Sarah fresh in my mind, I had shot down Kor's suggestion before it was even fully formed.

You could call in some of the guard from Goldek Gate, Kor said now. *There's more than enough time to get Sarah settled and send for backup.*

I sighed. *Fine. We'll land there, because it's convenient and because it's the best place around to tend to Sarah's needs, whatever they are. Then...we'll let Sarah decide.*

She would not be happy that I was forcing her to choose again, but the torched truth was...despite our early, astonishing success, this whole quest was doomed without her instincts guiding us.

We landed on a plateau above the shelter, the closest we could come since the entrance was narrow and hard to access by design. As soon as Kor helped Sarah off my back, I changed as quickly as was wise and hurried over to her, reaching her just as she was getting off Kor's hand.

"Oh, thank goodness," Sarah said with a gasp as she unbuckled her cloak and pulled it off.

"What's wrong?" I demanded.

"I'm much better now," she said ruefully as she slung the cloak over her arm. "Sorry about that. I tried to tell myself I could wait, but I was dying in that thing. It was nice in the rain, but as soon as we crossed over...."

She shook her hair out, airing it in the wind, and I noticed her clothes were damp with sweat, clinging unusually...tightly to her subtle curves.

I fixed my eyes firmly on her face and put a hand to her forehead. It was hot and clammy, and I fretted because I didn't know whether it was a fever or would pass in a few dek now that she was free of the cloak.

"We landed...because you were *hot*?" Yvera said icily as she made her way over.

"Yvera," I snapped. Couldn't she see this wasn't a minor problem? Sarah was drenched. How much moisture would she have lost if we had waited until Kellig? What if she had become dehydrated, or overheated?

Yet Sarah flinched, ashamed because she had finally asked for what she had *needed*.

"You did the right thing," I told her firmly.

"Come *on*, Ben," Yvera cried, gesturing at her. "Can't you see how pathetic and *useless* she is? At *best*."

And that's only if she's telling the truth, she shot at me privately.

I ground my teeth. "She's *not* useless!"

"No, Ben, she's right," Sarah said quietly.

Yvera ignored her and snorted again, folding her arms and sticking out her hip. "Oh, really?" she said dryly. "She could have gone after that gate on her own last night, hmm?"

I was so mad now, my eyes were beginning to soulflare. I could tell from the reflected glow in Yvera's own eyes.

"Asking for *help* once in a while does not equate to being weak or useless," I said in a dangerously quiet tone as I stepped closer to her, nearly nose to nose. "Even if it did, aren't you forgetting something? We both took the oaths to defend and aid amón in whatever way the Tree asked of us."

To my surprise, Yvera calmed somewhat, enough for her lips to pull into a smirk. As if daring me to hit her, with us this close. "But she's not even *amón*. She's *Earthren*."

Alright. *That* was it. If we needed to come to blows for me to knock some sense into my best friend, so be it.

I would give her one more chance, though, so I took a careful step back.

"Mock her now to your own regret, Yvera," I said coldly.

Uncertainty flitted through her eyes. She hadn't expected this degree of self-control.

"Why's that?" she asked nonchalantly, but her voice didn't have quite the same bite to it anymore.

I folded my arms and responded in a flat tone. "Because if she chooses to, she could well become more powerful than anyone here."

Silence, apart from the whistle of wind across the mountains, reigned for the space of about five seconds.

"What?"

Sarah was the one to break it. Only when her trembling voice registered in my brain did I realize the line I had crossed.

I met her eyes for one moment, my own narrowing and softening in regret for a second. Then I hardened again as I looked back at Yvera. I had begun this. Now I had to finish it.

Yvera finally unfroze and gave a forced laugh. "You're kidding."

"Absolutely not," I countered grimly. "The Tree made that part quite clear."

"Ben, what are you talking about?" Sarah said, voice still tremulous. "I was *there*."

"Let me clarify: I don't mean two nights ago, nor do I mean the Tree of Ice. I meant what the Tree of Flame told Avva and me when She first gave me my task one year ago."

"Your *task*?" Yvera cried, finally recovering her anger. "You didn't say anything about that, other than that She told your father to send us on some fool's errand to go look for an Earthren. Who would just...*appear*. Somewhere. *Without a gate*. That is all you told us. *All*."

"Yvera," Kor said quietly, intervening for the first time. "You know Ben isn't always authorized to tell us everything the Tree tells him or his father."

But Kor's eyes were on me as he said it, and the intentness of his midnight-blue gaze was telling.

He knows, I thought.

Kor knew I was holding back at least one big thing from them.

Which meant he had no doubt been trying to figure out what that was this entire time and had at least partially succeeded. I groaned inside, but I still had to focus on the *first* nest of wyrms I'd smashed open.

"Well, apparently there was *one* more detail that he *could* share," Yvera snarled, eyes never leaving me. "Care to reveal anything *else* to your lowly wings, O mighty Heir?"

"You suspected all along why we were looking for an Earthren," I said quietly.

She snorted. "Obviously, but I can't believe you think that small, weak, *human* girl will become the next White Lady, or be more powerful than *you*."

"More powerful? I do," I said flatly. Apparently the time for this particular truth had come. Whether I had prepared any of them for it or not. "Because she's not meant to become a mere *lady*. Rather, something more."

Silence again.

"But...Ben," Sarah said brokenly. "You said...you told me..."

I forced myself to look at her. To see the betrayal in her eyes. To feel the icy fingers closing over my flameheart. I deserved it all.

"I told you that you were meant to be their leader," I said quietly. "I...never used the word *lady*. You're a sovereign Tree's chosen, Sarah. Just as I am. Surely by now you can understand what that means."

Her eyes went wide, and she paled. She slowly mouthed the word, unable to even say it out loud. Even forming the word in her own language, I somehow knew she said the right one.

Queen.

She teetered dangerously, so much that I rushed forward, heedless of the voice inside that told me she might want me far from her right now. I threw an arm around her and pressed her to me. She stiffened for a moment, then relented, leaning in. Still, her eyes seemed glazed over, and her breath came in gasps, and she was cold. Far too cold. The sweat on her skin and clothes appeared to be stiffening, freezing....

"Sarah?" I said in alarm. "Sarah? Can you hear me?"

"You see?" Yvera said, recovering again enough to snort derisively. "A bit of truth, and she—"

"Yvera," I said, voice rumbling dangerously. "I cannot express my thanks enough for putting up with my nonsense and saving my life countless times over the years, but most especially this last, very difficult one. I know I have not made your job easy. I know you get so mad at me because you care and because you are right. So yell at *me* all you want. I won't say anything about that. Curse me, spit on me, hit me if it makes you feel better, I don't care. But when it comes to Sarah, this streak of nastiness you've gotten yourself into ends now. I'm giving you only one more warning: speak poorly about the future Queen of Ice one more time, and I will send you back to Crownhold."

Sarah flinched. But that was nothing compared to Yvera's reaction.

Her skin went a few shades paler. Her violet eyes widened. She took a step back as if I had struck her.

In a way, I had. It had come to blows after all, just like she'd wanted. Except I knew a way to hit her harder than my fist could.

A second later, her fury returned, and this time, it was directed right at Sarah. When her eyes narrowed to slits again, they were looking straight into hers. Her hands slowly curled into fists, every inch of her six feet or so of Battleblood fury going rigid. I half-expected her to launch herself at Sarah at any second.

Which made what Sarah did next seem suicidal.

She slowly took one step away from me, ignoring my quiet warning. Then two. Then a final third, putting a full body's width of distance between us. All while holding Yvera's gaze.

Some kind of message seemed to pass between them. Even without an inner voice, Sarah was communicating something to Yvera...and I couldn't for the life of me understand what that was.

But Yvera did. Her eyes widened and narrowed one more time, and her mouth pressed in such a thin line, her full lips became almost invisible. Then she spun on her heel and launched herself across the edge of the mountain, transforming while in motion so that in mere seconds, she was surging into the air in drakáform and flying away.

Within moments, she was fading into the distance.

Kor broke the silence with a low whistle. "Well," he said mildly. "That could have gone better."

I moaned, putting my head in my hands. "I know," I said, voice muffled. "But what else was I supposed to *do*?"

"Oh, I agree, you had to put your foot down," Kor said, folding his arms. "But you *should* have done it yesterday, in private. Or, ideally, long before that."

"I know, but I had no idea she'd be like *this*."

I raised my head with another groan and looked at Sarah. At least she was standing steadily on her own now. That was the smallest bit of comfort, but I took it.

"Sarah...I'm not going to apologize for her, but I hope you can believe me when I say she's not normally this...."

"Condescending?" Kor supplied helpfully. "Prejudiced? Tactless? Militant? Fire-filled? Stone-carved-stubborn? When has she *not* been all those things and more?"

"That's enough, Kor," I said shortly.

"Ben," Sarah said quietly, and both Kor and I looked at her in surprise. "I think you should go after her. She's your friend."

When I hesitated, she tried again. "Please, Ben. I don't want to drive a wedge between you two."

"You're not the one driving a wedge, Sarah," I said with a frown.

"She's got a point, though," Kor said, coming to stand beside her. "It looks like we're going to spend the night here after all, so you'd better go get her before she wastes too much energy. Besides, you two need to hash this out in *private*. Preferably somewhere high up and far away from anything flammable, breakable, or with delicate eardrums."

Kor inclined his head toward Sarah while giving me a pointed look.

I looked between Kor and Sarah, troubled. Then I glanced over my shoulder in the direction Yvera had disappeared to, then back at Sarah.

Kor put a hand on her shoulder. "Don't worry about Sarah. I can get her inside the shelter and call for the guard."

You...really think I should leave her to go after Yv? I asked silently, pained at the thought of separating from Sarah now without first making things right with her.

I do, Kor said sternly. *I'll keep Sarah safe*—and *smooth out the worst of her ruffled feelings, don't worry. You go take care of your rightwing's. She's the one who's going to find it much harder to forgive you.*

Normally, I would have agreed, but after seeing that betrayal in Sarah's eyes.... Perhaps I *should* go. If only to give her space away from me.

I looked at her, filled to the depth of my soul with regret. "Sarah...I am so sorry. This was not at all how I.... I *promise*, when I get back, I'll give you the explanation you deserve."

"I'll be waiting for it," she said quietly. Her brown eyes were sober but...not cutting anymore. I felt a twinge of hope.

"Stay safe," I said, looking between her and Kor as I reluctantly took a step backward. "*Both* of you."

And check her to see if she needs healing once you're inside, I told Kor silently. Sarah might have just been in shock, but.... *And get her to drink something, and give her food if she's hungry. And get her to sit down, if you can.*

"Like I said," Kor replied with a smirk. "We'll be fine. I'd be more worried about yourself right now."

I groaned in agreement, but I finally turned and began striding away to give myself enough space to change. When I was about a hundred erd away, I glanced back over my shoulder one last time at Sarah, unable to help another worried twinge, before I began to shift.

Yvera hadn't gotten far, and since she was the fastest flyer of the three of us, that meant her slowness had been deliberate. Probably hoping I *would* come after her like this.

I sighed, great gusts of steam spilling from my mouth, but as soon as I thought I was close enough for her to hear me, I said, *Yvera....*

She sped up suddenly. I growled and increased my pace as well.

Look, I said, carefully keeping my tone level. *I know you're mad, and I know it's at least partially my fault, so I'll give you this: one hit. One free hit, wherever and however you want.*

Silence for a moment, but Yvera slowed, so I knew she was thinking about it. *Wherever and however I want?*

I felt a twinge of nervousness. I knew from personal experience, both from these kinds of fights and from simple practices with her, just how hard she could hit. Right where it would hurt the most. But...if that's what it took for her to finally start letting out whatever poison had gotten into her blood lately....

One, I said, both in confirmation and warning. *Then I'll give as good as I get.*

Good, she said, then dove for the ground.

I stared. I had expected her to turn right around and come straight at me. Yvera was almost more draká than amá, so aerial fights were her favorite. Yet she alighted near a majestic natural arch in the red rock and changed into amáform.

If anything, that made me more nervous. This meant she had something in mind that might well debilitate me (at least temporarily), and she didn't want me falling out of the air.

Groaning, I soared down and landed where she had, then changed and carefully picked my way up and over the rivulets of rock to join her.

I eyed the arch apprehensively. "Yv," I shouted over the distance. "Should we really be doing this near something so...delicate? I have enough of the Conservationist Guild mad at me as it is."

Which was saying something, since they were mostly Peacegrowth. Of course, they were some of Peacegrowth's most...determined members.

"Oh, quit being a hatchling and come get your medicine," Yvera called back. She leaned right up against the arch, bending one knee and propping it against the rough surface. "What I have in mind won't hurt this rock a bit. If you take it to the next level after that, well...that's on you."

I eyed *her* now as I crossed the last hundred feet to her. Considering her temper from before, and her threats now, she seemed rather...casual. Almost...pleased. Her violet eyes glittered with clear anticipation as I approached.

Flame help me, I thought. *This is going to hurt.*

"Alright," I said peaceably as I stopped about ten feet away from her. I held out my hands away from my sides. "Here I am. Now, go ahead."

"Not just yet," Yvera said with a shake of her head. She pushed off the arch and then approached me.

I couldn't help it: I held up my hands defensively. "Wait, what?"

"You promised, remember?" she said with a raised eyebrow. She seized me by the forearm and pulled me over to the inside edge of the arch. "However I wanted."

"Yv, the arch...."

"As I said, this won't hurt it."

She grabbed me by the shoulders and turned me so that my back was now to the arch. Then she pushed me against it, hard enough that my head hit the stone with a small shot of pain.

"That?" I asked, baffled. "That was it?"

"Don't be a dimtorch," she said with a smirk. "Well, more than you usually are."

Her hands were still on my shoulders, keeping me against the stone. Then she stepped in close. Very close. Not a good angle for blows....

What was she *planning*?

"Yvera—"

"Shut up," she said.

Then she crushed her lips to mine.

I froze, brain in utter, shocked disarray. Not that I hadn't ever been jumped like this before, until I learned to avoid being alone with girls I didn't trust if mortally possible. But I had never, ever, in my wildest imaginings, seen this coming from *Yvera*.

Surely this was a trick, a distraction. She'd never tried something like that on me before, but that was surprising, now that I thought of it, considering how stupefied it made me. Then again, this kind of shock could be achieved only once, so she had saved it for maximum effect. Now, having completely disarmed me, she was going to deliver a blow that would knock me senseless with pain....

Right?

But as I waited, stiff with anticipation of the incoming suffering...it never came. Instead, Yvera continued to explore my mouth, as if fascinated. Her eyes were closed, which was ridiculous. She *never* let her guard down. Besides, how was she supposed to *hit* me if....

Only when she nibbled on my lip, when she molded her whole body to mine, did I finally understand.

This was it. The blow.

Well....

This form of revenge got points for uniqueness, that was for sure, and I was a bit relieved. This didn't hurt at *all*. But the physical reactions she was soliciting from me against my will or even desires were making me a bit sick. My mind and heart were screaming at my body that I *shouldn't be doing this*.

Not with her.

"Yv—"

I only managed that one word before she covered my mouth again, and this time, she used her tongue.

Alright, that was it.

I jerked my head to the side to break contact and snapped, "Yvera!"

I grabbed her by the shoulders and pushed her away from me, then met her gaze. Her eyes were glowing. Mine were no doubt blazing—but only from fury.

I clenched my jaw. "What. The. Hellfrost."

Yvera only smirked. "Don't tell me you didn't enjoy that. I've been practicing."

I stared at her. I could have sworn, before this moment, that my best friend didn't have a romantic bone in her body. She had never been with anyone, that I knew of. She had always said she didn't have time or the care for such frivolous nonsense.

"With *who*?" I choked out. Then, at the image of her in some dark corner, *practicing*...I gagged. The bile that had churned in my stomach at her kiss rose in full force. "Wait. Don't answer that. I *really* don't want to know."

Her smirk deepened, eyes satisfied. "Jealous?"

"Hellwinds *no*," I growled, shoving her away hard enough that she stumbled. "I don't want to think about it because *you're my sister*. Or the closest thing I'm going to get, anyway."

Even after that kiss, that press of her body against mine, her tongue in my mouth, I hadn't seen it. It hadn't sunk in. Not until *that* moment...when the glow in her eyes abruptly died. When the smile fell from her face. When the pain slashed across her suddenly vulnerable features, and she flinched away from me.

As if I'd struck her back, with even more force than she'd hit me.

My flameheart chilled and sputtered, nearly going out as I rethought my entire life in an instant. "Yv.... You.... You don't...."

A flash returned to her eyes, but it died as quickly as a sputtering candle. "And if I did?" she said quietly. "What would you say?"

Like the dimtorch I was, I could only stare at her and repeat numbly, "You're...my sister."

Or so I had thought.

Oh, I'd heard the rumors. I wasn't *that* blind and deaf. We had even joked about them together, rolling our eyes at everyone's assumption that there *had* to be something going on between the two of us—if only in the basest sense. They knew Yvera wouldn't become my consort, but they assumed we had to be friends with benefits, nonetheless. Most of them would have been shocked to discover that was the very *first* (and hopefully only) time we had ever made out—if you could call my slightly nauseated nonparticipation as amounting to that.

We had always shaken our heads when the gossipers couldn't understand the simple fact that we were inseparable simply because we were each other's first and most steadfast friend.

She always told me, whenever I became uncertain enough to ask, that there was nothing to the rumors.

She always told me....

She looked away, folding her arms tightly to her. I had never seen her so...broken. And guilty. "I always said you were like a brother to me because I knew that was what you needed me to say. I knew how badly you wanted a sibling, and I...couldn't take that from you. So, I tried to just be whatever you needed me to be. Hellwinds, why do you think I trained so hard to become the best? To keep you *safe*. To...always be the one to keep you safe. Most of the time, that was enough. Especially when, year after year, you didn't seem to prefer any girl over me. But the more times I told the lie, the harder it became to say, and then finally...she came."

Up to that last bit, my mind had been an empty, icy wasteland, utterly unable to function from devastation and guilt. Then a spark of intelligence reentered the wastes.

"She?"

Her eyes met mine, hardening. She straightened, some of the proud, strong friend I knew returning. "I'm not an idiot," she snapped. Her voice increased with volume with each subsequent word. "I *see* the way you look at her. It was bad enough from the very start, but it just keeps getting more nauseating by the day. Blessed Flame, Ben. You've only known her *five days*."

I blinked rapidly. Had it only been that long?

"Yes, *five*," Yvera raged, eyes beginning to burn. "While I have been at your side nearly every day for almost your entire life, and you have *never* looked at me the way you look at her."

So, this was it. The poison that had been festering inside her, the unfathomable reason she had taken such an intense and immediate disliking to Sarah. A dislike that had increased in exact proportion to my...like.

At some point, I would be angry for Sarah's sake. She had deserved none of Yvera's misdirected angst. Right then, all I felt was crushing guilt.

It was always my fault in the end. Wasn't it?

"Yv," I whispered. Suddenly unsteady, I reached back against the arch for support. "I...I am sorry."

Just like that, her anger died down. The soulflare in her eyes left. But I didn't feel relief. I knew that when the magma of her temper faded, it cooled into iron resolve. Shaken worldview aside, I still had enough confidence in reading her to know from her straightened, businesslike posture and folding arms that this time was no exception.

"Regardless," she said with a shake of her braid. "It's good we're having this talk. So maybe I'll finally get it through your thick skull that she's a threat, especially since you don't see her clearly."

"And you *do*?" I choked out.

"More than you do," she said with unnerving calm. "Five days, Ben. Five days, and you're as twitterpated as a maglark. Admit it."

My own temper flared again, giving me strength to let go of the arch and straighten. "Do you really want to be talking about this? Now?"

"Yes," she said coolly. "I brought it up, didn't I? Admit it, Ben."

I covered my face with my hands and took deep breaths. I could not believe she was making me do this, especially after her own fireball of a revelation.

"Ben," Yvera said impatiently.

I lowered my hands and spat, "Yes, fine. I admit it."

"Admit what?" she said, with all the obnoxious firmness of our secondary history teacher, Master Kelsa. Honestly...I was a bit surprised she had sunk low enough to imitate her. I had disliked her, but Yvera had *loathed* her.

I gritted my teeth. Then, it hit me, with a force that made my flameheart surge: I had nothing to be ashamed of. In fact, I did Sarah a disservice by being reluctant to admit it.

I raised my head, met Yvera squarely in the eye—and when she flinched, I reminded myself that she had asked for this—and said with quiet surety, "I admit that I have feelings for Sarah."

That wasn't being evasive, or even softening the blow. I still didn't know entirely *what* I felt for her, and with the hurricane of other feelings inside me right now, I wasn't about to try figuring that out on the spot. But what I had said, I knew to be irrevocably true.

"That will do," Yvera said stiffly, recovering quickly. "I had half-expected you to not have realized as much by now."

"I know I have officially earned the title of dimmest Heir in history," I said irritably. "But I'm not *that* dim."

"Good," Yvera said, lips twitching. "That means I haven't wasted all my time on protecting you for nothing."

"I should hope not," I muttered.

Now that my apology was given and at least somewhat accepted, and I was regaining my balance in the world, I was starting to feel the anger I was justified in feeling at her own part in her heartbreak. True, I was a torched idiot, but also, Yvera had known that, had *lied* to me to prolong my ignorance, *and* had made her own decisions knowing full well her own feelings and mine.

And she'd kissed me. Forcefully. Gah, was I ever going to get the taste of my sister's tongue out of my mouth? I would almost rather she'd hit me instead at this point. At least bruises faded.

Yvera raised an eyebrow. "But it still might be if you continue to blindly trust her."

It took me a half second to refocus. Then I growled.

"Not that again. You can't honestly believe that Sarah—"

"Five days," Yvera repeated, eyes hard. She held out a hand, with all her fingers spread. "What you feel could be natural. This kind of thing happens that fast sometimes, I'll admit it. But as your rightwing, *and* your friend, I need you to at least acknowledge the possibility that you might be...influenced."

I stared at her. "You...think that Sarah is...*spelling* me?"

The statement sounded so idiotic that I could hardly believe that Yvera had listened to it stoically.

Instead of rushing to correct or clarify, she merely said, "Yes. Or someone else working on her behalf."

I shook my head in disgust and disbelief, but before I could speak, Yvera pressed on with surprising earnestness. "Please, Ben. Just think about it. If the Devourer is really coming, then what better way to distract, harm, or even eliminate you than to...to entangle you with one of its agents?"

I folded my arms. I was beyond fury and into weary exasperation. "You realize that she's the Tree of Ice's chosen, right? Ignore our *own* Tree's hints to me, I heard the Tree of Ice's voice explicitly declaring Her intent to invest Sarah. Do you think She would have done that if there was even the slightest *trace* of consumption in her?"

I expected that to be the end of it. Yvera reverenced the Tree as much as Kor did not. In fact, she put my own devotion to shame, and I was the Heir.

Yvera just set her jaw. "That's why I said it could be someone working on her behalf. Maybe even without her knowledge. You know they say that the Devourer is getting more skilled at evading your detection, at creating consumed that don't even know they are—"

"The Tree of Ice was present enough to have felt even that kind of influence in Sarah," I said firmly. "Suppose you are right, and someone else is spelling me to feel for her, then who? Kor?"

Yvera snorted. "Of course not Kor. He's many things, but I don't think—"

"Then *who*, Yvera?" I pressed. "A love spell subtle enough for neither Kor nor I to detect it, yet powerful enough to make me feel what I do, would need frequent—at least *daily*—replenishment, and as you keep pointing out, we've had at least five days, which would require five renewals. *At least*."

For the very first time, Yvera hesitated, blinking. "Er. They...do?"

I put my palm to my forehead. I knew Yvera had passed every magical theory class she had been forced to take by only the narrowest of margins, but I could not believe that her greatest reason for holding onto prejudice against Sarah all this time was...ignorance.

Then again...wasn't that where all prejudice came from?

"Yes," I said through gritted teeth. "They do. This one would have needed a masterfully managed progression, too."

I hadn't started out feeling this way for her, after all. Love spells were devilishly tricky to handle, to get just right so that the victim was none the wiser *but* eventually overpowered. As such, the typical caster was practically doomed to overdo it. That's how the victim could usually spot a love spell: the sudden, overpowering lust or infatuation, coming from nowhere.

I knew that from personal experience. In fact, I'd known exactly what had happened each of the two times a spell had gotten through my precautions, and I had gotten away from the girl and to a cure right away. And they acted so *surprised* when I didn't fall immediately down at their feet. It was insulting.

As I said...I wasn't *that* dim.

"So," I said, glaring at her. "In the past five days, during which it has just been the four of us, and crossing three worlds—four, if you count my quick trip to Ythra—who could have done that? Hmm?"

"Well...." Yvera said, floundering. "What about...potions? Or charms?"

I spread my arms wide. "I have changed everything on my body right now several times, so that rules out charms. As for potions...you know those are the weakest of all, don't you? And that the effect runs out as soon as it passes through your system, just like anything you might drink?"

The body naturally resisted love spells or potions, just as it did with any hostile magic. Not that bodies were *immune* to love magic, otherwise people wouldn't try them, but it was generally benign enough that it didn't do any physical harm before the body could throw it off, and the body sent warning signals while it tried to do so. After getting hit with the second and hopefully last spell I would have to endure—and Flame, that one had been a doozy—I'd had a splitting migraine so bad that it was actually quite easy to ignore my sudden lust and push the girl away. That's where so many people went wrong with love spells: they assumed *more* was *better*.

Fortunately for me.

"Alright, I didn't know that," Yvera said, throwing up her hands. "Fine. You win that one."

She gritted her teeth, then took a deep breath. "But just because your feelings might...not be magically induced doesn't mean you should follow where they lead."

For the first time, my heart skipped a beat at her sudden shot far closer to home. "What do you mean?"

Yvera's face hardened. "I hate to tell you this, Ben, but even if she's not magically manipulating you, even if she isn't consumed or working with anyone who is...that doesn't mean she's worthy of you. She could still be dangerous to you—at the very least, as a weak and helpless distraction. I mean, look at what happened last night. She asked you on a walk, all by yourself, and—"

"Ashes," I said, abruptly furious. I didn't admit to myself at that moment that it was because her words now had the faintest echo of my own arguments against my feelings. Even if her perception was twisted by her own feelings for me, they cut too deep. "You're just so mad to discover there's someone I might actually want to marry that you won't see reason."

She paled and took a step back. "You might...what?"

I regretted the words immediately. She hadn't deserved that kind of blow, right then, delivered in that kind of way. But once again my temper had made me admit a truth I couldn't take back, so I had no choice but to go forward.

Still, I chose the coward's way first. Face growing hot, I said, "Surely you've realized by now...the political advantages...."

She was abruptly livid. "Don't you give me political drivel, Ben! You have never given in to that kind of pressure in the slightest before now."

I held up my hands in peace. "True. I'm sorry. It's a lot more than that. But Yv...you know that if I ever do decide to marry, politics has to come at least a little into it."

She knew what I wasn't saying: that it was the reason I could never marry her. She was no King's consort. And, despite her recent revelation that I had overly influenced her life's path, she had never, not even once, tried to be. She had chosen to become my rightwing. And that was—had to be—an entirely different thing.

Still, my reminder, as gentle as I had meant it to be, must have hurt her. Her nostrils flared and eyes flashed. "But you can't tell me you're seriously considering...marriage? Now?"

My face grew hot again. "Not...right now, obviously. Or right away. Even if we survive the invasion, there's a lot to consider...not the least being the will of the Trees and Sarah's...openness to the idea. But...because I'm the Heir, and that's the way I have to think...then yes. I'm thinking about it."

I hesitated, then took a deep breath. Yvera deserved the truth, all of it, delivered as kindly as I could. "No, I'm more than thinking about it. You should know that...when everything's over...and if I am at all allowed to...I intend to court her."

Yvera just stood there, frozen. In all the years I had known her, I had never seen her look so...lost.

I had never known someone with her drive. Her surety of purpose. Some-times it came across as arrogance, but I'd glimpsed her determination far too much to think it was just that. I'd frequently envied her for it. I'd counted on it as one of the bulwarks of my life.

But I'd been one of hers, in a far deeper way than I'd thought.

Her words echoed, sending tiny stabs with each one. *Why do you think I trained so hard to become the best?*

For the first time in her life, she looked like she didn't know what to do—as if I had always been her north, and now that her internal compass was spinning without rhyme or reason....

"Yvera," I whispered, flameheart chilling. "I...I am so sorry. I never meant to hurt you like this.... But you deserve the truth, and that is the truth."

"Five days," she whispered, staring at nothing.

Five of the most intense, wild, excruciating, and incredible days of my life, filled with suffering and a hope, growing wilder by the day, mingled with desire and connection that I had never felt before and somehow knew I never would again.

Avva had always told me I would just *know*.

And, blessed Flame...he was right.

You would think that I, of all people, would stop being surprised by that. But then, in this, at least, I had been determined to prove him wrong. Never suspecting, even after a year of searching, that the one who would tempt me enough to rescind my oath would be the very one to make it unnecessary.

But to my rightwing and lifelong friend, I simply said, "Yes."

She slowly hardened. I was used to watching her magma cool, but this...was more frightening. "Alright, then."

"Alright...?" I asked, dragging out the word as a question.

She shrugged. "I see how it is. Seems like I'm going to be the only one with the sense to keep an eye on her."

"Agh!" I cried, putting my head in my hands. Just when it seemed as if I had *finally* gotten through to her....

I lowered my hands. "Look," I said severely. "Let me make one thing clear—"

"Yeah, yeah," she said with a snort. "You want me to be 'nice.' Or you'll send me to Crownhold."

Since that was more or less what I had been about to say, I lowered my hand and closed my mouth, for a moment not sure what to do. "Er. Yes. And...you're fine with that?"

"Sure," she said with another shrug. "If Kor can fake being nice all the time, how hard can it be?"

"One," I said, holding up a finger. "He's not always faking it. Two, faking...has never been easy for you."

"But that's what you're asking me to do, right?" she said impatiently. "Because you can't possibly expect me to *actually* like her."

"Yes, I suppose," I said between gritted teeth. "That would be unreasonable of me, wouldn't it?"

She raised an eyebrow. "Yes, it would. Separate from my own feelings, my job isn't to like people, Ben. It's keeping you safe."

I glared at her for a moment.

"You know," I declared finally. "I think my life would be a hellwind simpler if my wings weren't so torched good at their jobs."

Her lips twitched. "It would also be a lot *shorter*."

I hesitated, then admitted grudgingly, "Also true."

"Just admit one more thing to me."

"What?" I said hesitantly.

She gave me a smirk, some of the energetic fire I knew and loved so well reentering her eyes. "I'm a better kisser than her, aren't I?"

I stared at her. "How should I know?"

She stared back. "What? But...."

As surprisingly painful as it was for me to admit, I said grudgingly. "We haven't...actually...."

"But last night," she said insistently. "On that 'walk' of yours. Surely she tried *something*."

My flameheart sank. I had tried avoiding romance so much of my life that I was clueless about how it actually worked. Just how bad of a sign was it that Sarah hadn't shown that kind of interest in me last night?

Too bad the one female in my life to whom I could entrust with all the details and ask for the answer was the one standing right in front of me. The one who had feelings for me herself and was therefore determined to think everything that Sarah did was evil.

"Nothing?" Yvera said in disbelief. And oddly now, she was flushing. "You mean I...."

"Overreacted, just a bit?" I said dryly.

"Not if you're planning on marrying her," Yvera snapped. "Which I can't believe you are when you haven't even *kissed* her yet. You know how dim that sounds, right?"

"I'm the Heir," I said flatly. Unless I wanted to be an absolute jerk—which no Heir should be—then interest and honorable intentions had to go hand in hand.

"Yeah, yeah," Yvera said with a wave of her hand. Then stiffened. "It's just...it seems I owe you...an apology."

I stared. I could count on one hand the number of times Yvera had apologized to me in so many words. "Undoubtedly, but for what in particular?"

She stiffened even further. And the heat in her cheeks rose. "It's just that...if I had known that particular detail, I might have...handled this differently."

Meaning....

And then suddenly, I understood. It should have been obvious, really, considering how much I too had been stewing about getting *even*.

"You wouldn't have kissed me if you hadn't thought Sarah had," I said flatly.

She shrugged. "I said I was sorry. Besides...I had to try *something* to get you to snap out of it."

I slowly closed my eyes, praying to the Tree for patience. "Yv...don't tell me you actually believe that fancytale that a kiss can end a curse?"

"Of course not," she said. But she was just as bad a liar as I was, and the discomfort in her voice gave her away.

Though what she said next had the ring of truth to it. "I was talking about snapping you out of the way you used to see me. As just a sister, I mean. I figured if anything could do it...that would."

I slowly opened my eyes and looked at her sadly. "Yv...I accept your apology because I've put you through hell, and that's not about to stop anytime soon. But you shouldn't have done it. You shouldn't have kissed me...much less with such...enthusiasm...without my permission, especially knowing how I felt."

She shifted awkwardly. "Well...you *sort of* gave it—"

"'Sort of' doesn't cut it," I said firmly.

I may have been ignorant in a lot of ways, but this much, I knew. My mother had made sure of that.

I pressed on. "You knew that wasn't what I meant at all when I gave you one hit. I know words are hard for you, but any words would have been better than that. I really, truly, sincerely hope that you find a partner who makes you happy. But if I hear of *anyone* who does to you what you did to me *without* your permission, I will punch the flameheart out of them. Do you understand me?"

Her lips twitched. "You're assuming that I won't have punched the flameheart out of them first."

"Oh, I am," I said darkly. "They'll have deserved getting it twice."

Any trace of a smile left her face, and she ducked her head. "I...understand. Sorry, again.... Do you...want a hit? I'll give you one."

I sighed and opened my arms. "What I want is to hug my friend...hoping she's still somewhat willing to be at least that.... Is that alright?"

She took a deep breath and raised her head to meet my eyes. "Yes."

My flameheart warmed and sputtered at the same time. That was my Yvera. Courageous to a fault.

"Come here," I said, and I crushed her to me.

CHAPTER ELEVEN

QUEEN

SARAH

WHEN BEN PUSHED OFF the plateau, we felt the vibration through the stone, not to mention the buffeting of his wings. Still not used to dragon take-offs, the sensation startled me enough that in my shaky state, I stumbled. Fortunately, Kor's hand was still on my shoulder, and he steadied me.

I watched Ben's drakáform slowly fade from sight with a surprising pang.

It's just for an hour or two, I told myself sternly.

This time, an inner voice whispered back.

Looking for a distraction, I looked up at Kor with a frown. "Does he *honestly* not know how she feels about him?" I demanded.

Kor snorted and let go of me. "As far as I can tell, he doesn't. Remarkable, I know."

He sighed as he ran a hand through his short curls. "I think it's because this is how they've always been. They grew up together. Her father was in the King's elite, her mother was in the Queen's and *died* protecting her. Queen Nyethra couldn't stand being at fault for two hatchlings losing their mother, so she took them under her wing, and with Yvera and Ben about the same age, it made sense to put them together; they've been inseparable ever since."

Kor stared off at Ben's vanishing form. "As far as I've been able to determine, Ben has always thought of Yvera as the sister he never got, and Yvera has always thought of him...as something else. She knows Ben won't—can't—choose her in the end. And she has no interest in the consort's duties in any case. But she seems to have always wanted something more from him, and the fact that she's never gotten it hasn't driven her away yet. In fact, she's dedicated her life to protecting him."

"And now Ben won't let her protect him from me," I finished soberly, gazing into the distance where Ben was now just a speck—or possibly just a bird.

"I'm not excusing her behavior any more than Ben is," Kor told me pointedly. "But you strike me as someone who likes to know *why*."

"I am," I said quietly. "So, thank you."

"Speaking of *why*s," Kor said with a casual stretch. "I gather Ben didn't get nearly as far as he should have with his explanations about your destiny."

"Queen," I repeated numbly, shaking my head. "Don't tell me you actually believe that."

"Actually, I do. I know it's a bit of a shock to you now, because you don't know how these things work. But really, even Yvera should have seen that one coming. There is only one plausible conclusion for you being the Heir of a sovereign Tree."

"But the person before me was a lady," I protested. "Right?"

"Come on," Kor said, clapping me on the shoulder and making his way to the edge of the plateau. "Let's get inside, before something nasty comes by and Ben has my hide for keeping you out in the open talking Covenant history and theory."

"Inside?" I asked in bafflement, but I trailed behind him.

"Indeed," Kor said, pulling a rope ladder out of nowhere. Which he attached with surprising deftness to two rings I hadn't noticed before.

I shook my head. Kor appeared so intellectual and scholarly sometimes, I had to remind myself that wasn't mutually exclusive with being good at things like tying knots.

"There," Kor said, pushing the rolled ladder over the edge and letting it flap down the cliff face. I didn't get close enough to see it fall, but I thought I heard a "thump" that hinted at hitting something below.

"A bit unnecessary," he said with a flirtatious smile. "After all, I can fall that distance easily, and carrying you, too. But I figured you wouldn't like that."

"Er, no. That's a pass."

He shrugged. "Suit yourself."

And then he stepped off the cliff.

"Kor!" I said in a garbled cry, rushing to the edge.

But sure enough, I saw him standing, perfectly fine, on a small lip of stone, only big enough for one drakón, twenty feet below. He looked up at me with a wink. "So good to know you care."

"Do that again and I might not," I snapped down at him.

"Noted. Come on then, before you attract attention. You don't have to do it my way. I gave you a ladder, after all."

I hesitated. "Just...what is down there? I don't see anything but cliff."

Kor smiled slowly. "Trust me."

"Oh, well, when you put it like *that*, how can I not?" I muttered to myself. But, against my better judgment, I turned around and began descending the ladder.

"Carefully," Kor said when I was about two-thirds of the way down.

Just then, a gust of wind blew, making the rope ladder wobble frighteningly. I froze and held tight. Then I felt something touch me, and I jerked.

"Easy," Kor soothed as he placed his hands back around my waist. "I'm just trying to help."

I hurried the rest of the way down, partly just to free him from having to "help." But I had forgotten how narrow the lip he was standing on was, and when I reached the bottom, there was nowhere for me to go but...right up against him.

Far from being as discomforted as I was by this, he wrapped his arms around me and inhaled the scent of my hair.

"Mmm. You have such an interesting scent, one not quite like I've ever smelled before. Like the smell that snow would have, if it had one. Sharp and clear."

"I have no idea what you're talking about," I said stiffly.

And yet...being this close to him, I smelled something too. Nothing like snow: rather, like...stars. The distant kind, burning like sticks of incense immersed in a licorice sea.

That analogy was so unexpected and ridiculous, I wanted to pinch myself. People didn't smell like things like that, even if they were wearing cologne or perfume.

And yet...I remembered Ben's scent, which I knew from repeated exposure by now was in even his smoky dragon's breath. And suddenly, remembering *his* scent, I was far hotter than I should be standing in Kor's embrace.

"What are you doing?" I asked, fidgeting.

"Proving a hypothesis," Kor said with a chuckle, relinquishing his hold.

I turned around and backed against the cliff to give as much room between us as possible. But...when I met his eyes, I wondered if that had been such a good idea. They were shimmering with sapphire light.

"And that is?" I growled.

He smirked, braced himself on either side of me, leaned in, and spoke with perfect confidence. "*You*, my dear Sarah, are attracted to me."

My heart stuttered, but I rolled my eyes. "Well, seeing as you're some kind of toned superhuman and magical badass, that's not exactly a Sherlock-level deduction."

Kor chuckled as he shifted to the side to deal with the rope ladder. To my surprise, when he tugged, the top came free and the whole thing tumbled into his arms. I really hoped that meant he had included some kind of magical release in the knots and not that I had been *that* close to plummeting.

With Kor...it could easily go either way.

With a flick of his wrists, Kor stowed the ladder in the ether. "Whatever a 'Sherlock' is, you're probably right. I've suspected it for some time, but I had to be sure."

"Why?" I demanded.

"Oh, my dear Moontouched," he said, with a wink as he leaned back in. "So many questions. Pity I can only answer one at a time. Suffice it to say for now that it's an important part of the next phase of my plan."

As he had spoken, he had placed his hand on the rock face behind me and sent a pulse of power through it. I was too distracted by his words and proximity to note how I would not have felt such a thing just a few days before, but now I could. Or to think about what the pulse had been *for*.

"What *plan*—"

Suddenly the rock behind me gave, and I stumbled into shadow. I would have fallen backward into the black precipice...except Kor casually stretched out his hand and caught mine.

"Watch out," Kor said innocently.

"*You....*" I fumed, beyond words as I straightened and looked behind me.

The rock face I had been leaning against had swung inward like a door, revealing steps leading down into shadow. If Kor hadn't caught me....

Of course, if he hadn't opened the door with me leaning against it, then I wouldn't have fallen, so I considered us even.

"You could have warned me," I snapped.

"I did," Kor said, face hardening for a moment as he held up the hand that had sent the pulse through the rock. "Didn't you feel that?"

I stopped. And remembered.

"Next lesson on survival," Kor said, tapping my forehead. "*Pay attention to all magic you feel.* Particularly if it's not *you* who is casting it."

He brushed past me to descend the steps.

"You distracted me," I muttered. But I followed.

"That was precisely the point," Kor said grimly. He waved his hand, and the rock slowly slid shut behind us. "Do you think the consumed play *fair*? Do you think their master does?"

I stopped in the utter darkness. "Uh...Kor...."

"Ah, yes. I suppose you need a light."

A small sapphire orb of light appeared, illuminating the passage; the floating light was much like one of my own except blue and completely still.

Kor pointed at the light and inclined his head to me with a look. "I would have made you cast that for practice, but I'm already getting us sidetracked enough as it is. Come along."

He turned and resumed his descent. His light kept perfect, almost robotic-like pace with him, as if attached to a stiff wire that led to his person. It's lack of independent movement, music, or...well, personality looked and felt very wrong to me. I carefully kept my eyes away from the light itself and focused on going down the steps.

"Some elaborate plan that was," I muttered. I seemed to be muttering a lot in these past few minutes. Kor had that effect on me.

Kor laughed. "Oh, that wasn't the plan I was referring to. That was just a brief lesson that came up in the moment. Don't you worry. A sharp mind like yours will catch on to what I'm doing in *that* regard soon enough."

That made me uneasy. "Just so we're clear...just because I'm a straight female, and therefore am attracted to you by default, does *not* mean I *like* you. Because I don't."

"Oh, I know," Kor said idly. "I'm rather counting on it."

I stared at the back of his head. "I don't get you. At all."

"I should certainly hope not. I'm a leftwing, after all. I wouldn't be doing my job right if you could."

We finally reached the bottom of the steps and came to a short passage. Kor pressed his hand to a panel that shimmered crystalline in the light of his floating orb. The panel flared sapphire, and then crystals began lighting up all down the hall and in the room beyond. Fortunately, the crystals glowed with warm, golden light very much like sunlight rather than cold sapphire. Even better, Kor dismissed his orb, thus removing an unexplainable itch I couldn't scratch.

"Welcome to a dramá shelter, of the variety built by the Strongshield in the Wirthen Desert," Kor said as he led me down the hall. "A shelter is an emergency place to...well, *shelter* for the night in case you are caught between holds. Safety and secrecy take precedence over comfort. Still, rudimentary as it is, it's going to feel homier than Brightflare hospitality. For one thing, it looks like we have it all to ourselves, for now."

We stepped into the main room, which was a large cavern—originally natural, judging from the weathered waves in the sandstone higher up, but down below, it had been carved out for various functions.

One entire wall had bunks built into the rock. Another, a basic-looking kitchen, complete with...was that a well? I didn't know what else that crank would be for. A few tables, some barrels, a board game with flat-bottomed glass pieces as tokens.

All in all, it looked like a pretty good doomsday shelter.

I pointed at the one offshoot corridor. "Please tell me that leads to a privy."

And that we won't have to go in those buckets from before.

"It should," Kor said with a chuckle. "Need to use it?"

In fact, I did. That had been the second reason I had asked us to land...except with one thing leading to another, it hadn't seemed right to bring up until now.

"Yes," I said, and strode toward that offshoot with a prayer of thanks to whatever higher power was listening, Tree or otherwise, and for more than just my relief now. I did *not* need to go to the bathroom in front of any of my drakón companions. But now, it seemed...particularly Kor.

By the time I got back, I heard Kor speaking with someone. My heart thumped with excitement—and surprise—and I hurried forward. How had Ben found and calmed down Yvera so fast?

But when I reentered the main room, I didn't see either of them, and Kor was merely sitting at one of the tables, talking into a scale.

And just like that, my restored good mood popped like a bubble. It was rather frightening how much my equanimity had become dependent on Ben. As if he were my personal sun, and life without him was just...cold and colorless.

That was surely *not* a good sign. Or a healthy one, considering Ben's indifference.

"Thank you, captain," Kor said with unusual formality. "The Crown thanks you for your service."

Then he tapped the scale, and the glow faded.

"That was very...bureaucratic of you," I said as I approached.

Kor smirked at me. "That is Strongshield: bureaucratic. And a Strongshield captain, no less. The Warflight likes to think it is above 'politics.' Little does it realize it is the ultimate bureaucracy. And just because I like to get under Yvera's skin doesn't mean I don't know how to talk their talk when needed."

"Of course," I said, rolling my eyes as I sat across from him. "So, what was that about?"

"I promised Ben I would call for backup." Kor propped his chin on the back of his joined hands as he met my gaze. "He didn't relish the thought of risking you out in the open another night, and frankly, I don't blame him."

I hesitated, then asked the ignorant-human question. "Is this...not where we were intending to go?"

"No, we were planning on stopping at a hold. One at the edge of the mountains and desert, with good views of both." Kor winked. "For Ben to take you stargazing, of course."

I rolled my eyes. "For me to look for a gate, you mean."

"And stargazing," Kor said innocently. "I might even have been able to lure Yvera away for some of it to give the two of you some cozy privacy."

My heart sank at his misguided perception of Ben's interest, but I wasn't about to let him distract me from the point. "But we stopped here instead. Because of me. And then Ben and Yvera got in a fight. Because of me. And now we're stuck in a dangerous situation again...because of me."

"You could look at it like that, feeling sorry for yourself. Or...."

"Or?" I asked with a sigh.

"You could think of it as *fate*." Kor said the word distastefully, but then he shrugged. "As so many of the things concerning you seem to be. Speaking of which...you asked me a question that I didn't give the answer to, and it boiled down to this: why are things different now than they were before, when the Moontouched were here?"

"I guess," I said reluctantly. I wasn't entirely sure I *wanted* to return to that subject.

Kor lowered his hands to the table. As he spoke, he pulled out a stylus and drew patterns on the tabletop in glowing sapphire light. "The answer is simple, after a bit of background. When the Covenants were first sworn, it was under the assumption that the small group of humans from Earth were leaving the stewardship of their Tree, the Tree of Ice, and binding themselves to the Tree of Flame."

He swiftly drew a circle, presumably Earth, with a tree in the center. Then to the right of Earth, he drew an arch I assumed was a gate, and an arrow leading to another circle, wherein he drew another tree. This tree was differentiated from the other by little squiggles on its branches that I assumed were heat waves or flames.

"They left with the Tree of Ice's blessing, of course, but they were *leaving* Her, with no intention of returning." Kor tapped the one-way arrow with the end of his stylus for emphasis. "Merging themselves, in a literal way we still do not understand, with the Tree of Flame's children, the draká."

He made seven pairs of dots underneath the world with the Tree of Flame in it, Ythra, then connected each pair with a line. He then drew five worlds around Ythra.

"When each clan received their own world, they planted an *offshoot* of the Tree of Flame on it for protection and guidance."

He drew arrows from five of the seven dot-pairs to the five circling worlds. Then, in each satellite world, he drew twigs, complete with little wavy leaves.

"It's that offshoot that governs each clan and chooses its leader," he explained as he continued to draw each twig. "But each offshoot is still, in some enigmatic way, the Tree of Flame. Just...a different facet of Her, so to speak. A piece of Her whole."

He tapped the Tree—the only one of the six he had bothered to draw as a tree, I realized.

"Therefore, all clan leaders that swear themselves to *their* Trees are in essence swearing themselves to the main Tree's rulers—the Monarch and the Heir. That's why they are merely Ladies and Lords, whereas the Sunfilled leader is a Queen or a King. Sovereign Tree, sovereign Monarch."

He drew a little crown over the Tree of Flame, then one over the sixth pair of dots.

I caught a glimpse, just a glimmer, at why the K was always translated with a capital in my mind. It still didn't entirely make sense, but Kor went on before

I could think more about it. He was on a roll now, only pausing for breath and for his drawing to catch up to his explanations.

"When Moontouched left—" Kor traced an arrow from the seventh pair of dots back to Earth. "—they *broke* the Covenants. For good reason, but when they pulled out their pillar, the building started to collapse."

"What?" I said sharply, looking up from his illustrations. Hadn't this been the detail Ben said no one knew but him and the King?

"Yes, yes," Kor said impatiently, misinterpreting my challenge. "Scholars differ on what effect it really had, but I'm almost certain by now. That's the only thing that makes sense. Why seven humans, seven draká, seven clans—seven, seven, seven—*if you don't need all seven for it to work?*"

He tapped each of the seven dots in turn.

"And I've studied the...well, for lack of a simpler term...the *strength* of the Covenants over the centuries more closely than any other scholar I know of. And I can tell you they are all weakening. The sungates, most blatantly."

Perhaps for thoroughness, or simply something to do while he talked, he began drawing arches between Ythra and each other world in the circle.

"I can't have been the only one to notice the trends, but either the Crown is hushing it up so well that they haven't told even me, or...they're idiots. And by now you should know that at least my mentor, Eskala, is *not* an idiot."

He sighed and tapped the crowned pair of dots. "But that's not all. There are indications that Monarchs used to be even more powerful than they generally are now. Kavarian is the strongest in a few generations, so with that resurgence, few people realize it. But there might be a reason it took so long for the Tree to find a suitable vessel to come after him...."

"Vessel?" I asked, troubled. I hadn't heard that term applied to Ben before.

But Kor didn't seem to hear. "And there's the reduced fertility rate across the clans, but most particularly in the Sunfilled. I know Ben told you two is our average births per mother, but for his clan, these days they're lucky to have *one*. People hoped that Ben's birth would signal better times, but so far, it hasn't."

"Why is that?" I asked. "I mean, why would they assume that?"

"The common people see the Monarchs as the center of it all, and there definitely could be something to that," Kor said with a thoughtful frown, tapping his stylus on his lips. "They seem to be either a lynchpin of the Covenants.... Or at least a measure of them. When the Crown is strong—magically strong, that is—and has a strong connection to the Tree, all seems to go well. When they don't...."

Kor shook his head. "At least, that used to be the case. But the last few Monarchs before Kavarian were good ones, and yet, I saw a steady decline in all measures I have identified to indicate the strength of the Covenants. A slow slide that even the Crown's best-intentioned efforts couldn't halt anymore."

My head was spinning. Despite Kor's helpful drawings and great pains to explain to a layperson and foreigner like me, I could hardly keep up. Which was frightening, because I understood enough to know these were all terrible things.

"Have you told Ben about this?"

"I've tried a bit, here and there," Kor said wearily. "But like I said.... Oh, Flame, what was it? Yesterday? Ben's been rather distracted. *Everyone* has been distracted, even Eskala. They're all so busy taking care of the immediate crises that they don't see what lies in the distance. And with the Devourer's impending invasion, that's only getting worse."

Kor looked up at me, and for the first time that I could remember...I saw a glimmer of fear in his eyes. "The Devourer is a genuine threat, one we *have* to face first. But just like last time the Devourer came, it's one thing to repel the invasion...and quite another to survive after. Once again, my people are on the brink of extinction, Sarah. And I'm the only one who seems to realize how close we are."

Every time I thought I could harden myself against Kor, dismiss him as nothing more than an arrogant, know-it-all, two-faced jerk...he did something like this.

I put my hand over his.

"That's why I'm here, isn't it?" I said quietly.

Kor's lips pulled into a faint smile. "You don't know how right you are."

He took a deep breath and pulled his hand back. "Sorry for getting us a little sidetracked again, but...perhaps this will help you appreciate the gravity of what I am about to tell you."

He tapped the arrow that took the Moontouched back to Earth. "As I said, the Moontouched left, and punched a hole in the barrel of Covenantal power as they did so, leaving it to slowly leak out ever since. Perhaps they were meant to be just like the other clans once. But now...we're so weak, we can't afford for them to be."

"What do you mean?" I said, my voice nearly a whisper.

"We need them to be something *more*," Kor said grimly. "Something *new*. The Covenants were formed in the first place to save the draká from themselves by changing them. Well, even if we hadn't weakened, the Devourer has learned all our tricks by now. And it has waited for the perfect moment to strike. To surprise it, and then survive afterward, we need to change again. Or...at the very least, ally ourselves with the ones who have."

He raised his eyes to mine. "You."

"I still don't understand," I said, shifting uneasily.

"The Moontouched came from us, but when you left, you returned to the Tree of Ice." Kor tapped Earth and its Tree. "You became Hers again. That could only have changed you, and we've only just begun to discover how."

Then he drew another line from Earth. But this time, he traced it to the space above the Six Realms, where he drew a seventh world, and beneath it, a single dot.

Me.

"Now, after a thousand years, the Tree of Ice has sent us you. But not so that you can restore things to the way they used to be. No. That's where everyone else who has guessed who you are—Yvera, Svyer, anyone with eyes who saw your doorgem—gets it wrong. "

He drew a sloppy twig inside the seventh planet, clearly not making an effort.

"*They* think you're simply going to go to the Tree of Flame and ask for a branch, and then go plant it on your own little happy world, become its happy lady, and thus become Ben's content little seventh vassal. Join the circle, fall in line. Make everything the way it should have been before. I imagine that's even what you thought."

Kor wiped the twig away with a dismissive swipe of his fingers. "But no. That's not enough anymore. Hopefully you understand why by now. You won't be rejoining Flame at all. You mustn't. You must remain something new, separate, superior."

He tapped the seventh world, where it rested above the ring of planets. "The how, then, is what you have already heard, and in fact told me. You are returning to the Tree of Ice...."

He tapped the tree inside Earth. And he made sure I met his gaze. "And you are becoming the Tree of Ice's sovereign Monarch. The White Queen."

I took a deep, unsteady breath.

Lady.

Queen.

Perhaps we were only discussing semantics, just as I had once underestimated the difference between Heir and prince. But by now, I *knew* those were different things. I still couldn't describe exactly how, but I knew it.

Now, I knew there was a difference between *Lady* and *Queen*. Even though...the Queen of Ice was still a leader of practically no one. Somehow, the lack of subjects made the title seem even more daunting. As if the weight of being a Monarch would always be the same...but I didn't have as many people as Ben did to share the load. I didn't even have *wings*.

And just like that, a mantle that had already seemed too heavy for me to put on became as crushing as a mountain.

"I...I don't know if I can do that, Kor," I whispered.

It was his turn to put his hand on mine. When I looked up, his eyes had that frightened look again. "Sarah...I'm not saying you have to. You still have a choice. But...I know enough about Trees to know that yours wouldn't have chosen you first if you weren't our best hope. And I'm afraid of what will happen to all the worlds, Earth included, if we don't have our very best."

The Tree of Ice had shown me Earth turning to shadow. Consumed in the Devourer's hunger. Turned to no more than bare, scorched rock.

The Tree hadn't said that Earth's fate was contingent on *my* decision. Just that *someone* had to receive Her power and return to Ythra to drive off the Devourer's assault, or all was lost. That someone didn't have to be me....

Couldn't be me....

Could it?

My eyes fell back on the table, running it all through my head again. And then one thing stuck out at me. The gear that didn't fit, the piece of the puzzle out of place.

I frowned, but inside, I was relieved for the intellectual distraction, and I suspected Kor might be too. I tapped the crown over the sixth pair of dots under Ythra, the only ones without another world.

"If Ben's father is the King because his world is the sovereign world..." I tapped the crown over Ythra. "...then why..."

My eyes traced to the seventh world above all the rest, and I tapped it. "...if I am to be the sovereign, do I have a vassal world? Why wouldn't I rule...Earth?"

It sounded ridiculous when I put it like that, but hopefully Kor would know what I meant.

"An excellent question," Kor said, eyes alight as he tapped his stylus against his lips again. "And one that occurred to me as well. I think—"

Just then, we both heard a clatter from the passage that led outside. Smooth as butter, Kor straightened and swiped his hand over the entire schema, erasing it as if it had never been. Which was a crying shame. Made me wish I could have taken a picture of it first....

"—that we shall have to pick up this pleasant intellectual pursuit another time," Kor said with a wink. He stood up, putting on an overly formal face. "Pardon me. It seems I have our backup to greet and get settled."

"Better you than me," I muttered.

As he passed me, Kor laughed quietly.

Oh, I'll miss you when you're gone.

I noticed he didn't say where he thought that would be. Or what choice he thought I would make. Just that either way...I would be "gone."

I sighed and looked down at the unadorned table. And thought too much about what—and who—wasn't there.

CHAPTER TWELVE

DUTY

KORIBEN

EVEN AS WEARY AS I was while Yvera and I descended the steps to the shelter, my flameheart pulsed faster. Foolish, considering how the last time I had seen Sarah, the quiet betrayal in her eyes had speared me through, and surely was about to do the same again.

Still, I hurried down and in, if only just to see that she was alright. I also remembered her paleness, her sweat-drenched skin freezing under the onslaught of her emotions....

Unfortunately, I was held up at the entrance to the main room by a Strongshield captain, immediately identifiable by her scarlet hair, even as short as it was, her red eyes, the cape half-draped over her scarlet armor, and the flame lines on her collar.

"Heir Koriben Sunfilled," she said, saluting by pressing her hand over her heart and nodding deeply. "It is an honor to be called on to serve you and the Crown on this day. I am Captain Yalla Strongshield of the Goldek Guard and am here at the request of your leftwing, Korinth Starkissed, with half of the First Flight of Goldek."

The First Flight would be their most elite, which was a relief. Half a flight meant about fourteen fighters, with most of them drakón but with at least a few amón—as was required by law and martial code. Depending on their skill set and risk tolerance, the amón could serve in many roles, ranging from command support to auxiliary combat, such as long-range targeting. The most dedicated of them could even keep up with drakón in a ground melee. Even Yvera had a solid foundation of respect for amón's contribution to the Warflight; I wouldn't have chosen her as my rightwing and future Warflight general if she hadn't. Which was why her attitude toward Sarah had been so baffling to me...until now.

"Excellent," I said, trying to smile and resist the compulsion to look around the captain for Sarah. I realized my mistake when Captain Yalla simply looked at me and waited, and I quickly yanked my full attention into the situation. I was dealing with a Strongshield, after all.

I first wiped off my smile—it had been a weak effort, anyway—and then saluted back with my hand over my heart and a nod, careful to not make it as deep. Strongshield were the most particular of the clans on rank, and you risked insulting rather than flattering them by giving more honor than they thought was appropriate.

"On behalf of the Crown, I thank you, Captain Yalla—especially for the swiftness with which you answered the call of duty."

Mollified, the captain saluted again. "It is an honor," she repeated. "I only regret that I could not bring more with me on such short notice and in such tight quarters. Had you lingered at Goldek Gate to consult with us, we could have done much more to serve the Crown."

It was a veiled critique, of course.

"Alas, if I had known what would transpire, I would have done so," I said with an apologetic incline of my head. I lowered my voice so that hopefully Sarah wouldn't hear. "Our plans were to continue straight to Kellig Hold, but as you can see, flexibility was required. My greatest charge at the moment is to protect and carry the young amón woman in there, whom you have no doubt met by now, and so, to tend to her needs properly, we were forced to shelter here."

There were other reasons, of course—ones that were entirely *not* Sarah's fault. But I didn't want to get into those, both because the captain didn't need to know them and because they wouldn't have been the most convincing to her.

Even though we needed to be discreet, I told the captain what I did because I could trust her with that much as a ranking member of the Warflight and because I needed her help to protect Sarah, and I hoped that would be enough.

Captain Yalla nodded slowly, accepting my indirect apology and explanation as valid. Spontaneity was alright—as long as duty demanded it.

If there was one word that summarized Strongshield, it was *duty*.

"Leftwing Korinth told me as much."

I kept my face bland, but inside, I thought irritably, *Then why did you need me to repeat it?*

But I knew why. I was higher ranked than Kor, so she needed me to confirm what he had said. Plus...though Strongshield would never admit to such a bias, everyone knew they mistrusted Starkissed's intentions as not being entirely pure.

Yalla continued. "Since guarding the young amón woman is your primary responsibility this night, I took the liberty of assigning two of my flight to her alone, one drakón and one amón—both female so that they may always remain with her. I trust this meets your approval?"

"Oh," I said, unable to help the sound of surprise from coming out. At least I kept my face straight. Maybe.

Inside, though, I cursed. Sarah was already unhappy enough with me as it was; I guessed she wasn't going to like constant supervision, either.

But I couldn't exactly tell Yalla now that there was no need for such a thing, when that would be entirely incompatible in her mind with performing their primary function in *being* here.

"Yes, excellent," I said with careful neutrality.

Yalla looked about as close to pleased as a Strongshield ever did. "Allow me to give you a summary of the other liberties I have taken thus far in establishing our protections for the night—"

Alarm horns blasted inside me that this could take a while, so I thought quickly.

"Ah, you see," I said carefully, nodding to apologize for the interruption. "Since my primary responsibility *is* Sarah, and I have been away for a time, I should reconvene with her to re-establish...contact. And so on. I entirely trust that you have done everything I could ask of you regarding our safety for the night, but if you would like to give a summary and begin strategizing, my rightwing is happy to oblige."

I placed my hand on Yvera's back, between her shoulder blades, and pushed her forward. Hopefully Yalla didn't notice the way my muscles had to bulge with the force required to do so. Unfortunately, the captain could not have possibly missed Yvera's glare back at me.

"Happy" was a blatant lie, and now we all knew it.

You owe me, Yvera snapped in my head.

Actually, I think we're about even now, I said cheerfully.

I nodded to the captain and laid my hand over my heart one more time. "Until next we speak, Captain Yalla."

"Until next. Flame go with you," she replied. Fortunately, her lips twitched in the slightest sign of amusement as she saluted back, so I hadn't entirely offended her by my handing her off.

As I passed her and entered the chamber, my flameheart lifted at that sign that she wasn't the most *hardcore* Strongshield I could have dealt with.

This half of the First Flight of Goldek had settled right in, which made me guess that this wasn't the first time they had nightsheltered here. Bunks were already claimed, and the first sleep shift were already in them, curtains (which they likely brought themselves, since shelters were generally not stocked with perishables like linens) drawn. A few of them with cooking skills were at work in the kitchen area, which explained the delicious aroma that had wafted up to Yvera and me as soon as we had opened the door. My stomach growled, even though it had only been a few deken since my breakfast. It was a small and quick one, though, while I had waited for Sarah to get ready, and I had burned a lot of energy since then.

Torch it, I thought. *I forgot to give Sarah something to eat.*

And she hadn't said anything. I sighed.

Fortunately, I saw her at one of the tables, eating from a bowl in front of her with half her attention while the other half was fixed with fascination on something a young amón woman next to her was working on.

I approached apprehensively, bracing myself for Sarah's reaction...but my fear was groundless. As soon as Sarah caught sight of me, she turned as fully as she could to face me on the bench she was sitting on and beamed.

Blessed Flame.... How could the world suddenly right itself around me so quickly? With just one smile? Just like that, it felt like I was no longer drowning. I could *breathe*.

"Ben!" she called excitedly from across the room. "You're back!"

I blinked, still reeling a bit from the smile. Could she really have already forgiven me? Just like that?

I crossed the distance to her as casually as I could, but I had to first wave, salute, greet, or clasp arms with the warriors of the First Flight as they did so to me. Sarah watched my slow progress with patience, still smiling, her eyes full of understanding. How could she know, without me telling her, that this was simply something I had to do? These people were here because I had asked them to be, because I had asked them to possibly put themselves in harm's way to protect her; I had to at least acknowledge each of them for that. And Sarah not just understood but clearly approved, her smile growing as she watched.

Only when the young woman sitting next to her called for her attention did she turn away.

"What's going on?" I asked curiously when I finally got to their table.

The blond-haired, spectacled young woman was fitting leather straps around Sarah's wrist, brow furrowed in concentration. The spectacles would have had to do with the crafting work she was doing, unless she was one of those amón who refused to have elective healing work such as vision correction done. I doubted the latter, because even though she was amón, I could see from the scarlet border of her uniform that she was Strongshield. She would be the amón half of Sarah's bodyguard set. The other was probably the Battleblood drakón who was leaning against the wall nearby and watching the pair with open amusement.

Far from resentful, at least at the moment, Sarah beamed at the young woman sitting next to her. "This is Alya. She's an artificer—did I get that right?"

"You did indeed," Alya said with a straight face, keeping her concentration on the task at hand. But then, she *was* Strongshield. Hopefully Sarah could read the smile in her eyes that was clear enough to me.

"And she's making me a watch!"

I blinked as I sat down across from her. "A what?"

I knew the noun *watch*, of course—but to me, the translation into Drona referred to people, a group that watched over a place or thing. Clearly that didn't apply to the device that Alya was fitting to Sarah's wrist as if it were some technical Starkissed instrument.

I tried to remember if I had ever seen Sarah so delighted. I had to stamp down a flare of jealousy of the young woman for getting that honor. Someone brought me a bowl of the same stew that was in front of Sarah; that distraction, and my forcing a smile and a nod of thanks to him, helped.

"Maybe I should back up," Sarah said ruefully. "I was talking to Alya about how much harder it was for me to tell how much time had passed since...."

She trailed off, cheeks warming as her eyes dropped from mine. I just cocked my head, clueless.

"She presented me with a fascinating challenge," Alya put in smoothly as she lowered the device and began making more adjustments with the tools scattered around her. "How to help someone who can't feel the sun and currently can't *see* it to keep time."

I looked sharply at Sarah and asked silently, *Did you tell her who you were?*

Sarah answered me as if she were continuing Alya's explanation. "That's how my *affliction* came up, you see."

I held back a sigh. I didn't like Sarah phrasing her differences that way...but an affliction was as good an excuse right now as any.

To my surprise, it was Alya who corrected her terminology, without even looking up from her work. "I would not call it an affliction. Does it cause you pain? Is it a danger to you or others?"

"No," Sarah said in surprise.

"Then a more precise word would be *divergence*. Or *condition*, if you must think of it medically. But with this, you will no longer be at a disadvantage, so I would not think of it in that way, either."

Sarah blinked.

"What did you come up with?" I asked Alya, curious despite myself now.

And begrudgingly grateful. First a drakón whistle, now a timekeeping device? You would think that I hadn't cared enough about Sarah to equip her with anything useful before whisking her off with me on a life-threatening quest.

Actually, now that I thought about it.... Technically, I hadn't given her anything. Even if her current belongings had been purchased in my name, Svyer was the one who had identified the need and gathered her things. If it had been up to me, I probably *would* have taken no more thought for what she needed than to get a saddle to carry her.

At least I did that much, I groaned.

"Sarah actually came up with the basic concept herself," Alya said modestly. "A round device that shows the progress of the sun as it travels around the circle, worn on the wrist as a bracelet to be easily referenced and not lost."

I stared down at the contraption. The small circular crystal or glass that would be the device's interface was inactive and jet black at the moment, but I could get the idea even now.

"Sarah...that's torched brilliant."

"I can't claim any credit," Sarah said sheepishly. "It...um...is like what someone *back home* thought of."

"But you said you combined two of their devices in one," Alya told her. "Something called a *sundial* and a *watch*."

Sarah had observed enough of how our magic and devices worked to combine concepts from her world and propose something that was doable for us. I shook my head.

"I still think you're torched brilliant," I said in admiration.

"I'm really not—" Sarah protested, cheeks warming further.

Alya interrupted. Which, for a Strongshield, was surprising. "There are other amón with your divergence, you know."

Sarah blinked at her. So did I.

"There are?" she asked.

"Not many, but a few," Alya said, still not looking up from her work. "And do you think anyone has thought of such an elegant solution for them before you? The answer is no. Perhaps the ideas were not all yours and the execution is mine, but as soon as I am back at Goldek, I will submit the patent to Crownhold and then offer the design free to the public in your name so that I can ensure that anyone who would like one can get it."

I stared at her. Then slowly, a small smile came to my face. Even with the Golden Heir as witness that Sarah was the originator of the idea, Alya was the actual creator, and I suspected she would add more of her own genius than she let on. Moreover, Alya was the one who would know how to create the schematics and submit the patent. She could have legally and ethically made gems off the design, if not the production. Probably not much, since the "divergence" was rare enough for me not to have heard about it, but some. Unless, of course, it became a trend—which, once Sarah's identity and role became public, it just might. Then Alya could have made her fortune.

But instead...Alya was going to give Sarah credit *and* make the design free once it was protected.

One could cynically argue that Alya didn't know what riches could lie in store for her and simply didn't want to be bothered with administrivia and measly profits. But from the way she was occasionally looking at and consistently treating Sarah, I suspected she had her own theories, combined with rumor, about this divergent amón she had been ordered to watch over. Alya was no idiot. No, I would wager she was fully aware of the chance she was giving up.

Sarah, understanding at least something of the magnitude of what Alya had just said, slowly closed her mouth and didn't protest again.

Thank you, I told Alya silently. *For more than you know.*

She pretended she didn't hear. But I wouldn't forget this example of Strongshield duty—at its very finest.

GIVEN THE ATTENTIVENESS OF her bodyguards, and the presence of the flight in general, it took a while before I was able to get Sarah even somewhat alone. In the end, I had to wait for most of the First Flight to go to bed after I convinced them that I and my wings, being on a different day schedule, could form most of the first watch of the night. Even then, Alya's Battleblood counterpart, Maliki, had to drag her away from her tinkering after they cast lots and Alya lost. While escorting Alya away, Maliki looked back at me, where I was sitting again at the table with Sarah, and winked. Then she settled herself in a distant corner.

I think I can keep an eye on my charge from over here, don't you? Don't mind me. I can't hear a thing over everyone's snoring.

I groaned inside. Was my interest *that* obvious? If so...what did Sarah see? More important, what did she *think*?

My own already limited confidence in reading signals had taken the beating of my life today. If I couldn't even tell that my lifelong friend was...interested, then I was doomed when it came to a near-stranger from another world. I had pondered that sobering fact as Yvera and I had flown back, and I had come to one grim conclusion: I couldn't try Kor's suggestion.

Even *if* a friendly kiss on the cheek and what Yvera had done were in distinct orders of magnitude entirely. I simply didn't trust myself both to keep it that benign and to gauge Sarah's reaction afterward. There was no justification for the experiment if a gain was unlikely and harm likely. And as for my petty desire to get even.... Well, Yvera had helped me let go of that too.

The irony of what I owed Yv for preserving what relationship I had already with Sarah wasn't lost on me. But I wasn't about to tell her about that.

So, on the flight back, I made myself a promise: I would *not* kiss Sarah unless she explicitly asked me to or gave me explicit permission. Or...kissed me herself. As much as that last bit might make me seem slightly hypocritical, I knew that in the unlikely event of Sarah kissing me without asking, I wasn't going to *stop* her to quibble about principles. In fact, I was pretty sure I would need to spend the very little cognitive functioning I would have left in different ways.

But that all was a distant hope. Right now, with the lights dimmed, with Kor at another table, muttering over his books and frequently calling one of his scribes on a scale to go research something else for him, and with Yvera wisely giving me some space by ostensibly caring for her many weapons at another, I had a bit of time and as much privacy as I was going to get to talk to Sarah about more practical and immediate matters.

"So...." I began eloquently. "I can't help but notice you're not mad at me."

"Why would I be mad at you?" Sarah asked in surprise, looking up from the mug of tsha I had just brewed for her.

My own mug was in my hands, giving me much-needed warmth and steadiness. I'd made a whole kettleful, just for this conversation.

Still mindful of how many people were in the room, no matter how many might be unconscious or too far to hear, I said carefully, "For not telling you certain things."

Sarah sobered. "Oh. That."

My flameheart sank. "Yes, that. I am sorry, Sarah. I truly am. I just...."

"You were trying not to overwhelm me, weren't you?" she murmured. "You were having to tell me so much, so quickly...."

I stared at her, baffled at what to say next. Because she already knew.

"Yes," I finally managed.

"Then I forgive you." She took a deep breath. "Probably more important, thanks to Kor, I now understand the details, and I now believe...that's what *could* happen to me."

"Oh," was all I could think to say.

Torch it. I owed Kor a big one. And he knew it, too. I knew better than to hope that he would forget this.

"But Ben," Sarah whispered, looking up at me with a plea for understanding. "I'm scared. I don't think I can do...*that*. It just keeps getting bigger and bigger and...I feel so small."

My flameheart ached for her, burning hotter even as it constricted. "I can see how you would feel that way. I feel the same way.... And I'm much larger."

She answered my weak smile with one of her own. "Then I must be doomed."

"Actually," I whispered, smile fading. "I think it means you're stronger."

Her eyes blinked rapidly, glimmering even in the reduced lighting. Her voice was tighter than before when she whispered back. "I don't feel strong."

I thought carefully before I answered. *Just because you don't feel like it doesn't mean you aren't. I think you are, and getting stronger, wiser, and more powerful by the day. But remember you don't have to bear all of this alone. You have me, Kor, and Yvera.*

Her eyes lowered at that. I didn't know what I had said wrong until she murmured, "For now."

"Always," I said impulsively.

When she raised an eyebrow in skepticism, I scrambled to find the truth that would convince her.

When I did, I said silently, *Maybe you've figured this out by now: who trains Kor and Yvera to do their jobs? I'll give you a hint: it isn't me.*

She pursed her lips thoughtfully, not seeming to guess where I was going with this. "Your father's wings?"

"Exactly," I whispered. "It takes one to train one."

Then I added silently, *So who do you think the Trees are going to command to help you?*

She smiled then, a spark reentering her eyes. "You."

Then, cheeks warming, she added hastily, "Or...your father."

I can assure you with absolute confidence that Avva will make as much time as mortally possible for you, I said with a smile. But my next words were the ones I secretly relished. *However...practically speaking, I'm going to have more of it to give. Once this is all over, I imagine I'll be spending more time in your hold than my own for a while—until you get sick of me and kick me out.*

A smile, bright as a star, grew on her face. It made my flameheart surge dangerously.

"You will?" she said in an eager whisper. "You'll stay?"

She *wanted* me to stay with her. She felt like she *needed* me. My head spun with just that thought. And the hope burned.

For as long as you need me, I said. And then vowed I would move earth and sky to make it happen, lesser duties be torched. *You are going to be the Crown's first priority for a long time, after all.*

"I..." Her eyes blinked rapidly again. "You can have no idea...how glad I am to hear that."

She ducked her head and took a sip of her tea; when she thought I wasn't looking, she wiped at the corner of her eyes. I needed to collect myself as well—to rein in my roaring hope before it did damage to me or her—so I focused on my own mug and let a comfortable silence fall.

After a dek, Sarah unconsciously fidgeted with the whistle at her neck, which made it catch my eye. I stamped out the spark of jealousy it still invoked as being unworthy, and as penance, I made myself say, "Do you know what that is?"

"This?" Sarah said, looking down at the object in her hand in surprise. "It's a whistle, right?"

My lips twitched. "Have you tried blowing it yet?"

"No. But I'm not about to right now." She frowned at me and glanced meaningfully at the bunk side of the room.

"Good idea," I said, taking another sip. Then said with a grin, "Although *some* people in the room wouldn't even hear it."

"What do you mean?" she asked, eyes brightening with interest.

"It's a drakón whistle," I said. I tapped the gem set into it. "*This* makes it so only drakón will hear it."

Sarah gave a surprised laugh, which she quickly muffled with a hand. "You mean it's like a dog whistle?"

"I don't know what a dog is, but I assume it's not a flattering comparison," I said with a grin.

"Oh, it's fine," Sarah said hastily. "I love dogs. I trust them more than I trust most people."

My flameheart fell a bit at that insight into her life, but I kept my smile steady. "In any case...I'm glad the boy gave it to you."

And I forced the words to be true.

"Why?" she asked innocently.

I grinned. "Well, for one thing, to get my torched attention while you're on my back."

She chuckled wryly.

My smile faded. "But also, if you have to, you can use it for its most important purpose: to call for help, with no consumed who might be nearby being any the wiser."

"Oh," she said. Her eyes widened as she looked back down at the whistle. Quietly enough she might have been speaking to herself, she murmured, "He *did* say the Tree told him I would need it."

My flameheart frosted over.

"Did he?" I asked, keeping my voice very controlled.

Sarah looked up at me in surprise, then understanding. "Oh. You didn't hear. You just saw."

"Yes," I said, trying very hard to appear calm. "Good eyesight in that form. Torched hearing. What else did he say? Tell me the whole thing, please."

She considered. "He said that the Tree had appeared to him in a dream and told him to get up and finish this for me. I guess he had already been working on it or something? For someone else? Anyway, he woke up and finished it, even though he said it took him deken. He said that the Tree said it was important, that I would need it."

I focused with excruciating intensity on my breathing for a few moments. When I felt like I was at least somewhat in control, I asked, "Is that all? He didn't say when you would need it?"

She shook her head. "That's all he said.... I just thought he had an ordinary dream, that he was just being sweet. But do you think the Tree really...."

"It could go either way," I said carefully. I poured myself more tsha, even though my stomach was clenched so hard I didn't know if I should drink it. "But...I think we have to act on the assumption that She did."

"By doing...?" Sarah asked attentively.

She was clearly taking this seriously. Then how could she remain so torched *calm*?

And she thought she wasn't strong.

I hesitated, thinking. Hard.

Then I groaned and said a word that my mother would have smacked me for, especially for saying it in front of someone like Sarah. Fortunately, Sarah only blinked, so hopefully the expletive didn't have a meaningful translation for her.

When I had a better grip on myself, I said quietly, "We can't do anything more than we have already done for tonight."

"Let me guess," Sarah murmured, eyes heavy. "You wouldn't have stopped here tonight if you had known."

"Don't blame yourself," I said, forcing myself to soften. "Maybe that's precisely why the Tree did things the way She did. She knows I can be a bit...hard to direct."

"You?" Sarah said with a faint smile.

"You would be surprised," I muttered, and left it at that. "What I'm saying is, as much as I don't like it...maybe this is where we're meant to be. Again."

Sarah's face tightened. Her voice dropped to a volume so low, I almost didn't catch the words. "But Ben...if anyone gets hurt...it will be my fault."

"Not yours," I said shortly. "Mine. Defense is my job, remember?"

Her lips twitched into a faint smile. "Then what's mine? Don't say 'offense.'"

I raised an eyebrow. "You could call it that."

She snorted softly.

I eyed her whistle. Now I had far greater reasons to hate...and be grateful...for it. "Just...don't take that off, alright? As in, ever. Except when you're showering or something, but keep it nearby even then. We don't know *when* you are going to need it. So...let's just hope it's only once, and that once is not tonight. But just in case...."

"I'll keep it on me," she promised solemnly, putting her hand over it to press it to her chest. Over her heart.

Flame, how much that beating thing inside her—that I couldn't see or hear or feel—meant to me now, whether or not it had a fire.

How much I...I....

I stopped myself there. Then redirected. *How much I want her to be safe.*

That was what I had to focus on tonight. That was my job, my duty.

Keeping her safe.

Chapter Thirteen

DATE

Sarah

I LIKED TSHA. I really did. Of course...I enjoyed sitting and talking with Ben even more, especially when we moved on to lighter subjects.

He asked me about my family, seemingly fascinated by every description and anecdote I told him. From his types of questions, he seemed baffled at how a family of my size *worked* but was determined to discover the secret. Many times, I caught a hint of envy in his voice, which made me think about my experiences in a new light.

I asked him about what life was like growing up for him, and I was just as fascinated by his descriptions of classes, hunts (and I don't mean the recreational kind), and shadowing his father. From what I gathered, his life ever since becoming Heir at twelve seemed to be a whirlwind of training, as if everyone was trying to turn him as quickly as possible into a paradoxical blend of politician, special agent, negotiator, priest, and general. And that was on top of his classes as a normal student; to my surprise, he said he had already graduated from all three normal levels of their education—two years early.

Why did people call him dim again?

When I asked him what he did for fun, he just stared blankly at me for a moment and then said hesitantly, "Um...sleep? And sometimes, when I'm lucky...cook?"

And I thought *my* schooling had been hectic and stressful. Suddenly, my added duties of babysitting, chauffeuring, and housework didn't seem like so much to ask. Especially in comparison with the rewards of being safe, sleeping in the same bed every night, and having people who genuinely loved me surrounding me every day.

Man...I was really missing them. *And* my bed.

Homesickness aside, I realized that Ben and I hadn't had a chance quite like this before. With nothing to be done except wait and talk (all while I tried to keep a feel out for any materializing gates), and with the dim lights and a relatively relaxed, public atmosphere that kept things subdued and casual, it occurred to me that this was almost like a...date.

Of course, that realization hit me while I was in the middle of telling Ben an anecdote about my mischievous little twin brothers, Noah and Jonah, so when I came to a stammering halt and my cheeks got hot, he had to stare at me in confusion until I got myself under control again. Fortunately, he let my odd reaction go without comment.

Enjoy it while it lasts, I told myself when it was his turn to talk. I just watched him, drinking him in and hoping my face didn't look as wistful as I felt. *This is the only date you'll ever get.*

But...unfortunately, in trying to prolong the moment by drinking cup after cup of tsha...I had to end it.

Ben laughed quietly when I stammered I had to use the facilities. He groaned, rubbed his eyes, and leaned back. "Don't worry about it. I didn't realize how long it had been.... I should...be checking in with Avva or doing something productive."

Yeah, I thought with a sigh as I left. *You should.*

It had been a small piece of heaven, though...while it had lasted.

To my surprise, I heard footsteps behind me and saw Maliki following. I flushed. "Er. Thanks, but you really don't need to...."

"Orders are orders," she said with a yawn.

At the same time, Ben said in my head, *Please, Sarah. For me?*

"OK," I said, dragging out the word uncertainly.

At least it isn't Yvera, I told myself as I turned around and continued.

At the end of the hallway was the privy room. It was rudimentary, and it was communal, since there were three seats in the stone bench right next to each other, but at the moment I had it to myself, and it had a curtain I could pull across the doorway.

Of course, my bodyguard stepped into the small room before I could do so.

Did I mention how small the room was? Just the stone bench and a couple feet of space between it and the door. Even standing to the side as far as she could, Maliki took up a lot of room.

"Do you...mind?" I said, pointing out into the hallway.

"Mind what?" Maliki asked blankly.

What was *with* dramá and their lack of privacy?

"Waiting outside?" I said, cheeks growing hot.

"Why?" She seemed honestly curious. "I'm female, like you. And I'm only attracted to men, if that matters to you. Otherwise, I wouldn't have been assigned to you like this."

"Fine," I said with a sigh. I drew the curtain closed.

I did my business as quickly as possible. Which was my one stroke of fortune, because just as I was pulling my pants up again, I felt a surge of magic behind me.

Pay attention to all magic you feel.

Even I knew by now that was way too much power for just a latrine cleansing spell. And it *felt* different from any kind I had felt before. It felt...sick.

"Mal—" was all I was able to choke out, but a knife and shield were already in her hands.

Not that they did either of us any good.

The last thing I remember was the lights in the privy room going out.

Chapter Fourteen

GONE

Koriben

My call with Avva was quiet and brief. Even though I stepped into the entry passage for a bit more privacy, this still wasn't the place to talk in detail about what was going on in either of our lives right now. Avva was just glad to hear that, for now, Sarah and I were safe.

The irony to end all ironies that day.

When I came back into the main room, I didn't see Sarah. Which was odd. My call had been short, but it was at least a few dek long. Frowning, I went over to Yvera. Since Kor's nose was still in his books, she was the wing I thought to have most likely paid enough attention to answer my question. For better or for worse.

"Has Sarah not come out yet?" I asked quietly, pointing to the privy hall.

"Nope," Yvera said carelessly, polishing her favorite dagger. Which was saying something, since she had many, of varying lengths, sizes, and edges, and knew how to use each with deadly precision.

"That's not...normal. Right?" I asked, flushing.

"How should I know?" she said coolly.

I hesitated. What was the balance in this situation between giving Sarah the privacy that was so important to her and looking out for her? And also keeping myself strictly away from any situation in which she was in any state of undress.

Surely Maliki would come out and say if Sarah needed healing. And yet...I worried.

"Could you go check on her, please?" I asked.

Yvera kept polishing.

"I know I said please, but I didn't actually mean *please*," I said flatly.

"I'll go."

I turned in surprise to see Alya approaching, rubbing her eyes. "Couldn't sleep," she explained. "Kept thinking about schematics. You realize this 'watch' is going to put my name down in the books, right?"

So, I was right, and she wasn't an idiot. And, apparently, not *entirely* altruistic. I was more amused by that than anything. And by the fact that either preoccupation or exhaustion had loosened her up a bit.

"Thank you," I said gratefully.

To her back, because she was already walking away. Then I settled into what was hopefully a casual, I'm-standing-here-just-because-I-want-to-and-not-because-I-can't-sit-down stance to wait for an answer.

I didn't have to wait long.

Not a dek later, I heard a shout that chilled my blood and froze my flameheart solid.

"Ben! Captain! Healer Alden!"

For one excruciating moment, as my flameheart struggled mightily to still beat even as a solid mass, I looked at the path to the privy.

I don't even remember running.

One moment I was standing frozen, the next I was staring down at Maliki's bleeding body.

And into the dark, cavernous hole that was now the back of the privy.

I didn't need to search the rubble to know Sarah was gone.

"Ben!" Yvera screamed at me.

But I was already through the hole, hammer and shield in my hands, my entire skin shifting to change my clothes into armor. I spared one single prayer to the Tree for Maliki's sake.

Then I was gone too, racing down that dark path, following the rancid scent that mingled sickeningly with Sarah's through the bored hole in the rock, with a speed that even my rightwing would be hard pressed to match.

If Yvera wanted to protect me this time...she would have to torched well catch me.

Or come the hellwinds along.

Chapter Fifteen

SHOTS

Sarah

I woke to the smell of rotten meat.

Even my subconscious knew that wasn't a good sign.

But, unfortunately, partial consciousness was all I had to deal with for far too long. No rush of adrenaline surged through my veins to fully wake me, even though I knew, in some vague sense, that I was in trouble. But I felt stuck that way, as if caught at the edge of some nightmare I couldn't fully wake from. Or, in this case...into.

Eventually, I noticed a sense of motion. Jolting. Of lying on something leathery, slightly hairy, and uncomfortable. Of a rough cloth tied so tightly around my mouth that it pushed through my lips. A gag, I realized. With no other leap of synapses to speculate why it was there.

Hearing trickled in next, like an absentminded friend suddenly remembering what it was supposed to be doing for me. Many little huffs, grunts, mutters. Patters of surprisingly small feet.

Memory came last. Or...what little of it there was to explain what was going on. A surge of sick magic, then...darkness.

Which surrounded me completely now. I could tell, even without opening my eyes, that there was no need for a blindfold.

Some bit of sense came back just in time to keep me from blinking them open. To lie there, still, even as the ability to move slowly trickled through my limbs again.

Then I heard a voice that sorely tempted me to flinch, to look, to scream, to run, to do *anything* but lie there still. A rasping voice. A dead voice.

"*She wakes.*"

Another voice answered. Not pleasant, but nowhere in the same league of nasty. It was small, grating, grumbling. "You said that your spell would keep her under for—"

"I miscalculated. She is healing quickly, and is more powerful than the master had expected her to be by now. Bind her."

"We can't stop now!" the voice protested, an edge of fear replacing the irritation from before. The jostling motion under me hadn't stopped when they had started talking. In fact, I now realized there was an edge of breathlessness to the grumbler's voice as well.

His next words gave me the last shot that I needed: the lightning bolt of hope.

"*All* the sensors we left behind have activated. The Golden Heir knows she's gone—he's coming after her. *Fast.*"

"*Fool!*" the rasper said, as if it sensed the surge of energy flowing through me. "Bind her *now!*"

Too late.

My hand grasped the gun in my holster, and then I did what Michael would never have wanted me to have to do with a gun: I began firing indiscriminately.

Lights flashed in the darkness as my glowing ice shards shot through it. Voices somehow both small and deep screamed, and I suddenly felt myself falling, tumbling off the flat-ish thing I had been lying on as it tipped. A stretcher? Even as I tumbled, I never stopped firing, never stopped holding out my hand in front of me and pulling that trigger. I used my other hand to brace against the stone before I hit it, then to push me up with strength and agility I didn't know I had.

Then, still firing behind me without even looking, I ran, tugging the gag off as I did so. Only when the screams and raging, rasping voice fell far behind did

I stop firing behind so that I could *really* run. But even after I broke into a full sprint, I had to keep firing ahead just for the light.

Light.

My ice shards hadn't glowed when I had practiced with the gun before. Had they? But now they most certainly did.

Ben had said that I might be able to make them glow. Somehow, I had done that without even trying, just by instinct. Well...thank goodness for that, I guessed.

He had *also* said I could use the light to lead him to me. Before, the light had faded from the shards almost as soon as they hit their targets, but now I focused hard on what I wanted them to do instead.

Stay lit, I pleaded. *Just long enough for Ben to see.*

When I shot next, and the projectile hit the wall, it stayed alight. That had the added benefit of letting me shoot at fewer intervals, thus conserving my energy—the gun's ammo—and momentum.

I *hoped* I had picked the right direction to run down this strange, round tunnel, but I was entirely disoriented and wasn't sure. If I was right, if I was running toward him, then hopefully the lights would tip him off early. If not....

Then hopefully I had left him a good enough trail of icy breadcrumbs.

Chapter Sixteen

SENSES

Koriben

A DRAKÓN'S SENSE OF smell was normally excellent, beyond anything an amón experienced. Adrenaline made it astounding. Right now, I could nearly navigate through the tunnel by scent alone—though I didn't risk it. Whatever was ahead could probably see in the dark better than I could, and I wanted to be able to anticipate their every move, so I cast some light orbs ahead of me as soon as I was far enough beyond the shelter to need them and I was sure Yvera wouldn't catch up fast enough to tackle me.

Also, now that I knew the scents were a few dek old, I put away the hammer and shield to give me another boost of speed.

I identified the scents long before I came on their owners. My brain cataloged the information coolly and immediately began strategizing.

The most plentiful enemy were jorgen. Greedy, knobby little things that lived underground, hated light, and usually only bothered us when they came out at night to steal a small herd animal or shiny trinket if they could. As such, they were usually only a nuisance, and I immediately dismissed them as any kind of threat.

Right now, they were only being used as pack mules and, once I reached them, would only be living shields.

My primary attention was on the other scent, the rancid one. The one with enough dark power to blast a hole through a shelter's protections and yet leave none of us the wiser. I didn't waste the brain power on trying to figure out how right now. No doubt Kor was solving that mystery that very second, or, if he was attempting to even somewhat keep up with Yvera and me, then he would as soon as we got back with Sarah.

We *would* get back with Sarah.

I didn't let myself think of any other option.

Most of all, I didn't let myself think of the scent of amón blood that was in the air as well, mingling with her cool aroma. I knew that if I let myself think about it for even a second....

No.

As I said before, my focus was on the second scent, the most worrisome one, although I had destroyed its kind before. I used the word *destroy* deliberately, because something had to be alive first to be able to be killed.

Rechal.

A twisted, dark spirit follower of the Devourer that had somehow gotten ahold of a dramá corpse—usually one killed by accident while alone or deliberately by consumed, since we always cremated our dead. The rechal would then possess the body, although why it wanted flesh was a mystery, since it mostly seemed to float around and be unable to *do* much with its rapidly decaying parts. Rechal primarily relied on their forceful, dark magic, their cunning, and any lesser creatures they could coerce into doing the Devourer's will. Hence the jorgen.

The tricky thing about rechal was their magic, which shouldn't be underestimated. But if you could shield yourself from it long enough to pulverize or burn their stolen remains to nothing, then the spirit would have to leave the flesh behind. To our knowledge, there wasn't a way to kill the spirit, but without a body, its magic was greatly dampened, and it could generally be chased off with weapons enchanted to cause spirit forms pain...or just plain, good old fire.

At least the one thing I *didn't* smell was the thing that had made this tunnel: a rock wyrm. That...would have been bad. Very bad.

But, fortunately, the tunnel was old, the wyrm long gone. How a rock wyrm had come so close to a shelter without detection, and why, was another grim mystery for another time. All I cared about in the moment was that Sarah wasn't currently being dragged along in its wake...or heading straight into its stomach.

Far in the distance, beyond a curve of the tunnel, jorgen shouts echoed back to me, and I saw faint flashes illuminate the curve. Then I heard the rechal shrieking in rage. It didn't sound like their getaway was going according to plan...which meant Sarah was fighting back.

SHE'S ALIVE.

That single thought pierced through the wall of focus I had put up to keep myself from being derailed, revealing by contradiction what I hadn't dared even think. The thought quivered through my whole being and made my flameheart roar, giving me an impossible burst of speed. I was nearly running up that outer wall by the time I made the curve, and in fact, I pushed off it with one foot to make the turn.

Sarah, I'm coming! I silently shouted, hoping she was close enough to hear.

The lights ahead originated, as I had suspected, from glowing shards of ice, but they were fading fast, revealing only briefly a chaotic mess of wounded, still, and cowering jorgen. And one abandoned, crude, empty stretcher.

Where is Sarah?!

At the sight of my own lights racing ahead of me, the jorgen screeched, and the ones who could move scattered. That would not do.

Not wanting to risk the smoke and stench of burned flesh in these tight quarters, instead of fireballs, I simply hurled lobs of raw power that mowed them over, crushing them against the floors and walls of the tunnel. Still, I missed some, and they ran on ahead.

Then I got out my sword, and as I overtook each one, I ran them through. I didn't bother sparing or questioning any of them; I didn't have that time, nor could I risk them coming at me from behind to stab my back later. I could see for myself that they no longer had Sarah, and I could gather why. As for where their ringleader was...I could guess that too.

Though I knew each second counted now, dealing with the jorgen and carrying my weapon had slowed me. Not much, but enough for Yvera to reach me just as I was overtaking the last ones.

Ben! Will you just come to your senses and allow more of the First Flight to catch up?

Come to my senses*?!* I cried as I ran through the very last jorgen without breaking my stride. *Have you lost* yours? *I wait a* second, *and Sarah could....*

How long could Sarah remain ahead of the rechal? How long could she hold it off if it caught up to her or she came to a dead end?

Yvera ran alongside me. At least she seemed to realize I was in too dangerous a frame of mind for her to try to physically restrain me without Kor as backup, so she was trying reason. Such as it was.

Sarah isn't worth risking your—

Asinine. There were more Sunfilled. One of them could take my place. There was only one Sarah.

But since I knew the emotion behind what Yvera was saying, and since I, too, wanted to try at least *one* shot at reason to get her to help me save Sarah, I interrupted with, *Yv, if she was me, if it was me ahead in the dark, and I was unprepared for what was coming after me, what would you do?*

I was too focused on what was ahead. Too trusting that Yvera would finally understand. Too ignorant of when I would cross her line.

I didn't see her grab coming until she had slammed me against the wall. My armor and helmet absorbed the worst of the shock, but the breath was knocked out of me for a second—both of which she no doubt had counted on. No one was more practiced in the art of hurting me without *hurting* me.

"That is not the same thing at all," she snarled out loud while her forearm pressed against my windpipe. "Ben, I *love* you. And you don't love—"

I blasted her against the opposite wall. Though I was beginning to see red, though my body, power, and instincts had now identified the person in front of me as an enemy, a small voice of reason yet remained, and it screamed at me to *run*. Before I did something I would regret to her and lost someone else I would mourn forever.

And so I ran. And in running, the rushing air helped clear my head enough to remember. To reign in the beast that was waking up inside. For a moment.

Don't you dare, I snarled back at her in response to her last words. *Don't you dare say that. And by the Flame, don't you dare try to stop me again. Either help me or get the hellwinds out of my way.*

Chapter Seventeen

REACH

Sarah

LET ME TELL YOU, running for your life is not all it's cracked up to be.

Movies make it seem so exciting, so energizing, so...doable.

When do those characters ever *breathe*?

I had done track, and even so, my heart was now hammering its way out of my chest and my throat was burning and my legs trembling and my feet throbbing and my lungs could never get enough air. The air here was too stale, and the tunnel was absurd. Whose idea had it been to carve all these bends, rises, and dips, anyway?

Not even cross-country had been this bad.

Of course, even cross-country hadn't required me to keep shooting glowing ice darts ahead just to see my path, each dart requiring a drain of precious energy.

I felt stifled, trapped in a never-ending nightmare. Like I was running forever through the intestines of some giant rock beast that would digest me for a thousand years.

I was suffocating.

As stupid as I knew it was, I slowed with each second that passed as I lost steam. That horrid, raspy creature and all its minions could be right on my tail, and I still couldn't help decelerating. One time I even slipped as I was making my way down a steep dip and half slid, half rolled the rest of the way down. I groaned and tried to ignore the flaming stings and bruises as I pushed myself back up and stumbled back into a run.

As much as I yearned to stop, as much as I wanted to just curl up and cry, then sleep for a year, as much as I was tempted to just surrender and let what came, *come*...I knew I couldn't. Not if I wanted to live. Not if I wanted to see my family again and end their grief.

Not if I wanted Ben to crush me in his arms again.

Kor had told me to trust my instincts—and to pay attention to all magic around me. (Why I kept listening to *Kor* was an existential question for another time.) Right now my instincts were screaming at me that the enemy was still behind me, and that enemy was prickling with magic gone bad.

I had to play a mental game with myself, a variation of the one I had used in cross-country. It went like this: I would shoot ahead. I would think, *I can only go that far*. Then, when I got there, I found I could go just a *bit* further, so I shot again.

I can only go that far.

Shoot.

Ben, please hurry.

Shoot.

Then I came to a fork, and I just about wept from despair. But I squared my shoulders, said a quick prayer, and ran to the right, shooting more glowing shards than usual and charging them with more energy to make certain Ben knew which way to go.

Of course...the disadvantage of that was the rasper would know too.

And then...just when I truly thought I could go no further, I felt something new. Something cool and fresh. Hope surged in me, giving me another burst of speed. I rounded a curve....

This time I really did cry, but from relief, to see silver moonlight ahead.

I ran with all the strength I had left...until instinct once again screamed at me to slow. I realized what was wrong almost as soon as I got to the end of the tunnel: the open sky I could see beyond was too open. It led to only....

I gasped and flailed back from the edge. The tunnel ended as abruptly as if it were a hole in a bread loaf and the rest of the loaf had been sliced off. Only a tiny lip jutted out beyond the tunnel mouth, with only a sheer drop down a nearly ninety-degree mountainside below.

There was no way down. None that I could risk in the dim light and limited time I had, anyway. If I was going to die, I would rather be facing my enemy than being picked off while clinging helplessly to a cliff.

As if to make the cruelty of my situation complete, I saw a white glow on another arm of the mountain. If the mountain were a crescent moon, I was in the thick center of the inward curve, and the glow was on the righthand slope, mocking me with its beacon of hope.

It was a set of doors, lined in white fire. Lest there be any doubt, I now realized I felt the pull—had felt it for some time now, strained for it, had chosen the right fork because of it.

Even now, the open air, the open, *clean* embrace of night was surging into me like ten shots of coffee straight into my bloodstream. My mind cleared, my trembling muscles stilled, even my pains and scrapes went quiet.

But for what? I was trapped, and all the buzz in the world wouldn't do me any good if I didn't know *how to use it.*

The gate, and the safety it offered, was within sight....

But hopelessly out of reach.

I couldn't help it. I let out a sob. Although, it kind of came out as a choke through my heaving breaths. So maybe whatever sadistic gods were watching me, waiting for any sign of breaking, wouldn't notice....

Then I smelled rancid meat.

I whipped around. And my overworked heart skipped a beat to see...

...only darkness.

Somehow...that was worse than anything.

And then I realized why: darkness meant....

"*No,*" I said in a quiet, strangled breath.

My lights, my breadcrumbs, my beacons of hope...were going out, one by one. Starting at the furthest I could see, then the next. Then the next. I knew better than to think the power in them was simply going out. Through the faintest threads of connection that I had with each one, I felt each being *crushed*. The darkness crept forward like a thing alive, swallowing each one whole.

Then the rasper spoke, its whispers carrying too well down the tunnel to be unaided by magic.

"That's it, little Moontouched. Wait for me. In fact, come to me. Come lay your tired head down on my shoulder."

As horrid as the voice was...there was an oddly...appealing quality to it. Something...soothing. Enticing. The rancid smell was turning sweet....

Despite my renewed energy, I drooped. Swaying.

Pay attention to all magic you feel.

The very air was charged by magic, carrying on or with that scent that I was inhaling by the lungful. So, though it felt like agony, I held my breath.

Clarity returned in an instant, allowing me to pop the lingering influence in my mind like a bubble.

I snarled a curse at it. Then I raised my gun.

But I had waited too long. The rasper's distraction had worked *just* long enough.

A harpoon of dark power shot out of the darkness, grasped my gun, and lassoed the weapon back inside. I winced from the sting in my trigger finger as I heard the gun clatter somewhere deep within the darkness.

"Yes, you see? There is no point in resisting, Moontouched child. I am more than a match for you now. Besides, I do not wish you harm, nor does the master I serve."

"B.S." I said, saying each letter with emphasis. At least I still had words to fling at the thing. Even if, even now, my parents' conditioning against profanity only let me initialize them.

Only after I said that did I realize the initials wouldn't make any sense to the creature. If it even had some way to translate my English like the drakón did. The spark of amusement I felt at it only getting nonsense from me, no matter what I said, made my lips twitch.

Hysteria, probably.

The attitude in which I said them was universal, though.

"It is true," the voice rasped in what was no doubt meant to be a soothing tone—though it should get its ears checked, because it could still make babies spontaneously cry. And all the while, the darkness inched closer. It was maybe fifty feet away now.

Forty-seven.

"Why would the Devourer hurt you?"

Forty-five.

"You are its precious one, the one it has waited and hoped for longer than the Children of Flame ever have."

"*B.S.*" I repeated. What was this guy doing? Reading straight from a villain script?

Now that I thought about it, though....

I narrowed my eyes. "What are you playing at?"

"Playing?" It hissed. "I play at nothing. I could crush you with the pinch of my two fingers."

Then why aren't you? I thought intently.

At the forty-foot mark, it finally hit me.

The monster had me *trapped*, at the edge of a drop, and all it had to do was send another lasso of power out to give me just a *push*, and I would fall to my death.

It had followed me swiftly enough that by the time I'd reached this dead end, it had only been seconds behind. Yet now it creeped forward inch by inch.

It was stalling. Either it *couldn't* kill me right now, for some unfathomable reason...or it truly didn't want to.

At least...not yet.

After all, if all it had wanted was to kill me...I would never have woken up.

I inhaled. "You really need me for something, don't you? I don't buy that 'precious' nonsense, not for a second. But you need me alive."

The voice in the creeping darkness didn't answer. Which was *almost* all the confirmation I needed.

To get the rest...I couldn't believe it, but I was about to take a page from Kor's playbook.

I put on what I hoped was an overly heroic face. "Well. I suppose if something as evil as you needs me alive, and all hope of rescue is lost, then I had better end myself, for the greater good."

And I took an exaggerated step back.

"*Stop!*" it cried in alarm.

It sent another lasso of power out that lashed around my waist and jerked me back from the edge. The power burned where it touched me, even through my shirt, and after it retreated, I felt so nauseated I nearly threw up. I shoved down the bile with monumental will. I didn't want to let my guard down in front of this thing, even for a second.

Well, I thought grimly. *At least that worked.*

Not to mention that *two* could play at the stalling game.

"Cease this pointless resistance," the voice rasped in a rush, as if trying to distract myself from my suicidal thoughts by...making me more despondent.

It seriously needed some psychology coaching.

"Your weapon is gone, your lights are vanquished. I have filled the tunnels with darkness and illusions. The Heir of Flame will never find you in time."

Just like that, I remembered my last weapon.

Never, eh? I thought.

Moving swiftly, I brought the whistle up to my lips and blew, sending an absurd amount of power into it, hoping more power meant further reach.

The whistle, of course, was silent to *my* ears. Before I could wonder if it had worked, the orange gem flared, and though I heard nothing, I *felt*...something.

Something coming nearer. Something burning with power and carefully harnessed rage. Coming in fast.

Not a moment too soon, because after another stab of power from the dark, my whistle grew too hot to press to my lips and hold, and I dropped it back to my chest with a hiss.

The darkness was twenty feet away, and the stench was mind-numbingly bad. I was finding it hard to keep my breakfast/dinner soup down now.

"Stop making this difficult, child!" But for the first time, I heard an element of nervousness in its own voice. That's when I knew I wasn't hallucinating the oncoming storm. "I am not your enemy, nor is the Devourer!"

I decided it finally deserved the full impact of my Earthren curse, so I said it in full, and savagely so. "*Bull. Shit.*"

I got a bit more satisfaction from that, knowing it could understand me. Though...it might still not even know what a *bull* was, come to think of it. But surely it knew what the other thing was, since it smelled of the stuff, and it could get the idea from there.

But I had to keep stalling, so I didn't leave it at that. "You know what your 'friendly' Devourer had its minions do to welcome me to the neighborhood, the *moment* I arrived? *It had them strap me to an altar to sacrifice me.*"

The epiphany hit me like a hammer to the chest, knocking out the air that I had won back.

"You need me alive...." I said breathlessly. "...to sacrifice me."

I remembered with crystal clarity how, only hours ago, I had guessed out loud to Ben that the Devourer was trying to kill me to end me as a threat. And while that had an element of truth to it, now I realized *why* Ben hadn't answered, why his eyes hadn't met mine, but instead stared sightlessly ahead, glowing with fury.

Ben already knew what the Devourer intended to do to me. Or guessed. So no doubt Kor had, maybe even Yvera. Probably I would have too, if I hadn't been so new to the way things worked here. But it made sense to me now, in a sick way. Why merely *kill* your enemy when you could also use their death...to your advantage?

Suddenly...that drop behind me didn't sound so bad after all.

For the first time, the rasper chuckled. And that deathly sound was enough to send goosebumps down my spine. "I was not lying when I said you were precious, that the Devourer has waited millennia for you. Or rather, to be more precise...for your Blood. Which I have only a few drops of now, but soon—"

If he said anything more, the words were drowned out in a bestial roar. Somehow, even with the unsettling element of humanity mixed in, I recognized the sound.

A solid wall of golden fire surged down the tunnel, burning away the darkness. I caught one glimpse of a floating skeletal frame in a tattered robe—only a black outline in the searing light—before it was swallowed up in an ear-splitting shriek of agony.

I wasn't speaking metaphorically: the banshee-worthy shriek damaged my eardrums and send a blinding flash of pain through my skull that had me crouched with my own scream of pain.

And that is why I didn't see or feel the enemies swooping in behind me until it was too late.

Ben had been my reason for stalling.

This...was the rasper's.

Cold, stony hands scooped under my shoulders and wrapped around my chest. I screamed, the sound faint in my ears, but as I rose into the air in buffeting flaps from the wings behind me, all I could do was thrash and kick my legs. The arms were as solid and unyielding as rock, not only making them impossible to pry off me but also making my gravity-induced pressure against them bruising.

The second-worst part of it all was how much better I could see the moongate from this view. Unbeknownst to anyone but me, the arched double doors still sat, glowing from the light of the two moons in the cloudless desert sky.

A breathtaking view. Or it would have been, but for the small army of stone, batwing angels like my captor lifting me away from it....

The worst part was hearing Ben's agonized shout in my head.

SARAH!

I looked down, but if he had glimpsed me, he was now out of my sight, given my rising angle above the opening.

My eyes stung at the pure unfairness of it all. Again, with my hope *so close*...and so far.

Both so close I could *feel* them....

Wait....

Feel?

But there it was. Two connections, two pulls, two anchors. One going to the moongate...the other into the tunnel.

Time slowed, each wing flap from my captor taking minutes, heartbeats lasting eons. I could *feel* what Ben felt, almost see what he saw as he put one foot in front of the other in slow motion, as his flameheart throbbed inside his chest.

It really is a fire, I thought in a daze. A literal *fire*, in the region where his heart should be. Never mind right then how that could function as an organ. My much greater concern was that the fire was burning dangerously low, even as it pulsed dangerously fast.

Ben was nearly at the end of his strength; it was night, and he had used nearly all he had to get this far, to get this close to me. And yet still he ran, even knowing it was too late to save me from a fate worse than mere death. Still, he reached for me, with his mind and heart, not even understanding how. Still, he pleaded with me, begged me, even though he didn't know what for.

But, as another crystal-clear memory from this morning came to me, suddenly *I* did.

If I was going to die...then it would be how I chose. It would be serving, rather than harming, the ones I loved.

Ben, I said, opening the void where my power rested. I hoped he could hear me. Our connection was so strong at this point that I was almost certain he could.

Take it. Use it, if you can, to find my family...and tell them I loved them.

Without waiting for his reply, I poured nearly everything I had down the conduit between us...and into him.

Nearly.

I would have given it all, every single, last drop. I would have thrust it all on him, even as his understanding of what I was doing grew and he cried, *Sarah, STOP!*

I would have died for him. And...not just to have something worth dying for.

But a Presence entered that void, and Its voice echoed through that eternal moment.

Cease, My child. All is not lost this night. Reach out for your other anchor...and pull.

Hoping I had done enough for Ben, and figuring I had nothing else to lose, I stopped pouring into him just before I ran dry. Then I reached for my other connection, the one to the glowing gate only I could see...

...and pulled.

Chapter Eighteen

MAD

KORIBEN

"NO!" I ROARED WITH my mind and voice and power.

But I felt the enigmatic yet undeniable tie between Sarah and me sever as swiftly as a sharpened ax slicing through a neck.

Just as I reached the mouth of the tunnel.

I looked out, chest heaving, flameheart roaring with a strength that should not have been possible, as if Sarah had dumped an entire *sun* inside of me.

An entire soul.

How could a heart be so alive and so dead at the same time?

When it was consumed with rage.

My burning eyes riveted at once on the flight of arrel in the sky. I didn't know which one had taken Sarah—and therefore, which one now held her lifeless body.

I didn't care.

"Ben?" Yvera said, panting voice uncertain as she slowly approached me.

She might as well not have existed. I couldn't hear her through the blood pounding in my ears. I couldn't even see her through the red in my vision. I simply backed up to get a running start.

"Ben!" Yvera shouted in disbelief, reaching for me.

Too late this time. Her fingers only just grazed my back as I charged forward and dove off the cliff.

She had cause to worry. Not that I cared or even consciously heard her. What I was doing should not have been possible in the middle of the night, even with two bright moons, let alone after having spent all my fire.

But I didn't need a sun now. Not with a supernova inside me, taking the place of my heart.

I changed. I expanded. I *exploded*. Muscles, sinew, bone, teeth, wings, tail—all came into being with the force of a Brightflare mine detonation. I changed so fast and became so massive that my tail shook the mountain behind me when it struck, causing a landslide. And I wasn't even bruised.

Then, popping my jaw with satisfaction, I *roared*.

That roar alone caused more rockslides—everywhere this time, across the Korpeth range. Precariously balanced boulders that had somehow withstood the test of time and been the inspiration for countless Strongshield ink paintings and poems collapsed. Desert trees that had fallen into and been held up by their neighbors for perhaps years made their final descent with thundering cracks. Ground animals screamed, night birds fled the skies, a pack of argen howled.

That roar echoed for *elden*. It would have shocked anyone with ears from Goldek Gate to Kellig Hold and perhaps beyond.

That roar shook the world.

Which was *just* what I had intended. I wanted everyone, everywhere, even those who had no part in creating my suffering, to feel something of it—and tremble before me.

The arrel—a stone creation all the Devourer's own, made in solemn mockery of Royal half-forms—scattered. Which was just as well, because I craved the challenge.

The only singular, miniscule voice that remained of my humanity screamed at me that Sarah's body was somewhere among them, that I should take at least enough care to retrieve it.

But what good is it now? my agonized fury raged. Her body was going to be burned in any case, for surely that was what even her family would have done, had I delivered it to them. Better to do it now, and cleanly, and erase as quickly as possible any remnant of the empty shell, before I ever had to see it....

I never said I was in any state of reason. In fact, I was entirely mad.

In *every* sense of the word.

Fire spewed in great sweeps from my jaws. That alone wasn't enough to kill those paradoxical beings of flying stone...but it made them brittle.

Heedless of the temperature with my scales protecting me, I knocked the super-heated arrel out of the sky with limbs and tail. Either that alone was enough to make them crack apart, or the blow, combined with the heat, used up the magic that gave them existence and they fell from the sky like the rocks they were and shattered on impact, creating more delicious destruction.

In desperation, some arrel aimed for my wings, but even as large as I was, I was too agile for them. I dove, corkscrewed, rose, and twisted in the air in a deadly, flame-filled dance they couldn't match. I was a behemoth of destruction, too large and powerful to defy, let alone survive.

Never did I see Sarah's body. But never did I look. Never did I want to.

It wasn't Sarah anymore.

Neither was I Ben. Or Koriben, or an Heir, or a Sunfilled, or even my father's son.

All identity was replaced with loss, and all thought with rage.

And then...all too soon, there were no more arrel.

That...that wasn't enough. No, not nearly enough. That had only whetted my appetite. My hunger roared, and so did I out loud.

I lashed my tail against a pillar of sandstone, sending it crumbling. I landed on top of the highest peak and bellowed into the night as I smashed my foot into the ground, sending gaping cracks through the stone.

Then, with my mind and power, I added words to my roar.

IS THAT ALL YOU CAN DO? IS THAT ALL YOU SEND AGAINST ME? I DEFY YOU, DEVOURER. SEND YOUR LEGIONS. SEND YOUR LISH. I WILL DESTROY THEM ALL. I WILL AVENGE HER DEATH ON YOU A HUNDREDFOLD. I WILL BURN, AND I WILL BREAK. I WILL CRUSH, AND I WILL TEAR—

A voice unexpectedly cut into my mind, piercing like a sapphire spear through the red. A voice I...knew. Using a name I recognized as...mine.

Saying...the last words I had expected to hear.

Ben, you torched idiot—she's alive!

Chapter Nineteen

IDIOTS

Sarah

For the second time that eternal day/night...I woke excruciatingly slowly.

But, oddly enough, smell came first: moist, relatively warm air wafted in and out of my nostrils, so different from before. Sight came next as I blinked open my crusted eyes, even though my mind couldn't make much of my blurred and unfocused vision. The perspective was strange, too. Like gravity had tilted sideways.

It took maybe five seconds for me to realize that the world wasn't on its side—I was.

Focus returned slowly, like a camera lens adjusting, and I saw a stone balustrade and roaring waterfall beyond. I blinked rapidly, realizing another problem: the light. I had just been in darkness. Hadn't I?

But now all was bright around me, and that was painful, but it was also safe, and....

A light hovered in my range of vision, bobbing in concern, as if asking me what I was doing collapsed on the floor. I was indeed, prostrate as if I had fallen on my side while reaching for something.

What....

Then it all came rushing back to me with painful suddenness, and I gasped in more than mental pain. Because I felt aches and bruises and cuts everywhere, not to mention a throb in the back of my head that was sending spears of suffering through the rest of my skull, as if not content to suffer alone or in silence any longer. My mouth felt as dry and rough as sandpaper; I swallowed, but nothing went down.

And then there was the ringing in my ears...my hearing still not entirely healed from the rasper's final revenge.

I moaned and curled inward, wanting to just sink back into oblivion.

I had just...surged to one of my gates. Just like Ben could do to his. I wondered if it just about killed Ben every time he did, just like this. If so, I could understand why he did it so seldom.

The light continued to hover. Then another joined it. Then another, and another. The combined light was searing, and I snapped out, "Will you just go back to bed and leave me alone? Everything's fine now, right? Let me just...*be.*"

But the lights were bobbing against me now, as if pleading with me to move. Finally, the ringing in my ears died enough for me to recognize an urgency in their hum.

Apparently, I wasn't quite out of adrenaline, since one more shot kick-started my system into life again.

"What is it?" I croaked, propping myself up on my forearm.

They whirled around me in relief for a second, then formed a line leading toward the north end of my hold. Well, that message was as clear as a neon arrow: I was meant to follow.

I moaned. "This had better be dang important. Like, life or death important."

The lights kept up their urgent hum.

Like a shipwrecked survivor crawling with her last strength onto a beach, I first pulled myself forward with my arms. Fortunately, movement seemed to warm my aching muscles and lend me further strength, and I was able to push up onto my knees and then to my feet a few moments later.

I still felt more zombie than human, but I was able to shamble after my moving dotted line of lights.

The human part of me still apparently had a sense of humor, because I thought with weary amusement, *I feel like I'm Pac-Man.*

Though this dotted line simply kept moving on ahead of me, so perhaps a better analogy was.... What was that one in which you swallowed things to increase the length of your tail and tried not to run into yourself? I still wasn't swallowing anything, though, so that didn't fit either....

While the thirty percent of my brain that was still functioning tried to figure out what classic arcade game my life had turned into, I found, to my surprise, that my lights were leading me through the tiered seating room (still hadn't figured out what that one was for) and to....

The ice room.

I needed a better name for that.

Ice...Rose Room?

Nope, still not it.

Fortunately, the lights spared me the effort of opening the doors and did so by themselves with a few mysterious twirls. I followed them inside with even greater reluctance, at a total loss. Plus, my body still remembered how exhausting my last entry into this room had been.

Fortunately, the room's illuminating crystals stayed on this time, even after the doors shut behind me.

To my surprise, I noticed there were some additions to the room. Three, to be exact.

Three suns floating over three of the seven pillars, with a planet orbiting each one. I was grateful that I wasn't here to solve that puzzle now, because the lights floated to the furthest northern end of the room, the one that had, in the previous two times I'd been in it, formed the tip of the hold's leaf shape.

Right now, that tip was somewhat concealed behind a giant pane of solid ice, so smooth and clear that I would have mistaken it for glass, had it not been for the frost around its edges.

The lights hovered around it, their hums urging me forward.

I did so. Then winced at my reflection on its surface. I...had seen better days.

"Mirror, mirror, on the wall," I murmured, and idly reached out to touch the surface with a finger.

I should have known better.

One of the last drops of power I had surged through my fingers and into the ice mirror.

An instant later, it became a movie screen, and the whole room my surround-sound theater.

I staggered back as a deafening roar exploded in the room, and I cried out as I flinched away while covering my poor, abused ears. Meanwhile, I blinked at the scene in front of me, trying to make sense of it.

Well, there was a night sky, some desert, some mountains....

Looked a lot like where I had just come from, actually. My perspective could have been on the side of one of those mountains. In fact, there was something familiar about that plateau I was looking out on....

Wait....

I knew that roar. Even though it had an edge I didn't think I'd heard in it before, and I was certain I never wanted to again.

Then a familiar figure literally dropped into view and rose from his crouch. To stare straight at me.

"Sarah?"

"Kor?" I stammered. "Can you see me? And...hear me?"

Was this not just some recording or metaphorical vision?

Was this what was happening right *now*?

"I can," he said quickly, rushing up to me. Or...to whatever surface he saw *me* through. "You *will* describe to me in detail how you are doing this—and how you got back there—*later*. But we have a bigger problem right now. *Way* bigger. Right now, I need to know two things for certain: Are you healable and not immediately dying? And are you not in any immediate, life-threatening danger?"

Well, that was oddly specific. And encompassing a lot of states between total wellness and excruciating agony.

"Yes, and yes," I said, dryly. "Thanks for the concern."

"You're welcome, but I have to admit, I have ulterior motives—"

Just then, another roar ricocheted through my magical, invisible surround-sound system. If it was bad for me, it must have been even worse for Kor, because he bent over with pain and his hands clasped over his ears.

"*Ben, you torched* idiot," Kor shouted furiously, squinting in pain as he forced himself upright. His voice echoed in a way that made me wonder if he was using both his mouth and mind to project the words. Probably a necessity to make himself heard through the roar. "*She's alive!*"

The roar abruptly cut off. My ears rang in the silence that followed.

"Kor," I said uneasily. "What's going on? Is Ben—"

A golden...dragon...suddenly appeared in my field of vision, just beyond Kor. It landed on the mountainside with a force that brought Kor—ever smooth, ever graceful Kor—down on his knees, and it peered down at the two of us with one enormous eye, all that it could use at one time to examine insects like us while it was this close.

But...that was impossible. That couldn't possibly be *Ben*. I knew by now how big Ben was, but this....

Unless this ice mirror was getting proportions way out of whack, only the dragon's eye and the inside corner of its toothy maw could even fit on my "screen." Kor, standing in front of it on the plateau...looked like a grasshopper facing down a bear.

And yet, as soon as Kor climbed back to his feet, face it he did—feet braced, shoulders down and back, fists clenched, chin up.

I had my gripes about Kor...but now I knew to never, ever call him a coward.

"*Look*," Kor said, pointing back at me. His voice kept that dual vocal, yet echoing quality. "*Just look at her, Ben. That's Sarah. She's back in her hold. She's alive. She's alright. She's safe.*"

Ben.

He had called that...that Godzilla-shamer...*Ben*.

"*She's alive. She's alright. She's safe,*" Kor repeated, as if speaking to a child.

Or...someone who was dangerously unstable.

My heart pounded as I stared into that slitted golden eye. I put both hands on the mirror—and was reminded that it was made of ice and not glass by the burning chill. Yet, in that moment, I didn't care.

"Ben?" I stammered.

The dragon's lip curled, and it let out an ominous, low growl. Its teeth bared, and it leaned back, enough that I had a terrifying glimpse of its entire maw opening.

I thought I could guess what was coming next.

"*No, Ben, no!*" Kor cried, pure terror entering his voice.

I still didn't think he was a coward. If he hadn't been scared now, I would have thought him a fool. *I* was frozen in fear, and I wasn't even there.

Kor rushed on, speaking as quickly as he could. "*You'll bring the shelter down, and half the mountain with it! First Flight are in there, the rest in the tunnels, and Yvera too! You could kill them all!*"

My heart froze.

"Kor, what's wrong?" I choked. "Why is he doing this?"

He looked back at me, eyes wide. As if I were his only hope. "He says it's an illusion, that I'm tricking him! Sarah, you have to *give* me something! Some way to prove to him it's you."

I still didn't understand what was going on, what had possessed—and super-sized—Ben, and why on Earth proving that I was *me* would solve things. But if Kor said that was what I had to do....

I looked up at that maw that was glowing from a fire building deep inside...and blurted out the first thing that came to my mind. "Your mother taught you to make your bed!"

"Sarah...." Kor said in a strained voice.

I continued in a rush. "She taught you to make your bed, because if you couldn't do the simple things, the hard things would be harder. She always knew you would become the Heir, long before you did. You told me all of that, remember? As I was helping you make your bed, here, in my hold. We were alone. No one else could have known you had told me that but me."

Kor turned back to Ben. He didn't shout the words out loud this time, but I could almost see him thinking them at Ben with all his might.

Ben stopped inhaling. The flickers of flames at the back of his throat died. He slowly closed his maw. Then he turned his head to look at me again.

"You showed me how to fold the corners," I said, babbling now, too relieved that it appeared to be *doing* something to stop. "I told you I was a tosser, you said that you slept like a log. You sang as you cooked us dinner. A song about a star of some kind, falling in love with a moon? You stopped when you noticed me watching. You said your mother taught you to sing, and cook. And that your father told you to keep it up, even after she was gone. When you talked to me on Yvera's scale, you wouldn't let me look at your bedroom because it was messy. I told you I liked tsha, that it tasted like sunshine. You made me breakfast when you came back, said it was the least you could do after getting me up to open the gate for you."

Ben continued to stare, watching me.

Then...just about the time I ran out of breath...he began...shrinking.

That's the only word I could think of to describe it. He just became...not *less* than he was before, but condensed, concentrated. Reining it all in into a smaller, more controlled package. Until finally, he became his normal size, half on, half off the plateau—because he had condensed forward rather than to the center. But he didn't stop there. He kept changing back, except slower than normal, slow enough that I looked away because the sight was a bit nausea-inducing for my already overstrained body and pounding head. I glanced back when he lost his scales.

Finally, he was, at long last, human again.

Ben again.

Except...as far as I could tell from his crouched position on all fours...completely naked.

He raised his head, blinked dazedly at Kor and me, and wobbled.

"I...need a dek," he said woozily.

And then collapsed.

A FEW HOURS LATER, I cracked open the new Romskal gate—blazoned with a set of scales inside a sun—to let Kor in for the second time.

The first time had been shortly after Ben had collapsed, when Kor and Yvera had carried his unconscious body in. Both had been anxious to get him into my hold as quickly as possible. I thought it was to heal him, but as soon as they were inside, Kor had let out a breath of relief.

"He should be safe enough here," he had panted to Yvera.

She only grunted in reply.

I felt a chill. "What do you mean? I thought the danger was over out there."

"Danger is never over as long as it's night," Kor grunted. "*Flame*, he's heavy."

And Kor had the relatively lighter end: Ben's legs. Yvera had her arms hooked under Ben's and was leading the way backward toward the dormitory. Ben's head lolled lifelessly, and that distressed me more than I was going to admit. I just followed along beside them, feeling helpless.

The only good thing I could see about the situation was that they had found Ben some pants. And left his chest bare.

Although I tried very hard not to take advantage of that last benefit.

"But," Kor added darkly. "Ben had to go and make it even *more* dangerous by challenging the Devourer to send its legions."

I gaped. "No."

Kor cast me a sidelong glare. "Is that the most shocking thing you've seen or heard tonight? Speaking of which, I need some answers. Now."

So while Kor and Yvera panted and carried Ben all the way to his bedroom, Kor asked his questions, and I answered as well as I could. That seemed to satisfy him for the time being, at least. After the wings unceremoniously dumped Ben on his bed, Kor examined me, healed me of a hit I'd taken to the back of my head since it seemed to be my most worrisome injury, and declared that he had to go back, muttering something about leftwing-type stuff he had to do that reminded me of the US political cliché "damage control."

A couple hours later, he contacted Yvera by scale, who passed the message along to me, then I hurried back to the gate to open it again.

When I cracked the doors open wide enough for him to slip through, I saw with relief that dawn was lighting the desert sky, hopefully bringing at least a temporary reprieve from the threat of "legions" coming down on the innocents of the Wirthen Desert.

I also saw with surprise that most of the fighters who had stayed with us that night were at a respectful distance away from the gate. Less respectful were their unashamed stares at me and at the gate that had materialized on their mountain slope.

"Er...Kor...." I said, looking back at them as he slipped through the ice. "What happened to secrecy?"

"Ben happened," Kor snapped. He groaned and put a hand to his forehead. "Don't worry. I only told them what was necessary. And then swore them to secrecy."

As I closed the doors, I thought of what I saw as dramá proclivity for gossip and near utter lack of privacy, and I said skeptically, "And that'll be enough?"

Kor looked at me balefully. "*Blood* oaths, Sarah. Every single one of them swore with their blood. They can't tell even if they were tortured to."

Fortunately, the doors closed fully just then, because I suddenly felt weak. "What?" I whispered.

He sighed and slung an arm over my shoulder as we began a slow walk back to the dormitory. "What do you think took me so torched long? Well...that was one of the things, but it took the longest."

"Was that...necessary?"

"Yes," Kor said with grim simplicity.

I sighed but let him leave it at that. "You look tired."

"I am torching beyond tired," Kor said, rubbing his eyes with his free hand. "But I'll get some rest soon. Speaking of which, how is Ben?"

"No change," I said fretfully. "Still sleeping like the dead. Are you sure...."

Kor moaned and removed his arm from my shoulders. "For the last time, Sarah, he'll be *fine*. He's not even hurt—or if he was, his change back healed him.

He's just burned dry. He just needs to sleep for a day, and then eat his weight or more. Then he'll be the Ben you know and adore again, don't worry."

My cheeks heated. "But did you have to put him in a *coma*?"

"Magic-enhanced deep sleep," Kor corrected with a finger. "Not a coma. There's a slight medical difference, but it's there. Besides, the answer is *yes*. We couldn't risk him waking up before all of...that...was out of his system."

I took a deep breath. "You still haven't told me what *that* was. Kor...what happened?"

Kor looked at me sidelong. "The short of it? *You* happened."

I stared back. "Me?"

"I'm not saying it was your fault. Hellwinds, if I had been in your shoes, with the limited knowledge you had, I might have done the same thing. But yes, Ben was like that...did those things...because of you."

"I don't understand."

Kor sighed. "Many drakón...become more draká in times of great emotional strain, Yvera being the prime example, but the Royals...."

He paused, then seemed to choose his words with care. "When someone who is...shall we say, *close to* a Royal is endangered or killed, Royals have been known to go a bit...mad. Berserk, really. And that's exactly what Ben did when he thought you were dead. He probably didn't even realize what was happening to him. In fact, the person you think of as *Ben* might not have been in there for most of that time."

"What did he do?" I whispered as we stopped in front of the dormitory arch. Kor rubbed his forehead.

"Compared to what he could have done in that state? Not much. He wiped out the arrel—those things that were flying away with you," Kor added hastily when I blanched. "Nothing more than glorified spelled rocks with barely enough sentience for independent action, so don't you lose sleep over *them*."

Kor took a deep breath. "Other than that, he knocked down stuff, smashed some rocks, gave everything living within elden a minor heart attack, but...that's it, I think. The greatest fallout is more about information, but I'm trying to mitigate what I can of that now."

Kor shook his head wearily. "We got lucky. *Very* lucky. Mostly thanks to you and that...ice communication spell of yours. Of course...Ben's berserker rage might have been much easier to contain if it weren't for you, too."

I suddenly put it together. "I gave him power," I breathed in horror.

"To put it mildly," Kor said with folded arms. "Sarah...I don't know how to describe to you how what you did changes *everything*."

"What do you mean?"

Kor held up a finger. "One: Giving someone else power directly has never been done before. It was thought to be impossible. I can use my power *on* you; that's how I healed you. I can give you gems infused with my power that can save you having to charge them yourself. But that is it. My spark is my spark alone. Yours is yours. That was...until you gave me a boost sometime at the beginning of this interminable day."

"*That's* why you asked me what I'd done, and told Ben you had to think."

"Exactly. That alone could have been our Realms-shattering event of the day. Figures that we would only have to go up from there."

He sighed and held up a second finger. "Two: Ben changing at night should not have been possible. Someone as powerful as Ben can remain in that state for a while after the sun goes down *if* he has already paid the price of the change. But not even a Royal has ever been able to shift in the middle of the night without a direct boost from the Tree of Flame, and Ben was across the cosmos from Her. That fact was no doubt what the Devourer had been counting on when it sent its minions to take you.

"But Ben's change is not as huge a leap, since we already know by now that you are strengthened at night. Put that together with number one, and the result is not too surprising. To us. But only the four of us, plus maybe the King, had known that quality of yours before tonight. Now everyone who heard and saw Ben is going to be wondering how in the *blazes* did he change *at night* on *Romskal*. And everyone, of course, includes the Devourer and any consumed with sense. Because of course, in that state, Ben wasn't going to be torched *subtle*."

My eyes widened in understanding. "That's what you meant, about the main fallout being information. That is why you made the First Flight swear blood oaths."

"Yes," Kor said grimly. "But I can't track down every torched soul who heard and saw Ben that night and make them do the same. And there will be many. Ben was heard and seen for elden. Word is already spreading like wildfire. I just contained the worst of the gossip—I hope—with the most immediate and knowledgeable witnesses."

Kor grimaced. "Alright, that's not giving them enough credit. They'll do their best, I think—in addition to the oaths. They're the First Flight of Goldek Gate. That means they're its elite. They're dutiful to a fault, and they're not stupid. They know the significance of what they saw and took part in tonight, and I made sure they knew how important it was to do what they can to keep this quiet. I spun a story, and I made sure they could recite it forwards and backwards."

"What story?"

"Not important right now," Kor said with a weary wave. "I'll tell you later, since you'll need to stick to it too, but I need to get going on more containment work, and I still haven't fully answered your question."

"There's more?" I asked, baffled.

"One more thing," Kor sighed. "And it is, perhaps, the most significant, believe it or not."

"What?" I whispered.

Kor held up a third finger. "Three: Ben didn't just change. Surely you noticed his...size."

I could only nod.

"A drakón's size, as I think you've already learned by now, is determined by the drakón's capacity for power. I'm the strongest magic user among us not because I have the largest capacity—I don't, that's Ben—but because I'm the most *efficient* and *effective* at using what I have."

I nodded. "Ben said about as much."

"Hopefully in a way that was properly complimentary to me," Kor said with a tired attempt at his usual smirk. It quickly faded. "But since a drakón's capacity is set in stone after they become drakón, a drakón's size is likewise stable, growing as they grow and stopping when they stop. Just as you don't grow a couple inches just because you're feeling energized, a mature drakón's size should always stay the same, no matter how much power they *currently* have."

"Oh," I said, beginning to realize where this was going. "Ben...should not have been that big. No matter how much power I gave him. That wasn't his normal size at all."

"To put it lightly," Kor said grimly. "Sarah...I'll just keep it simple by saying that there has, definitively, *never* been a drakón or even a draká that...big.... For a very good reason."

I just stared at Kor for a moment. I didn't need to be told what that reason was. I, too, had stared into that maw licking with tongues of flame, and wondered if it could have swallowed the world.

"Why?" I whispered. "How?"

Kor looked at me with heavy eyes. "I...don't know. I think you can understand why that terrifies me. And everyone else. Maybe even gives the Devourer pause."

My heart went cold. "Ben. He was so mad that he..."

"...challenged the Devourer," Kor finished. "I'm not even going to bother hoping that message never reaches it. Even if the Devourer wasn't listening—which I doubt, since it would have been watching the progress of your kidnapping closely—too many consumed would have heard."

"No wonder you wanted to get Ben away," I breathed. I couldn't help a reflexive glance at Ben's room. I felt a surge of protectiveness to a degree I had never felt before. And powerlessness. What could *I* do to protect someone like Ben? Let alone from....

"For the sake of everyone in the Wirthen Desert as much as his own," Kor agreed darkly. "Once the Devourer saw Ben was out of reach, I hoped it wouldn't waste 'legions' on making a statement. And it seems I was right, for now. But I certainly didn't breathe easily until dawn came. That's...another reason I had to go back."

"To be with them, in case."

How...brave. And noble, actually. Seared forever in my mind was the image of Kor facing down the berserking behemoth his friend and Heir had become, and now the memory had an added layer of awe from all that Kor had just told me. He, more than anyone in that moment, knew what was at stake, what was unknown, and how much he risked by trying to stop Ben.

Kor just kept surprising me. It made me wonder. All those times he *was* an arrogant, know-it-all, manipulative jerk, how much was an act? How much of it was him thinking that was what he was supposed to be, *had* to be, and how much of it was who he really was, or at least...what he wanted to be?

Kor, fortunately, didn't seem to read my thoughts this time. He simply shrugged tiredly. "I had to. You had to be safe, Ben had to be away, and Yvera had to be here to protect both of you. So that left only me to stand with them to face whatever hellwind of a mess we might have gotten them into. And meanwhile...."

I smiled weakly. "Damage control."

Kor blinked, then smiled slowly. "I like that phrase. I might steal it."

I chuckled. "I thought you might."

Any humor then died. "Kor...I am so sorry—"

"Don't apologize, Sarah," Kor said with abrupt severity. "You were the catalyst, but *you* are the least at fault in all of this mess. You were just doing what you thought was right when you had no other hope. For that much spine, that much spit in the Devourer's face.... Well, I'm torched proud of you."

To my surprise, he pulled me in and hugged me, tightly. When he let me go a few moments later, he cleared his throat. His eyes were glistening.

"I...know I didn't act this way before," he said, blinking rapidly, "but I am...relieved to see you're alright. Ben wasn't the only one you scared last night."

Then he sniffed, some normalcy returning to his expression. "Though *I* had the good sense to wait for evidence that you actually *were* dead."

I had some guesses why Ben had thought the way he had, things I hadn't described in detail to Kor or had avoided mentioning entirely. But I still wasn't going to bring them up now.

"Still, I'm—"

Kor held up a hand and glared hard enough I shut my mouth. "If you need someone to blame, blame Yvera and me."

I snorted. "You?"

"Yes, us. It's our job not just to protect and aid Ben—and now, by extension, you—but also to make sure things like last night don't happen. I saw how hard Ben was pushing himself, and us, to find those gates, but because I'm nearly as scared as he is at how little time we have, I let him. But now I see I let him get too close to the breaking point, and that's on me. I'm trying my best to make up for that now, and that started with, as you put it, 'putting him in a coma.' If that's what it takes to make him *rest* right now...then that's what I'm duty-bound to do."

"I see," I said heavily.

"So," Kor said, straightening and placing his hand over his heart. "Since I know Yvera won't have the decency to apologize to you personally, please accept from me the formal apology of the Heir's wings that we did not protect you and Ben better."

"Apology accepted, although it's unnecessary," I said with a faint smile. "You're only human, Kor. If you know what I mean."

He chuckled as he ran a hand through his hair. "I think I do. Now...I had better get back to my duties so *I* can get some rest, and you had better get back to Ben. Magic-induced sleep or not, I can't predict when he'll wake up, and we need you to be there when he does. Just...in case."

That had been Kor's only assignment to me before he had left. *Stay with him,* he had told me with burning eyes. *Don't leave his side for anything other than grabbing something to eat or using the privy.*

So, even though I didn't know why at the time, I had remained dutifully at my post until Yvera had poked her head in to grudgingly convey Kor's request for me to let him back in. At the time, I had thought my assignment to Ben was because he was sick somehow, which was why I had fretted so much. Now...I still worried, but at least I finally accepted that it seemed like he was going to be physically well.

If not exactly safe.

I wanted to ask Kor more about what he thought the Devourer might do about...Ben, but I also could see how tired the leftwing was and didn't want to hold him back from getting his own reprieve. That question could wait for now.

So, I only asked the one I couldn't keep down any longer.

"Kor," I said. I was at once both dead serious and growing hot. "Do you think Ben...did what he did...mainly because he felt guilty at not protecting me like he'd promised, or because he...?"

Kor gave me a look. The one that only Kor could give, the one that said, *I can't believe my lot in life is to be surrounded by torched idiots.*

"I will let you figure that one out."

Not letting myself be deterred by chagrin or squeamishness, I took a deep breath for courage and said, "If I could do that, I wouldn't be asking."

Kor's condescending expression faded, replaced with one of intent examination. I squirmed, but I remained in place, determined to get my answer now that I'd paid the excruciating price of asking it.

"You honestly can't, can you?" he said.

"No," I said with as much evenness as I could muster. "Sometimes I get a glimpse that he might be.... But then he does or says something that makes me rethink everything."

Kor sighed. "He would, the dimtorch.... Look, Sarah, we *will* talk about this. It's high time we did. But I really do have to...."

"Right," I said hastily, stepping back. "You have more important things to worry about."

"More urgent," he said pointedly. "But not necessarily more important."

"Really?" I said dryly. He couldn't honestly be saying that my pathetic romantic woes were more important than saving the worlds.

And yet...the quelling look he speared me with seemed to imply just that.

"*Yes*. Far more important than it seems anyone else has guessed—except me, per usual."

He sighed and waved as he turned and began walking to his room. "Go back to Ben, Sarah. And get some rest yourself—so long as you stay with him. Grab a bedroll or climb into bed with him for all I care. Trust me, sometime later, we'll *talk* about this."

I suddenly wasn't so sure I wanted to anymore. At least...not with Kor. But...who else did I have to go to? Yvera?

Ha. Had anyone been listening in on my thoughts and been in the position to suggest her to me, I would have told them they were even more of "torched idiot" than I was.

CHAPTER TWENTY

SLEEP

SARAH

I HURRIED BACK TO Ben's room. To be honest, I had no problem with my assignment. I might have stayed at Ben's side anyway, just from sheer worry, so I was secretly relieved to be ordered to do so. Even the time I had spent talking to Kor had been difficult; with each passing second, I had felt a stronger magnetism pulling me in Ben's direction.

And I wasn't just talking about an emotional kind.

The pull, the connection I had felt with Ben from before, had snapped back into full force the moment Kor and Yvera brought him into my hold. If anything, it felt stronger. I'd been trying hard ever since to not think about what that meant.

I paused at the threshold of Ben's room to look at him. And sigh.

I hated seeing him like this. I understood and even supported Kor's decision now to keep him under for a while longer, but still....

Ben was normally so...alive. So strong and radiant and *there*. Right now....

At least I had managed to roll him onto his back from the side position he had been in when his wings had dumped him there. Even Yvera hadn't seemed to care much for his comfort beyond bringing him to his bed and leaving to go do her own version of damage control—whatever she could do by scale, since she had to stay with me and Ben. On my quick errands over these past few hours, I'd often passed her room while she was shut inside and talking to people; other times, I caught glimpses of her pacing around the Rim, or heard her working out her angst in the training room. I'd known better than to disturb her with any of the questions I'd just asked Kor.

So I had distracted myself from my questions and worry by taking care of Ben. After shifting him to his back and positioning him in the ways I thought would be most conducive to long-term comfort and circulation, I'd adjusted his pillow to support his neck better and plumped it up for good measure. If I had run my fingers a bit more than was necessary through his golden hair to get it out of his face, well...there was no harm in that, right?

After much heaving, I had given up trying to pull his blanket out from under him, and I'd gone to the storage room to find him another one—the absolute biggest and fluffiest comforter remaining. I then spread it over him and tucked it right up to his armpits, pulling his arms up to rest on top of the covers as I'd seen him sleep before.

And then...there didn't seem to be anything else I could do. Yet I had whiled away the hours until Kor had called me trying to find anything else. I got incense sticks from the storage room, ones that smelled soothing and clarifying to me, and I brought them back and lit one in a beautiful ceramic tray that had been stored near them, presumably for that purpose. I tidied a bit, since already Ben had a bit of clutter going on; impressive, considering how little time he had spent in the room and how he could just carry whatever he needed with him. It made me wonder what his bedroom back in his home looked like. Finally, I made tsha, just so he would have the smell of that, too, and put a mug of it in the nook on the other side of his bed.

After that, I had...paced. Stood. Sometimes, when I thought I could risk it, I sat in his desk chair. But I couldn't let myself rest, as exhausted and aching as I was, because I knew that Kor was back out there and could be facing danger. Plus, I knew he would need me to let him back in.

Now....

Ben lay right as I had left him: like a dead soldier on his bier, straight and still, face utterly expressionless. Even the comforter didn't help, since the biggest and fluffiest one remaining was as white as a shroud. From this distance, only the subtle rise of his chest indicated to me that he was still alive.

Neither did anything in his current, very human repose give any indication of what he could—and just had—become. A thing that no one, even among his own kind, had ever been.

I knew what he could be. In my head. Feared it, even, and rightly, in my gut. And yet, in my heart....

That fleshy organ in my chest, so different from his, only tightened from seeing him so...powerless.

It made my own feelings of helplessness become suffocating.

I sighed again and turned around to go search the storage room for a bedroll. With Kor safe and sound in my home, I could finally let myself sleep, and *oh*, how my body said it needed it.

I didn't find a bedroll, per se, but I did find something just as good: a mat so cushy, it was practically a mattress that could roll, and I swore it felt like memory foam; it was big enough that it was all I could carry at one time, and I had to go back to my bedroom for a blanket and pillow.

Really, was there anything I didn't have now? Aside from a computer, a cell-phone, a car, and all the expensive, high-maintenance things I used to consider necessities on Earth. Now, they didn't have nearly the same pull. I'd survived this long without thinking much about them at all, in fact. The only *thing* I still wished I had was some reliable way to contact my drakón companions, like they did with their scales, but I was sure Kor would start helping me figure that out, too, now that we had a hint.

And, of course...a way to call my family. A way to get at least one single message to them: that I was alive, alright, and, for the moment, safe. Just as Kor had told Ben about me.

I didn't include a way home on that wish list, because that had already been promised to me under certain conditions—and I now had a glimmer of hope that they were actually achievable.

I still didn't understand the *why* behind what the Trees were asking us to do. My intellect was with Kor; it seemed a lot of highly dangerous trouble and a needlessly condensed timeline to gain something that They had the power to give not just now, but years ago.

But, also like Kor...I was having a hard time disbelieving the fervor of Ben's faith. As if faith were catching...it was becoming my own. And I hadn't forgotten that in the time of my greatest despair, my Tree had reached out to me, and by showing me the way to reach, She had saved my life.

True, maybe my life wouldn't have been in such danger in the first place if She had just *told* me I could suck myself through my gates just like Ben could through his. But then...could She have? Was this something that I could just be told? Or did I have to first want it so *badly* that I would trust Her and try with all my might?

I didn't know. But...dang it, I wondered if Ben was on to something.

And that wondering had frightening implications of its own, giving less comfort than fear. Because if the Trees were right, if They were *always* right....

Then They were right about me.

I shook such thoughts out of my head as I spread my blanket over the mat. I still had days to make my decision. Right now, we *all* had earned some time to not think about such heavy things and get some sleep.

But then, as I lay down and curled up under my blanket, facing Ben...

...sleep didn't come.

Gazing at him, studying every facet of his handsome face with an abandon I usually wasn't allowed since he was normally conscious and *self*-conscious...the word for what bothered me most about seeing him like this finally came to me.

He looked alone.

But what else could I do? I had already done everything that seemed humanly possible to get something into his subconscious that he *wasn't* alone. And I was here, wasn't I? Sleeping on his very floor to keep him company and be right there when he woke up.

And yet...his connection pulled at me.

Then Kor's second offhand suggestion, the alternative to the bedroll, came into my mind—so insidious that I wondered if he'd slipped it in deliberately.

Nope, I told myself flatly. *I'm not doing that to him. Even* just *to sleep.*

And for good measure, I turned myself over so that my back was facing Ben.

That just made the pull suddenly worse, stronger than it had ever been. Surely that was just my imagination, right? I glanced over my shoulder, and it decreased slightly, but it was still too strong to ignore. I would not be able to get any sleep like this, and what good would that do anyone? I had to be rested and prepared to give one hundred percent again as soon as the others were. Our lives depended on it.

Finally, after a solid minute of struggling...I made a compromise.

I forced myself to lie still while I laid my ground rules.

Number one: *Just sleep.* I wasn't even allowed to touch him. As...much as that was going to be humanly possible, with him taking up almost the entire bed. The beds in the single-person rooms (meaning not the ones with bunks) were as wide as queens and longer than kings—a generous allotment...for humans. Not for Ben. Straight as he was lying now, his feet were nearly off the end.

Number two: I was going to stay on top of his blanket, and I would drag over my own and hope he didn't get too hot if mine shifted to cover him too. Assuming he *could* get too hot....

Number three: I was only going to sleep there for a bit, and then the very next time I was conscious enough to think about it, I was going to get up and move back to the mat. I would not risk making him uncomfortable by being there when he woke up. Somehow, in my mind, it was more honorable to do this while he was totally unconscious than...when he was not.

Yeah, there were some problems with that last bit of logic.

But I didn't know what else to do. His sense of loneliness was almost overpowering now. Maybe I was just crazy, but...what if I wasn't?

Last, but not least, number four: The door stayed open. I had already kept it open that entire time, for good reason; I had left it open while setting up for sleep, even though my makeshift bed was visible from the door, and I had longed to close it for a bit more privacy before I'd lain on it. But even though my plans had shifted, the door was going to stay wide open, and if Yvera killed me in my sleep for what she saw when she peered in...so be it.

She'd assume worse if I closed it, so I was dead either way.

I got up slowly. And then, trying not to think about what I was doing...I dragged my pillow and blanket to Ben's bed and climbed over him to the other side. That choice of location was necessary, given how much room Ben took up. I would probably be fine, but given my tossing tendency, I would relax better if I were against the wall, knowing I couldn't fall off.

I squeezed my pillow into the space between the wall and Ben's own, then I cocooned myself in my blanket, and not just because that was my preference: it also kept my hands safely to myself. Then, settled in on my side next to him, I returned to gazing at his face, abruptly and blissfully content.

Because the pull had eased, back down to just a magnetic awareness. And somehow, without changing his expression at all, Ben looked much less alone.

My eyes were suddenly impossible to keep open, even with a view this good and rare. They drifted close...and I was immediately under.

Chapter Twenty-One

AWAKE

Koriben

I DRIFTED AWAKE SLOWLY. For a time, it was hard to remember where and when I was. All I knew was that I had been under great strain, enduring great pain, but that made little sense. Right now, I was warm and comfortable and content beyond imagining.

I was with....

I first identified the smell: Sarah's scent, swimming around me, enveloping me in its cool, clear embrace. Far, far closer than I was used to.

And then I felt the small body pressed against my side, unmistakable even through at least a couple layers of blankets.

But instead of waking me up, that jolt of adrenaline drug me back into that dark place, that place in which I had curled up in agony at her loss while something else used my body to rage and destroy.

I gasped for air, eyes blinking open but unable to see clearly. All I saw were blurs. All I could remember was that pain....

I struggled to breathe, clenched my fists, fought the urge to burn....

"Ben, Ben!"

First Sarah's sleep-cracked voice pierced through my fog and then her face filled my vision. Suddenly, I could see clearly, now that I only saw her. Suddenly I could breathe, with her pressing down on my chest.

"I'm here," she soothed, propping herself up on my chest with one arm and putting the other hand on my face. "I'm here, I'm safe. So are you. We're all here, we're all safe, we're all alright."

Something about the words seemed familiar, but the memories were still sluggish in returning. Still, the fire in my blood and agony in my flameheart died at this irrefutable proof that they were no longer necessary.

"Where...are we?" I croaked. I could have looked around, but I didn't want to look away from *her*. Or risk reminding her of her hand on my face and making her withdraw it.

"Back in my hold," she said comfortingly. "You're in your room here."

And so are you, I thought in wonder, but didn't dare say it out loud.

Not just in my room. She was....

Flame help me, I had better not even think it.

But Sarah did. Her cheeks warmed, and she began separating herself hastily. "Sorry, I should—"

I felt a surge of the fear, agony, and burning return, and I gripped her arms as if grabbing a lifeline.

"No!" I cried.

At her startled look, I took a deep, shaking breath. Even if I couldn't quite control what I felt or let go of her yet, I had to explain. "Er, that is, if you don't mind, could you...stay? For a bit longer? I need...."

I didn't know what I needed. Other than for her to *not leave*. But I couldn't think straight enough to put it into words that didn't sound...crazy. Or desiring.

Oh, there was an element of desire, but believe it or not, most of what I felt in the moment at the thought of her leaving was fear and pain. Some of the darkness still clung to me, ready to drag me back, and I didn't know if I could resist it if she left.

Finally, I managed, "Having you here is very...comforting."

Comforting. That was a good word, right? A much milder term than what I felt, like calling an ocean damp or a sun warm. But accurate enough. And not crazy, right? Friendly?

That seemed good enough for Sarah, because she relaxed and even settled back down. Knowing she wasn't about to leave, I was able to relinquish my hold so she could do so.

Though I longed to reach out in some other way or at least turn on my side to face her, I held myself still, with my hands at my sides.

Thank the Flame for the blankets between us—one over me, and one tangled around her.

She yawned. "That's good with me, because my body says it wasn't quite ready to wake up yet."

"Sorry," I said sheepishly.

"Oh, don't be sorry," she said dismissively. "I'm the one who should be apologizing, again. I was supposed to keep an eye on you, but I shouldn't have settled down here to sleep. It's just...you looked so lonely."

Her cheeks warmed again. "Silly, I know."

"Not silly," I insisted, but inside I felt a chill at the degree of her intuition. How much had she already guessed, even subconsciously, about how I felt about her? About how much I *needed* her? Right now, she felt more necessary than air to breathe.

When her expression remained doubtful, I continued. "Like I said, having you here is...comforting."

What I didn't say is that I didn't know what I would have done if she hadn't been *right there*. And if her very presence and scent hadn't been soothing me from before I was even conscious.

My next words slipped out before I could think better of them. "I think...I needed you. And still do."

Oh, Flame above, that wasn't brotherly, was it? What would she think? What would she do? Was she about to—

But to my intense relief, she only smiled contentedly and relaxed further. She pulled her blanket up over her shoulders and tucked her chin. "That's...nice to hear. I like being needed."

That gave me pause. I focused so much on taking care of her because that was what *I* liked doing. Why hadn't I ever stopped to think before that she...might want a chance to do the same?

As a friend, of course. To show friendliness. And friendship. And....

Yup, I had better shut up.

So of course, I blurted, "I've always needed you."

Oh, hellwinds, her proximity and scent must have been making my already fog-filled brain even worse. What was I about to do next? Propose?!

Proving how far gone I was, part of me began considering the merits of doing just that. Then, if she said yes, maybe I could do something about the distance that remained between us....

Thank the Flame, all she did was blink. Then smile again, this time in amusement. "Really? You don't seem to. You're so...self-sufficient."

Ah, she was still thinking of *friendly* needs. I tried to subtly let out a breath of relief—and desperately rein myself in.

"Well, I suppose I don't like asking for help," I mused.

It wasn't a luxury I was used to. Normally, everyone else wanted me to help *them*.

Her smile deepened. "I guess that makes two of us. What a pair we are. Both of us like helping but don't want to be helped."

I chuckled, partly to hide the warmth increasing—completely unnecessarily—in my face at her calling us a pair.

A pair of friends, I told myself.

Torch it, how many times did I have to say some variation of the word *friend* before I got a grip?

I smiled crookedly. "I'll try to be better about that."

"And I'll try to have a better attitude about being helped." Sarah sighed. "Since I need so much of it."

My smile faded. "You won't forever. And it's not a bad thing that you do now."

"It's a dangerous thing, though," she said quietly, not meeting my eyes. "If I hadn't been so helpless, then...."

Oh.

Oh, Flame.

It was coming back. The darkness roared up to claim me, and this time, it had memories.

Alya's scream, my sprinting down the tunnel, running through the jorgen, Yvera holding me back and me knocking her away, facing the fork in the tunnel and nearly pulverizing something from despair, hearing Sarah's whistle to the right, running again, seeing the rechal almost on Sarah....

Seeing Sarah....

Seeing red.

"Ben! *Ben!*" Sarah said, near shouting to break through to me.

Her face filled my vision again, driving off the red. I gasped again, inhaling and exhaling wildly as if I had been drowning.

This was why I was so afraid for her to leave me. Because my subconscious knew that as soon as it could no longer suppress memory....

"I'm here, I'm alright, I'm here," she repeated urgently, over and over again. She was on my chest again, and the solid weight of her, as light as it was, was supremely comforting.

But no longer enough. I wrapped my arms around her and crushed her to me. One hand lingered on her back, the other tangled in her hair at her neck.

She is alive.

With every breath, I inhaled her scent, felt her lungs move against my chest, and repeated that to myself.

She is alive.

I didn't know how long she let me hold her like that. Longer than it took for the darkness to finally settle. Not entirely leave—but it became content to linger as shadows rather than swallow me whole. Longer than it took for my trembling to stop, my breath to ease, and my flameheart's pulses to slow.

Longer than was necessary.

And yet...she didn't seem in a hurry to move.

Before the embers of hope could surge, I remembered her words from just before. *I like being needed.*

I was in need, so she was content, maybe even happy where she was right now.

That didn't mean she would have chosen to be there had I been perfectly alright.

Yet another, horrible doubt concerning her pierced through me: I was always going to need her. And I was not always going to be able to hide that fact. Even if my need was subconscious, she might gravitate toward it, toward the simple happiness it gave her to help me.

Then how could I ever know if she...felt anything more?

Perhaps more important...would it be wrong of me to ask to court her? Would she say yes and then convince herself to love me simply because she would finally see the depth of that need? Where was the line between persuading someone to feel for you and taking advantage of their good heart that couldn't help but respond to your pleas?

But...did I have the strength to do anything else but plead anymore? I was *barely* holding myself back from acting until after...the after. Honestly, one of the few pillars of support I had left was the fear that the Trees would not allow it.

There was a certain way to find out the answer.

But, like a coward, I couldn't bear to ask Her for fear the answer was no. If it was to be no, then...at least I could have these days of pretending. Of putting off the inevitable until some future point that was safely out of sight for all the other mountains in its path right now.

I wanted—I *needed*—these days of having her all to myself, before our duties pulled us apart and other people pressed into the void.

This wasn't so bad, this friendship. Especially right now, with her lying in my arms. I could live with that for a few more days before ruining it. Right?

Too soon, she shifted. But to my sharp relief, she only pushed up onto her forearms to examine me.

"Better?" she asked uncertainly.

I forced myself to think of the retreating darkness, and not on my choking flameheart, to make the words true. "Yes...better. Sorry...about that. Not every-thing came back at once."

"Don't mention it. That's what I'm here for." She seemed to really mean it, too.

She hesitated. "Does that mean you now remember...everything?"

I frowned. "I think there still must be some holes.... I remember the arrel grabbing you, then...."

"Don't force it," she urged gently. And...was that a bit of relief in her eyes? "It will come if it will come, but there's no need to bring it up now."

I looked at her. Then said, "I'm a torched idiot, aren't I? Here I am, falling apart and needing you to keep me together, and *you're* the one who...."

"Don't worry about me," she said with a thin smile. "I think...I'm going to be OK. But if it hits later, I'll let you know."

I just stared. How could she possibly think herself *weak*?

"How?" I whispered. Before I could stop myself, I reached up and brushed her face in awe. I tried to make the motion casual by tucking some of her hair behind her ear.

Thank the Flame, she didn't seem to mind. Her eyes were thoughtful, her focus inward.

"I think..." she said slowly. "...it's because I did everything I could. Everything. The gun, the running, the lights, the whistle. Stalling until you could get to me—because I *knew* you were coming for me. And everything I could do...was enough."

"How did you do it?" I asked. "How did you get away? I can't remember. I couldn't have flown up to save you, not at night."

She looked away, and something in my mind stirred. But I was distracted by Sarah's answer.

"There was a gate, Ben. On the same mountain. I could see it. Then the Tree came to me, and She told me to reach for it. So I did. And...then I woke up here."

I inhaled sharply. "You can surge to gates?!"

She smiled. "Moongates, at least."

"Sarah," I said excitedly, grabbing her by the shoulders. "This is incredible!"

It was a Flamesend, that was what it was. Literally. The relief I felt at knowing that Sarah could get away from danger like that...I couldn't describe.

"I don't think I can do it before the gate appears, Ben," Sarah cautioned. "I think I need to *feel* it's there; I need that connection. And I don't know how far away I can do it from...."

"The distance you're able to manage might increase over time," I said eagerly. "That's the way it was for me."

She shrugged, but she seemed doubtful. "Maybe."

"Sarah, I don't think you realize—this is a torched miracle." The best news I'd received in days, by far. Unable to contain my relief any longer, I pulled her into me for another tight hug.

Thank you, I said fervently to the Tree. First to mine, out of habit. Then I said it again to Sarah's, in case She could hear me, too.

Sarah laughed in my ear. "I think you're way more excited about this than I am. Is it nice having something in common?"

That gave me pause. I let her push away enough to meet my eyes again. "I...suppose that's part of it. But I'm just so torched relieved that you have that option now. If something like that were to happen again...."

I shook my head and sighed. "I really am an idiot. I should have had you try it sooner."

"It worked out," Sarah said soothingly. Then added thoughtfully, "I think...I had to learn it that way. It was hard. *Really* hard. It took everything I had left by that point, and I only had enough faith in myself because of everything else that had happened. I don't think I would have been able to do it if you had just pointed at a moongate and told me to try."

"You're talking as if the Trees put you in danger to teach you," I growled.

She held up a finger, still thoughtful. "No, hang on a minute, I'm having an epiphany. What if...the Trees are so smart, They know how to use what is going to happen *anyway*? What if They know how to turn the Devourer's machinations into...victories? And our own choices into lessons?"

I raised an eyebrow. "Are you sure you didn't grow up hearing the High Priestess lecture on the Tree's wisdom every Flameday?"

Sarah laughed. "No, but I'm assuming you did. And I think you're beginning to rub off on me."

"Hopefully in a good way," I said ruefully.

Her smile was bright enough to send my flameheart roaring. "Only in the best way."

Chapter Twenty-Two

BUZZ

Sarah

BEN MUST HAVE STILL needed rest, because after a few minutes of talking about more normal, calming things, his eyelids drooped, and he yawned. He made a valiant effort to keep talking and keep focused, but after a few fits and starts in which he couldn't remember what I had just said, he conked out entirely.

This time, his sleep looked much more natural. It helped that he was snoring just the slightest bit. Far from being bothersome, it was kind of adorable.

I just watched him and smiled, taking advantage of yet another chance to just drink him in. This time, with not just his permission to be there, but his request. That added the sprinkles, whipped cream, and cherry on top.

Ben *needed* me.

Oh, how good it felt to be needed. But most especially by him.

I didn't know how long I had slept, but I was wide awake now. Judging from the buzz increasing in my blood, night was falling, which also explained the drop in Ben's own energy. So even though I would have rather stayed until he thought it was getting weird and kicked me out, I sighed and began slowly extricating myself.

I thought for sure I would wake Ben, since I had to pull out of his arms. But though he tightened them once and muttered something unintelligible, when he loosened his grip and I tugged again, he let me go, his arms flopping back down by his sides.

Either he was a deep sleeper normally, or he had *really* needed this recovery time. With how hard he had pushed himself...who knew?

Probably Yvera, but I wasn't about to ask her.

Speaking of Yvera, though, I was a bit surprised to wake up not stabbed through the heart or something. And Ben hadn't been quiet, especially when his memories were returning. She must have been out cold or really busy.

I stopped at Ben's bedside before I left. At my own recollection of his pain, when he had crushed me to him as if I were a life preserver, I felt such compassion for him, I couldn't help but tuck his blanket back up and lean in to pull some hair out of his mouth again. This time, before I could stop myself, I brushed a kiss to his forehead.

Three words rose to my lips and almost came out. I stopped them just in time and hastily backed away.

Just a reflex, I told myself shakily.

Born from years of tucking in younger siblings at night.

That was all.

Still, I turned straight around and left, closing the door quietly behind me.

Hopefully the worst was passed. But because not all his memories had returned, I would still come back to be there the next time he woke. Just in case he needed me.

But right now, I had some needs of my own to attend to.

I heard Kor's and Yvera's voices drifting from the kitchen and slowed my steps. Remembering my utter failure the last time to snoop or at least prepare myself for what I was getting into, I hesitated, coming to a stop.

Just then, a light floated down to me. I was about to tell it I didn't really need a secret passage this time, but suddenly Kor's and Yvera's voices were in my head, and I knew the emanating source was the light.

—absurd, Kor was snapping. *Sarah is the Tree of Ice's chosen. You can't be making accusations like that without proof, Yvera.*

Ah, Yvera's old soapbox. Sarah can't be trusted, because reasons.

I know, but—

But nothing, Kor snapped. *You're letting your flameheart blind your head—again. This idiocy must stop, and it must stop now. Say one more word against Sarah without evidence, and I will drag you before the Tree of Flame myself, with or without Ben's support. In fact, I should do that right now, before you nearly get us killed again.*

Last night was not my fault, Yvera snapped.

Something metal banged in the kitchen, as if one of them had slammed a cup or pan on the stone counter. From Kor's next words, I bet it was him.

"*Last night was almost* entirely *your fault,*" he raged, loud enough that I could understand him partially with my own ears. I couldn't remember hearing him so furious.

As if remembering Ben and I were supposed to be sleeping, he lowered his voice again and spoke with great control. *If you had been keeping a better eye on Sarah, she might not have been taken, or at least her absence might have been discovered sooner. But even when Ben* ordered *you to check on her, you refused.*

You—

Don't you dare put this on me. This is your *job, Yvera. I was doing* mine. *But while you were playing with your toys and throwing a fit because Ben spent time with Sarah and not you, the Devourer took her. Do you understand what that could have meant? What it could have done with even some of her Blood? Let alone all of it, fresh and hot out of her heart?*

Yvera said nothing, but her face must have been stubborn enough that Kor let out a sound of frustration.

When are you going to get it? We need *Sarah. You* need *Sarah. And most of all,* Ben *needs Sarah.*

No, he doesn't, Yvera said stiffly. *He's just gotten it into his head—*

Oh, sorry, excuse me, did you not see the hulking golden behemoth last night? Strange, because when it came up to me, it torched took up the entire sky. *He became* that *because of Sarah. At night. Now, imagine what he could do with the power she could give him if he were in control.*

I inhaled sharply. That was not where I thought Kor had been going.

Kor went on dryly, *That's called a battle advantage, so it shouldn't be too hard for even you to grasp. Especially if it saves our lives in less than ten torched days.*

Yvera said sullenly, *I still don't think it was my fault. Sarah had her own bodyguards.*

Alright, Kor said sharply. *Try this one on for size. From what you and Sarah have told me, I've pieced together that Ben was seconds from reaching Sarah in time. Seconds, and all of this could have been just a normal, success-ful rescue. But I'm betting that somewhere in your efforts to make him "see reason," you delayed him by at least a few seconds. Am I wrong?*

Yvera was silent.

Maybe Sarah being taken wasn't your fault. But everything that came after Ben thought Sarah was dead? That's on you.

I didn't know he would—

Kor let out a hard laugh. *How much of a dimtorch are you? Well, consider that your one warning. Now you have your irrefutable proof of yet another reason you can't let Sarah come to harm.*

My priority has to be Ben—

Grow up, Yvera. Get it into your head that this isn't you and Ben running around on adventures anymore. Knock it into your thick skull that his im-mediate safety means nothing if the Realms fall to the Devourer.

Kor sighed. *Ben was doing his duty, Yv. And by not focusing on the greater picture, by not helping him with his duty and instead hindering him in it, you failed in yours. You* failed *him, rightwing. In every way that counts.*

There was a loud clatter and shattering, accompanied by a burst of magic. I winced, hoping that whatever had broken was replaceable.

I wouldn't try that again if I were you, Kor said coldly.

Then his voice softened. Marginally. *I understand you are in pain, Yvera. But you* chose *to accept Ben's offer to be his rightwing, knowing it would come to something like this. Now, either get your head on straight and* be *that rightwing Ben and I need right now...or step down. Before I remove you myself.*

You dare— Yvera snarled.

Oh, I am torched past daring, Kor said, coldness reentering his voice. *I am torched past* tired *of doing* your *job* and *mine and then cleaning up after* your *messes. You slip up one more time, you let harm come to any of us again through your petty narrowmindedness—and that counts double for Sarah—and I will bring my concerns about your objectivity to the King again. And you know he won't give you another chance.*

Silence again, but this time accompanied by a storm of footsteps. I pressed to the wall of the dormitory in alarm, wondering if Yvera was coming this way, but fortunately, she went another.

Perhaps she went to hit something in the training room. Hopefully something that regenerated or was invulnerable.

I looked at the light hovering in front of me.

"Thank you," I whispered. "You knew that wasn't a conversation I should stumble into, didn't you?"

Or, heaven forbid, be discovered listening to with unskilled eavesdropping. Yvera had enough reasons to want me dead now as it was.

The light bobbed in confirmation.

Since I didn't want to run into either wing right now—figuring even Kor needed some space—I took a steadying breath and said, "I'll take that secret passage now, please."

THANKS TO MY LIGHT guide, the private privy in my "special" bedroom, and a touching delivery of a snack brought by some other lights, I got back to Ben's room with no one being the wiser.

Except Ben.

Who, when I carelessly pushed opened the door and stepped inside, was standing in the middle of his room, pulling on a shirt.

My cheeks flamed as hot as if I had caught him *un*dressing.

"Oops, I am *so* sorry—" I began babbling, backing out and making to close the door.

"For what?" he asked curiously, seeming completely unbothered.

I paused. "For...barging into your room? Without even knocking?"

He shrugged. "No harm done. Besides, you probably figured I was still asleep, right?"

"Yes, that's *exactly* what I assumed. Or I wouldn't have done that. I promise."

He chuckled and put a hand on my shoulder as he passed me. "I know. Thanks for coming to check on me. Now, let's go find some food. I'm *starving*."

When I just stared at him and didn't move, he looked down at me. "What?"

"You're looking...a lot better."

Which was...*odd*, considering he had just been too tired to stay awake not that long ago. And so dead asleep when I left that he hadn't noticed me pulling away from him or kissing him on the dang forehead. And I had only been gone a few minutes.

Ben shrugged. "Guess that second nap really helped. How long was I out, by the way?"

"The second time? Only long enough for me to go to the privy."

Ben blinked. "Excuse me?"

"Seriously. You fell asleep while we were talking, I started getting my Moon-touched buzz, so I left to use the facilities, then—"

My brain finally caught up with my mouth.

I was no longer buzzed. In fact, I felt...normal, actually. Not like I wanted to go to bed, but also not like I wanted to do laps around the Inner Rim.

And now that I thought about it, I felt *well*. All my aches, bruises, and scrapes were all gone, and they had been since I woke up. I raised my palm to look at the scrapes that should have been there from when I'd fallen in the tunnel and...they weren't.

Unless Kor had come into the room while I was asleep to heal me....

The rasper's awful voice came into my mind. *She is healing quickly.*

Healing quickly...was a drakón power. Up until this point, all my abilities seemed different from Ben's somehow, almost reversed. Fire, ice. Night, day. Sun, moon. Gate surging was the closest one that had come to being the same, but I was almost positive I could only do it with my own gates, and with more limitations than Ben had—if only because my gates weren't always "on."

So unless this broke the pattern, and I was suddenly developing Wolverine-style healing....

"Sarah?" Ben said slowly.

"Nothing," I said numbly, then turned to walk down the hall. "Come on. Let's get you some food."

Ben reached out, grabbed my arm, and brought me to a halt. His expression was stern now. "Sarah, what's wrong? What aren't you telling me?"

I looked up at him hesitantly. This touched on memories he still might have suppressed, and for good reason. Would talking about it trigger them?

What's more...what would he think of me saying that I thought we were developing some kind of...magical symbiotic connection? Even just putting words to it in my head made it sound ridiculous. Not to mention...manipulative. Trying to make him see a tie between us.

And yet I could *feel* it. The magnetism. It was latent now, perhaps because both of us had finally gotten what we needed from each other and reached equilibrium, but it was there.

"Sarah," Ben said slowly. Something he was reading in my expression was hardening him. "Tell me. Please. Whatever this thing is, I need to know."

He did. What's more, he had a right to. No matter how disgusted he might be by the idea.

I took a deep breath, then nodded. "Alright, I'll tell you. But it's only a theory, mind you. Just...wild conjecture."

"Sarah, I promised to always listen to you," Ben reminded me.

"You did," I said quietly. I turned. "Still...I think you're going to want some food in you before you do. At the very least...some tsha."

"This is new," Ben said with a strained smile as we began walking again. "You, telling me to eat. With some secret you're reluctant to tell me."

"Well, I *did* say you were rubbing off on me."

Even more than I had thought.

Chapter Twenty-Three

MONSTER

Koriben

"ALRIGHT, TIME TO SPILL," I said to Sarah.

We were both in her kitchen, where I had stuffed my face while she made us some tsha. Kor and Yvera were elsewhere; Sarah muttered something about Yvera probably being in the training room and having no clue where Kor was. She brought over the tsha just as I had finished what had been a heaping plate of food. I could have eaten another, but Sarah didn't know that, and I wasn't about to wait any longer.

"Just a minute, let me pour," she said as she tipped the kettle over our mugs. I would have pushed her, but I noticed how her hands trembled, making the steaming stream waver.

When I had woken after she left, I had seen the mug of tsha she had made and left for me in the nook next to my bed, and I had been so touched that I had drunk it, even though it was long since cold. Now, even though her nerves were frazzled from whatever was going through her head, she was determined to give me as much comfort as she knew how.

Sometimes—alright, most of the time, but especially in that moment—I wanted to kiss her breathless. But I was pretty sure that wouldn't help her nerves right now.

And...it would break my promise besides.

So, instead, I let her finish pouring and then sit across from me. She wrapped her hands around her mug, and I took a sip of mine. She smiled and just shook her head at me.

"What?" I said.

"It still amazes me you can do that. I don't know why, when, of all the many impressive things about you, it doesn't even rank in the top ten."

My flameheart surged. She thought there were many.... I stamped down the coals with savage force.

"Do what? Drink tsha? You do that."

"But I have to wait for it to cool first," she said, as if explaining the obvious. "If I were to take a gulp like you just did now, my entire mouth would be scalded. Badly."

I blinked. "Oh."

I made a careful mental note to mind the temperature of all foods and liquids I gave her. Then put down my mug.

"Sarah, it's time."

She sighed and met my eyes. "I promise this is relevant. How...do you feel right now?"

I blinked. "Fine, I guess. Fuller now."

"It's night, right?" Sarah asked.

"Yes...." I had no idea where this was going.

"Do you feel...like you normally do...at night?"

I paused. "Well, now that you mention it, no. I feel well rested. Which is odd, considering...."

Flickers, memories. Flying in a night sky.

Must have been a dream. Although, it felt more like a nightmare....

I frowned, refocusing. "Considering it's night. But then, I guess I must have slept during the day."

I stilled. Thought about the daylight differences. Did some rough calculations. "Sarah...how long was I asleep?"

"Exactly? I don't know how to say," Sarah said uneasily. "But...the entire day, at least."

So my estimate was close. That...wasn't a good thing. "The entire *day*? Why did you guys let me sleep an entire *day*? And...come to think of it.... *Why* was I asleep? If the last thing I remember is...."

The arrel snatching Sarah. Lifting her out of my view, kicking and beating uselessly at it. Me, running uselessly forward with all my might, even though I knew I couldn't go after her on wing, not even in half-form; I would have been no match for an entire flight of arrel with only the half.

Although, in that frame of mind, I might have tried anyway....

"Ben?" Sarah asked, piercing through my foggy memory.

I blinked, coming back to the present. To her.

"Sarah...." I said quietly. "What did I do?"

She took a deep breath. "That's what I need to talk to you about. And...it's actually more like what *we* did."

"We?"

She hesitated. "This is also related, I promise. How do you feel about sun-gates? I mean...what's your connection with them?"

She was making me more baffled by the dek. "Connection with them?"

"I mean, how do you interact with them? Use them?"

"I...go through them. Same as anybody."

Sarah sighed. "Let me try again. How does it feel when you are around one? Does it feel the same to you as it does to everyone else?"

"Oh. Um...I know it's there. I can sense them, even if I can't see them. Even if I'm worlds away, in fact. That's a Royal thing."

"And what does that feel like?" Sarah encouraged.

I thought hard for a moment. No one had asked me to describe this before. "Like...a sight that's not a sight? Like, even if I closed my eyes, I would still see something, some dot of power there. It's how I surge. I see a dark map of all the gates in my mind's eye, like constellations, and I...trace a route through them to where I want to end up."

"Oh," Sarah said in surprise. "That's...interesting. Thanks for telling me. But...you just 'see' them? You don't feel a connection with them? A...pull?"

"No," I said definitively. "Do...you?"

"Yes. Once they're there, I feel like there's this conduit between me and them. Whatever energy I have to give it, whatever I want it to do, I work through that channel. And it has this...pull. Like gravity, almost. When I surged, it felt like I was fully embracing that pull. Reaching for it."

"Interesting," I said. A bit fascinated, but still puzzled. "But why bring it up?"

She looked down, fidgeted. Tapped her fingers on her mug.

I reached across the table and placed my hands over both of hers, wrapping my own around her mug as well.

"Sarah...." I said gently. "Whatever this is, I will listen and believe you."

"I'm not worried you won't believe me," she said with a sigh. But she met my eyes. "I'm worried you won't like it. That it will make you uncomfortable."

"Just tell me and find out. Remember, I'm asking for this."

She nodded and took a deep breath. "When the arrel took me...I felt two connections. Two pulls. One was to the gate on the mountain...."

"Where did the other go?" I asked in confusion.

Her eyes dropped, and her cheeks warmed. "To you."

I stilled. "To...."

"I felt two pulls," she repeated. "The gate was pulling at me. And so were you."

I felt numb. "I remember that," I whispered.

Straining with all my might for her. I thought...it had just been emotion. My soul yearning, pleading. Had it been something...more?

"What else do you remember?" she whispered.

"I...I remember...your voice. In my head. *In my head.*"

I stared at her. And gripped her hands so tightly they probably hurt, but she didn't protest. She only looked up at me with those wide eyes.

"You told me to take something. You made it sound as if it was a goodbye. You told me to find your family and tell them you loved them."

Loved. Past tense.

And then....

I gasped as I remembered the feeling, almost as if it were happening again. "You poured a *sun* into me. A *sun*'s worth of power, Sarah. *Into me.* Do you understand that?"

"Now I do," she said quietly. "Kor told me it should have been impossible."

"Not just impossible...."

I trailed off, because the memory kept going.

The power, the connection—snapping. So suddenly. As if.... As if....

I became still. Only because I could see her, sitting in front of me, feel her living hands, warm from the tsha, under my own, smell her, hear her....

Only because of those things did I not break again at just the memory.

"I thought you were dead," I whispered.

Sarah got up. My hands just fell limply onto the table. I couldn't move. I couldn't breathe.

She came around the table.

And then she ducked under my arm and sat on my lap, wrapping her arms around my neck.

Suddenly, I could breathe again, and I did so in great heaves. I could move again, and so I wrapped my arms around her and crushed her to me. But also carefully, mindful of how fragile this precious body was.

And then I felt it....

Power. Cool, sweet power, trickling like a fresh mountain spring from her to me.

"You're doing it again," I said dazedly. "You know that, right?"

"I figured you needed the boost," she said sheepishly. "Do you want me to stop?"

Never.

It wasn't much, but it was as powerful and heady as the most intoxicating wine. It should not have been enough to fill me, and yet it did. My flameheart didn't just surge. It *roared*. As if I were standing naked in the desert sun on Ythra at high noon.

And that was only from a *trickle* of her power.

"I...think you should," I said in a choked voice. "Thank you, but...I don't know how much more I can manage."

Not to mention how much longer before I lost all inhibitions and crushed her lips to mine to drink straight from the source.

"Oops, OK," she said, cutting it off. Not as abruptly as before, thank Flame. This time, it slowed in the more natural way of things, first to dribbles, then drops, then nothing.

"What...happened? Before? You were pouring power into me one moment, and then the next...."

"I...think that was me surging through the moongate," Sarah said sheepishly. "I'm sorry. I didn't think about how that would feel to you. I...really didn't even understand what I was even doing. At all. I thought I was dead either way, so I figured I might as well die in a way that gave you something, and the Devourer nothing."

I remembered the echo of her emotions now. Somehow, I had felt something of them. The despair. The crying out in unfairness. The surprised awareness of my own consciousness. Then her determination.

There was a very good reason I had thought she was dead: she had told me she would be in all but words, and even her words had hinted at it. And then, when I felt her go....

I'd had a sun's worth of power inside me, and nothing but the knowledge that she had just died to give it to me.

And then...all I remembered was red.

Sarah was continuing, but her words seemed muted, distant. "Then the Tree of Ice came, just before the end. She stopped me and told me to reach, so I reached and ended up here. Like I told you."

"Sarah," I said slowly. "What did I do with all that power you gave me?"

She fell silent. I let her go and pushed her back, lifting her chin to force her to meet my eyes. "*What did I do?*"

"You still don't remember?" she whispered.

Darkness. Grief. Curled up inside of myself while another part of me, the part I tried so hard to keep hidden, raged free. And flew. And roared. And burned.

I blinked rapidly. "I...I don't know. It's all blurred together, mixed up, confusing. I don't think...I was entirely *me*."

And then it hit me: I had thought Sarah was dead. What else would I have done?

Really...I was a torched idiot. But then, I had never done it before, so I hadn't recognized the signs, either when it was coming on or after when remembering. I had hoped to never have done it, to never have that degree of mad destruction weigh on my soul, but....

I clenched my jaw. "I...went berserk, didn't I?"

Sarah winced. "A...bit."

"And by that, you mean a lot," I said flatly. "Flame, Sarah. If I went berserk...with that much power...."

Worse and worse.

I went cold with shame. "How bad was it? Just tell me now. Don't spare me. Did I.... Did anyone...."

"No one died," Sarah said quickly. "Well, except if you count the arrel. Kor said you killed them all. But that they didn't...really have lives to lose?"

I let out a breath. "No, not really. Is that truly *all* I did?"

"You're going to have to ask Kor for more details about what you actually did," Sarah said ruefully. "I was gone by then. But I gather you smashed some rocks and stuff. And roared really loud. And...um, became bigger than any dragon ever before."

"What?" I said flatly.

"Yes, Kor told me that should be impossible, too. But apparently, with what I gave you...you did."

That explained a few things, mostly about why what limited memories I had were so...off, the perspective wrong—for other reasons than letting my most bestial side take over. I really felt like I was sifting through the incoherent remnants of a nightmare.

"Ben...you were...."

She shook her head, eyes wide.

My flameheart chilled. She had no words for what I had become.

So I would say them.

"You mean I was...I *am*...a monster."

I dropped my arms to free her, in case she wished to leave.

Had I finally done it? Had I finally horrified her enough? In her eyes, was I once again a monster?

But wait. Then...why had she...slept beside me? Why was she here with me, even now, let alone in my *lap*?

Her eyes flashed like twin moons. "You are *not* a monster."

I shook my head slowly. I couldn't let myself hope. She didn't know better now, because of her newness, but that meant I had to make her see.

Even if it extinguished my heart.

"Sarah, you don't understand," I said with difficulty. I had to drag each word out from where they wanted to hide, to bury themselves, hoping they would never be discovered. Especially by her.

"That's the danger that lies at the core of every Royal. Always. The Tree chooses us for our good souls before She ever entrusts Her power to us, and She does all She can ever after to teach us to use it only when necessary, to rule by love and justice and reason whenever possible. But any time you give anyone power like this, there's danger. The danger that they'll allow their head to be corrupted by what's in their heart and start ruling by force. And if they did that...no one would be able to stop them but the Tree.

"Everyone knows that. Everyone fears me—*rightly*—for that. I have tried all my life to be someone they would not have to fear. I have taken every oath after oath to only serve, not rule, over them, and strived until I thought I would lose my mind to keep each one. But in the end, I failed. Because no matter how hard I tried, I always had the potential to become a monster. And now I just did."

Sarah clenched her jaw for a moment. "How is it you can't see that everything you just said—aside from the last bit—is proof that you are *not* a monster?"

I blinked at her. "Excuse me?"

I had been baring the darkest part of my soul to her...and she thought it was light?

"Ben," Sarah said slowly. "A monster is someone who, with complete con-sciousness of what they are doing, hurts others for pleasure or gain. *That* is something you will never be."

I stared at her. "But I just—"

"Were you fully conscious of what you were doing?"

"I...don't...know."

I honestly didn't. It was all so hazy, so confusing.

"That might be a hint," Sarah said dryly. "But here's another one: Kor doesn't think you were."

That gave me pause. When it came to questions of intelligence or sanity, Kor didn't hold back his punches.

Moreover, he was my wing. It was part of his solemn duty to *contain* me, for the good of everyone else, and Kor took duty as seriously as a Strongshield. If he felt I was too unstable or corrupted, he wouldn't hesitate to drag me before the Tree for trial and judgment. If he was showing me mercy....

Sarah pressed on. "Would you do the same thing now, now that you're fully yourself again?"

"No!" I said with reflexive horror.

She raised an eyebrow. "See?"

"But, Sarah, that's beside the point. I could—"

"No, that is *precisely* the point. We are talking about whether you, Koriben Sunfilled, are a monster. Would you, Koriben Sunfilled, in full possession of yourself, hurt anyone who didn't deserve what was coming to them?"

"I sure *hope* not," I said in frustration. "But if I can't always be in full possession of myself—"

"How many times have you done this, Ben? I'm not talking about losing your temper or being human—or draká, or whatever. I'm saying going full berserk."

I gritted my teeth. "Once. But I should have never. My father has never—"

"I *told* you to stop comparing yourself to your father!" Sarah said with surprising vehemence, slapping my chest lightly with both hands. "He has ruled a different era entirely than you will. He needs to be a different King than you will be. But, for the sake of the argument...."

Sarah took a deep breath and softened. "I'm sorry, Ben, but I don't know how else to get this point through to you. How...did your mother die?"

All fire left my blood, retreating to my flameheart, leaving only ice behind.

The words came out only with extreme difficulty. "She...got sick."

Sarah's face became infinitely gentle. Her warm brown eyes shifted silver and *glowed* from the sheer force of her compassion for me. She curled her fingers against my cheekbone, just past the edge of my beard, so that her cool touch seared itself straight into my skin.

"Was it right away?" she whispered. "Or did your father have time to...."

"He was prepared as he could be," I said hoarsely.

I, on the other hand....

Sarah cupped my face with both of her hands. "There was a point, I promise, and it's this: the way your father lost the closest person to him, and the way you thought you lost me—whatever I mean to you, I don't know, but I must be important—were completely and utterly different. What do you think he would have done if he and your mother had been in our places?"

Avva had loved Avvi with a passion that eclipsed the sun—and still did. If he had lost her like that.... So suddenly, so violently, having failed her so deeply...when it hadn't been her choice...*their* choice....

I could only stare into those soft silver eyes. "I...don't know."

How could Avva have even made that kind of choice? It had confounded me when I found out, and I had been a boy. Now, as a man, having tasted something of what he had known of love....

I would give anything—anything—to protect Sarah and keep her here, with me, like this. How could Avva have just let Avvi *die*?

How, if ordered to...was I even going to let *go*?

"Stop comparing yourself to your father," she repeated gently.

Easier said than done, I thought as I gazed at her with equal parts longing and despair.

"Here's another epiphany," Sarah said, face turning thoughtful. "You are so convinced you're a monster...because that's what everyone else thinks you are."

My head spun from the change in direction. "What?"

"I have heard people call you some variation of stupid more times than I care to count," Sarah said in exasperation. "But Ben, you are *not stupid*."

"I...." I didn't know what to say.

She didn't need a response. "That's only *one* example of how they belittle you and push you around whenever they can. They do it teasingly, but underneath the teasing, you sense their fear. So, you internalize it. You try to make yourself as small and unthreatening as possible. You hide from the crowds. You wear plain, loose clothes that conceal your strength instead of armor, even when you could be personally in danger that day. You *try* not to break their things. You smile and blush and constantly apologize for who you are. Then when they see that weakness in something they fear, they take advantage of it, and it feeds this descending spiral of fear and shame until you think you're a monster. And so does everyone else."

I felt like she was punching the air out of my lungs with each sentence. I couldn't speak or breathe or do anything but stare at her.

I thought...she didn't see me. Not for what I was. She couldn't have. Because if she had...she would have pushed me away like all the others.

But she saw *everything*.

More than I ever had.

"In a way, I get it," Sarah said with a sigh. "They have grown up being told Royals are dangerous; it's what they want them to be, after all. You're a necessary evil that they tolerate because they need you and even like you most of the time, because you bend over backward to make yourself *likeable*. But then they see you doing your job to protect them, and they can't help but get nervous. So, they try to defend themselves in the only way they can, which is to push you away or push you down. Because as much as most people seem to like you, subconsciously, they think they know better than to get too close to the fire."

She shook her head. "But that's where they are wrong. If they only got close enough, they would see that the fire would never burn them. Or if it did, on accident—because it can't be perfectly safe and still be able to protect them—it would feel horrendous about it afterward and do everything it took to make amends. It would never mean to hurt them. And that is the crucial difference, the difference they never see because they stay too far away. But I know better now. Because now I know *you*."

She put her hand over my flameheart. Could she feel how much it throbbed at just that touch, let alone at all she had said? Could she feel how it pulled toward her, yearned for her, as it had pulled to and yearned for no one else ever before?

Her eyes were glowing silver again. "Ben, you have the biggest heart—figuratively and literally—that I have ever known. I know you would never mean to hurt me, and if you did it unintentionally, you would move heaven and earth to make it right. Yes, I still might be frightened occasionally of what you can *do* sometimes, because I am human, and I have healthy instincts to help keep me safe. But that's different from thinking you're a monster. That's different from being frightened of *you*."

She cupped my face again and then leaned in so close our noses brushed each other.

"Koriben Sunfilled, Heir of the Tree of Flame—but more important to me, my friend: I, Sarah Lind, see you. *And I am not afraid of you*."

I felt like she had set off a soundless explosion inside of me, deep inside the deepest part of me, and the silent shock waves rushed out to touch every particle of my being, altering each one in its path.

Inside the darkness, in the deepest place within me...a star was born.

Chapter Twenty-Four

PULL

Sarah

Ben just sat there, stunned and unmoving, for longer than it took me to count to thirty.

I think that finally got through, I thought with weary amusement.

Which meant...I should stop pushing my luck and get off his lap.

If my life were the kind of telenovela my Latina mother loved, this would be the part when Yvera would walk into the room, see Ben and me, and then either stab me or gasp in betrayal and storm off, saying she was leaving forever. Then, Ben would go beet red as he suddenly realized the romantic implications of this position, shove me off—gently—and run after her, explaining that it "hadn't been like that."

I hated those telenovelas, and only watched them with Mom when she had no one else to cajole into it, and even then, it was an act of pure love on my part—unlike the actions of the overly dramatic, spineless characters, who really just needed to stop playing the victim, *think* for once in their life, and get their act together.

I got my down-to-earth nature from Dad. Which isn't to say that we weren't romantic. We just both thought that love meant cutting out all the pettiness and thoughtless passion and simply doing what was right for the other person. Always.

Which was why I was being Ben's friend, first and foremost.

So, I told him, "I am going to get off now. Not because I don't want to be near you—I do. But because of how this could look if Kor or Yvera walked in."

And...cue Ben's face going beet red.

"Er. Yes. Good idea."

So, I slipped off his lap and rounded the table, sitting back down in my seat on the other side.

Not a moment too soon, because just then, Yvera strode in, hair sticking to her face with sweat, a towel over her shoulders, breathing just a tad more heavily than normal.

Man...was I psychic?

"Ben," she said in surprise, stopping in her tracks. "You're awake."

The tables were placed perpendicular to the arch leading to the Rim, so both Ben and I could see her without turning around. Ben glanced to the side at her, red creeping up his face again, but he tried to hide it by taking a sip from this mug.

"Yes," he said when he lowered it. "And feeling more rested by now than I apparently have any right to be."

His eyes met mine for a moment and then narrowed. He seemed to realize the part we hadn't gotten to, before being derailed with helping him process his memories: I was the reason he had woken up wide awake.

Yvera hesitated, looking between the two of us. To my surprise, when her eyes slid over me as if they couldn't quite bear to really look at my face, it wasn't out of disgust. She seemed to be...chagrined.

Her eyes darted back to Ben. "Are you...feeling alright, though?"

Ben sighed and ran a hand through his hair. "I'm myself again, if that's what you're asking, Yv."

"Oh. Good. Well. Good. I...need a shower."

Without another word, she turned and strode through the kitchen toward the washrooms.

"Is she...feeling OK?" I asked, blinking.

"That," Ben said, dryly, "is the usual way Yvera apologizes. By showing a smidgeon of concern for how she could have possibly hurt you...and then running away."

"What was she apologizing to *you* for?"

Ben looked over my shoulder to where Yvera had gone. The faintest of smiles was on his face. "I'm...not sure that apology was entirely for me."

I stared at him. "You're kidding."

"Nope," he said, taking another sip. "But I'm sure hoping. It's the first time I've had a reason to, at least."

"She couldn't even look at me."

"And that's what makes me think it was at least partly for you," Ben said with a crooked smile. "The more guilt she feels, the less she looks."

He filled his mug again and gave me a pointed look. "Now, enough about Yv, and torched enough about me. I think there's something else you need to tell me."

"Ah, yes, that," I said, and it was my turn for my cheeks to warm. "I didn't know what I was doing. Honest. I only just figured it out, in the hall back there, after you got up."

"What *did* you do, though?"

I took a deep breath. "I know this is going to sound crazy, but...that connection I first felt between us? It's...still there. Or rather...it's back."

"Back," Ben repeated carefully.

"Back," I repeated with a helpless shrug. "When you felt it cut off, that was me surging through my moongate. Then, I guess the distance was too great.... Or something. I don't always see my gates like you can, Ben. They're not always in my mind's eye. They have to be active, I have to be nearby, and I have to get that connection."

"Why did you switch to gates?" Ben demanded. "We were talking about this...."

My heart clenched. Was he disgusted?

Did he honestly not feel it too?

I gestured to him helplessly with both hands. "Because that's the closest thing I can think of to what I feel between the two of us. You feel like a gate to me."

Ben cocked his head, expression unreadable. "I...feel like a gate to you."

"Yes," I said heavily. "I...I'm sorry if that makes you uncomfortable, but—"

"It doesn't, not at all," Ben said dismissively. "Stop worrying about how I feel about this, Sarah. I'm just trying to understand. This is as new to me as it is to you. But I want to know. I need to know. So don't hold back anything you're feeling or thinking. How else am I supposed to help you?"

I didn't want him to *help* me, as if I had a condition. I wanted him to say I wasn't crazy.

Dang it, I wanted him to...feel it too.

"Do you...honestly not feel anything?" I asked in a small voice.

Ben paused, thinking, then scrutinized me.

Then closed his eyes. "Sarah...could you do me a favor?"

"What?" I asked in surprise.

Keeping his eyes firmly shut, he said, "Go somewhere—anywhere—in the hold. Don't tell me where. Go out into the Rim first before you pick a direction, so I have a moment to spell my ears and nose so I can't track you by smell or sound. Find your spot, and stay there, unless you hear me shouting for you to come out."

My breath caught as I finally understood. And then it beat faster with hope.

"Alright," I said as casually as I could.

I got up and walked at a carefully controlled pace out of the kitchen and into the Rim. Then I considered my choices of hiding places.

The Room of Ice (that sounded more ostentatious than "Ice Room," right? No? Well, I would keep thinking) jumped out at me first. It seemed to be a special place, a place of power. But that...also made it obvious, probably the first place Ben would think to look.

A light floated down to me, anticipating my need once again, and I smiled.

Let's make this game of hide-and-seek a bit more of a challenge, I thought.

As I paced around the rim of the sunken seating area in my "special" bedroom, I fretted I had made a mistake. It had only been a few minutes since I'd gotten there, but still.

I had already thought of the problem of Ben being unable to open my special doors, and I had asked my guiding lights if they could let him in, but *only* if Ben started looking in the right places. As in, literally putting his hand on the invisible door to the secret passage. The lights had bobbed and hummed enthusiastically, so I figured they both understood and could do that.

Now...was it fair to expect Ben to figure out the rules of the puzzle I'd set for him? He wasn't stupid, I knew that, but this was out of his—

The bedroom door swung open, and a blinking—and hunching—Ben squeezed through.

"Ben, you did it!" I cried in excitement. And not just from relief that I hadn't made a mistake.

Unable to contain myself at what seemed like pretty conclusive results to me, I ran to him and jumped into his arms.

He laughed, gave me a squeeze, then said a bit too loudly, "Hang on, let me...."

He set me down and then touched his ears and nose, then shook his head sharply and inhaled. "Flame, that feels better. I *hate* not being able to smell. Loss of hearing isn't so bad, but gah, I feel like I can breathe again."

He put his hand on my shoulder as he gazed around the room, the wondering look returning. "Sarah...."

"It's a bit much, I know," I said, cheeks heating. "Why do you think I don't sleep here?"

"Oh, it isn't that," he said dismissively. He looked down at me, eyes narrowing. "It's...that it's here at all. How long have you known about this?"

I paused to think. "Since...the morning you came back from Ythra? I asked a light to lead me to my room. And this is where it brought me."

Ben chuckled. "And let me guess: you decided to keep this little secret to yourself until now."

"Yes," I answered. Unashamedly, since it seemed he wasn't mad.

"I don't blame you," he said, giving my shoulder a squeeze. "It's your hold, after all. You deserve a piece of it all to yourself."

He looked back at the bedroom door, perhaps thinking of the Outer Rim, which had led him here. "Have you discovered anything else, going through there?"

"No," I said with a shrug. "Haven't had time to explore, really."

He sighed as he looked back at the room. "You'll have time, some day. Still, for now...this seems nice. Fancier than what I've got back home. I wouldn't blame you if you started using it. You'd make Kor torched jealous."

As tempted as I suddenly was for that very reason, I shook my head with a laugh. "Oh, no. Like I said, this is too much for me. I'm not a...."

I trailed off.

"Queen?" Ben finished quietly. "Strange, because this room seems perfect for you to me."

More than just his words, something in his eyes made me swallow.

I looked away hastily and gestured to the sunken seating area with its plump-looking cushions. "Er.... Why don't we have a seat and pick up where we left off?"

With much better privacy, I thought with relief.

Not that I was planning on trying to pull one on him, mind you. But I liked not having to look over my shoulder, wondering if I was about to be stabbed.

"Sounds like a good idea," Ben said with a nod.

I walked to the steps leading down, then, seeing he hadn't immediately followed, turned back.

Ben was looking at the closed door. And smiling in satisfaction.

"Ben?" I asked curiously.

"Nothing," he said innocently as he came to my side.

I descended first, since the steps were only wide enough for one person at a time to maximize seating space.

"Oh, I get it," I smirked as I settled down on a cushion. It, and the bench backing, was filled with that substance like memory foam but surely not exactly that. "You're waiting for me to congratulate you on such a successful win of hide-and-seek."

"Yes, that's it," he said solemnly as he sat next to me. Then, with unusual casualness, slung an arm on the top of the bench behind my shoulder. "Feel free to start."

I laughed. "Congratulations."

Then I sobered. "Did you really do it by...."

He became genuinely serious now. "Yes. I wouldn't have found the door—this place, you—otherwise. You picked a good place for this kind of test. I could still...*see* you. Even through all the walls. Not actually you, not as you look like, but see...something. The same thing when I 'see' gates. Like a star, I guess. I could even see you must have been pacing."

He smiled crookedly. "Were you just impatient, or did you have so little faith in me?"

"Hey, I worried I had been unfair," I said, cheeks warming. "I don't like being unsporting."

"Well, that was a good sport, alright," Ben said with a shake of his head. "I couldn't, for the life of me, figure out where you must be. I just kept walking toward you as best as I could until I hit the wall, then...."

He shrugged. "You know the rest."

I took a deep breath. "So...we both feel as if the other person...is like a gate."

That made me feel less crazy, so that was a relief, but I'd be lying if I said I wasn't a tad disappointed, which I knew was silly. It was far better that Ben wasn't burdened with this...pull.

Gracious, maybe this room hadn't been such a good idea. I knotted my fingers together firmly in my lap.

"It seems we do," he said soberly.

I hesitated. "What...does that *mean*?"

He ran a hand—the one not resting behind my head—through his hair with a sigh. "Torched if I know...."

He looked away. "I assume you don't...with anyone else...."

"Nope," I said definitively. I had seen both Kor and Yvera by now, and I felt nothing out of the ordinary with them. "Can you see anyone else? Kor, or Yvera?"

Surely if merely being emotionally close to a person was a factor, those were suitable test subjects for him.

Ben shook his head firmly. "No. I have no idea where they are right now. I can't see them at all."

"Then perhaps it has to do with how we reached out to each other, that one time," I suggested. "It started the connection."

Ben hesitated. It looked as if he thought of something but wasn't sure whether to say it.

"What?" I asked gently. "Ben, I need the same honesty from you that you asked from me. The only way we're going to figure this out is together."

He sighed, then nodded. "You're right. Complete honesty, then. Maybe...it didn't start then. Maybe that's only...when it was fully forged."

"What makes you think that?" I asked, although my heart skipped a beat.

"Just, little things that have come to me," Ben said with a frown. "First, I remembered...how I *knew* you were gone. Not consciously, at first. But I was so uneasy. And then when we discovered the hole, I *knew* you weren't there, even though you could have been...buried."

He took a deep breath. "But I didn't waste time searching the rubble, because I knew."

"What else do you remember?" I asked quietly.

He looked away, growing pink. "Mostly just.... For days now, I've always felt more energy when you're around. Even when I had no reason to feel that way, like at night."

He looked at me questioningly. "Can you think of anything?"

Now that he mentioned it...I already had.

I took a deep breath. Then reached behind to touch the back of my head. "I don't remember much about going to the privy. I think I must have been hit by something in the explosion, and it knocked me out. Or that...thing...."

"Rechal," Ben said darkly. He bent the arm behind me at the elbow to gingerly touch the place I was touching on my head. "Are you still hurting? Why didn't you say anything? Sarah, head injuries aren't something to be ignored!"

"No, see, Ben, that's the thing," I said. "I woke up much sooner than the rechal expected me to. It said I was *healing*."

Ben's fingers still dug under my hair, and once they found my scalp, sent warm energy into me. But it seemed he could at least somewhat multitask, because he also shifted to gaze at me. "What?"

"That's what it said," I insisted. "I shouldn't have woken up from that kind of hit, or at least not have been able to fight back and run like I did. But I was healing."

Ben lowered his hand slowly.

"You feel just fine," he said at my questioning look.

"Kor finished the job," I said quietly. "He only had the time and energy to heal what he saw as the worst injury before he had to go back to Romskal for a few hours."

I carefully didn't say why. We had been derailed by that conversation enough for tonight. There would be time enough later to tell Ben about all the other implications of his dramatic transformation and rampage, now that I'd relieved his immediate concern of not having harmed any innocents.

Besides, Ben didn't seem curious about that now.

"The worst?" he demanded, shifting further away from me for a better look.

Before he could go too far, I said hastily, "I'm fine, Ben. There's not a scratch left on me. Thanks to you."

He blinked but settled back. "Me?"

I smiled thinly. "You're not the only one who woke up feeling a lot better. When I did, every scrape and bruise was gone. So, either I'm developing a super-healing ability, like you drakón have, or...."

Ben stared at me. "Or I healed you, even in my sleep."

I hesitated, but then told myself, *Honesty*.

"The pull I feel from you was particularly strong when I was settling down to rest. *Very* strong. So strong, it wouldn't leave me alone until I...came over." My cheeks grew warm. "That's why I was there when you woke up. Sorry."

"Don't apologize," he said with a thin smile. "Like I said, I was very glad you were there. And if I did you some good, too, then I'm even more glad. I just hope I didn't take too much from you."

I shrugged. "I feel just fine, so I don't think so."

He sighed. "Let's hope so."

He looked away and thought for a minute. I let him. I needed time to gather my own thoughts, letting all the things we had learned over the past day/night/day settle.

As if he had been thinking about the days, too, Ben sighed. "As much as I dislike the thought that I took from you to recover faster, I'm glad we don't have to waste more time. We have too little of it left for me to spend more sleeping."

"You needed the rest, for more than just the obvious reason," I chided. "We've been going like a whirlwind ever since you found me. How much sleep have you even gotten each night since? You can't do that to yourself forever, Ben. Not even for ten days. You have to rest sometimes, or you're going to burn out, and then where will we be?"

Ben smiled at me.

"What?"

"You sound like my father again."

"Are we wrong?" I said in exasperation.

"Of course not," Ben chuckled. "Why, between the two of you, you probably contain the wisdom of a Tree."

"Then listen to us: rest. We've done well so far. We've earned a break."

"I *have* rested. And as much as we've done, we need to do more. We have half as many gates to still find."

"Is the glass half full or half empty?" I demanded. When he looked at me, I waved a hand dismissively. "Earthren phrase. It means you need to see the positive side of things. We've found *three gates* now, Ben. Half the gates, in less than half the days. Can't you at least be a little excited about that?"

"I am excited about that. And about some other benefits we've gained recently as well. You can surge. I can always find you. Those are all things I'm relieved and grateful for."

He shifted, frowning. "I'm not saying we should charge back out there right this dek. I see that I'm a lot at fault for how unprepared you were to defend yourself. I should have given you more than a gun. I intended to do more...sometime. But I see now that I had better make that 'sometime' before I drag you out of the safety of this hold again. Or...you might not make it back."

His hand on his leg clenched into a fist.

I sighed. Well, at least training me would give him something productive to do that was *relatively* restful.

"Alright," I said, straightening. "You want to go to the training room?"

He looked at me in mild alarm. "Now?"

I blinked. "Wasn't that what you were saying?"

He shifted, looking away. "I.... Well.... We don't need to go *right* now. These seats are rather comfy and...."

I stared as he trailed off and started going red, still not looking back.

Heaven help me, I thought numbly. *Is he trying to be...*alone *with me?*

Was *that* what his satisfied smile at the door had been about?

My heart pounded, and my hands became clammy.

Don't lose courage now! I snapped.

I tried to say as casually as I could, "That's fine. I'm good with sticking around for a bit."

Ben relaxed as he looked at the fountain in the center of the seating area. "You're right. Maybe I do need a moment to just breathe."

Ben was a terrible liar, and that rang with all the bells of an excuse. I couldn't think of any real reason for his sudden reluctance to leave except...interest.

Was it finally time? If it was, could I do this?

Could I stop myself? I had never wanted anyone or anything like I wanted the incredible man sitting so casually next to me. And that had been before the pull, a very literal magnetism drawing me in. And right now...it was every bit as bad as it had been when I was trying to sleep. I found I had already leaned in, just from the force of it.

"Ben?" I asked, just a tad breathlessly.

He glanced at me in surprise. Then his expression changed, becoming intent. His golden eyes began to glow, ever so slightly.

That...was a good sign, right? Dang it, I wished I knew drakón tells better.

Good or not, ready or not, I couldn't hold the question back any longer.

"Do you think—"

A light floated between us, its hum apologetic. A moment later, it projected Kor's voice.

"Sarah, I can't tell you how sorry I am to interrupt, but this is urgent. I assume that in whatever secret hole you've burrowed yourself into, Ben is there as well. Would the two of you meet me in the kitchen, please? It's time to discuss some things."

Chapter Twenty-Five

RSVP

Koriben

I am going to kill him, I thought as I followed Sarah through the dark passage that led back to the dormitory. *I don't care what this is, I don't care how important. I am going to get the message from him, and then I am going to kill him, slowly and painfully.*

I couldn't have mistaken that look in Sarah's eyes. Could I? I knew I was a dimtorch about this, but what else could it have *possibly* meant? Why else would her eyes begin to soulflare when nothing in our environment or our conversation would have brought up such intensity of emotion? And with her leaning in so close.... Then there was her temperature. She normally ran cool, and that was a cool room, so the increase in her heat had been striking. And her *scent* as her power stirred....

Gah, I nearly went mad with just remembering, nearly grabbed her in that dark tunnel and pulled her up and to my mouth.

But....

I couldn't. I had promised. She had to ask. Or...give permission.

I could ask. Surely that was allowed now. Now that I had seen a request in her eyes, which I didn't think even *I* could mistake, for something of a very different flavor than friendship.

But...the Trees....

So ask Them first, you dimtorch, a voice in my head said impatiently.

I...would.

I would finally ask Them. And I would face Their answer.

I couldn't put this off any longer. Even as cowardly as I was about it, the next time Sarah asked—*Flame Above and Below*, please *let her ask again*—I had to have an answer.

That resolution made...I went straight back to plotting how to murder my leftwing. I studiously ignored the fact that he had potentially saved me from committing a transgression against Their will. If he hadn't interrupted, then at least I could have gotten *one* kiss in before They denied more to me.

I had that settled just in time for Sarah to push open the door to the dormitory and step out.

"Fascinating," I heard Kor say.

Sarah yelped and spun in the direction of his voice. "You...." she growled, fists curling.

Her display of aggression was so adorable, it helped take the edge off my temper, so that I was able to fix my face into something merely stern as I squeezed my way through the small doorway.

Kor was ignoring Sarah and studying the door with interest. "So, I was right. *That's* where the entrance to the other passage is. Or at least one of the entrances."

"You knew?" Sarah exclaimed. Then huffed and turned to push the door closed. "Of course you did."

"Of course I did," Kor agreed. He pointed to his room, which was one of the two on either side of the door, the other being mine. "That's my room, after all. You thought I wouldn't notice a hollow space on two sides of it?"

"How.... Never mind," Sarah said, stomping off to the kitchen. "Come on. If this is so darn urgent, let's get on with it."

Her temper was doing wonders for mine. It gave me yet another sign that maybe, just maybe, she was finally interested after all. If she was this mad with Kor....

Kor looked back at me with a smirk. *Sorry for interrupting.*

Torch it. Now I couldn't even punch him without admitting that he *had* been interrupting anything. And...admitting that I was mad that he had. I'd almost forgotten my resolve to not tell him I had changed my mind about Sarah. That was still the best policy with Kor, until and unless the Trees *and* Sarah said yes.

So as much as it killed me...I pretended not to be bothered. Though passing him by *sorely* tempted me.

Just one hit, a voice in my head wheedled. *Just one....*

But I kept my fists to myself and followed Sarah into the kitchen.

Yvera was already there, carefully avoiding eye contact with everyone as she ate a kalla fruit. I inwardly winced at what she must have thought of Sarah and me being somewhere alone together, but...I wasn't going to stop. I just wished there was something I could do to help her.

She was my friend, after all. Sister, practically...but I should stop thinking of her in that way if it bothered her so much. I guessed that was the one thing I *could* do.

"Thank you all for coming on such short notice," Kor said, making his entrance last. "I am certain you are all on pins and needles to know why."

For once, Yvera summed up all three of our sentiments when she said, "Cut the dramatics, Kor. Spill, or shut up and let me go to bed."

"Fine," Kor said, rolling his eyes. "For you, dear rightwing, I'll cut to the chase. The urgent matter is this: Olsdak Hold has formally invited Ben as the guest of honor at the Moonfair, and I think he should accept."

Silence. Yvera was incredulous, Sarah confused, and I....

"I am going to kill you," I said flatly. "*That* is your 'urgent' matter?"

Kor's eyes were wide with innocence. "They have given us the next deken to respond. It couldn't wait."

"Fine, then," I said, throwing up my hands. "Here's my response: *no.*"

I turned to find something I could beat the stuffing out of. Then, after getting in a more reverent frame of mind, find a private place to ask the Trees a long overdue question.

"Ah, Ben," Kor said. His voice was deadly serious now. "Once you've heard me out, you are going to accept. Trust me."

I paused. Turned. Then glared at him. "What can you possibly say that would possess me to accept an invitation to the *Moonfair, now*?"

Kor smirked. "What if I told you I am eighty percent certain that's the next moongate location?"

We all stared at him, and his smirk only widened.

He lived for these moments.

"Do I have your attention now?"

I took a deep, calming breath. "But the others have all been remote locations, Kor. Olsdak is..."

The second-largest hold on Oshal, and its cultural heart. But I didn't need to tell Kor that. It was his ancestral home, the hold of his birth—as familiar and beloved to him as Crownhold was to me.

If I didn't know better, I would have thought Kor was letting his fondness for Olsdak cloud his judgment. But I *did* know better, so I bit back the comment. If I accused my scholarly leftwing of bias, especially before hearing his evidence, he would bite my tail off.

"Ah," Kor said. "I have thought about that. Has anyone else thought it odd that Peacegrowth didn't get a world until *after* the Moontouched left, and yet there, on Ykran, we found the first moongate?"

Again, we just stared.

This time, Kor huffed and folded his arms. "Really? No one?"

Sarah raised her hand, like a polite student in a classroom. "Uh, I'm new here."

"You get a pass, Sarah," Kor said without looking at her. Instead, he glared at me. "Ben doesn't."

I...deserved that one.

I sighed. "What's your theory? In brief, please."

"In brief, it goes something like this: the Moontouched *always* knew they were going to leave."

Kor let that sink in for a moment.

"What?" Yvera snorted. "Nonsense. Even I know they left because the Lady—"

"That was the reason they gave. But the theory that makes the most sense is that somehow, they always knew it would come to that. How do I know this? Well, we have had abundant evidence by now that the Moontouched had, at least at some point, some kind of foresight. That's how they built and supplied this hold with technology we have only just invented ourselves or haven't yet. That's how they wrote Sarah's name on an archival that predates their departure—and *yes,* I have done tests on it to prove it."

Kor declared the last triumphantly. As if any of us were about to challenge him. He paused, then when none of us did, he huffed a bit and went on.

"So, with that kind of foresight, knowing that they would one day have to leave...they began to prepare immediately. Long before they actually did. Perhaps centuries before. Did you think this hold could have been built in a quick scramble in the aftermath of the Lady's assassination?"

He only paused slightly this time. "No! It would have taken years, at least. And that was after they even built a moongate to come to this world. Which would have required the help and approval of the Tree of Ice. Which means that even the Trees always intended for the Moontouched to leave!"

Kor paused to catch his breath.

In the silence, Sarah said numbly, "But...why?"

To even my surprise, I was the one to answer, quietly. "Because They knew. They knew that the other clans would never respect the Moontouched properly, they would never treat the amón as they deserved. They gave us our chance...but They prepared the Moontouched for when They knew we would ruin it."

"They may have known that, Ben," Kor said, softening to a surprising degree. "But...and I can't believe *I'm* the one saying this...the Trees know how to make flames from the coals. They also knew that we would reach this point again: the point of change or die. So, by removing the Moontouched for a time, They prepared for our salvation now. They took away the Moontouched...to allow them to change into what we need today."

Could that...be true?

"Alright, that's great," Yvera said impatiently. "But how does this relate to...anything?"

"Right," Kor said, taking a deep breath. "I got sidetracked, sorry. Being on the cusp of rewriting our entire history is getting me a bit excited."

"Rewriting our *entire* history?" I said.

Kor smirked at me. "Oh, *yes*. Because, you see...at least some of the Moontouched never left. In fact...I think most of them did not."

Silence.

"What?" I said flatly. Had Kor finally lost his mind?

"Stay with me," Kor said, smirk deepening. "Remember my paper on how drakón are now more widely distributed in the population?"

"Yes...." I said uncertainly.

"That required me to pour through an obscene number of bloodlines. But it meant that I noticed a trend: a lot of the bloodlines with the heaviest concentrations of amón began at the same time. The time..."

He paused for dramatic effect. "...around the Moontouched departure. Now, I know what you are thinking—or should be, if you were keeping up. 'But Kor,' you say. 'Records were spotty back then. Blood registrations were only just beginning to be standardized and made mandatory. Plenty of people were registered for the first time during that century.' And you would be right. Except for one thing: these amón-heavy bloodlines that I was noticing often had *an exact match* with one of the Moontouched records we have. An exact match...except for the last generation."

Kor grinned triumphantly, waiting for...a gasp, or applause, or something.

His face fell when it didn't come. "Really? You all *still* don't see it?"

"OK," Sarah said. "Since I'm the new one, I'm not afraid to say it: What?"

Kor groaned. "Alright. Maybe if I explain in terms even an Earthren can understand, these two dimtorches will finally get it."

"Hey," Yvera said irritably.

"Look," Kor said, pulling out his stylus. He went over to the kitchen wall and began frantically drawing.

While we watched him scribble, I thought hard about what Kor had said so far. I think I almost had it. I caught a glimpse of what he was saying. It was just so...*enormous* that I wanted to know for sure. I needed every bit of Kor's evidence and logic before I would accept the same leap.

When he had something he was satisfied with, he pointed to the first diagram. It was a shape that I and even Yvera were well familiar with: a single line at the bottom that branched as it rose into two, then those two branches split again, and those four branches split again. Kor had stopped there, probably for the sake of time.

"Sarah, this is a bloodtree. Does that mean anything to you?"

"Oh!" Sarah gasped. "That's why it looked familiar. It's a family tree. You've just made it more...tree-like."

"Excellent," Kor said with relief. "That makes this next part easier."

He tapped the first bloodtree again, this time on the branches. "You see these runes?"

"I can't read those," Sarah said.

"You don't need to for this purpose," Kor said dismissively. "Just know that each of them represents a clan. Can you see how this bloodtree represents a *unique* heritage for *this* person?"

He tapped the trunk of the bloodtree.

"I...guess?" Sarah said hesitantly. "Are you sure that combination couldn't happen twice?"

"A blood*tree* like this is just a shorthand representation of a blood*line*. In other words, the bloodtree has the barest of details that someone can draw by hand. Just trust me when I say that the original blood*line* has far richer detail that uniquely identifies each branch, and therefore—" he tapped the trunk "—the person in question."

Sarah nodded slowly. "OK. Like a DNA test. I can accept that."

"Say this represents a Moontouched bloodtree. We actually have quite a few of them in our records. Relative to the clan size, Moontouched were some of the swiftest and most compliant adopters of the blood registration practice, before it even became a mandate. So, surprisingly, we estimate that *most* of the Moontouched clan is accounted for somehow in our blood archives."

"Blood...archives?" Sarah said, making a face.

"Another time," Kor said, holding up a finger. Which he then tapped on the trunk. "This person—let's call him Haman—is a Moontouched. Because we always thought Haman left for Earth, our bloodtree for him ends here. No descendants of Haman that we know of. Are you with me?"

"Yes," Sarah said firmly.

Kor pointed to the second diagram.

"This is a bloodtree that goes both ways. These are the ancestors—" He tapped the branches above the trunk. Then he tapped the roots below. "—and these are the descendants."

"Got it."

"*In our records*, this person is identified as 'Aman.' Aman lived at the same time as Haman. At *exactly* the same time. Yet, because he is 'Starkissed,' he is fully accounted for, backward and forward, all the way to today."

Sarah's eyes were widening. Even she was catching on now.

Yet, since Kor had started this, he was going to finish it. He was about to give the final flourish, after all.

"If these were two different people—Haman and Aman—there would be differences in the ancestor portion of their blood trees. Yet, if you lay them over each other, like so...."

Kor dragged the first diagram over the second. Since I had already seen this conclusion coming, I had the mental capacity to appreciate how brilliantly Kor had drawn each chart. Even freestyling, even in a hurry, he had made them...

To overlap torched near perfectly, runes and all.

In case the conclusion was not now self-evident, Kor turned back to us and pointed. "These are *not* two different people. *Haman*...is Aman. *Aman* was not...or at least was not *born*...Starkissed. But he died one."

Again, silence. This time...judging from his smug expression, it seemed to be the kind Kor could appreciate.

"How is that possible?" Sarah asked with a frown. "Can you change your clan?"

"Drakón can't," I said quietly.

"But amón *can*," Kor added.

"And most of Moontouched by then was amón," Sarah finished in a murmur, eyes wide.

Kor's eyes glimmered. "Precisely. This is not an isolated instance. I first noticed a few cases, and then I and my scribes began searching for more. As of today, we think we have found a match for *eighty percent* of our Moontouched records."

"Eighty," I breathed. "Flame Above and Below. This...changes everything."

Then my eyes narrowed at the familiar percentage. "Wait, when you said you were *eighty* percent certain—"

"I'm getting to that," Kor said. "Don't you dare interrupt my dramatic conclusion. Because you're right. This changes *everything*."

He paused, making sure all eyes were on him. "The Moontouched *never left*. Not entirely. Not even mostly. Only the ones who could not hide themselves went to Earth. The rest disbanded, scattered across the Six Realms, and joined other clans. Oh, they were smart about it. They always went to a different world than the one they were first registered on, and usually they resettled in the remotest parts of those worlds that they could."

"The remotest parts...." Sarah breathed.

Kor smirked at her. "All the better to blend in, you see. Those were the regions that were most likely to not already be registered. The most likely to not care too much where you had come from and why you wanted to join their clan when you got there. The areas with the faintest records of population numbers, where a spike would not be noticed even by scholars studying for centuries afterward. The places where no one would notice them quietly continue to build moongate after moongate, and perhaps even continue to help with the work on this hold. The only clue they left behind as to where they had gone—and they were so careful about everything else that it *must* be a deliberate clue—"

He pointed to the bloodtree. "—is their bloodlines."

And, of course, no one had noticed the patterns in those bloodlines un-til...Kor. Because no one else besides Kor had bothered to study the *amón* ones. At least not in such depth. And no one else had his brilliance to see the first few patterns.

"Kor...." I said, shaking my head.

"Say it," he said with a grin. "You know I've earned it."

He had, so I said it.

"You're a torched genius."

"Alright, this is great," Yvera said flatly. "Moontouched descendants are among us. Yay. But *why* am I staying up for this?"

"As I said in the very beginning," Kor said innocently. "Because of the dead-line for Ben to respond to the Moonfair invitation, which is due in about half a deken now. It isn't my torched fault it's taking this long to convince Ben to say yes. He could have just trusted me, told me to send whatever reply I thought was best, and you all would have been on your merry way. But no."

I pointed to the bloodtree. "You still haven't explained what all of this has to do with that."

"I'm getting there. Now, I said that the Moontouched usually resettled in remote regions. But we have so far found one very notable exception."

I suddenly saw it.

"Let me guess," I said flatly. "Olsdak."

"Indeed," Kor said, looking at the bloodline fondly. "After all, the Starkissed always *were* the greatest allies of the Moontouched, which is perhaps why such a concentration dared settle together there. In fact, the founder of the hold, Olsdak herself, was...."

"Let me guess," I said with a sigh. "Moontouched."

"The daughter of one, since Olsdak *was* drakón, so she must have been Starkissed at least by the time of her becoming. But from how she sheltered so many Moontouched under her wing, you could say she did not forget her roots."

"But what makes you think that just because so many settled there that they broke their pattern to build a *moongate* there?"

"Because the Olsdak Moontouched were among the *first* migrators. Before the assassination, in fact. Think about it. What would they need to build the first moongate? Allies. A secure, secret location, but with access to resources, artisans, sophisticated tools.... And *a* lot of magic users. A greater concentration than the Moontouched normally had, with so few drakón among them—and after the assassination, the Moontouched drakón left."

I sighed. "All of that...pointing to Olsdak not just being a good place to check for a moongate, but that Olsdak is likely to have been the *first* moongate, perhaps created before even the assassination."

"Believe it or not," Kor told Sarah. "I had a logical reason for suggesting we go to my home realm first. I already had my suspicions by then, but the past few days of my and my scribes' research have only strengthened it."

"I won't say I'm sorry," Sarah said with a raised eyebrow.

"Oh, I'm not asking you for an apology. This way is better. This way...our arrival can be timed for the Moonfair."

"Kor," I groaned. "The Moonfair is the absolute *worst* time of the entire year for me to visit Olsdak."

"You mean the *best*," Kor smirked at me. "Think about it, Ben. Just think. What other time in the next six days are you going to be able to snoop around Olsdak without looking like you're snooping? Because...you've been invited."

That gave me pause. There...really was no other time I could go. Not in the next six days. If I turned down the invitation, I couldn't exactly show up a few days earlier or later and say, *Excuse me, my Crown business that has me rocketing around too much to attend your sacred festival has taken me here outside of it. Don't mind me poking around in dark corners looking for a thousand-year-old moongate.*

I had thought that the one good thing about this mad rush of a quest was that I would be able to turn down the invitation this year guilt free.

And now....

I moaned, putting my head in my hands.

"In case that isn't enough to convince you, I have other reasons," Kor said.

"I tremble to know what they are," I said with a sigh as I lowered my hands.

"Don't worry *too* much. I saved the most important for first. But there is the fact that you missed last year."

"I had krathenis!"

Kor narrowed his eyes. "Which I almost think you got on *purpose*."

My eyes darted away from his, and my cheeks warmed.

"Ben!" Yvera exclaimed.

"I won't do it again," I muttered. "Don't worry. I learned my lesson."

To my intense surprise, the unending agony of krathenis was *slightly* worse than being the centerpiece of the Moonfair. Slightly, but enough.

"Whatever the reason, you missed," Kor said. "Now it's more important than ever to the Starkissed that you go. The King won't be able to this year, for obvious reasons, so Crown representation falls to you."

"They don't care about Avva for the Moonfair, anyway," I muttered.

Not the old widower. All they cared about was having *me*, the bachelor Heir, for their torched *pageant*.

"What is—" Sarah began.

But Kor spoke at the same time and held the stage. "And there's a final reason, Ben. Right now, your public image needs a bit more...humanizing."

I blinked. "Why?"

"Oh," Sarah breathed.

I looked at her. If even Sarah could immediately understand....

"Ben, the only thing the Realms are talking about right now is the fact that you turned into a berserk, nearly mountain-sized draká. *At night*. And then challenged the Devourer itself."

I gaped. "I did *what*?"

"You don't remember?" Yvera asked incredulously.

"No," I said numbly. "My memories are...spotty. What did I *say*?"

Kor began reciting, no doubt from near perfect memory, his deadpan voice a stark contrast to the words. "'I defy you, Devourer. Send your legions. Send your lish. I will destroy them all. I will avenge her death on you a hundredfold.'"

Sarah started at the last words, as if they were new to her.

"I said that?" I said numbly.

"Projected it with your inner voice for elden," Kor said flatly.

That kind of projection should not have been possible, but since it was hardly the most shocking revelation right now, I didn't even think about it.

His quotation struck chords of familiarity in my mind...but in a much different key now.

Now they filled me with horror.

"Oh. That..."

...had been perhaps the most recklessly idiotic thing I had ever done.

I was a dead man.

Of course, in six days...we might *all* be dead. So perhaps I wasn't in much *more* danger than everyone else....

I looked at Sarah. "Why didn't you tell me?"

"I told you to ask Kor for the details," Sarah said, biting her lip. "I wasn't there. I didn't hear that."

"We'll talk later, Ben," Kor said impatiently. "Long and hard, trust me. But right now, we only have about a quarter of a deken to respond before they find someone else to take your place."

"His place for what?" Sarah asked.

Kor ignored her and pressed on, feeling me begin to cave. "You have been so much out of the public eye for the past year. They all know you're doing secretive, dangerous things. And now *this*. And they're understandably nervous—for you and about you. Right now, they need to see you, Ben. *This* you. Not the Ben who is protecting them. The Ben who is one of them."

I looked at Sarah. She gazed back at me soberly.

This is your choice, she whispered silently to me.

I tried to hide my start at hearing her in my head. So that hadn't been a onetime thing, or something she could only do in the most pressing of circumstances. Now she had an inner voice....

At least with me.

You have nothing to prove to them, she continued. *And nothing to prove to me. Only do this...if you want to prove it to yourself.*

Prove to myself...that I was no monster. Surrounded by practically half the Starkissed clan and a good fraction of all the others, all descended on Olsdak for the fair. With everyone staring at me, more convinced than ever that's what I was.

Could I...do that?

Perhaps...I needed to find out.

I took a deep breath, nodded slightly to her, then looked at Kor.

With the grimness of someone accepting a duel to the death, I said, "Alright. Tell them...yes."

CHAPTER TWENTY-SIX

WON

SARAH

THIS MOONFAIR THAT HAD both Kor and Ben so worked up (in opposite ways)...was in two nights.

Ben was not happy about that fact. He paced the kitchen in agitation the entire brief time Kor was gone to call whoever he had to talk to in order to give Ben's acceptance, and as soon as Kor got back, the two of them picked up right where they left off.

"Kor, you realize that will mean *two* of our remaining days spent just...."

"What?" Kor challenged. "Recovering? *Breathing*? Getting some torched sleep? And don't you think you've gotten the least of us, Ben. You don't know how many night deken I have burned to keep up with the pace you've set us and do my job to help you. Speaking of which, those two days will be a Flamesend for my and Eskala's analysts to continue identifying the most likely locations of the two moongates *after* Oshal. Not a second of those two days will be wasted by anyone, Ben. Including you and Sarah."

"Us?" I asked in surprise. And hoped that the warmth in my cheeks didn't show. A silly reaction, since I was ninety-five percent certain Kor wasn't suggesting anything romantic.

But...the momentary smirk Kor sent me didn't entirely rule that out, either. After all, Kor never seemed to have only one reason for what he did.

But that look had only lasted for a second before Kor returned his attention to Ben, expression once again grim. "Yes, the two of you. Ben, surely you've realized by now that you need to give Sarah more training. I hate to say it, but the danger to her is only going to increase."

Ben sighed. "I have."

"So," Kor said, "if these two days—one day, really, since we'll have to spend much of the second at Olsdak—of training her are what keeps her *alive* for the rest of them...are they a waste?"

Ben didn't even hesitate now.

"No," he said grimly.

Kor softened. "I know you're anxious and frustrated at the delay. But I promise you, everyone who can be trusted with the secret of the moongates at this point is doing double shifts to ease our way. If anything, this 'delay' might just save us time and danger. Yvera has even begun directing your elite on protective measures for Sarah for the next three realms."

Ben looked at her, startled. "You have?"

"Don't look so surprised," Yvera grumbled. But she didn't meet his eyes. "It's my job."

She stood abruptly. "Whatever else you have to say, Kor, it can wait until tomorrow. I'm going to bed."

As we watched her go, spine rigid and stride long, I thought, *That...was another apology.*

It fit all of Ben's criteria, anyway.

"Though it pains me to say it...Yvera has a point," Kor said reluctantly. "You...*we all* should go to bed. Even you, Ben."

"I'm not tired," he said mulishly. "I've slept all day, and...."

His eyes couldn't seem to help a dart toward me.

"Try it," Kor answered with a raised eyebrow. "I think if you lie back down, you would be surprised. No matter how much energy Sarah has given you, I highly doubt you can rely on it as a replacement for sleep."

Ben and I both stared at him.

"What?" Kor said. As a sign of just how tired he was, he didn't even smirk. "You think I can't put two things together? Go to bed, you two."

But, as he turned away, he couldn't seem to help sending one last silent tease to me.

Preferably, together.

Then he left. Leaving Ben and me alone.

"Well...." I said brilliantly. Then, in a desperate scramble for anything to come after that, I said, "What's a Moonfair?"

Ben groaned. "It's a seven-day festival that celebrates Oshal's lunar new year. It's the most...*enthusiastically* celebrated Starkissed holiday. And they love their holidays."

"So...." I said, trying to get to the heart of what Ben's problem with it was. "Lots of people?"

"Thousands," Ben said grimly. "Starkissed come from across Oshal to Olsdak to celebrate, and a fair number from other clans, too—because everyone knows no one throws a party like the Starkissed do, and this is *the* Starkissed party. Half the reason the hold is so big is to accommodate the crowds. It has the most guest rooms of any hold, and the permanent residents don't seem to care that they mostly stay empty when a festival isn't going on."

"Is that why you didn't want to go?"

Because something was clearly eating at him, making him reluctant even after he knew that was where—and when—we *had* to go. And his dislike wasn't anything new, if he had gone to such desperate measures to get out of it last year. I didn't know what krathenis was, but if it was enough to take a drakón like Ben down for the count, and he'd given it to himself on purpose....

Ben hesitated. Then, to my surprise, his cheeks started pinking. "The crowds would have been bad enough. Especially since we're trying to keep you out of the public eye. What Kor's plan about that is, I have no clue, but he no doubt has one."

"Then...?" I was baffled by the growing heat in his face.

Ben gritted his teeth. "Starkissed are...the ultimate romantics. The reason the Moonfair got started at all is because of a ridiculous play written by their most beloved writer centuries ago, and the kickoff event of the fair is a...sort of abbreviated version of it—a pageant. And of course, they like no one better to play one of the two central characters than...me."

I blinked. Then a laugh escaped before I could suppress it. Fortunately, Ben didn't seem to mind. "*You*?"

Ben sighed, even as he went almost entirely red. "Rather...an unmarried Golden Heir. Because that's what the romantic interest in the play was. So, by their logic, *who better* to fill the role than..."

I grinned. "The actual Heir."

The fact that Ben was being dragged into playing the role of a leading man in a romantic play wasn't bothering me nearly as much as I thought it might have. Most of that was because of Ben's obvious, excruciating reluctance. But at least a part was because...I kind of wanted to see that now. Just to giggle at Ben's adorably awful, unwilling reenactment.

Far from being offended, Ben seemed a bit relieved at my amused reaction. He managed a faint smile. "As you've probably guessed, I'm always torched terrible at it. I keep hoping each year that they'll give up on me and ask someone else, but...either the symbolism means too much to the planners...or they're sadistic. I haven't figured out which."

I grinned further. "If they're anything like Kor...it could be both."

"True," Ben agreed darkly. "If you ask me, it's almost too convenient that Kor found a way to pin me down for it this year. I thought for sure I could pass."

"Sorry," I said with a chuckle. "What happens if the real-life Heir is married? Or female?"

"They don't care about the gender," Ben said dismissively. "The original character *is* male, but they're happy to swap the genders of the leads for the sake of the pageant production. In fact, if I had been attracted to men...which I'm not, by the way..."

He grew red again.

Then, when I just kept grinning, he cleared his throat and finished. "...they would have been happy to accommodate that too for the sake of a more 'authentic connection,' or whatever the torched ashdust that means. No, the only line they won't cross is if the Heir is engaged or married. Something about that 'authentic connection' again. In that case, they get someone else to play the part until there's an available Golden Heir of marriageable age again."

"And what's that?" I asked curiously. "Marriageable age, I mean?"

Asking for a friend.

Ben rubbed his neck, looking away. "Customarily, nineteen, but as young as sixteen summers with the clan's Tree's permission."

So, I had a couple more months, unless I wanted to ask a Tree....

Wait.... What was I *thinking*?

Fortunately, Ben seemed oblivious to my minor inner crisis. "So...guess how long I've had to do this."

I smiled, adding in some sympathy now. "Since you were sixteen."

Ben groaned. "Yes. Four *years*. Well...I suppose, technically three. But I had to face the dread of it last year until I found a way out, so I count that one too. And now...this will be the fifth."

Only just in time, I stopped myself from saying, *Maybe you won't have to do a sixth.*

Where had that audaciousness come from? I, Sarah Lind, *flirting*? Much less so...presumptuously? What the heck had gotten into me?

All I knew was that between Kor's insidiously premature pushes and Ben's seemingly unconscious pulls...I was going crazy.

And on that note, I stood up and stretched with hopefully believable—yet not *too* believable—casualness. "Well...Kor is right. I had better...go to bed...now."

I could not believe what I was doing. But I couldn't seem to stop, either.

For better or for worse, Ben didn't seem to catch on. His focus was on something else now, and he nodded to me absently. "Good idea. Get some rest. That way you'll be all the more prepared for training tomorrow."

I was more relieved than disappointed. I wasn't thinking clearly right now, anyway. Better take a bit more time.... Not to mention, start slower.

But I paused as I passed him and asked sternly, "Are *you* going to bed?"

He smiled thinly. "Soon, I promise. There's just...something I have to do."

At my pointed look, he chuckled. "It's something important that I've put off, and if I don't do it now...I might lose the courage. I'll go to bed after, I promise."

"Alright, I suppose that's good enough," I said with a smile. Then I gave him a hug, as I might with any sibling. "Goodnight, Ben."

He wrapped his arms around me, and to my surprise, kissed the crown of my head.

Was that...a friend thing?

"Safe sleep, Sarah," he said quietly. "I...."

I tried very hard not to freeze, to just remain calm and content in his arms. But...with my head against his chest, I could feel his flameheart...and it seemed to be throbbing nearly as fast as mine.

"I am very glad you're alright," he said finally. "You're right: you are important to me. Thinking you were...gone, and that I had failed you, was perhaps the most pain I've ever felt."

My throat tightened, and I didn't know what to say. But I had to try.

"You didn't fail me," I said finally.

He pulled me up and crushed me in. "Yes, I did. But *you* didn't fail *me*, you strong, brave young woman."

I could hardly breathe...for more than one reason. But I never wanted him to let me go.

He truly thought...I was strong. And maybe, just maybe...I was.

"YOU SEEM QUIET," I said to Ben.

We were finishing up breakfast. He had been in the middle of making a Thanksgiving meal's worth of food when I woke up and wandered through the kitchen to the bathrooms. (Really, one of the main things tempting me at this point to use my "special" room was the convenient personal bathroom.)

By the time I had my shower and changed and came back, he was setting it all out on the table. Fortunately, he didn't seem to expect me to gorge and let me serve myself, making no comments to get me to eat more. In fact, he had seemed unusually...subdued.

Ben looked up from his plate and blinked. "What? Oh, sorry. Just...thinking."

"Did you sleep?"

"Yes." Ben grimaced. "I hate it when Kor is right. Which...is most of the time. Did you? Sleep, I mean."

"Eventually," I said. I had spent far too much time tossing and turning, feeling the pull. It had gotten worse for a while...then, perhaps when Ben himself had fallen asleep, it mellowed enough for me to finally drift off.

Ben grimaced. "I'm sorry. I'm not sure how we're going to manage your night energy, but we'll think of something."

That hadn't been a problem, since he'd taken the worst of it off me. But I wasn't going to correct him. The pull was my problem; he was the cause, but since he seemed totally unaware of what he was doing, he wasn't at fault. Besides, I wasn't sure it was him at all; it could be reflecting *my* needs and desires more than his, despite what the gravitational direction made it seem.

It just made me glad that my gates were only "on" when I needed them to be.

To change the topic, I asked, "How did your...thing go last night?"

"Thing?"

"The...whatever you had to do before going to bed."

He looked away. "I...did it."

"Did it not go so well?" I asked gently.

He took an unusually long time to chew and swallow, and he still didn't meet my gaze when he answered, "It's done. That's the important thing."

With a forced attempt at cheer, he raised his head and said, "So...you ready for an exciting day of discovering what you can do?"

I laughed at how much he sounded like a tired summer camp leader. Although, even despite the lack of enthusiasm, half the girls would still have been up for any activity he was remotely a part of. Goodness, if he had *lifeguard duty*....

But I made myself focus and channel my own mock eagerness. "Yeeesss. So excited."

"Good, because I have some ideas."

"You do?" I asked in surprise.

He took a swallow of his tsha. "Yup. So brace yourself. And eat some more of the daka. It's good for you."

I smiled. That sounded more like the Ben I knew.

BEN STARTED ME OFF with target practice as a warmup, since that was something I was already familiar with. Fortunately, either Kor or Yvera had retrieved my gun for me from where they found it in the tunnel, and it was waiting for me in the training room again.

When I could nail the dead center of the target every time, Ben turned on multiple targets scattered across the entire wall; they alternated in some kind of random toggle mode, with the challenge being to shoot at the one that was currently on. Finally, he made the targets move.

And I don't mean just back and forth like a fair game: they bounced all over the place, and increased and decreased in size as they did so. That required more skill and focus than simply willing the shards into accuracy. At Ben's suggestion, I attempted to make them *follow* a target, like a heat-seeking missile. I got better, but I was still going to need more practice before I mastered the technique.

He then let me take a break—which was much needed, since I was the gun's battery, and my energy levels ran low quickly.

"Part of that is probably because it's day," Ben explained. "But you also need to increase your available stores by pushing your boundaries slightly further each time, just like how you build a muscle."

As he spoke, I took another swallow from the canteen he'd given me. Ben said he'd added something for energy and hydration, which explained the sweet, citrusy taste. Better tasting than an energy drink, in my opinion—and was probably healthier, too.

"Emphasis on how *I* build muscle," I teased, poking his biceps. "Do you drakón have to do *anything* for those?"

To my surprise, Ben cocked his head in confusion and said, "At first, yes."

I blinked. "Wait, what?"

He shrugged. "We have to build up our muscles the same way, too. Why do you think Kor is so much leaner? He simply hasn't bothered to do more. Other than our metabolism and healing, the primary advantage we drakón have is that once we gain the muscle, it can take years for us to lose it."

I stared at him, looking him up and down more boldly than I would have normally.

"What?" he said self-consciously.

I took an angry swig from my canteen. "OK, now the fact that you're so ripped is even more unfair *and* impressive—*at the same time.*"

"'Ripped'?" he said, repeating the word in English.

Strange. The translation magic in their blood normally interpreted my slang better.

My irritation popped like a bubble, and my cheeks grew warm. "Er...very...muscular. In an attractive way."

"I gathered that's what you meant. I just...." His cheeks were growing pink now, and he looked away hastily, hand on his neck.

I stared. Was he honestly so unaware of how he looked?

He clearly hadn't earned those muscles because of vanity or for the attention. Of course he hadn't—he hated attention. He had paid the price for them...to protect. To do his duty. When he would *rather* have appeared weaker and less imposing.

Man...just when I thought he couldn't get any hotter....

After an awkward pause, Ben—still going beet red—asked, "Well, ready to start on the next thing?"

"Sure!" I said hastily.

Even though I would have liked a little more of a breather, I knew I owed him one.

"Good. Because it's actually time to work on those muscles—and aerobic capacity—of yours. Catch me."

With that, he took off with all the grace and speed of an Olympic runner.

And I had missed the starting gun.

"Wait, what?" I cried.

"I have a lead now!" he shouted over his shoulder.

I moaned, but then started running after him.

Ben couldn't have been going at his full speed, but he still led me on a crazy chase through the entire hold (aside from the "secret" parts, probably only because he couldn't open the doors on his own and would have had to slow down because of his size in any case). He would dodge around things, jump over others, and even hurdle or push off them parkour-style, such as when he launched over my kitchen counter with only using one hand. All the while he would keep an eye on me and mentally instruct me how I was to do the same, with proper form—even if he often had to modify for me. For the kitchen counter, he let me use both hands to push up and swing one leg at a time.

How merciful of you, I shot at him silently, glad for the sake of my breath alone that I could now speak to him this way.

He only laughed.

Goodness, how I loved and hated the sound of that laugh at the same time. I didn't know if I had ever heard it so...alive.

Whenever I couldn't go anymore, he would stop a safe distance ahead, but he would insist that we weren't done. He would guide me through some stretches to keep me from freezing up, and as soon as I caught my breath, he would take off again.

I despaired of ever coming close to catching him. Even when I thought I had him cornered in the storage room, he merely ran around a shelf and zipped right back out before I made the first turn.

When we whizzed by the bathrooms, we passed Kor coming out of the men's side. I nearly crashed into him and only dodged just in time. By then, I was panting my lungs up through my throat and could only gasp, "Sorry! Gotta...get him."

"Kill him slowly!" Kor shouted after me. "Make him suffer!"

"She has to catch me first, Kor!" Ben said with a laugh.

How does he have the breath to laugh? I moaned to myself.

This was, by far, the strangest running lesson I had ever had. But also...by far the most fun.

Even if most of the time I felt like I really did want to kill him.

Which...might have been part of the point. After all, this was fun and games now. But...it wouldn't always be.

We had been through the rest of the hold at least twice by the time Ben risked leading me toward the Rose Room (*No, that's still not it....*), and then I thought I might just have him. But either my lights had finally misinterpreted one of my needs or they had gotten themselves into the same sadistic bent as Ben, because two of them left their light nests and floated down to open them.

Ben had slowed his pace—perhaps deciding what to do—but at the sight of the opening doors, he rushed forward once again.

Then I had a glimmer of an idea.

As we passed through the room, I pulled the cold of it into me with all my might. All I had been intending was to get a boost. But unexpectedly, the more I pulled, the more the temperature dropped. Even the few shadows there were in the room stretched themselves toward me. Ben stumbled in surprise.

Very good, he said as he ran out of the room. *Now see if you can do something with what you've gained.*

I felt a flare of anger. He hadn't said magic was allowed! *I thought this was about building muscle. And aerobic whatever.*

It is, but you've earned a bit of a cheat at the end.

Use it how?

It's your magic. Let it guide you.

That wasn't exactly the hint I was hoping for. Even if my magic was different, surely Ben had some ideas on how I could use it. But then again, this wasn't the time for deep theory. I wasn't going to have *time* to learn deep theory. The very next day, I could be in a situation in which I simply had to reach for my magic and *do* something with it. So, for better or for worse, gut was what I had.

As we raced through the long room with tiered seating, Ben said, *If you can catch me by the time we reach the training room again, I'll give you a prize.*

A...prize?

My mind went to last night.

And suddenly, I had all the power and motivation I needed.

I stared hard at his back. I thought about how much I wanted to reach him and let that desire fill my entire body. The pull suddenly increased tenfold, and my magic rose to answer the call.

And suddenly, it hit me. It had been so *obvious* I couldn't believe I hadn't seen it before.

Ben...was a gate.

Then it was almost too easy; in fact, it would have been difficult to stop myself. I responded to the pull by reaching for it.

In sharp contrast to my normal overthinking, I didn't consider how what I was doing might have been dangerous, how I might have spliced Ben and me together or knocked him over or hurt him somehow. The very thought of hurting him by doing this wasn't possible.

This felt too easy, too natural, too *inevitable*. Like finally stopping to resist the pull of gravity. Like finally taking wing.

And that's exactly what it felt like when I *blurred*. I had no other word to describe it. My vision became a tunnel, laser-focused on Ben's back as he dashed the last few yards to the training room. And then, everything I was became a silver blur as I surged, taking flight.

I became solid just in time to hit his back with a *thump* and instinctively wrapped my arms and legs around him to keep from falling.

The second before he stumbled into the training room.

Far from being shocked, far from being disappointed at his loss, Ben was....

"YES!" he shouted in a sound of pure, jubilant triumph that echoed in that stone room. He bent over slightly, fists clenched from the force of his celebratory energy. As if *he* had been the one to win.

"Yes, yes, *yes*, you brilliant, incredible woman!"

He pulled me effortlessly by my arms and shoulders—as if I weighed no more than a backpack—around and into his embrace, crushing me to his chest. But, I noticed, not so hard that I couldn't catch my breath.

"You...knew?" I panted.

"I *hoped*," he said with a joyous laugh. He shifted me up and moved his arms on me to support my lower half more as he leaned back so we could make eye contact. "You said I felt like a gate to you, so...."

I inwardly winced from the chagrin that he had figured it out long before I had. And...heaven help me, I hadn't ever seen him this happy before. He glowed—*literally*. More than just his eyes, his skin and his hair were taking on a sheen of light.

I...didn't think I had ever seen a more majestic sight in my entire life. It truly was like I was looking at an angel.

Thank goodness he would only think my breathlessness, heat, pounding heart, and sweat were from the run.

Because they were the only words that came to my short-circuited brain, I stammered, "Is *that*...what all of this...was about?"

He set me down—to my severe disappointment—with another laugh. "Not entirely. If all you got was some good conditioning, that would have been enough for me. I wasn't even sure you would have the spark for it right now. But when you pulled power from the ice room, like I'd hoped you could...."

Ice room again. It made it sound like a mundane *refrigerator*. I was really going to have to come up with a better name.

"You're a good loser," I said with a weak attempt at a smile. His glow was only just beginning to fade.

He shook his head with a chuckle. "I may have lost the chase, but I won *my* prize. Flame Above, Sarah. Don't you realize what this means? Now I can always find you, and you can always reach me."

"Maybe," I cautioned. "This will need a lot of testing. Distance, line of sight—"

He pulled me in for another hug. "I don't care about that right now. For the first time since I lost you, I feel like I can truly breathe again. It's a sign, Sarah. It's a sign that we can *do* this."

I didn't see how...but who was I to take that from him?

"Now," he said with a brilliant grin as he pulled away. Then got down on one knee. "Ready for *your* prize?"

I inhaled sharply. *No*....

When he pulled something gold out of thin air, my already overworked heart nearly had a heart attack.

But then he held it out between his thumb and pointer finger.

It was, most definitely, *not* a ring.

Of course it wasn't. Even *if* Ben were ever to propose, most likely dramá customs were different from mine. With savage force, I reined in my equal parts disappointment and relief and fixed my expression into one of—hopefully—curiosity.

It was a thick, gold, tear-drop oval, about the size and shape of the space in the middle of my fingers if I were to pinch my thumb and index finger together. It had a convex surface on the top, thickest in the middle, and a flatter surface on the bottom. Almost like a....

I stared. "Is that...one of your *scales*?"

"It is," he said with a smile, proffering it to me.

I took it with a reverence that it didn't deserve. I almost didn't even register the minor shock of power, like static electricity, I felt as I did so. "But it's so small."

He chuckled. "It's one of the first I ever shed. All the way back when I was a small, gangly twelve-summer. Soon after I became a drakón and the Heir in the same day."

I looked back up at him, feeling a bit dazed. He had given me...one of his first scales. From back when he had only just found out who he was and had to be, when he was feeling the weight of what all of that meant sink onto his much smaller, weaker shoulders....

Just like me.

The timing and the gift of the scale itself probably meant little to him.

But it meant everything to me.

Something in my eyes made him blush. "Normally, people prefer the largest scales possible for this, but I thought this one would be easier for you to keep in a pocket or something."

"For this?"

"For...calling," Ben said self-consciously. He shifted his fingers again, and another scale of his normal size appeared. "I...spelled them for you this morning, and that one in your hand imprinted on you as soon as you took it. Really, I'm a torched idiot for not giving you something like this sooner. I guess...I was overly optimistic that you wouldn't need it. I couldn't think of the alternative."

I inhaled sharply. "You mean...I can use this to call you? Whenever I want?"

"That's the idea," he said, blush increasing.

"*Thank you*," I breathed.

I couldn't help but throw my arms around him, lean back just enough to kiss him on the cheek, and pull in again.

Now...I could call him. Even after he left. Even if he never showed an interest in anything more than friendship, he still had at least offered me that: a connection that wouldn't die even when we were worlds apart.

Hadn't I just been thinking yesterday that this was one of the few things I had left to want? And now...I had it. And this was far better than anything Kor and I could have come up with using ice and lights. This came from Ben. He had literally given a piece of himself...to me.

I knew that didn't mean the same thing to him. That he had given out dozens, maybe even a hundred or more of his scales. That, to him, this gift was only a practical, friendly necessity. A sign of trust. A recognition for the need for communication. Just like giving me his phone number. That was all.

But if I kept his intent in mind and expected nothing more from him, I could treasure the scale all I wanted inside—and that was with my entire being. As pathetic as that might sound, I was past the point of caring.

I may have won the chase...but I had just lost my heart.

"You're welcome," Ben said, voice oddly tight.

Could he sense in even the slightest part what had just happened inside of me? Even if he did, judging from the way his arms tightened around me...he didn't seem to mind.

I pulled back sharply, a horrible thought occurring to me. "What if it doesn't work for me?"

Ben cleared his throat and spoke normally. "I'm sure it works for you. You may be of Ice, but you're also amón—one of us, in some way. The doorgems work for you, remember?"

I let out a breath of relief and nodded.

Ben continued. "And even amón can work call scales. It's just torched more inconvenient for them to carry them around. That's why I gave you such a small one. But here, let's try it out to make sure."

"How do I use it?"

"It's simple. I think I told you that once." He smiled as he looked away from the scale to meet my eyes for a moment, and I smiled back.

"All you have to do is hold that, give it a bit of power, and say my name."

"Ben? Or Koriben?" I asked, feeling a flutter of excitement. And nervousness. Oh, how I wanted this to *work*.

"Either is fine," Ben said. "Whatever feels most natural to you. The name isn't strictly necessary, actually—it's more of the intentional thought *of* me that counts, but people often find that easiest by saying a name out loud."

Heart pounding more than it should have after the rest I'd had, I held the scale up in front of me, gave it a drop of my power, and whispered, "Ben."

I didn't even have a moment to doubt. The golden scale immediately glowed.

"That means it's contacting mine," Ben said, holding up the scale in his hands, which had glowed at the same time. "Even if I have to put it away in my ether storage, I'll *feel* you calling."

He tapped his scale, and immediately the surface of the two scales changed to show the front-facing perspective of the other.

"It works!" I cried, unable to help a little jump of joy.

Ben chuckled. "See? Nothing to worry about. And easy as anything."

"How will I feel if you call me?"

Ben tapped the scale again to end the call. "Put the scale in a pocket or something."

I slipped it into the front pocket of my pants. Ben tapped his scale again, said, "Sarah," and it glowed. Immediately, I felt an awareness of the scale in my pocket, like a mental notification going off in my brain, and the thought of

Ben came to me—and the very faintest impression of his voice saying my name, so muted that I wasn't entirely sure I hadn't imagined it. But the rest of the indicators were clear enough.

"If you don't or can't answer at the moment, just ignore the feeling, and it will go away," Ben said. "Just try doing that now, for practice. Trust me, once you get enough scales...it will be necessary."

I chuckled wryly and pushed away the thought of Ben, as hard as that was. Then at least the magic part faded away, as did the glow on his scale, even if my thoughts immediately returned to him.

"If you *have* to concentrate," Ben said, "there's a way to block the feeling entirely, but I don't think we need to go over that right now. You only have that scale, and you should probably get the feel for it."

"Plus, if you're calling, it's important," I said.

His smile faded. "For a while. But...once this is all over, and you're comfortable enough in your role to kick me out, we can just...talk. About absolutely unimportant, nonurgent things. At least...I'd like that."

"So would I," I said quickly.

"Good," he said, standing. But there seemed to be some heaviness in his eyes that wasn't there before.

"Ben...." I said uncertainly.

"Nothing," he said, giving me a strained smile as he grabbed my dropped canteen and handed it to me. "Just...thinking about the invasion...and everything."

Then why won't you look at me? I wanted to ask. But was too afraid to.

I couldn't make sense of him. It sounded like he wanted to still be friends after everything. Good friends, in fact. What was wrong with that? That was probably just the slow and steady start we both needed to build something more, if *more* was ever going to be a possibility.

The fact that my heart would now shatter if it wasn't was beside the point. I knew...or thought I knew...how relationships were supposed to work. You could fall in love quickly, sure, especially in circumstances as strenuous as we had been through together. But that was exactly why my head was telling me we should take our time. Because there was more to choosing a partner for *life* than heart flutters and hair-raising danger. Until after, when the dust all settled, how would we truly know?

And yet, you know, a voice whispered inside.

I ignored it by taking a swallow from the canteen. But when it spoke again, I nearly choked.

You said you saw him, that you saw his heart. And that you aren't afraid of him. Are you going to make that a lie?

Now that I knew my heart was lost, was I suddenly afraid of Ben, in an entirely different way? The next time he needed me to look into his eyes and say it, *could* I?

I gritted my teeth. *Yes. He would never mean to hurt me.*

But he could. In a far greater way now than merely killing me.

And suddenly, that was more terrifying than anything.

"Excellent!"

Ben and I both turned in surprise to see Kor striding into the room. "Looks like you two are finished running about like gigal that got into the sundew."

Heedless of my sweat, Kor threw his arm around my shoulders and winked at me. "That means it's my turn."

"Your turn?" I asked in surprise.

"I asked Kor to help you work on your magic," Ben said. Although from his scowl, it looked as if he were regretting that decision.

Then I saw Ben's eyes dart to Kor's arm.

Feeling warm, I started stepping away, but before I could do more than shift slightly, Kor swung me around and began leading me out the door, never relinquishing his hold. If anything, he walked too close for my comfort.

"Don't worry, Ben!" he said with a smirk over his shoulder. "I'll bring her back in one piece in a deken or two. Although, who knows? She might prefer *my* teaching style to yours."

"Watch yourself, Kor," Ben snapped. "Sarah, if he gives you any trouble, tell me."

"Ah, come on, Ben," Kor called back in a mock wounded tone. "She likes me!"

"Kor, what are you doing?" I hissed.

I didn't look, but I could almost *feel* Ben's eyes searing holes through Kor.

Just trust me, Kor said, smirking.

"You always say that to me right before you're about to do something I really don't like."

We were far enough away by now that Kor risked a whisper. "But it's always for your own good in the end, don't you agree?"

"No!"

"How short-sighted. I'd hoped for better from you, at least. Ah, well. A leftwing's work is never truly appreciated."

"And how is *this* part of your job?" I shook his arm off and gave him a shove.

Kor gave me a sidelong look. "Think about it, Sarah. Think really hard about why you should be thanking me right now."

Then it finally hit me. I groaned and put a hand over my eyes. "Your 'plan.' The one that requires me to be attracted to you. You aren't trying to tick Ben off for making me uncomfortable. You...are trying to make Ben *jealous.*"

"*There,*" he said with a grin, tapping my forehead. "I told you that you would figure it out quickly. Now, before Ben comes after us, go dry off. Don't shower, just get dry. Then meet me on this side of the Oculus."

I blinked. "The what now?"

Kor raised an eyebrow. "The room of ice."

"Why did you call it an 'oculus'? In *English*?"

Kor shrugged. "If it's in your language, you can tell me why it's called that better than I can tell you. That's just what the archival said it was called."

I groaned. "You've accessed the archivals."

He scowled. "Don't get your tail in a knot. I haven't accessed anything. That's what the original message to you called it."

I blinked. "It did?"

Kor just groaned, so I supposed I had to just trust that his memory was better than mine. Or go check that message again, if it was still there.

Oculus. I tasted the word. And scowled when I had to admit that it fit. I didn't know why, but....

Kor's smirk returned at my expression. "You're welcome. Now, like I said, go get dry, and meet me at the west entrance."

I gave him a baleful look. "And then we're going to do what?"

Kor was all innocence now. "Practice your magic of course. In the most obvious place—for you—where we would do such a thing. The thickness of the walls, the inability of anyone but you to open the doors, and the nauseatingly thick spells against eavesdroppers are entirely coincidental in my choice of location."

I groaned. "This is 'the talk,' isn't it?"

Kor winked. "Come and find out."

Chapter Twenty-Seven

PUSH

Sarah

"What *is* an oculus, if you don't mind me asking?" Kor said as the doors slowly swung shut behind us. He stared up at the ice-rose skylight in interest.

He was wearing a thick coat to ward off the chill. I had grabbed the one Svyer had given me but was waiting for me to be cold enough to put it on.

"I...don't exactly remember," I said with a frown. "Something about a lens, I think? I didn't bring a dictionary with me, so I can't look it up, sorry."

"Ah," Kor said sagely. "That's why the meaning didn't come through when you said it."

I looked at him in surprise. "Your blood only translates the words *I* know?"

"Of course," Kor said, tapping my head meaningfully. "Because the translation comes from here, silly."

"Of course," I said dryly. "Silly me."

He chuckled and began walking around, examining the recent additions above three of the pillars. "Ykran, Yonvey, Romskal. Fascinating. Clearly representing the three gates we have already found."

"Ah," I said. "Yes. I knew that."

Kor stood in the center of the room, and thus the seven pillars, and looked around slowly. "The others must be for the other realms. All seven, so it must count this one."

"Not Earth?" I asked, curiosity piqued despite myself.

Kor shook his head slowly. "No, I don't think you are meant to rule Earth, Sarah."

"Why do you think that? Not that I *want* to rule Earth, mind you. Or...anything, really."

"Earth already has her children. From all that I have studied about Trees, They are very particular about giving each kind of child stewardship only over themselves. You are not meant to be human, Sarah. Therefore, you are not meant to rule over humans. You must be given your *own* world, and so you have been."

"Oh," I said, surprised by the simple logic of it. And unable to help a pang of loss.

Not meant...to be human. I hadn't thought of these changes that had already taken place inside of me quite like that before—as a loss of humanity. Before, I had only compared myself to the drakón and despaired at how much less I had than them, at how much harder it was for me to keep up, at how much more vulnerable I was. I hadn't thought about what I no longer shared with my birth species....

If they had ever been mine to begin with.

All disconcerting thoughts and feelings, to say the least.

Did I really *want* to keep changing? Did I really want to give up the only people and planet I had ever known for the most formative years of my life...forever? If I did, what *was* I? And what did giving it up say about me?

I didn't have an answer.

Nor did Kor let me find it.

"Nevertheless, despite your sovereign world, and your origins from Earth, and your allegiance to the Tree of Ice, the Trees still seem to include you with the Six Realms. Curious, isn't it?"

"Let me guess," I said dryly. "You have a theory."

"All in good time," Kor said with a distracted wave. "Hmm...the formation of the pillars is almost like a seven-pointed star.... See?"

I stood where Kor did and followed his finger. With no lines in place, and looking at it from the side instead of above, I had difficulty holding the shape in my head, but I could almost see it.

"What does that mean?"

Kor smiled slowly. "The symbol of the Moontouched was a seven-pointed star over a dark moon."

"A dark one?" I asked in surprise.

"The banner was black, the moon outlined in white but left black inside. Only the star was solid white."

"Huh," I said, thinking about that.

I felt like there was some significance there. What with the *Moon*touched name and all, I would have figured a brighter and fuller moon, the better. Then why use a dark one in their symbology?

Then again...had I ever gotten any power from the moon *itself*? Or was it from something...else?

I felt like I was just on the cusp of understanding something huge, something crucial, when Kor unknowingly interrupted once again.

"Well, thank you for indulging me in a few dek of examination," he said, clapping my shoulder. "I couldn't resist."

"Since this is one of the few places in the hold that you can't snoop around without me," I said dryly.

"Alas, yes," Kor said with a sigh. "You really *will* have to help me with the archivals at some point, but Ben will not give you time for that for some days to come. Speaking of *Ben*, though...."

I groaned and covered my face with my hands.

Kor snorted. "You were the one who asked me about him."

"Yes, I know," I said, lowering my hands. "It's just...I can't believe it's come to this. Going to *you* for advice on Ben."

"I'm hurt. My dear Sarah, I am a leftwing of the Golden Crown. It is my *job* to give Ben, and by extension, you, advice on these matters."

"Somehow," I grumbled, "that makes it worse."

Kor sobered and put his hand on my shoulder. "Then pretend I am a friend—which, I really am, by the way, no matter what you might think of me."

"I consider you a friend too," I said with a sigh.

"Excellent," Kor said, giving my shoulder a squeeze. "Now, asking strictly as a friend...how are things going between you and Ben?"

His expression remained sober and eyes unusually kind, which helped more than I cared to tell him. He always disarmed me when he got like this, dang it. Threw off the act and became...a friend.

"Going?" I said, cheeks warm. "That...kind of implies that there's something to *go*, doesn't it?"

Kor blinked. Then frowned. "What do you mean?"

I took a deep breath. "I mean, *nothing* is going on between Ben and me. Nothing more than what you've seen. We're friends. That's it."

Kor let go of my shoulder and took a step back. "Friends," he repeated.

"Yes, friends," I said again, pain lashing through me. I folded my arms to hold myself together, though my eyes stung dangerously. "Ben has never done or said anything but—"

Kor held up a hand. A muscle twitched in his jaw. "Wait. Nothing? He hasn't even *kissed* you?"

I glared daggers at him. "He might have come close. Once. Maybe. But you know what happened? Some *genius* decided to interrupt about an 'urgent' invitation to a Moonfair!"

Kor blinked. "I.... Well, that was not my best timing."

All the anger abruptly drained out of me. After all, I was assuming that I had even been reading Ben right. But at the very least, if Kor hadn't interrupted, I would have an answer.

That would have been better than nothing.... Right?

"You think?" I said wearily.

Kor abruptly shook his head, as if just waking up. "Wait, *what*? What were you two even *doing* all that time you were all cozily shut away?"

My cheeks warmed. "Talking. What did you think we were...?"

"More than talking!" Kor snapped. "More than just kissing, in fact!"

My jaw dropped. "Wait, you honestly thought...."

Kor shook his finger at me. "Oh, don't you think Ben doesn't want to do that with you. Because he most certainly *does*."

"I...." And only got that far before my mind short-circuited. "*What?*"

Kor moaned. "I cannot believe this. I cannot believe Ben...."

He paced away, running his hands through his hair.

My heart felt like it was being wrung like a towel. "Please, Kor. Don't say these kinds of things to me."

Kor paused, took a deep breath, and visibly calmed himself. "Apologies. That was unprofessional. But also, because I'm being your friend right now...I'm torched mad on your behalf that Ben is doing this to you. To *both* of you."

I took deep, painful breaths. "Ben isn't.... Kor, this is my problem. My fault. I just need to either be patient or give up. Just like Yvera."

Kor had calmed to the point that kindness had reentered his eyes. He came back to me, and this time, he grasped both my shoulders.

When I wouldn't meet his eyes, he said, "Sarah, look at me."

Reluctantly, I did. The depth of compassion in those sapphire eyes was even more painful for how rare a sight it was. "Do you trust me? I mean, *actually* trust me?"

"Trust you how?" I rasped. I was seconds from tears now.

Kor answered gently. "Trust me to know Ben as only his years-long friend and leftwing could know him? And if you can't trust me, I can bring Yvera into this, too, because she knows this part just as well as I do."

I laughed shakily. "You bring Yvera into this, and she'll just answer by running me through."

"As if I would let her," Kor said, with only the tiniest of smirks. Which quickly died. "Do you trust me? If I swear I am saying nothing but the objective truth, will you believe me?"

I looked into his eyes, and as mine finally overflowed, I nodded.

"Agh, Sarah," Kor sighed. He pulled me into his arms and tucked my head against his chest. "It *will* be alright. I promise. You know why?"

"Why?" I whispered.

"Because...Ben loves you."

I froze.

Kor must have felt it, because he insisted softly, "That is the absolute truth, Sarah. I will swear it before the Tree of Flame Herself. And I *don't* mean 'as a friend.'"

How could *Kor*...be so wrong?

"But Kor...." I said thickly. "If he...."

"Yes, fair question, isn't it? But this is *Ben*, Sarah. I'm sorry to say it, but you could not have picked a man who would be more determined to break his own heart rather than allow anyone to love him."

I blinked rapidly, then pulled away from Kor so that I could see his expression. "I...don't understand."

"Neither do I," Kor said with a sigh. "And trust me, I have tried harder than anyone else, for years. I told you when we first met, if you'll recall, that Ben has never been...interested in relationships."

"I remember that," I said quietly.

"I told you that to give you fair warning that he would be a bit...stubborn. But I thought that once he truly fell for you—and I knew he *would* fall for you—his resistance would cave. Only after we first spoke did I discover that at some point, Ben got it into his head that he could never marry."

Kor grimaced. "He may have even made a vow along those lines—that would be just like him. The noble idiot."

I stared. "A *vow*? Why?"

"That's the question I've been trying to figure out ever since. And I have a theory. But since Ben refuses point-blank to talk about it with me, it is still *only* a theory."

"What is it?" I asked, heart thumping.

Kor looked at me heavily. "It has to do...as a lot of things with Ben do...with his mother."

"Oh," I whispered, eyes widening.

Kor nodded. "I think you see where I am going with this. Nyethra's death was...devastating for both her husband and son. But Kavarian was a hundred and thirty-four at the time. As much as he loved her with a love that has had ballads and plays and novels written about it, he had ways to cope. Ben...did not. He just...broke. And I mean *broke*, Sarah."

Kor sighed. "That was when I first met him. I'd come to Crownhold for my tertiary. When I first saw him in the state he was in, I remember being afraid for the Realms, thinking, *Flame help us, our Heir is a block of wood*. He was that dead—for *months*. He did what people told him to do, went where people told him to go. But that was all."

His expression darkened. "Fortunately for us all, Yvera kept him away from the worst people and out of the worst of trouble, or Ben might not have survived."

He gave me a look. "Again, I am not excusing Yvera's behavior.... But there are good reasons why she is so protective of Ben. And so suspicious of anyone who might try to take advantage of him."

I swallowed. "I understand."

Kor's lips pursed. "And...I began to help, too. Flame only knows how, but...somehow I found the patience and sympathy for the poor fool. Or maybe I was just too terrified for us all not to do what I could to shore him up. And slowly...he got better. Came back to some semblance of aliveness, anyway. But Yvera says he has never been quite the same ever since. And I think...that included his attitude toward love."

I inhaled. "He...doesn't think he can survive that kind of pain again."

Kor nodded slowly. "That's what I think. So you see the problem, Sarah? I swear again by the Flame, Ben *loves* you. It is nauseating to watch how he looks at you, as if you're the Flame Above come down to walk among mortals. He would do *anything* for you...except allow you to love him back."

My heart was pounding. I shook my head. "I can't.... This is...."

And yet....

It was as if all my interactions with Ben were the pieces of a jigsaw puzzle, and I didn't have the picture on the box to know what it was supposed to look like. Every time I got a glimpse, the pieces would never quite seem to fit. Every time I thought I saw a *look* in his eyes, every time I thought a touch was more than just friendly, or that a word meant something more...the dang piece would not go in where it was supposed to go, and the whole thing would slide again into disarray.

I still didn't have the box to really *know*. But it was as if Kor were describing to me what it was supposed to be, and that helped the pieces fall into place.

I stared at Kor, heart pounding even faster. I swallowed. "You *swear*?"

"By the Flame," Kor said with deadly seriousness. "I have *never* seen him look at anyone like he looks at you. But...if you can't believe me, believe what you saw."

"What do you mean?"

"You saw what Ben became because he thought he lost you. I told you that Royals go berserk for people they were 'close to.' Well, that was putting it a bit mildly, because I didn't want to get into this discussion at that time. Now I'm telling you the full truth. Royals only go berserk for *their own blood*: a mother, a father, a sibling, or...a consort. Just those relationships. That is *all*."

"All?" I whispered.

Kor nodded grimly. "That's all the Tree would risk. The rage is a protective mechanism the Tree gives her Monarchs and Heirs to discourage anyone from using their families against them. Because even the consumed now know that if any harm were to come to them...there would be hellwinds to pay."

I looked away, feeling goosebumps crawl up my spine.

"Now, Sarah. Tell me honestly. In the deepest depths of your intuition...do you think Ben considers you a sister?"

I paused, waiting in the stillness for the answer as the pieces finally fell into place, and I saw the picture.

I met Kor's eyes and said firmly, "No."

Kor smiled slowly. "Then what does that make you? In Ben's subconscious, at least?"

My lips twitched. "Alright, I accept he loves me. But his *consort*?"

Kor smirked and folded his arms. "It is quite sudden, I know, but that's the way Royals generally are. I have a theory about that, too. One that I won't go into right now, since our time is precious before Ben can't help himself but interrupt. But suffice it to say that, in his right mind, Ben isn't so presumptuous. He probably hasn't even dared think the word. He probably still believes he'll somehow resist proposing and is coming up with all sorts of excuses why he shouldn't. Nonetheless, in the deepest part of his soul, that is what he wants you to be. Desperately. It was always going to be all or nothing with him. For all his mature life, he somehow gave nothing. Until he met you."

And now I have...everything? I thought in a daze.

Not...quite.

"Kor, if Ben's reluctance is that deep, I...don't know what I'm supposed to do."

"Don't sell yourself short. You've done a valiant job so far. In fact, it was your guileless little nudges that made me hope Ben had given in—physically, at least."

My cheeks grew hot. "I guess...that's at least somewhat fair. We touch a lot, even around you two. But...last night...you honestly thought we were...."

"Yes," Kor said emphatically, gesturing to me with both hands. "I see how you look at each other. And yesterday I saw you *sleep* with him, for Flame's sake."

My cheeks were flaming now. I knew that had been a mistake.

"While he was in a *coma*."

Kor raised an eyebrow. "And when he woke up?"

I glared at him. "He was busy processing. Give him a break."

"Oh, I don't doubt he was. But after that, I'm equally certain he started processing something else entirely."

Forget my face. My whole body was too hot now. Thank goodness I hadn't put on Svyer's coat.

Kor growled in frustration. "But it figures that, on top of being ice-dead stubborn, Ben would be so torched *noble*."

"Hey," I huffed. "I like that about him."

"You might not for much longer," Kor said grimly. "I don't think you realize how long Ben might be able to keep this up. He is altogether too content with the status quo between you. If you let him, he'll just be your friend forever."

My heart thudded. Painfully. "Forever?"

"If you keep things the way they are, yes. You're giving him a lot of what he wants already right now, after all. The sad truth is, Ben desperately needed a friend like you, someone who could just be with him and be there for him, accepting who he was without reservations. Now he has himself convinced that's all he wants and needs."

I hesitated. "I...don't want to take that away from him. Or myself."

"Nor should you. In some ways, you have done him more good in this past sevenday than I have managed in six years. But that means, to move things along, you're going to need *me*."

Kor winked.

I groaned. "Your plan."

"The next phase of it, to be exact. I've been working on this little project since the moment you arrived."

As if Kor's behavior toward me and Ben had been a separate, smaller puzzle, suddenly all those pieces fell into place as well.

I frowned at him. "From the moment you first met me, you were already pushing us together. Why? And why do you care? Don't say it is because you are my friend. You weren't back then."

"True enough," Kor admitted with folded arms. "But I *was* Ben's. And his leftwing besides. Which meant I had been searching for his ideal mate long enough that I knew it when I saw it."

I narrowed my eyes at him. "I don't think that's it. Not even by half."

Kor smiled slowly. "You're listening to those instincts of yours much better than when we first met, aren't you? Excellent."

I rolled my eyes. "Are you going to answer the question or not?"

"Eventually. But as I said, our time is short, and we haven't even begun discussing the next phase. Which, it seems, we should begin without delay."

"Making Ben...jealous," I said uneasily. "Are you...sure that's a good idea?"

Kor raised an eyebrow. "I wouldn't have proposed it if I didn't."

This was once again beginning to smell too strongly of Mom's telenovelas.

For a moment, I had the bizarre, tangential image of Kor and Mom sitting down together to watch them over a bowl of popcorn....

Which strangely felt a bit too much like it could actually happen one day for my comfort. I could almost picture Kor lounging back with his feet up, could hear his chuckles as he predicted every dramatic twist, and could see him handing Mom tissues when she cried during the sad parts.

And then my brain sort of fried for a second.

I shook my head quickly to dispel the image.

"Look, maybe I should just talk to Ben. Just tell him how I feel, then see what he—"

"Oh, no, that is exactly what you must *not* do," Kor said, pointing a finger at me. "Ben doesn't talk about these sorts of things, Sarah. That's the whole torched problem. Every time in the past that I tried to talk to him about anything to do with feelings and relationships, he shut me out. And ever since you got here, that has counted double."

Yes, I thought. *But that's* you *talking to him.*

Kor wasn't finished. "You try talking to him about this, and you risk him shutting down entirely. Or pushing you away 'for your own good.'"

I hesitated. "Are you...sure?"

"Trust me," Kor said grimly, putting his hands on his hips. "He's that imbecilely self-sacrificing. We have to first bring him to the point at which he realizes, for himself, that he cannot live without you. Otherwise, if you confess how you feel to him too early, he will convince himself that he can and *must* live without you. He'll throw away even your friendship, push you away, and shut you out. All in the name of doing what is best for you."

My mouth went dry, and it was suddenly difficult to swallow.

"What...makes you think that?"

Kor closed his eyes and took a deep breath. "Because that is what I have seen him do to nearly every single person who cares about him."

"What?" I whispered.

"He and Svyer used to be close, Sarah," Kor said gently as he opened his eyes. "Nearly as close as he is to Yvera. They are cousins, and they visited each other often. But over the years...she's just stopped trying. He almost never answers her calls. He avoids spending time together if they're in the same place. He keeps most interactions with her about Crown business, rarely talking about her or himself. His excuse is always that he's *busy*. But you know what a terrible liar Ben is."

I nodded slowly.

Kor sighed. "What's more, I have seen the pattern repeat with anyone else who tries to show a genuine care for him. There's a reason Ben was in such desperate need of a friend...but that reason had more to do with him than anyone else. The only ones he hasn't pushed away by now are his father...and Yvera and me. I think we're exceptions because he knows we can handle ourselves nearly as well as he can. He thinks he doesn't have to worry about losing *us*. But anyone else, particularly anyone he sees as vulnerable...."

I inhaled sharply. "Like...me."

"Do you understand what I'm saying now?" Kor said gently. "I'm not proposing that we do this because I want to create some drama. It's because you can't simply *talk* to him. Not before he's decided for himself that he *can't* push you away. Or he *will*. And I'm afraid the little incident with losing you once will only make things worse. He has this twisted conviction that anyone who gets too close to him is bound to get hurt sometime...and he is afraid he won't be able to bear the pain and guilt when they do."

I was stunned into silence. I had wanted to dismiss Kor's suggestions as being just that—wanting to create drama. But his breadth of experience in studying and handling Ben far exceeded mine, and his reasoning struck far too close to the epiphanies I had already had about him.

Ben saw himself as a monster. Not usually in so many words, but that was what it boiled down to in his subconscious. And anyone who got close to a monster...

...was bound to get hurt.

Or worse.

Kor continued kindly. "I genuinely believe that Ben is not leaving us with many options, and our window to influence him is short. This...tenuous status quo between you won't last for much longer. Either because you, understandably and rightfully, will break it. Or because Ben will *see*. But if he gets even a subconscious inkling of how much you care, he will pull apart. First emotionally, then the moment you two no longer have to work together so closely...he'll be gone. Which means we have only a handful of days to convince him—*without* him realizing that's what we're doing—that he can't live without you."

I put my head in my hands for a moment. When I lowered them, I took a deep breath. "Kor...I understand what you're saying. But...jealousy?"

That just seemed so...petty. So underhanded and manipulative. It went against everything I stood for.

"It's the next logical step, Sarah," Kor said with a helpless shrug and spread of his hands. "Maybe the only way to get him to let you stay...is to make him *fight* for you. To make him see that the only thing worse than losing you...is losing you to *someone else*."

I folded my arms and looked away, biting my lip while I thought. "Kor...you're assuming that this is the right time for Ben to enter a relationship. Or that I'm the right person."

"Torch that," he began angrily. "I told you, Sarah. I tried for years to find *anyone* that remotely had all the qualities Ben needed—"

I cut him off with a raised hand. "Alright, fine. Assume I'm the right person. Is this *really* the only moment? What if I just talked to Ben, let what comes come, and then just...waited for him to work through things and heal?"

Kor took a deep breath. "That's the thing, Sarah: I don't think he will. Not until we unstop whatever plug is festering inside of him—and the yank it takes might seem cruel to you. What's more, the Realms can't take that kind of risk. We *need* Ben to get over this, yesterday; he can't keep pushing away his support network and be the Heir we need right now. And most of all, we *need* the two of you, working together, side by side, with nothing held back."

I stared at him. "That's it, isn't it? You think...the survival of the *Realms* hinges on a *relationship*?"

Kor smiled tiredly. "I have a bit more to go on than that. But that is the core, yes."

I shook my head and said flatly, "You're bonkers. You know that, right?"

Kor's eyes glowed sapphire for a moment, and his face was deadly serious. "I'm really not. I'm one of the few truly sane people in all the Realms, actually." I snorted. Kor groaned.

"Sarah, we really don't have time for this," he said anxiously, looking at the door. "I predict Ben will interrupt in about five dek, and when he does, we need to be at least *pretending* to make some progress on your magical defenses. Are you or are you not with me on this?"

I looked at him. Looked away. Then looked back at him.

Then a little voice inside me said, *Why not?*

I grimaced. "Alright. But I hope you know what you're getting into. I am going to be horrible at it."

"Oh, I know," Kor said, chuckling with relief. "That's why I needed you to be attracted to me. You just let me do most of the work and keep stammering and blushing like you do. All I need is your permission."

I looked at him sidelong. "I have...boundaries."

"Nothing major," Kor said innocently. "Nothing that can't be done in public, since it will only be in front of Ben. I'll make each time count, promise. And anytime I'm pushing your comfort zone, just tell me."

"How do I do that in front of Ben?" I asked with a glare.

"With your inner voice, silly," Kor snorted.

My jaw dropped. "How do you.... And I thought that was just with Ben!"

Kor raised an eyebrow. "Have you *tried* with anyone else?"

My cheeks heated. "No."

"Try it sometime," Kor said, backing up from me. "And if it doesn't work...we'll come up with a code or something. Now, to business. I'm going to throw some magic at you, and you are going to block it."

"Wait, what? *How—*"

But with no further warning, Kor threw up his hand and sent a wave of sapphire energy crashing toward me.

Just like that, the magic in the room surged into my blood. I threw up my own hands, as if to brace myself, and shards of ice speared from the ground and up into a solid semicircle around me. The magic crashed as harmlessly against it as waves against a wave break before dissipating, leaving the angled spears of ice untouched.

Kor lowered his hand and whistled. "Impressive. I wasn't expecting you to be able to block that."

"Then what exactly did you expect that thing to *do* to me?" I cried.

"Oh, don't get your tail in a knot," Kor said dismissively. "All it would have done was knock you back a bit. It would have been a nice lesson on always being on your guard."

I clenched my fists, for a moment too furious to speak. Eventually, I said flatly, "I hate you."

Kor grinned. "Oh, I know. Like I said, I'm counting on it. I'm not intending to actually win you away from Ben."

I huffed. "As if you *could*."

His eyes glittered. "Oh, be very glad I'm not even going to try. You might end up liking this charade more than you—"

A knock at the east door. When Kor and I looked away from it to meet each other's eyes again, he smirked and said, "I told you so."

"Let him in, would you please?" I asked wearily, looking at the lights that had drifted down to me like polite butlers.

I wasn't sure I liked that Kor had predicted Ben's behavior so exactly. On the one hand, it was reassuring; maybe I really was right to trust that Kor knew what he was talking about, and maybe I was justified in going along with his plan as being the only option. On the other hand...I didn't want Kor to be right. For so many reasons more than pride.

If he was right about how much was at stake....

Ben slipped through the doors as soon as he could fit. Since he came through the east doors, he was on the other side of the ice-spear wall from me, near Kor, so he had an unobstructed view of its pointy glory. Even I was impressed by now: it was nearly waist-high to me—a formidable defense from low attacks or melee charges. And it was pretty, in a deadly sort of way. Almost like a giant's tiara.

Ben stopped. And blinked. Whatever he had been expecting when he walked in, it hadn't been this.

"Nice, isn't it?" Kor told him with a wink and a nudge. "It took us this long for her to be able to throw it up, but I think it shows promise, don't you?"

I blinked. Somehow, that was technically true. And it was as backhanded as a compliment got.

"It shows more than promise," Ben said evenly as he sent him a glare. "I just hope you didn't knock Sarah down too many times before she got it."

"Not a one," Kor said, with a smile that was perfectly calculated to make Ben think he was lying.

I stared at him. How many times...had Kor lied to me with the truth?

And what could he be lying to me about now?

CHAPTER TWENTY-EIGHT

QUESTIONS

KORIBEN

I WATCHED KOR WORK with Sarah for a bit longer, but though she was able to dispel the ice she had summoned, she must have been getting tired, because she wasn't able to create another nearly the same size.

"Enough, Kor," I said after her third attempt was only about a foot high. "It's time to give Sarah a break."

"I can go longer," Sarah protested, face warming. But I noticed she looked more present now than she had before I had said anything.

Her lack of focus was another sign that she needed rest, but I wasn't about to point it out and make her feel worse, especially in front of Kor.

Instead, I told her gently, "Ice room or not, you've been working hard all morning, and it's day. You can work more with Kor in the evening, when you have more spark."

"Good idea," Kor agreed—a tad too quickly.

I glanced at him suspiciously, but he just straightened his coat and crossed the distance to Sarah.

"Well done today, Sarah," he said warmly, and to my surprise, he gave her a hug and then a flirtatious kiss on the cheek as he pulled away. "We'll pick up again tonight."

I was suddenly severely questioning my judgment in suggesting such a thing. What made me downright sick was the warmth increasing in Sarah's cheeks and her shy darting look away from him.

"S-sure," she stammered.

"I could use the time myself for some more calls and study," Kor declared, waving as he walked toward the door. "Until then."

He blew a kiss over his shoulder in Sarah's direction and disappeared from sight.

"What was *that*?" I said flatly.

Sarah shifted, not meeting my gaze. "You...know him better than I do."

That I did. And that...was Kor in full flirtation mode. Which always meant he wanted something. Usually that wasn't actually romance—instead, information or favors or just plain entertainment. Although, no matter the cause, he...could be quite persuasive.

"Was he making you uncomfortable?" I demanded. "You know you can tell him to just torch it, right? He'll listen. And if he doesn't, he'll answer to me."

"He wasn't," Sarah said, finally meeting my gaze.

When I just gazed back in disbelief, she bit her lip and then added, "He...was actually being very nice to me. I know he made you think he knocked me around, but he didn't. He was...kind, in fact."

Flame, no, I thought in horror.

Kor was only flirtatious *and* kind...when he was actually interested—and Flame help the object of his interest in resisting him.

I just stared at her, feeling completely disarmed, blindfolded, and spun around so that I didn't know which way the enemy was.

Sarah grew more self-conscious under my stare by the second, shifting from foot to foot and folding her arms. "Um...now that you mention it, I think I could use a nap. Would you mind...?"

I shook, mentally slapping myself out of my tortured daze. "Of course not. Go ahead. Sleep, eat, shower—do whatever you need to do. Just come find me when you're done, and we'll work on whatever you have the energy for."

"Thanks!" she said with relief.

She walked so quickly past me out the door that it was nearly at a run.

I stared after her, flameheart sinking as my insides twisted. She hadn't seemed so uncomfortable around me since we first met.

What was happening?

Blessed Flame, I silently begged. *Don't let me lose her now.*

To anyone.

But most especially...to Kor.

I TRIED PACING IN my bedroom, but though it was my only private sanctuary in this hold, it was too confined for my restless worry. When I could somehow stop thinking about Sarah, something else would come in to take her place.

I had my pick of Realms-shattering problems to fret over right now: the lish, which was still at large and had thus far avoided every hunt for him or her; the fact that I now had a mountain-sized target on my back from challenging *the Devourer*; the swiftly passing days until the invasion, in which we somehow had to find three gates, get to Earth, bring Sarah's family to the Tree of Ice, and get back to Avva; the invasion, which we would somehow have to repel, and the aftermath we would have to survive; oh, and the Moonfair tomorrow, which, in case you were wondering, ranked about equal to the lish in my mind. And that was setting aside the old but still relevant worries: the sungates failing, the crushing pressures of being Heir, Avva...fading.

I needed something to *do*. Somewhere to *go*. I needed to feel the change in my blood and take off into the sky. Everything always seemed simpler as a draká, especially floating in a sea of blue. Nurtured by the Flame Above, safe from all that lay in wait below—malicious foes and demanding subjects alike.

But for a lack of any of those things, and most especially the lack of Sarah as she rested in her own room...

...I would take something or someone that I could hit.

And there was one person I could always count on for that.

I found Yvera in the kitchen, eating a kava.

"Want a duel?" I asked brusquely.

She spit out the pit into her palm and threw it in the compost bin. "Flame, *yes.*"

Needing no other explanation, she followed me to the training room.

Sometimes, I could kill her. But always, I loved her. Most especially when, with no questions asked, she let me try to kill her.

"Terms?" I asked, since I'd been the one to make the challenge.

"Staves, no armor, no magic," Yvera said without hesitation.

Interesting. She wanted a fight with few holds barred, but kept some distance, was an entirely physical outlet versus magical, and guaranteed that we would both walk away bruised and limping.

She could have been reading my mind.

Yvera chose the largest of the training rings and, once I'd stepped inside, activated it. A precaution that was more habit than strictly necessary under her terms, since we wouldn't be using any magic and didn't have any bystanders to worry about. But I wasn't going to protest, because when it came to the two of us, you never knew. If we got carried away, I wasn't about to make Sarah mad at me for accidentally scorching her training room walls.

We both summoned our staves, saluted with our hands over our hearts...and then launched at each other.

Yvera was always a beauty to behold in a fight, whatever its nature. For someone who was so abrasive in every other context, in battle, she *glided*—danced as smoothly as the wind and swiftly as the oncoming storm. Even when she was being as ferocious an opponent as she was now, her face was never more at ease than in a duel, her smile never more genuine.

She smiled widely now, and I found myself smiling back.

"It's been too long...hasn't it?" I mused through some pants as I used both hands on the stave to block a particularly forceful blow and shoved her back.

"Hellwinds, yes," she agreed.

"Sorry," I said ruefully.

She shrugged, a magnanimous response for her. Of course, that could have just been a distraction from her wicked side swipe, which I took squarely on my forearm.

"Ouch!" I complained, cringing at the sting. Bruise one, to Yvera. "I *said* sorry!"

"Did you want a fight or not?" she grinned.

I growled at her and charged.

We focused purely on the fight for a while, using each other as we always did to vent all the frustration we felt at life. Then, intensity used up, we finally settled into a kind of pattern—almost a glorified drill session. Really, the fight was over at this point, and when we tallied bruises, we concluded Yvera had won. (Big surprise there.) We just didn't want to stop yet. Besides the now companionable rhythm we had going on, keeping our muscles warm and limber helped with the healing that was actively erasing the damage we'd done to each other.

"Now," Yvera said. "What is it this time?"

"Huh?" I asked, pulled back into the present.

"What's got you so worked up?"

I blinked. Yvera didn't normally ask. It was one of the reasons I came to her for something like this.

"Take your pick," I said as we traded overhand blows. "It's not exactly a relaxing time to be either of us right now."

"Torched ashes," Yvera declared. "It's Sarah, isn't it?"

I gave her a careful look. "Are you sure you want to talk about her?"

"I brought her up, didn't I?" Yvera snorted. She looked away. "I know I haven't been...your friend a lot lately. But if you want to talk...."

I stared. Then chuckled. "Careful, Yv. I think you're setting a record for the most apologies in two days."

She broke our pattern by swiping at me harder than usual, but I had been ready and blocked her easily.

"Do you *want* to talk or not?"

"I appreciate the offer, Yv. I do. But no."

"Is it just because I...." Yvera took a deep breath. "Look, Ben. I'm working through it. It just came as a shock, that's all. But I...I learned my lessons, and I'll be alright. Eventually."

She smirked. "I'm not saying I'll ever *like* her...."

At my glare, she chuckled. "What did you really expect, Ben?"

I sighed. "Miracles, apparently. You're both important to me. I don't want to lose either of you."

"And you won't," Yvera said conclusively. "Not me, anyway."

I winced—between blows, so Yvera knew it wasn't from a physical pang. Her focus on me sharpened. "What is it?"

"Nothing," I lied. Poorly.

Yvera thought for a moment, then her eyes widened. And narrowed savagely. "What did she do to you? Hellwinds, Ben, if she's playing with you—"

She began striding forward for the exit.

"No, Yv, it's not *her*," I cried, catching her around the waist as she passed and yanking her to a stop.

She glared at me, shoving me off. But I noticed she stayed in place. "Then what the—"

"It's *Kor*, alright?" I snapped.

That gave her pause. The worst of the fire died in her eyes, and she cocked her head. "Kor?"

I ground my teeth. But if Yvera was going to give Sarah hellwinds unless I made her see it wasn't her fault....

"He's...flirting with Sarah."

Yvera looked at me like I was stupid. "Ben, Kor would flirt with an *ugle* if it would come up out of the tar pit long enough. And he thought it knew something *useful*."

"You think I don't know that?" I snapped. "This...is different. Sarah said he was...kind."

Yvera stared. Took a step back. Then, eyes firing up, said, "That—"

She called Kor a name so profane I blinked. She went on, for at least ten seconds—I counted—and punctuated the end of her string of colorful curses with a stomp of her foot and a heavy breath.

"Feel better?" I asked dryly.

"Do *you*?" Yvera demanded with a glare.

I cocked my head and thought about it. I had thus far tried to avoid thinking about Kor even more strictly than about Sarah—for the simple reason that cold-blooded murder is wrong. Even if my sick rage was screaming at me right now that Kor deserved it.

Plus, I didn't have time to find a new leftwing right now.

"Slightly," I said finally.

And by slightly, I meant that the growing cold sun of fury inside of me was momentarily slowed in its expansion.

Yvera took a deep breath. "Look, Ben. I don't know what torching Kor's problem is. This really isn't the time for *any* of this ashdust, in my opinion."

She said that with a pointed glare at me.

Then looked away with a scowl. "Torch me, I can't believe *I'm* the one having to say this, but Ben...if Kor is flirting with Sarah...then flirt *harder*."

I stared. Then swallowed. "Yv...."

She met my eyes again with another glare. "You can't possibly be telling me you think *she's* the one, but you're just going to roll over and let Kor *take* her?"

"She's not a *thing* to be *taken*!" I snapped. Then took a deep breath for calm. "She has the right to choose what is best for her. And Yv...I'm not sure I'm it."

There. I'd finally said it. The real thing that had been festering inside of me all day—the bright spot of my time with Sarah excepted—made only more virulent by Kor's advances.

When I had asked the Tree last night if I could be with Sarah...I had received no answer.

Nothing.

Not even the slightest brush of awareness or presence.

Now, the Tree didn't *always* answer. I knew that as well as anyone. She wasn't at our beck and call, and She didn't usually bother to tell us what we already knew or could figure out if we tried hard enough.

But this had been a question I was certain She *would* answer. I didn't know the answer and thought for certain I couldn't unless She told me. And it wasn't some idle curiosity: it made the difference between me making a grave transgression against Her will or not. Surely the Trees of Ice and Flame would want me to respect the new Realms order They were slowly establishing.

And yet...nothing.

And that nothingness...horrified me.

What was I supposed to do with it? How was I supposed to answer Sarah now, should she ever look at me that way again?

Would she...ever look at me that way again?

Should she?

Were Kor's flirtations a Flamesend...saving Sarah from me? Was *that* my answer?

I was so wrapped up in my inner turmoil that I didn't see Yvera's hand until it was too late.

It slapped against my cheek with a force that threw me off balance, making me stagger back.

"Yv!" I spat, gingerly feeling my stinging jaw. Yet another thing for my spark to spend itself healing....

"*Ashdust*," Yvera snarled. "Torching. Ash. Dust. Snap out of it, Ben. '*Not it*'?"

"Look, Yv, what I meant was...." I swallowed with difficulty. "What if what I feel, what I want...goes against the Trees' will?"

If there was one thing Yvera respected, it was the Tree.

She folded her arms and frowned. "Well, that's torched stupid."

I gritted my teeth. "How?"

"She's going to be a Queen, right? That's what you said, isn't it?"

"Yes," I said tightly. "But see, that's exactly why—"

"And who would the Trees *want* her to marry except someone who's going to be a *King*?"

I froze.

"I mean, really," Yvera continued. "That's a Tree-related rank thing, isn't it? I know I don't pay much attention to that kind of stuff, but even I can put that together. No one is going to be her rank in the Tree's eyes except you, Ben. That's fact."

She wrinkled her nose. "Except your father, I guess. Ew.... Nah. Can't be. I'd rather see *you* marry her than *him*. 'Cause that...that's just gross."

"She's going to be Queen," I repeated slowly, still dazed. "And someday, I'm...."

For the *very* first time...I had a reason to be glad I would become King.

Yvera rolled her eyes. "Come on, Ben. I put that together the moment you first said her title. And you've known about it for longer than any of the rest of us have. How could you possibly *not* have seen that coming?"

The Tree...didn't answer stupid questions.

And I may have asked a *very* stupid question.

"Who else?" I whispered, staring at nothing.

And then I felt it.

The faintest brush of the Tree of Flame's driest amusement, like a desert wind blowing through my soul.

Then it was gone.

But it had still lit a bonfire.

"Not Kor, that's for torched certain," Yvera said with a snort. "I'd also rather see you marry her than *him*."

I came out of my daze enough to smile thinly at her. "For someone who just a couple days ago said she was in love with me, you seem strangely willing to marry me off."

Yvera rolled her eyes again. "I always knew you would marry someone else, Ben. It was just a matter of when, and how much I'd hate her. But, like I said. If someone has to marry that girl, it had better not be your dad, because *ew*. And it better not be Kor, because...*Kor*."

She gagged. "So, I guess that leaves you."

She approached me with a fire returning to her eyes and poked me in the chest. Hard—probably drawing blood. (I wasn't kidding. Yvera's two vanities were her hair and her nails...and she kept the latter pointed. And drakón fingernails weren't the flimsy, brittle variety.)

"So you listen to me, Koriben Sunfilled," she said, leaning in close, eyes burning violet. "Don't you dare let that arrogant, conniving, torched son-of-a-krathen *win*."

I looked down at her. And slowly smiled.

"Oh, don't worry. I *won't*."

Chapter Twenty-Nine

LK

Sarah

I TOSSED AND TURNED in bed—*knowing* I needed rest so that I could be ready to make the best use of this precious training day. And yet, my thoughts wouldn't quiet. All I could think about was what Kor had told me, and what I had agreed to—and when I could avoid thinking about that, I remembered.

I must have run through every single memory I had of Ben, from the first moment I saw his human face underneath me to when I'd practically run from him in the Oculus just now. It was like my vision had had a dark filter, not allowing me to see him clearly. And now, with the filter off...I was belatedly dazzled.

Ben...*loved* me.

All those looks he gave me, all those little touches, all those things he said, all those crushing hugs, all those little things he did to care for or protect me...I had put down to just him being kind, protective, noble. And he *was* kind, protective, noble. But he had another motivation that glowed straight through them all, tying them together into a bright tapestry of...love.

I...had been a blind idiot. It was so painfully obvious now. No wonder Kor had been so frustrated with the two of us. *Look at these two silly love-struck fools, too caught up in their own insecurities and fears to see how the other feels.*

I had thought with foolish pride last night that I had finally seen Ben clearly. But I hadn't. I had seen the darkness that he thought was far darker than it truly was and decided that was a completeness of being.

I should have known better. Hadn't *I* been the one to say Ben had the largest heart I had ever known? It was like my subconscious had been screaming at me, *Stop feeling sorry for yourself and LOOK AT HIM.*

Look up.

Reach.

You didn't truly see a person—*truly* see them—until you saw their absolute purest core that lay *beyond* the darkness, both above and beneath it, as the sun was to the void.

And now that I had seen Ben's...I would never be the same.

How...could I have lost my heart and somehow gained it back, full and overflowing...in the same day?

There was one problem, though, and it cast a pall of clouds between me and the sun: Ben's own inhibitions. And if Kor was right...they were far deeper and more insidious than mine. I had felt sorry for myself so many times in my life, thinking of how hard it was to move around, to have such a large family that needed constant work, and to feel lost and forgotten in all the shuffle.

And yet, now I was learning how *lucky* I had been. How provided for, sheltered, surrounded, loved. Any price I had paid in giving up after-school activities to babysit, all those times I thought I could scream from wanting some privacy, all those times I craved more individual attention from hectic parents.... Those things had hurt...but the pain was fading, and the prices no longer seemed so great.

Not in the face of the ones Ben had paid.

All his parents' individual love, adoration, and attention hadn't been enough to save him from the heartbreak of losing his mother and the burden of serving his people. If I had grown up feeling a bit squeezed, he had grown up in a crucible, with everyone on all sides trying to either change him...or kill him. And he, desperate to make himself not a monster, had tried to become everything that the good ones wanted him to be. But it was never enough, and his pain was too great to hold on to them—especially the ones with the most potential for more pain. So he cut them off, all in the name of serving them *better*.

Then circumstances had thrown us together, and he had latched onto me like a drowning man to a lifeline. I saw that now. I felt tempted to doubt the purity of his love because of it, but I shook off that shadow, refusing to let it drag me back. No. Ben *loved* me.

But...with *that much* love...how long was it before it became too much for him, and he let go of me too?

A quiet knock on the door made me jump—even though it was the volume carefully calibrated to test whether the occupant was awake enough to hear and respond.

From the closeness of the pull, I knew exactly who it was.

I scrambled out of my bed and to my feet, ran my fingers frantically through my hair to get rid of the worst of the bedhead, straightened my clothes...and took deep breaths to at least somewhat slow my pounding heart.

Calm down, I told myself sternly. *He loves you.*

That only made it worse.

This would be the first time I would truly look into his eyes with that knowledge. I hadn't managed, back in the Oculus. I hadn't been prepared, hadn't had the space to process. That was why I was so distracted and half-hearted in trying to replicate my first ice wall, and given half the chance, that was why I had run.

Well, that...and to save myself from the horror of keeping up Kor's charade alone. I'd tried to say true things, but I thought Ben still saw through me. I wasn't much better at lying than he was.

Now, though, I had no excuses. I had to look him in the eye, knowing all that I knew now, without flinching.

I, an Earth-born amón...was going to stare straight into the sun.

I walked slowly to the door, trying hard not to tremble....

And opened it.

Ben stood there, smiling down at me.

I looked into his gold eyes instinctively, and then thought, *Oh.*

It was the *Oh* that you think just before a totally unexpected tornado hits you.

And that was all my brain got out before it was scrambled.

"Ah, you're awake," Ben said naturally. "Good. Got the rest you needed?"

When I just continued to stare, his smile faded to concern. "Sarah?"

I shook my head sharply, wishing I could slap myself without looking even stranger. I faked a yawn and blinked blearily. "Oh, sorry. I guess...I'm not quite awake yet."

His growing concern shifted to an apologetic smile. "Oh, sorry. Did I wake you? I can come back—"

"No, it's fine," I said quickly. "I was already waking up, so your timing is perfect. What's up?"

His face became serious. Unusually serious. "I need your help with something. Something very important, and something only you can do."

My heart picked up the pace again as my mind ran through all the terribly dangerous, exhausting, and painful things he could ask of me.

"I'll do it," I said immediately.

His eyes softened, and my heart sped. "You don't even know what it is yet."

I tried to make my shrug nonchalant. "Because it's *you* asking...I'll do it. What do you need?"

He grinned, all seriousness fading with a disorienting suddenness. "I need you to teach me an Earthren recipe."

I blinked at him. "Come again?"

His grin faded but didn't entirely leave. "Sorry, I meant to tease you, but now I see that was in poor taste. I really do want you to teach me, though."

"No, no," I said, holding up one hand while I put the other over my slowing heart. "I think my sleepy brain is catching up. It was funny, really."

In a retroactive, stress-released hysteria kind of way. I had to suppress a mad giggle for fear I wouldn't be able to stop.

"But...you really want me to teach you a *recipe*? Like...a *cooking* recipe?"

He took a deep breath, sobering. And I was pretty sure it was genuine this time. "I recognize...that your family must be going through hellwinds right now.

I don't know what they must be thinking, but if they've given up hope and decided they've lost you...."

My heart clenched and my eyes stung at the compassion on his face and in those golden eyes.

No one, not even Kor, had expressed any concern for my family. Except, of course...him.

He cleared his throat awkwardly. "I know...something, just a bit, of what they must be feeling right now. And when we reach them, they're going to have a hard time believing that I did my best to take care of their daughter and sister while she was in my care. So...I want to be able to *do* something for them, to prove it to them in a small way. And the only things I know how to do well are kill things...and cook."

He reddened a bit. "Since the first seems like a bad idea...."

I chuckled, finally getting what he was after—and my heart melted.

What did I ever do to deserve a guy like this?

Well, technically, *you still don't* have *him,* my pessimistic side said.

Shut up, my lovesick, starry-eyed side answered.

"That's so sweet," I said, finally crossing the threshold of my room to stand right next to him and beam up at him. "Sure, I can help with that."

"Oh," he said, looking a bit dazed.

My heart began pounding again as I realized, for the first time, the effect *I* had on *him.*

I, Sarah Lind...made Koriben Sunfilled, Heir of the dragons...flustered. Just as much, if not more, than he made me.

Would wonders never cease.

He looked away hastily, putting a hand on his neck. "Great. Good. Great.... Um.... What are we making?"

I frowned thoughtfully. "Well, it has to be something I know by heart, something that uses things we have here, and won't take too much time...."

I was mindful of how precious today's time was.

"Don't worry about time," Ben insisted. "I'm getting hungry, anyway, which means you probably are too. And weren't you the one saying we needed to celebrate and enjoy the moment a bit?"

I nodded absently, only half listening as I thought. "I think maybe...pancakes?"

"*Olith*?" Ben said curiously, saying the word *cake* in his language. "As in, *olith* you make in a pan?"

I smiled. "I'll show you."

WE HAD TO GET creative, of course.

First, I wanted to write down the recipe so that I could reference it. I had our tried-and-true family recipe for pancakes down pat, but I quickly realized that replicating it here was going to be a slow process, and I didn't want to keep thinking through the whole thing all over again.

But when I asked Ben for something to write with, he simply handed me a stylus just like Kor had.

It was surprisingly heavy, and I realized suddenly that it must be made of some kind of dark rock. It was cut in the shape of a writing utensil—no doubt designed for Ben's much larger hands—and polished as smooth as a river stone. But a *rock*.

"Er...." I said hesitantly. "This is cool and all that, but I was hoping for a pen or pencil and some paper."

"Why waste the paper?" Ben asked curiously. "What's wrong with that?"

"I'm all for saving paper," I said hastily. "But I want to be able to carry the recipe around. If I just write it on the counter or something...."

I tapped my kitchen counter demonstratively. "That's great while we're in here, but not when we go to the storage rooms."

"But I'll have my tablet for that," Ben said, still confused.

I blinked at him. "Excuse me? You have a *tablet*?"

"Yeah," he said. Then he pulled it out of thin air and laid carefully it on the counter in front of me.

It was...a tablet. In the original sense. In the sense of a rectangular...rock.

I blinked and held up the stylus. They were the same shade and smoothness, with only the slightest of white striations to disturb the perfection and hint at their shared origins.

"They're made of the same aldstone," Ben explained, guessing something of my thoughts. "Then magically imprinted on each other to make the bond unique. Whatever you write with this..."

He gently took the stylus from me and scribbled a handful of characters in their rune-like script on the counter. Then he tapped his...tablet.

"...I can bring up on this."

Just as he said, the gold letters slowly appeared on the dark stone, fading into being like ink seeping through paper. I looked between the letters on the counter and the ones on his tablet: they were perfectly identical.

Ben put his finger on the tablet again. "It's the same thing as with the archivals. In fact, the tablet, in turn, is connected to my personal archival. Whatever is stored on here, I can back up there, once I return."

He blushed. "Which, given my track record with breaking things...I try to do as often as I can. This is my third tablet. But fortunately—or unfortunately, for the sake of the records I'm supposed to be keeping for posterity—I don't use it that much. So...I haven't lost much after breaking or losing each one. The archivists just shake their head and get me another one."

"Neat," was all I could say. Really, I was a bit in awe. It was yet another piece of evidence of what I had already long ago concluded: dramá culture might look simple—almost Medieval, even—on the surface. But through magic and ingenuity, they had a level of sophistication in some things that we Earthren couldn't match.

"I can get you a pen and paper if you want," Ben said, reddening. "But if you write it with this..."

He offered the stylus a bit hopefully. "...then I'll have it forever."

When I only smiled softly, he looked away and said quickly, blushing again, "I mean...as a reference. For making this pan cake. Again."

I...had seriously been blind before. But then, I had been turned inward. Self-pity and insecurity did that, after all. To truly see *clearly*...you had to get out of your own way.

I took the stylus from him without another protest.

As I hovered the stylus just under the word already on the counter, curiosity pricked at me.

"What did you write, just now?" I asked idly as I began listing the ingredients on the countertop. The tip of the stylus glided smoothly and soundlessly, so it couldn't have been completely stone. Unsurprisingly, *my* "ink" was white with a silver sheen.

Ben didn't answer long enough that I glanced up from writing out the recipe to look at him.

He was fully red now. "'Sarah.'"

When I only blinked, thinking he was addressing me, he quickly clarified.

"Er, that is...I wrote your name...in Drona."

The first thing he had thought to write in demonstration...stored now on an archival stone that would go down in the public record of his life one day...was my name.

At one point, I would have dismissed that as coincidence or mere kindness. Now, even though I responded the same way I would have before by merely nodding and returning my attention to my task...my chest constricted, and tears pricked my eyes again.

The question burst out of Ben, as if he couldn't hold it back. "How *is* it spelled? Or...written?"

Without looking up—because if I did, he might see how much I knew—I left aside the ingredient list and raised the stylus to rest on the same "line" but a few spaces after the runic Drona version of my name. Then I wrote it out, letter by careful letter.

Sarah.

"Oh," Ben said, blinking at it as he leaned in. "That's so...smooth. And pretty."

I could see why he thought that. I'd been showing off a bit. I didn't normally write my name in cursive unless I was signing something—and even then, it was usually illegible. But this had been my finest cursive work since middle school.

"Thank you," I said with a smile as I traced the first gold letter with a finger. "I like your version too, though. There's something strong about it."

The three letters—if I had separated them correctly into three—were all angles and edges, triangles, squares, and lines and dots. They had fortitude, as if meant to stand the test of time.

The two versions of my name couldn't have been more different.

"As it should," Ben said with surprise. "In Drona, it means *sera*."

He said my name again slowly, but with emphasis and concentration, as if trying hard to get more than just the meaning *"hey, you"* across to me. And so he did.

Valiant.

I gaped at him. It was a small thing, really. What was in a name, anyway? Especially in another language. And yet....

"You're kidding. *Valiant*?"

"Of course I'm not kidding," he said with a frown. "From the moment you told me it, I thought it was perfect."

He didn't just think I was *strong*. He thought I was *valiant*. Every time he had said my name, he was calling me...valiant.

From the moment he'd met me.

He cocked his head. "What does it mean in...your language?"

"English," I supplied absently. "It doesn't mean anything in that, though; it's just a name. It comes from Hebrew, which is much older. In that language, it means 'princess.'"

I blinked, making the connection for the first time.

"Princess?" he asked intently, scrunching his face as if trying to pierce through the meaning his blood was trying to convey to him.

I shook my head. "You don't have a word for it. The closest equivalent is...well, what you are. Heir. Except, the female version."

"Oh," he said in satisfaction, figuring out the puzzle. "Well, that's perfect too, isn't it?"

"A little *too* perfect," I said dryly, refocusing on recipe-writing.

"You still have a choice, Sarah," Ben said gently.

Goosebumps went down my arms at him saying my name. Would I ever be able to hear him say it again and not think of what that meant to him?

I sure hoped not.

"What does your name mean?" I asked, turning the focus onto him.

"Oh, Koriben? It means 'oath binder.'" Ben then gave the same sort of grimace I had after saying "princess," as if he, too, were making a connection he hadn't before.

"I like it," I said as casually as I could, keeping my focus on writing. "It suits you, too."

It might explain a bit of his commitment to making and keeping promises. No matter what they cost him.

"Thanks," he said in surprise.

"Which is the 'Ben' part?" I asked, trying to hide my intensity. That part mattered to me. I wanted to know what *I* was telling him every time I said his preferred name.

"Binder," Ben said with a shrug.

The pull hummed between us, thrumming like a plucked string at his own casual mention of the word.

That gave me pause. I stopped writing for a moment, worried I would slip and make some garish error in this timeless public record of my family's favorite pancake recipe. I had been writing this slowly for a reason. Well...given the many distractions, more than one reason. But this was the main one. After all, this was my first official contribution to the store of dramá knowledge. It wouldn't be my most momentous, but it was my first.

Oblivious, Ben went on. "Kor and I share the first part, which is common in male names: Kor, 'oath.' Except his name, Korinth, means 'oath keeper.'"

Nothing to read into there.... Probably.

"Except you go by 'Ben,' and he by 'Kor,'" I said, trying to keep the conversation casual. I was still recovering from the pull's vibration.

Was there anything to their choice of nicknames? Particularly Ben's?

"Well, yeah," Ben said with a chuckle. "'Kori' for me and 'inth' for him aren't exactly easier to say, are they?"

So no, then. Just coincidence, finally.

I answered with a chuckle of my own. "I guess not."

Ben hesitated, then asked with a bit of pink, "Does...my name mean anything to you?"

I paused again. "*Koriben*, no. Not to me. But *Ben*.... That's short for another Hebrew name borrowed into English: Benjamin."

"What does that mean?"

I was by no means a Hebrew expert or name etymologist, so the only reason I knew the answer to that question was because I'd once gone through a phase of looking up the meanings of every person I knew, and I had an uncle on my dad's side with that name. He'd always been my favorite uncle....

OK, I was trying very hard now to not make this weird in my head.

I focused on the answer to Ben's question. "*Benjamin* means 'son of the right hand.' Kind of weird, if you think about it. Strangely close to right*wing*."

"Not right*wing*," Ben said tightly.

I was surprised by his tone into looking at him. His expression was controlled. "*Hand*. The Monarch...is often called the Right Hand of the Tree. The one the Tree can trust to go and do in Her place what She cannot. I *am* the son of Her Right Hand."

I blinked at him. "'Ben.' *Son*."

Or even, adding in an English twist...sun.

I shook my head and refocused on the recipe. Again.

"Interesting," I said.

"Interesting," Ben agreed in the same tone.

We were quiet for a minute while I finished. Then, with mutual relief, we both got to work.

I had to talk through every single ingredient to give Ben an idea of the qualities I needed in each and then find the closest equivalent. The flour we had in the storeroom wasn't wheat, but Ben assured me it had gumming properties like gluten and would rise with a powder that must have acted like baking soda. The eggs we found in the chilled section of the cold storage room were enormous, making me wonder if dramá raised ostriches or something; I only grabbed one of those and was sure we wouldn't use all of it. We could make scrambled eggs with the rest.

After debating for too long about this ingredient or that and proportions of each, we gathered our finds and brought them to the kitchen. The measuring got tricky, since dramá didn't use cups and tablespoons, so I just tried to add whatever looked and felt right.

"This is all very experimental," I warned Ben as he stirred for me. "Don't get your hopes up."

He chuckled. "Avvi would always say that, no matter how it turns out, food is the best adventure, especially when you go on it with..."

He cleared his throat. "...er, the people you are close to."

I smiled, leaned against the counter, and just tried to freeze this moment in my mind forever: Ben standing there, a streak of flour on his beard, an unconscious smile on his face, peace in his golden eyes. Diligently stirring whatever crazy, doughy mess we had made together. The only thing that could have made this better was....

"Could you sing something?" I asked impulsively, before I could think better of it.

He looked at me in surprise, coloring a bit. I expected him to refuse outright, but then his eyes grew thoughtful. Calculating, almost. "Do you...like it when I do?"

"A lot," I admitted. "You have a good voice."

His lips slowly pulled into a smile, his eyes flashed with a challenge. "I'll sing if you sing with me."

"How am I supposed to do that?" I asked in surprise. "I *highly* doubt we know any songs in common."

"I'll teach you," he chuckled.

So, as we stood together and I showed him how to pour and flip pancakes, he taught me a jaunty love song. Turned out I was the least composed of the two of us as he coached me through the words and melody; the romantic theme didn't seem to strike him as deeply, thank goodness—probably from familiarity. I tried to focus on the cheerful tune and not the meanings and avoid looking at him, and eventually I settled in. I could tell the song was meant to be danced to from the way Ben's feet began to tap and his hips shift to the rhythm.

That should have been my warning.

By the time I poured the last of the batch into four small rounds, I was able to remember some of the lines. So, as I sang comfortably along with Ben, I didn't realize he had dropped out until it was too late: I had already sung a full line of the other lover's response. I looked up at Ben in mild alarm, but he just grinned widely as he answered with the next line. I laughed, and the next time it was my turn, I picked up the song, and we sung the duet as I finally understood it was meant to be sung.

Then, the moment I flipped the last of the pancakes and he turned off the hot plate...

...Ben snatched my hand and spun me.

"Ben!" I spluttered, but I was laughing too much to make the irritation convincing.

Thank goodness he didn't expect me to focus on two new things at once, because he carried the entire rest of the song as he danced us around the kitchen. I kept up as best as I could, but I knew I couldn't be doing anything right. Still, somehow he didn't seem to care. His eyes simply glowed, and his hands gently guided me through spins and turns and lifts.

He ended the song with a lift, and this time, he didn't put me down. He kept me up there with him, his nose nearly brushing mine. His eyes didn't just *glow.*

They burned.

I swallowed with difficulty through my panting breath, and my eyes widened. My heart pounded even faster than it had during the dance—and it had already been beating fast. Instinctively, my arms wrapped around his neck, even though I wasn't sure that was what I was supposed to be doing at all.

But all Kor's warnings were flying out of my head. This felt too right, too inevitable. Turning away—unthinkable.

I could see the glow of my own eyes for the first time reflected in his.

"Sarah," Ben whispered, voice edged with something that made me shiver. The way he was looking at my lips made them burn and part in anticipation. "Can I—"

"When are you two going to be *done* already?" Yvera said irritably as she strode into the kitchen. "I'm starv—"

She froze when she saw us.

I looked at her anxiously. This had been exactly the scene I had been trying to avoid. For *all* our sakes.

But to my shock, it didn't play out at all as I had expected.

Yvera...snorted. "Fine. I can wait."

Then she grabbed a fruit from the bowl on one of the tables and cast us an irritated, pointed look that said, *Hurry the torch up, will you?*

Then, biting in, she strode out.

And Ben, far from dropping me and running after her...hadn't even looked her way. Or looked away from me, even though I noted that the fire in his eyes had died.

"Er, Ben?" I said, clearing my throat awkwardly. "I think...you had better put me down."

He only raised an eyebrow. Where were his blushes and stammers now?

"Because of Yvera, or because you don't want me to hold you?"

With all of Kor's warnings rushing back in, I didn't know what the right answer was. "Um...because of Yvera. And just...not now."

Ben sighed but nodded, as if he had been expecting that answer.

He gently lowered me back down. I worried I'd hurt his feelings, but he gave me a reassuring squeeze on my shoulder and turned to walk back to our pancakes, whistling the tune to the song we had just sung.

I followed him in a daze.

From the way my lips were still burning at just the *memory* of being so close to his...I was pretty sure that the pancakes could taste like sawdust, and I wouldn't notice.

Chapter Thirty

PLANS

Koriben

ALL IN ALL, I considered the afternoon's experiment a success.

Oh, and the pan cakes were surprisingly good, too. Despite being not much like what I thought of as a cake.

But the meal hadn't been the point. As pure as Sarah might have thought my intentions had been in asking her to teach me a recipe, what had originally given me the inspiration was racking my mind to come up with some way to ask her for a favor—since she liked to be helpful—that entailed spending time with her.

I felt surprisingly little guilt about the ploy. Probably because I did fully intend to make her family pan cakes, for the exact reason I had given her. As soon as I thought of the Earthren cooking lesson, I knew I did need some way to show them I had tried...and *would* try to take care of her. And if they were, right in that moment, feeling anything close to the desperation, guilt, and rage I had felt at losing her.... Well, I shuddered for them.

But as I ate the results of our painstaking work with Sarah and my wings, along with the rest of the egg and some sausages I had quickly fried up, I almost couldn't sit still for satisfaction.

Because now, I was almost certain that if I asked in the right way and with the right amount of Sarah's beloved privacy...she would let me kiss her. And that made me *very* happy. Happier than I could ever remember being, actually. More filled with fire and fizzy energy than I had any right to be as the sun lowered in the sky.

I couldn't be as mad at Yvera for her interruption as I had been at Kor for several reasons, foremost being that, without her, I might not have realized that I was Sarah's intended mate and taken the risk to "flirt harder." And Flame, had it paid off. I couldn't help but feel a bit of smugness directed at Kor as he sat obliviously next to me and tried to flatter Sarah with compliments about the pan cakes.

My smugness increased when she didn't seem moved.

She was rather quiet, actually. Had been, I realized, since our near kiss. But before I could worry that I had misread everything and upset her, she met my eyes. Her cheeks warmed, but she didn't drop my gaze. Then her lips slowly smiled, and her eyes flashed silver for a moment.

Then I knew she was remembering, just as I was. And the memory was a good one.

I grinned back.

"Ben? *Ben!*"

"What?" I asked, suddenly realizing Kor had been trying to get my attention.

He sighed. "Discussing plans for tomorrow? The Moonfair?"

"Oh, right," I said.

Somehow, I had forgotten about that torched thing. That just went to show how high I was soaring right now if I could overlook the looming mountain of the Moonfair for even a second.

Ashdust. Now I had another reason to curse it. The chances of giving Sarah the privacy she needed during the Moonfair were scarce. I was just going to have to make the most of tonight with her....

Kor grunted. "As I was saying, I think Sarah should leave tonight."

"Wait, *what?*"

"If Sarah is going to be blending in with the part of your retinue arriving early—"

"*What?*"

"I think you're going to have to start again, Kor," Yvera said dryly as she stabbed another piece of her pan cake—with a little more savagery than usual, but even if I could have cared in the moment, I would have let it slide.

Kor sighed. "I knew you were taking this too calmly."

"I'm not letting Sarah be separated from me!" I snapped. "Who else can prot—"

"And how else do you propose avoiding announcing who she is to the entire Six Realms?" Kor said impatiently. "The two things on everyone's lips right now are that you are coming to the Moonfair, *and* you'll most likely have this Moontouched amón everyone's heard about with you."

"You didn't put that in your acceptance, did you?" I demanded.

"No," Kor said slowly, as if I were a hatchling. "I specifically said she would *not* be coming with you. But that isn't going to stop people from assuming it, Ben. You have been inseparable from her in every public setting since she was first seen. And they have her description now: small, young, dark-haired, tan, and beautiful."

Yvera rolled her eyes at the last adjective, and Sarah raised an unimpressed eyebrow. I tried to hide my unjustified irritation with Kor's flattery—no matter how accurate in this case—under my entirely justified anger at his outlandish proposal.

"Then we disguise her," I said impatiently. "I'm not letting Sarah out of my sight."

Kor took a deep breath, visibly striving for patience. "That is precisely what everyone is going to expect, Ben. There's no disguise we can offer Sarah as long as she *is* with you that will save her from being recognized. We can change the color of her hair, maybe do something subtle enough about her eyes, but any deeper illusionary magic that could obscure her height or alter her skin is going to be spotted immediately. Therefore, the only way to protect her identity is to separate her from you. From all three of us, actually."

"*No*," I said vehemently. "Absolutely not. The Tree entrusted her to *our* care—"

Kor interrupted with a flat voice. "If you won't trust my judgment in this, would you trust the King's?"

That had perhaps been the only thing Kor could have said that would have given me pause, and he torched knew it. I clenched my teeth. "*Avva* thinks this is a good idea?"

"He does," Kor said stiffly. "He agrees with my reasoning that separation is necessary for Sarah's anonymity. Therefore, he has offered Eskala, her rightwing, and all her elites to safely take Sarah to Olsdak."

I hesitated. That was no small gesture on Avva's part, especially at a time when Avva desperately needed Eskala and all her people at *his* side to prepare for the invasion. It expressed more support for Kor's idea than I liked.

Meeting my eyes, Kor said quietly, "The King also thought you might need the gentle reminder that you aren't in charge of this quest the Trees have given us. As you yourself keep telling us...that is Sarah. He said if you fought me on this, but Sarah agreed, that you could consider it an order from him."

I winced. Kor might as well have slapped me. I could almost hear Avva's soft, yet firm rebuke echo through his words.

With a heavy flameheart, I looked at Sarah, already knowing how she would answer.

"What Kor said makes sense," she said evenly. "I'll admit, I don't like the idea of going along with strangers. But I trust all of you to know that *they* are trustworthy and that they will keep me safe."

I groaned and put my head in my hands. I officially had no choice. And yet, even now...I didn't know how I was going to do it. Never before had I felt such a savage desire to rebel against a direct order from my father and King, and never thought I would. Avva always knew what was best, just as surely as the Tree did.

Or so I had always thought. But Sarah, as always...changed everything.

"You'll be heavily guarded at all times," Kor said to Sarah, voice softening now that her decision was made and my authority shoved aside. "You'll be given the uniform of a healer's assistant and safely ensconced with Eskala and her retinue in the King's Wing. Some of her and even Ben's elites are there now, making sure everything is secure and that we don't have any more...surprises."

"Speaking of surprises," I said grimly, glad for the momentary distraction, no matter how distasteful in and of itself. "Any news on how a rock wyrm's tunnel near the shelter *and* an explosion forceful enough to knock a hole into it entirely escaped our notice until long after Sarah was taken?"

"Rock...worm...." Sarah said faintly, paling.

"I...can explain later," I told her reluctantly. I would if she made me. But I didn't want to add to her nightmares more than I had to.

Rock wyrms...were one of the few things even I had to fear, no matter the time of day. Even though they were smaller than their cousins, the sand wyrms (those were truly a nightmare to behold), rock wyrms were the more deadly for their preferred hunting grounds and their preferred prey: the mountains...and us.

A sand wyrm only got one of us if it had the opportunity. The rock wyrm sought us out. And no other monster could break through a hold's interior defenses like it could, or devastate a hold's population so thoroughly if it got in. They didn't seem to care that they always died in the process; not content to grab a mouthful and go, they were inexorably drawn to the power in our flamehearts like insects to flame and feasted until we killed them. Given their slow reproductive and growth rate, and our diligence in exterminating any that came too close to our holds, their numbers had dwindled toward extinction over the centuries in their quest for their relatively newfound sport, but they mindlessly gorged whenever they could anyway.

They were devilishly hard to kill, too. Since we often had to fight them in the confines of their own tunnels or our holds, we usually couldn't use our drakáforms. Their hides were impervious to all but the sharpest, magically enhanced weaponry, and even then, the only good in attacking it from its sides was to annoy it or slow it down (with only one notable exception, lauded in many a ballad or novel, when a Queen had once sliced one clean in two). We had also developed a poison that seemed to pain it enough to distract it from gorging if we could shoot a few tipped arrows far enough to get past the rows of teeth into its only unguarded portion: the tender flesh that came after. However, the only fast and surefire way to kill one was to get a direct hit of scorching flame far, far down its throat. And, if my people were unprepared with a sufficiently powerful team, such as in a hold incursion, doing that too often required a sacrifice.

I had hunted rock wyrms a handful of times—with a specialized team of elites following it down one of its tunnels, before it broke into the hold it was heading for. Given their deadliness, rock wyrm sightings were serious enough to call in backup as high up as the Heir, especially if the wyrm was getting close.

But I had only been in one rock wyrm hold incursion in my entire life. And I never, ever wanted to repeat the bloodbath that was that day.

Ever.

Just remembering was making me curl my fists and take deep, steadying breaths. A mindhealer's careful attention and many talks with Avva were the only reasons I was still sane after Ilyam.

"Yes," Yvera said grimly, supplying me with a much-needed distraction. "Kor and I just got the report this morning. The silencing of the explosion is the simplest explanation: the rechal created a torched good sound dampening and magic capturing bubble around the explosion, which would have prevented us from hearing or feeling it."

I sighed. "That would have taken skill. An older rechal, then. But I see how that could do it."

Yvera nodded. "The tunnel is where it gets trickier. It was dated to only be a month old, give or take a few days."

I frowned. "Interesting."

More like disturbing. The tunnel was old enough that the scent was stale, yet new enough to have avoided the seismic tests that the Strongshield did periodically across the Wirthen Desert to find the wyrms or signs of their passage. It could have been an unconsumed wyrm, just minding its own deadly business. And yet, if so...how would the Devourer know about the tunnel before we did?

That made me think it was consumed after all, and the tunnel deliberately created with close access to the shelter. But that presented a more disturbing question: What had the Devourer been planning to do with it? With its invasion so close, surely it hadn't gone through that trouble just on the off chance it could snatch a few people nightsheltering there. Unless....

I had just been on the cusp of a horrifying realization when Yvera continued, "The exit hole that we all...ended up at had been concealed with consumed magic."

"So, consumed rock wyrm, most likely," I said.

"Most likely," Yvera agreed.

Fantastic. My favorite kind. If *normal* rock wyrms were obsessed with finding and eating us, then imagine what one given a few nudges in the right direction would do.

As a matter of fact...that sense of direction was the only difference we could discern between a normal rock wyrm and a consumed one. That and being on a planet it had no business being on, but now there had been sightings of both kinds of wyrms on every one, so that was becoming less of a determining factor by the century.

"Have—"

Anticipating my question, Yvera said with a raised eyebrow, "All holds in the Wirthen Desert have been notified and are now on high alert. Hunts are underway as we speak."

"Good. Thank you."

"Don't thank me. They passed the information on themselves before even giving us the report."

"As they should," I said with a nod.

Kor added, "I warned them it could now head rapidly for a hold. The Devourer might have kept it in check long enough for its trap to spring, but now it might point the wyrm in a direction and let it go create some mayhem."

Sarah was looking slightly ill, which meant she had guessed enough of what a rock wyrm was to get the picture.

I turned my gaze quickly to Kor. So the hunch I had been coming on had been right. "You think that trap was meant for us, too?"

"I do," Kor said grimly. "It's too much of a coincidence, and too much bother for too little gain otherwise."

"But how would the Devourer know *we* would nightshelter there?" Yvera demanded. "A month ago?"

"Same reason we were there at all," Kor said quietly. "I think we now have to assume that the Devourer knows the location of the moongates. *All* the moongates. Even the ones we have not yet led it to."

Silence fell over the table.

Yvera was the first to break it, with a bit of profanity. "Kor...you had better be wrong."

"Oh, I hope I am, Yvera," Kor said grimly. "But I don't think so. Think about it: it probably spied on their very construction. And though it could not or did not act on the information at the time, it would have remembered. We've given it a bit of a chase with our fast pace and backward direction through the Realms, but now I think it has now figured out our goal and our pattern."

That...was some of the worst news I had heard since the fact of its impending invasion. I just sat there, too devastated by it to even take part in my wings' discussion for a few moments.

"But the rock wyrm tunnel was a month old," Yvera said, pressing the table with her pointer finger. "Sarah got to the Realms seven days ago, and we only began this mad hunt a couple days after that."

"Seven...." Sarah said, blinking.

Did it seem like a lifetime ago to her too?

"Yes," Kor answered Yvera. "But the Devourer would be a fool to not expect the Trees to make some effort like this in the days leading up to its second invasion. And it is no fool. Probably the only reason Sarah is alive is because she came to *Ykran*, the last of the worlds. If she had come to Ythra...."

My flameheart sputtered and my fists slowly clenched again.

Yvera drummed her fingers. "If the Devourer knew we were going to stay at that shelter, why did it only send a rechal and some jorgen?"

"Only?" Sarah muttered.

Kor spread his hands. "Like I said, I think we gave it a bit of a run *at first*. It had the tunnel dug in advance, but it hadn't had the time to sneak in a proper ambush force the night we were there. It was improvising the rest. But I don't think we'll catch it so unprepared for us again."

And that was the terrible reality of it. From now on, the Devourer would know approximately when and exactly where we would be taking Sarah. And it would be readying ambushes at each place.

I ground my teeth. "And you thought it was best to stop for a day."

"Yes, Ben, and I still think it was the right thing to do—for that reason. We have lost our element of surprise. With that protection gone, it is time to involve the people and resources we have at our disposal to keep Sarah safe and accomplish our mission. But all that coordination requires *time*."

Kor paused and made sure he had my eye. "We can't do this alone anymore, Ben. Perhaps we never could. But we got lucky—or were Flameblessed. I'm not sure which I prefer, but seeing as I'm alive, I suppose I'll take either. But I won't count on either for a day longer. We *need* Yvera directing your elites to help us. We *need* all the research my analysts can do. And we need to coordinate with the King and his wings. So that is what we have done, ever since you collapsed at my feet after exhausting your berserker rage."

The memory of it suddenly came to me: coming to myself to find myself on all fours in front of Kor. And...Sarah, as if standing in a bright window in the mountainside....

I shook my head and dismissed the image as being one of the absurdities inserted by the nightmare.

I sighed. Then slowly nodded. "You're...right. As usual. The time for going at it alone...is over. And I was torched stupid for extending it for that long."

Kor smiled thinly. "Not stupid. It's a method that has worked well for you so far in your life—and it won us three gates in so short a time it confounded even the Devourer. But this is getting bigger than us, Ben. Sarah is our only hope to truly repel the invasion *and* survive after...and the Devourer knows that too. It isn't about to let its centuries of planning go to waste for one amón girl and the Heir and his wings standing in front of her."

Sarah spoke up quietly. "The rechal. It said the Devourer wanted my blood."

We all turned to look at her.

She had come far in these seven days. Where once she might have shrunk under our stares or the frightening subject, she now stared back at all of us calmly, shoulders relaxed, chin up.

Yvera broke the silence with a snort. "Of course it wants your blood. It wants all Royal blood."

Sarah asked the question I had been dreading. "Why? The moment after I arrived, the moment its consumed captured me, it tried to get them to sacrifice me. Why?"

Kor and Yvera looked at me. It seemed they weren't going to take the burden of the revelation off my shoulders.

"Because if it had...everything might have ended there," I said quietly.

"How? The Trees could have sent—"

"By sending you, the Tree of Ice signified you as Her Heir. You haven't been invested yet, so your transformation isn't complete. But it would have been enough to change you—to change your blood to *the* Blood. The Royal Blood of the Covenants. And with that Blood...the Devourer can break our gates...and make its own."

I let that sink in, watching her lips press thin and her breath sharpen. Still, she stared so bravely, so valiantly back at me. Living true to her name, in all its meanings.

I forced myself to think enough about the words so that I could say them, though they were so terrible each felt like they burned my mouth and darkened my flameheart as they came out.

"If it had sacrificed you and gotten all the Blood that it could, it would not have had to wait for the Dark Solstice. It could have opened gates across the Six Realms and launched its invasion almost twelve days before the Trees were expecting it, and long, long before we were prepared to meet it. The devastation to our defenses would have been catastrophic, our extermination swift and complete. The Devourer would have won the Six Realms, and our Tree would have fallen...and the Tree of Ice would not have been able to stand alone against it when it came next for Earth."

Sarah took several deep breaths. Then said, "I...see. Does that mean it wants your Blood just as badly?"

"You're something a step above me, Sarah," I said gently. "I'm an Heir. The spot of King is full. You have no one above you. You *have* the Blood, the potential of a Queen now, and it has been waking more strongly in you by the day. So, the answer to your question is probably no. It likely wants your Blood more than it does mine."

"That's one reason the Heir is allowed to run more risks," Kor explained simply. "The Heir has more power than anyone but the Monarch, but less potential for harm if captured and sacrificed."

"So, the Devourer could do the same degree of harm with my blood...as it could only do with your father's," she murmured.

"Yes," I said heavily.

"And I have the most vulnerable Monarch's blood that it has ever had a chance to get," she finished.

I winced. "You're not...."

"Don't lie about this, Ben," she said calmly. "I have no wings, no elites, no *clan*. I don't even have most of my power. I'm ignorant and naive and untrained. And I'm just an amón—no dragon inside of me. *That's* why it wants me. Because I'm vulnerable...and it's a torched coward."

We all stared at that ending. That had not been what *I* had been expecting, at least.

Kor suddenly chuckled.

"*Sera*, indeed," he said with a flirtatious smile. To my consternation, he reached across the table to pick up Sarah's hand and *kiss* it. "You live up to your name in every sense, my dear."

Can I kill him? I silently asked Yvera. *Please?*

I was bunching my fists under the table to hide the force of my rage.

Sure, Yvera teased, so that I knew she wasn't serious. *I'll help. First, we drug him with icebane. Probably in his favorite wine, that red one from Romskal. Then, just in case he has the antidote or can still get some magic out, you bind him, since you're better with the magic stuff, and I'll shoot him from a distance with a—*

Yvera, I said tightly. *I didn't need you to be quite that encouraging. Or detailed.*

She rolled her eyes. *Then you shouldn't have asked* me.

True. Joking aside, Yvera probably had a plan to kill everyone, including me. You know...just in case.

As we'd silently communicated, I'd kept my eye on Sarah to see how she would respond. She slowly withdrew her hand without changing her expression, perhaps still too sober to duck or blush. But I didn't *think* she enjoyed Kor's flirtation.

"Unless there's something else you need to tell me about blood sacrifices, perhaps we had better get back to discussing the Moonfair, especially if that means I'm leaving soon."

Soon.... Flame Above, the sun was still lowering, past its zenith now.

No, no, no, *no*.

Handing her off to someone else to protect, *even if* it was Eskala, her right wing, and all her elites, would have been impossible enough.

But without the private moments I had been planning with her?

"Yes," Kor said, studying the invisible sun for a moment. "Although I think we have covered most of what we need to discuss for now. I'll go inform Eskala of your acceptance of her escort and arrange for her to meet us outside the Ykran moongate in four deken."

"Four *deken*?" I said, the bottom of my stomach dropping out.

"Yes," Kor said absently. "That should be just enough time for her to arrive at the gate and for you to give Sarah some last defense pointers and help her pack. We need to give Eskala as much daylight as possible to bring Sarah to Olsdak, after all."

I...had nothing I could say, about any of that. My hands were tied by an order from my King to let her go, and if Sarah *had* to go today, then Kor was right: the sooner, the better. And I couldn't waste what little time I had left with Sarah on anything but preparing her as much as I could and distracting her as little as I could help.

But Flame Above....

How was I going to do this?

CHAPTER THIRTY-ONE

PARTING

SARAH

As WE STOOD IN my hold in front of the Ykran gate, waiting for Eskala's signal, I played around with my new watch, hoping no one would see my nervous fidgeting for what it was.

Alya had made the finishing touches on the watch while Kor had spent those couple hours until dawn with them and, just before he left them, she gave it to him to give to me, telling him to pass along her apologies that she couldn't do more in the time she had and that she would send a far superior one when she could. Kor claimed that he had simply forgotten to give it to me until now, which, given the million things that he had had to do and think about since then, could have even been true.

But he didn't have to make as much of a show as he did of putting it on my wrist in front of Ben, finishing with another kiss on the back of my hand and some drivel about how it would help me keep the deken until we could be reunited. Forget faking acceptance of his attention, I just had a hard time not visibly gagging.

If I hadn't already had irrefutable proof of Kor's courage, that would have been it. Ben's glares in his direction now were bordering on murderous. I wasn't sure how much more of this charade would be healthy, for either of them. Perhaps there was another benefit to me leaving the three of them for a bit.

Alya's watch was...amazing. Sure, it didn't play music or have an AI assistant, but I wasn't sure I wanted those things—on my wrist, at least—anymore. For now, it was all I could have hoped for.

The circular interface was about the size of a quarter. Most of the time, it was dark, maybe to save energy or simply not be obnoxious. But if I tapped it once, it would show Ythra's day and night cycle over the Temple of Flame—which apparently was the dramá equivalent to Zulu time—demonstrated with a sundial pie chart. The golden glowing portion was for the remaining sunlight, which would slowly decrease as Ythra's day went on.

The notches etched around the rim were practically invisible when the watch was inactive, but when it was active, the notches showed up against the gold like hour lines on an analog watch. Which was exactly what they represented: whatever a "deken" was, it seemed roughly equivalent to an hour, since there were fourteen notches. Kor explained that at dawn, the watch would fill completely with golden light, and the notches would count down the fourteen deken of daylight as the sun crossed the sky over the Temple. When the golden pie was entirely gone, that indicated nightfall, and the watch would fill with white light instead, presumably to represent a moon, and the cycle would repeat for fourteen deken of night.

When I asked about seasons, Kor said that no matter the time of year, that full circle with the fourteen notches would sufficiently approximate actual day and night above the Temple, since it was on Ythra's equator.

So, yes, the watch couldn't show me the *current* day/night schedule, but I was getting a sense of that of my own, even if it was in the reverse way the drakón did; even now, I could feel that my weakest moment of power had passed, and it was slowly building again.

Besides, with how much we were world-hopping right now, I wasn't sure local time would have been useful to me anyway. I was surprisingly comforted to have an anchor within time and space again that would always be the same, even if it didn't reflect my current surroundings. Plus, I would finally be able to understand and express time to Ben and his wings, an ability which seemed increasingly important now that we were beginning to coordinate with others and separate.

The notches had another purpose. If I tapped the interface again, it would show another golden pie, this one representing a quarter of a deken, with each of the fourteen notches representing a dek. It was only after watching a dek pass that I finally confirmed to myself it was *roughly* a minute. So four revolutions of the golden pie in this setting would roughly approximate an hour.

And if I tapped a third time, it would act like a day counter, with the golden pie now decreasing at an indiscernible rate to show how many days remained in a fourteen-day cycle. Two of those cycles would apparently constitute a dramá month. Coincidentally...or not...Kor said that I had met with the Tree of Ice and been given our mission on the nineteenth night of their eighth month.

Meaning the five days that remained in the pie accurately represented how many days we had left before the invasion. I had told Ben just last night to think of the glass as half full, but with that dark chunk staring me in the face....

Right now, if Ben was even trying to conceal his anxious energy, he was doing it poorly. Often, he paced, but if he managed to stay next to me, as he was now, he drummed his fingers, shifted from foot to foot, or let his gaze wander restlessly.

"You have the whistle?" he asked absently.

For the third time. He had been the one to help me pack, after all. He once again had my things in his ether storage, ready to hand them off to someone in my escort party.

I just took a deep breath for patience and once again made a great effort to slow my own heartbeat. I had been fighting a double battle against my own fears and his contagious anxiety, but I was determined to win it for his sake. My calm probably didn't have enough potency to influence him in turn, but I knew that if he saw I was nervous, his agitation and reluctance to let me go would only increase.

I answered him by raising the whistle off my chest to show him. "Yes, right here."

I preempted his other questions by following up with their answers. "And I still have your scale in my pocket."

I patted the pocket with my other hand, where the scale rested comfortingly, even though it was now a different pair of pants. While Ben and I were packing, my lights had brought me, without prompting, a sturdy, loose, serviceable pair of gold pants and matching shirt.

I only realized why they looked so much like a uniform when Ben saw what the lights had brought, grunted, and said, "Well, you might as well wear those. They're practically identical to the healer's uniform they're going to be giving you to wear anyway. Saves you having to change under someone's wing or something."

I stared at him, but he had seemed perfectly serious.

Dragons, I thought in exasperation.

Neither of us, nor even Kor when he saw me in my partial "uniform" and expressed satisfied approval, talked about why my lights would have something like this just sitting around for me. In my size. The only thing the lights hadn't provided to complete the uniform was....

"Are you cold?" Ben asked. "Do you need to wear your own coat until they give you the healer one?"

I couldn't wear Svyer's pretty gift of a coat on this trip, unfortunately, since that wasn't part of my disguise and would have been too recognizable besides. In that case, I didn't want to pack it at all; I had left it hanging on a hook in my room, secretly thinking of it as a kind of good luck totem. A sign of faith that I would be returning to this hold, to that room, for it.

"No, I'll be fine until then, Ben. Besides, I wouldn't have a quick place to put it after I switched, unless you held up my bags for me."

"I could—"

I shook my head. "That's just one less thing we have to do. Besides, I want to leave it here where I *know* I won't lose it and where it will stay safe and nice."

Ben raised an eyebrow at me. "It's a nice coat, but coats are meant to be used. They're not much good otherwise."

I just smiled back at him. For someone who tried so hard not to break things, he didn't seem to have as much regard as I did for keeping nice things nice. But I could see why. After breaking or ruining so much, he'd stopped letting himself become attached a long time ago. Plus, he'd grown up as practically a prince. New things, things specially given to you and for you, without being handed down from sibling to sibling or some other family member, were nothing "new" to him. The cost of replacements didn't seem to be an issue, either.

And, well, as Svyer had said...he was male—and not the *Kor* kind of male, which I was coming to appreciate.

I continued before he could protest further. "I also have a pack, with sunscreen and my essentials and more food than I can eat in a day, let alone a few hours, inside."

That sat at my feet. Again, it wasn't my usual pack, which matched Svyer's coat, but a leather shoulder bag that looked much more standard issue.

"And I have my gun."

I patted the small of my back. When Ben had taken me back to the training room after our late lunch for some more self-defense lessons, we had found a waistband holster that would allow me to conceal the weapon with the uniform's loose shirt and the coat they would give me. It helped that the gun was unusually slim and small compared with the average Earthren pistol—perfect for my small hands...and now, for concealment.

Ben had made me draw it what felt like over a hundred times before he was satisfied I could do it quickly and from various positions—including one in which he'd pinned my dominant arm, forcing me to draw it with the other.

"And the...knife," I said reluctantly, with a final pat.

My most recent acquisition was on a belt on my hip. Again, the sheath, belt, and even hilt looked standard issue, but Ben assured me the knife was of superior craftsmanship. I trusted him on that, but I was less confident that I would be able to use it effectively, despite Ben's lessons on grip, stance, and thrust. I could tell Ben was worried about that too, but I didn't know whether he was worried about my lack of confidence, was genuinely worried about my skill, or was simply worried about a scenario that would force me to use it.

Regardless of how either of us felt about the knife, it was one more weapon Ben could give me, and this one, with the coat, completed the uniform, so it would have weakened the disguise for me to not have that much. Apparently not even Peacegrowth healers were pacifists. In the Six Realms, where the dramá were besieged by the Devourer's consumed or their escaped descendants *every single night*...no one could afford to be.

Technically, Ben had given me yet one more weapon, but that one was in my mind and body. Since packing and changing didn't take long, he spent most of those four hours teaching me ways to escape, disable, or hurt even an assailant as big as him.

The number of tactics I, a one-hundred-and-twenty-pound, eighteen-year-old Earthren female, could use against someone of superior size and strength had surprised me—and I had grown up with an older brother obsessed with self-defense. But then, beyond after-school karate, Michael had only been able to really indulge in that interest after he left home, and though my parents gave tacit approval for him to show us things when he came to visit, I'd avoided his lessons with the others like the plague.

Part of it was my parents' dogma on nonaggression was too ingrained by the time their own thinking had shifted; part of it was simply not being ready to process being in a situation in which I would need what Michael could teach me. I was too old and aware of the realities of the world to think they were merely superhero lessons like Michael let the younger ones think, and I had none of Rachel's spunk. I let Michael take me shooting, because I could pretend it was just a target sport. But that was it. As much as that worried and pained Michael, he quickly understood that pushing only made me more fearful and reluctant, so he let it go.

Now I had been through more life-threatening situations than I let myself count, and I had somehow survived. I was so far past processing that I jumped at the chance to learn what Ben offered.

Even though, while he was teaching me how to get out of a choke hold, I pointed out to him, "Ben, this stuff...most of it is assuming that whoever is attacking me is at least somewhat humanoid."

Ben let go for a moment and kneeled to be level with my eyes. His were the hard gold now. "Sarah...I hate to say it, but that's exactly the sort of agent the

Devourer could send against you this time. Who else would be able to get into Olsdak undetected to get to you?"

I went cold. Though the monsters I had encountered thus far had been the stuff of nightmares, somehow they didn't seem as frightening now as the thought of someone human—or amón or drakón—attacking me: a dramá, born free, who had betrayed their own people that thoroughly. Who had chosen to work with their race's sworn destroyer...for what?

I could only think of the desire for power or pleasure at causing pain.

That...was the true kind of monster.

Ben's eyes grew heavy as he saw I understood, and he nodded. "It happens, Sarah. Some of us turn to the Devourer. It can't make all or even most of them lish, especially not the amón, but it's happy to use them as agents among us until they're caught. There aren't many, and it's hard for the ones there are to avoid the methods we've developed to detect consumption, so they stay on the fringes. They avoid Avva and me if they can because we have enough of the Tree in us to sense the Devourer in them. And they *never* go near a Tree, theirs or the One on Ythra.

"But Olsdak isn't the Starkissed capital, so it doesn't have Oshal's Tree. With all the foreigners flooding in for the Moonfair, and with the Devourer most likely knowing exactly when and where we will be to find the next gate...."

"That's what you think it will do," I murmured, chilled with understanding.

Ben closed his eyes and nodded wordlessly.

I debated swiftly, then allowed myself one slight indulgence. The gesture wasn't much more than what I had already done, anyway.

I cupped his face with both of my hands, allowing my thumbs to brush along the upper edge of his beard. His eyes shot open, wide with surprise, but they were soon glowing after they met mine.

Even though his expression remained deadly serious.

"Ben," I said quietly. "I'll be fine."

He sighed. "You had better."

My lips pulled into a thin smile. "After all the work you're putting into me...how could I be otherwise?"

His lips twitched, as I'd intended. "Well, now I have to admit to an ulterior motive in teaching you these sorts of things now."

"Oh?" I asked, curious.

"There's...a lot of drinking at the Moonfair. Not so much on the first night, but that night often has its own risks. Starkissed...and the others who come to their festivals...get very...physical."

"Ah," I said soberly, nodding to show I understood. Still, I deliberately kept my hands on his face to show him I had no qualms about *him*.

But apparently he needed that kind of separation right now, because he reached up with both of his hands to lower mine. But I noticed he still held them.

"I know I am way overthinking this," he said quickly. "You'll be guarded at all times—there should never even be a risk from that quarter. And people generally mean well. But, with the drinking...and you being so different...."

He blushed. "This probably won't come as a surprise to you by now, but we dramá tend to not be very...subtle in the way we express interest. Or *deny* it. Generally, we have no qualms about asking for what we want and saying no when we don't want what's being offered."

You being an exception to that rule, I thought with a secret smile.

I could see what he was getting at, though, so I spared him some awkwardness by saying it calmly. "You're worried that, since I'm so nice and quiet, someone will misread me and make me uncomfortable, and I won't feel like I can tell them no."

His blush increased. "Er...yes. Like I said, I am being paranoid, since it should *never* be an issue, but...Flame, I'll feel better if I know you can tell someone no in a way that will not just get the message to their drunk brain but also make them wince when they remember you."

I smiled. "Thank you for your concern. It's good of you. And for teaching me these sorts of things, because they're useful, they're important, and it gives me confidence to know them. But, like I said before, either you or the dramá in general have been rubbing off on me. I don't think I'll have a problem telling anyone *no*. And shooting them in the foot if they don't listen."

At first while listening to me, Ben had appeared relieved. Only when his face fell just a fraction at my last couple sentences did I realize how he could have interpreted them.

I...had not been telling Kor no. And Ben had been hoping that was only because I didn't feel like I could.

He recovered quickly with a broad, genuine smile, gripping my shoulder. "Good. I'm relieved to hear it."

He spoke truthfully. He truly seemed worried about drunk Starkissed and guests. But one currently sober Starkissed had him more concerned than ever.

And then, of course, when we met in front of the gate after packing, Kor had to do the whole show of putting on the watch and kissing my hand again, with Ben looking so stonelike that *Yvera* had poked him to get him to snap out of it.

I sighed inwardly after finishing my re-inventory with Ben and looked at my watch again. I didn't know how much more of this jealousy game was wise; the goal was to help Ben get through his mental block, not give him an aneurism. And how long would it be before Ben thought I was wishy-washy—or worse? At some point, he could rightly expect me to make a clear choice.

Hopefully Kor was right and that would be the point at which Ben realized he was ready to make his own.

Relax, Kor told me, once again eerily seeming to read my mind. *Everything is working out just as I'd planned. We're getting him right where we want him.*

I frowned at the gate to subtly show my doubts about that.

Oh, come on. Don't tell me that your time with him in the kitchen this afternoon didn't have a different flavor to it.

It...had. That was the first time Ben had been unmistakably something more than friendly. Daring, almost. And he had suddenly changed plans, making time out of a day he had meant to jampack with training, to spend just *being* with me.

After...Kor had begun truly flirting with me.

Could just be coincidence. Could just be a natural progression of our relationship, one that might be hindered by Kor's machinations.

Or....

Kor pulled out a scale and stepped away to answer it. When he walked back, putting it away, he said, "Eskala and the flight are over the mesa. Given how many of them there are, they'll wait to land until the gate materializes, just in case."

I winced as I pictured knocking aside or, far worse, splicing a dragon in two as the gate came into being.

"But they'll be on the lookout for an ambush?" Ben demanded.

"Yes," Kor said dryly. "These are *elites*, Ben. Led by the King's leftwing, come for the express purpose of guarding Sarah. In broad daylight. Try to remember that."

"How about this?" I said as a compromise. "I'll try to just open the doors on this side, so the gate will activate, but not the doors on the other. Not until Eskala gives the signal that they've landed and all is clear."

The drakón blinked at me. But at least Ben quickly looked sheepish for underestimating my grasp of strategy.

Kor chuckled and brushed my cheek. "Clever as always, darling. If you can manage that, that will do just fine. I'll call her back to let her know."

After he turned away, I couldn't help rolling my eyes at his back, which made Ben smile, even if the smile was pained. I quickly turned to my own task by walking up to the doors and putting my hands on them.

Please, I said. *Only activate. You can open on this side, but don't open on the other just yet.*

As silly as it might seem to talk to stone doors...it had worked for me thus far. Until I had the luxury of finding out if the request was key, I would keep right on doing just that.

Sure enough, the doors pulled the energy they needed from me, and the lines in the stone glowed. I felt the gravitational pull come into full being, so I knew I could let go and step back to allow the doors to swing outward. They did, and judging from the darkness on the other side of the crack, the others weren't doing the same.

"Very good," Ben said, putting a hand on my shoulder and giving me a more genuine smile.

We waited a couple minutes, then Kor looked up from his still glowing scale and nodded. "All clear."

I nodded back, reached through the icy curtain, and pushed on the outer doors.

They slowly swung open.

Ben made to move ahead of me, then visibly controlled himself and took a deep breath. "Please?" he asked me. "Wait for a dek?"

I smiled, since I knew the request hadn't come from arrogance, but rather a desire to determine the safety on the other side for himself. I nodded for him to go ahead.

"Good call," Kor said with a wink as he and Yvera passed on either side of me to flank Ben. "The highest rank should go last, after all."

I rolled my eyes again. If I were around Kor for much longer, they might get stuck in an upward position.

I watched the blurred forms of the drakón I had come to think of as my teammates stride out onto the mesa to meet the other team. Dragons of all colors and sizes were everywhere, as were amón (or drakón in humanform) hurrying about. The mix of small patches of sunlight and large shadows cast by the great, hulking forms and busy people reminded me absurdly of a childhood memory of going to watch hot air balloons inflate early one Fourth of July morning.

Ben, unmistakable even through the ice and fifty feet or so of distance at this point, stopped and talked to a Battleblood drakón male nearly as tall and even more muscular than he was, dressed in full purple scale plate. A Starkissed woman taller than Kor came up to them—Eskala, I assumed. Another drakón, this one Peacegrowth, judging from the green hair, came up to Ben and took each of my bags from him as Ben summoned and handed them over.

Ben turned to look my way. *Ready or not, it's time to come out. Close the gate behind you.*

I'd been expecting that last bit. Since my drakón couldn't exactly stay in my hold without me to open my gates for them, Ben and his wings were going to fly hard with the remaining Ykran daylight for the second-closest sungate to the mesa and nightshelter somewhere on the Battleblood planet of Ekrel to throw friends and foes alike off my scent. Meanwhile, I would go with Eskala in the opposite direction to the closest sungate, teleporting directly to Olsdak.

Feeling a surprising flash of nervousness, I took a deep breath and stepped through the curtain.

The hot, humid, noisy air of the jungle mesa hit me in a wave. I found myself glad for the hulking dragons all around and the shadows they cast, although the shade didn't seem to do much in the cloying air.

I tried to ignore the stares all around as I turned back to the doors and—not wanting to bother with manual pushing—simply raised my arms and politely asked them to close.

After taking the energy they needed from me, they did, and as soon as they swung completely shut, the glowing lines in the air faded, and the door once again disappeared completely. I tried to ignore the murmurs, but just before I turned around to face Ben, I caught sight of a curious young amón man wave his hand through the empty space where the doors had been.

My lips twitched as I began walking to join Ben and the wings. I had done the same thing the first time I had closed one of my gates from this side, with much the same look of wide-eyed incredulity, I was sure.

"Sarah," Ben said with unusual formality when I reached them. "This is Eskala Brightflare, leftwing of the Golden King."

His gesture went straight past the Starkissed woman I had pegged as being Eskala and to a much smaller, unassuming figure that stood between the two new drakón, having joined the group just before I had.

I hopefully hid my surprise. Eskala was not at *all* what I had been expecting. For starters...from her unusually short stature—being a few inches shorter than even me—her brown hair, and her blue eyes, it was abundantly clear that she was...*amón*.

More than just that, though, she wasn't anything like what I had expected a leftwing to be—nor the sort of person Kor would go dreamy-eyed over. I had been dreading a female Kor, made somehow even worse by her femininity: all curvy seductiveness, extravagant flare, and frightening cunning.

Eskala...was the opposite of what I had been picturing in every way—except in being female. She was slight of figure and quietly dressed in a gold uniform with orange trim that didn't entirely suit her pale, freckled skin and looked identical to my quick glance and untrained eye to the many other gold uniforms about. Her brown hair was tucked into a wispy bun, no doubt made untidy by the flight over. Her face was unadorned with any trace of makeup, although her eyebrows were tidy and her eyelashes unusually long.

She was pretty, I gave Kor that. But, at least to me, it was in an unconscious, platonic, aunt-next-door sort of way. And when she smiled tiredly at me, I saw intelligence in her pale blue eyes, but her weariness concealed well the brilliance that had earned her protégé's declaration that she was the brightest mind in all the Realms.

"Eskala," Ben continued quietly, gesturing to me. "This is Sarah Lind, declared Heir of the White Crown of Ice."

I realized then why I had felt a bit of stage fright—more than what simple stares warranted—and why this whole procedure struck me as being oddly formal.

This was the first time I was openly being presented as the Moontouched Heir.

We still weren't going public, not until I had made my final decision. Kor had assured Ben that every single member of the company had sworn themselves to secrecy. But they all knew why they were there. So, there was no other way to introduce me to the King's own leftwing, a formal representative of the Golden Crown in a way Ben simply hadn't been.

"Heir Sarah Lind," Eskala said soberly. "On behalf of the Golden Crown, allow me to formally welcome you, at long last, to the Six Realms."

To the surprise of everyone around except Kor, Eskala bowed with her hand over her heart. Though I had seen the heart salute before, I took it that *bowing* wasn't standard protocol among dramá, even when greeting a long-lost heir to a newly created throne.

That realization made my cheeks warm even more.

There, though, Eskala broke with formality. She came forward and took both of my hands in hers. "Ah, Sarah dear. I can't even say what a delight it is to finally meet you."

Her voice completed my aunt impression of her. It was kind—an elegant alto, but soft and warm.

She cast a teasing smile at Ben. "I understand dear Koriben's reasoning for keeping you to himself, but the King has felt the cruelty of it, that's for certain."

Ben colored slightly.

Eskala's smile faded, and she made me meet her eyes.

"The King prayed long and hard for you," she murmured, quietly enough that only our immediate circle would hear. "Harder and longer than you know. You cannot imagine what a burden your arrival has relieved from his shoulders—*our* shoulders. The time has come for the Covenants to be forged anew—stronger than ever before. And not a second too soon."

Looking into her eyes...I saw it now. The intelligence—but more, the *knowledge*—to make me tremble. She, more than any other mortal except perhaps the King she served, knew just what was at stake.

She gave my hands a squeeze, smiled warmly, and parted. "Come, dear," she said. "Say your goodbyes, if you haven't already. We had best be off before trouble comes calling."

Kor didn't need any more invitation than that to lean in to kiss my cheek. "Until tomorrow," he said with a wink as he pulled away.

To my surprise, Yvera stiffly offered her hand. Hesitantly, but not wanting to offend or embarrass her, I reached up with my own. Fortunately, Yvera acted quickly enough to save *me* from the embarrassment of trying to shake her hand by reaching further for my forearm and clasping it, and I curled my fingers around hers not a second later.

Right, I thought, cheeks warming. *Arms, not hands.*

As we met eyes while pulling away, Yvera said silently, *Do anything to hurt Ben or betray his trust, and I will tear your heart from your chest. Slowly.*

I was almost relieved. *That* was more like the Yvera I knew. I nodded to her to show I understood.

I turned hesitantly to Ben next, not sure what was acceptable in this situation. He hesitated, too, so that was no help.

Then I thought, *What the heck?*

I rushed forward and hugged him tightly. He let out a breath of relief and lifted me up to his level for a proper, crushing hug.

"Be safe," he whispered in my ear.

"You too," I rasped.

I held him with all my might, trying to soak in the warmth and feel of him. I rested my head on his shoulder and let his hair brush my face and fill me with his warm scent one last time.

For now.

Three words came to me again, unbidden, and once again almost spilled from my lips. But I once again caught and swallowed them just in time, though they went back down with difficulty.

A man cleared his throat pointedly, and Ben slowly and reluctantly let me down. Of course, not to be outdone by Kor, he leaned down and kissed me on the forehead, brushing away some of my hair and tucking it behind my ear to do so. My cheeks were flaming, but to my surprise, his weren't even pink.

Perhaps that had something to do with the agony in his eyes as he pulled away.

He kept his hands on my shoulders for a few final moments. *Call me the moment you get to your room in Olsdak*, he said. *The very* moment. *Do you understand?*

I nodded solemnly, and he finally let go.

"Take care of her," he told Eskala. The words weren't a command, but a plea.

"I would give my life for her," Eskala said simply.

"As would I," the Battleblood man at her side said, smiling grimly. "She'll be safe with us, Koriben. Don't you worry. You have my word on it."

Ah, that would be *Eskala's* rightwing. Who the smirking Starkissed woman was, I had no idea, since I was pretty sure Kor had said something about Eskala's leftwing staying with the King. Maybe she was just filling in?

"Come with us, dear," Eskala said, putting an arm around me. She looked back at Ben. "You three had better get going. You are going to need all the daylight you have left to reach Ankon before sunset."

Ben nodded stiffly, but he didn't move, and his eyes remained on me.

Eskala sighed but then smiled indulgently and began leading me away. Her rightwing and the woman followed.

She whispered in my ear. "Perhaps if we get you settled, he might be able to tear himself away."

My cheeks heated, and I was about to turn to look over my shoulder when Eskala warned in another whisper, "*Try* to avoid looking back, dear. You'll only make him linger longer if you do. Korinth will let you know when it's safe to get one last look at him."

Dear *Korinth* must have been reporting some extra details to his mentor about Ben and me. She hadn't seemed the least bit surprised at our emotional farewell or Ben's reluctance to entrust me to her care.

The fact that the King's leftwing seemed entirely fine with Ben's feelings for me was a bit...disconcerting. It made me wonder if Kor wasn't the only one who was hoping we would get together—for the good of the Realms.

We only walked a few moments longer before she brought me to a ladder that had been hooked to a saddle on a deep emerald-green dragon, who somehow managed a kindly expression as they turned their neck to look down at me—and kindly expressions didn't come easily to giant, toothy snouts and slitted reptilian eyes.

"Up you go," Eskala said cheerfully. "The healers already up there will have a coat for you and help you get settled."

One of them waved down at me, smiling.

"Thank you," I told her as I approached the ladder.

"No need to thank me," she answered. "Apologies that this isn't the honored position you deserve. We will give you a proper escort to Crownhold the first time you visit after your investment, I promise you that."

"I'm fine right where I am now," I said with a thin smile, and I began climbing.

This ladder was nice—much better than relying on Kor to lift me up and down in the palm of his dragon hand. I wondered a bit grumpily why my drakón hadn't used something similar for me. Then I thought about the logistics of setting up the ladder, which would require at least two normal people to raise and maneuver, and...there I had my answer. There was no way Yvera or even Kor would indulge me in that much labor when they had a much simpler system that worked for them. Ben might have done it for me...but that would have required me riding on one of the other two.

When I got to the top, I saw a much larger saddle than the one that Ben had for me, one specially fitted in between the dragon's spine spikes and with multiple seats. Two of the four were filled, and one young man was standing by the second from the front, waiting for me.

He helped steady and lift me past the final step on the ladder while cheerfully introducing himself as Kade. To my surprise, Kade appeared to be Starkissed, if I was catching on to the reasoning behind the varying colors of their uniform trims. So not all healers were Peacegrowth; that only made sense.

He helped me into my green-trimmed gold coat, and given the awkwardness of standing and balancing on drakáback, I appreciated the help. Then he straightened me out, declared with a grin that I would "pass," and led me to my saddle seat.

Just as Kade was helping me get buckled in, I heard two things at once.

A familiar roar. And Kor's inner voice teasing, *He's doing this for you, so you had better make it worth our while and look.*

My eyes shot to the sky, where three dragons circled in skillful formation around the mesa, close enough that I felt the buffeting of their passage. I had seen Ben's drakáform from many angles by now, but up until this point, I had been too close to get the full majesty of him all at once, and never so magnificently displayed.

Now I did. As I saw him turn sideways with his back facing me, glistening like gold in the sunlight from head to tail...he took my breath away.

His drakáform had always made me tremble, from the first moment I had seen it. But now it did so in the best possible way.

As the golden behemoth whooshed past for the last time, I caught his slitted eye for one split second. Then he roared again as he turned and beat his mighty wings to climb higher into the air, the violet and sapphire dragons following in his wake.

"An impressive sight, our Heir, isn't he?" Kade teased with a wink.

I didn't even have the attention to spare for a blush; all my focus, all my yearning, followed the golden dragon as he slowly grew small in the distance, and the pull stretched and thinned until it dissipated like smoke.

"You have no idea."

Chapter Thirty-Two

DREAM

Sarah

ON THE FLIGHT TO the sungate, I did what, a week ago, I never would have thought possible on drakáback: nod off. But the dragon was so warm, and the wind cool and dry up at our height, and with a spine spike behind me to lean against....

I felt a poke and roused with a start to see Kade pulling his arm back and grinning at me around the spine spike between us.

"Better get tightened down," he shouted back. "We're coming up on the gate."

So we were. I could see it on the mountain ahead, currently in the four o'clock position as we rounded to face its front.

Now that I wasn't so nervous, knowing what to expect, I had to admit that sungates were always an impressive sight. Not only did they always seem to be placed on the highest point around, the perfect, freestanding arches towered higher than they had any right to for seemingly being made from just stone. And with the sun setting in the sky now, the flames filling and licking at its frame illuminated the entire mountainside in their glow, casting light and shadow like dappled sunlight on water.

I looked toward the sinking sun and bit my lip. I hoped Ben and his wings either had or were still going to reach the other gate in time. They all had seemed confident they could, but if we were only just reaching the *closer* one....

Of course, as I quickly learned, managing a flight of dragons this big was a tricky business, and not all of them could or even should fly at the speed that Ben and his wings usually did. I began to understand a bit why they seemed to like flying in a V formation, like birds. More than just the practicality of gifting their downbeats to help support the ones behind them, it provided a clear sense of direction to the whole group and kept them from getting in each other's way. At this height and with their size...a simple bump or stray wing could be deadly. Especially to the amón on board.

If simply flying together was a skill, getting a flight this big safely through a sungate was a masterful one. To my surprise, the violet dragon that had led the way this whole time—Eskala's rightwing, carrying her himself judging from the lone figure on his back—and his flankers pulled off and began rising and circling hundreds of feet above the sungate. Most of the other dragons did the same, but at a lower level than him, forming two stacked circles. The only exceptions were a purple and a red dragon who went through immediately, one right after the other.

At some direction I didn't hear or see, other dragons began breaking away from the lower ring when they reached the front of the gate and dove through, one by one. After about half of them were gone, the dragon carrying us began adjusting their wings as we came around the turn. By then, I had fully tightened my straps and was leaning forward in the saddle, ready as I would ever be.

Though I might somehow be comfortable enough on drakáback to nod off...I didn't think I was ever going to get used to the moment of stillness as the dragon carrying me turned...then dove for the wall of fire.

My way is so much better, I thought as cramps clenched in my abdomen.

And that was the last thought I had time for before we plunged through the light and were squeezed like toothpaste through the darkness of the void, then spat back out on the other side.

As always, I was panting slightly and had to shake my head and blink rapidly to clear my vision of spots. I didn't get a good look at our surroundings until we were circling lazily above them in yet another ring.

Then I gaped.

Olsdak...was an island. A gorgeous, tropical island that was mostly mountain but still had long strips of pure white sand, on which crowds of people were already frolicking or basking. (Figures that dramá would be into sunbathing, and quite a few of them in the nude.)

The water around the island was crystalline, and deeper out, the purest blue I had ever seen. Dragons dove into and swam around in the water with abandon, and one playful tousle between a blue and an orange deep out into the ocean caused a minor tsunami on a beach that had people yelping, running for cover, and shouting at them.

Few trees dotted the slopes, but what ones that were there were bedecked in strings of glowing blue lights and tinkling wind chimes that sent a sweet music all the way up to me. The trees often sheltered beautifully carved pergolas, benches, fountains, or gardens, with ornamented paths carved into the rock to lead from one to the next.

This didn't look at all like what I'd come to think of as a hold. It looked like an exotic (and terribly expensive) *resort*.

I realized I had begun to think of all dramá as being serious, deadly, and hard-working—that their lives were far too dangerous for relaxation, play, and beauty for its own sake.

That could genuinely be the case for some regions and clans, but that didn't have to be the same everywhere. My last seven days of near constant danger and skirting the outskirts of civilization...*may* have skewed my perception of their kind as a whole. Just a bit.

I didn't get nearly long enough of a chance to examine the dramá paradise below before it was our turn to land. After only a few passes, the emerald dragon banked and glided toward one of the smallest of the landing circles carved from and built out of the mountainside. Though it was one of the highest landing pads, it was small enough that only a few drakón could be on it at once, hence why we had had to wait a bit for our turn. And the others were going to have to wait even longer, since there were four of us amón who needed to dismount.

The moment the green dragon touched down and drew in their wings, people were rushing in with a ladder. As I had suspected, two attendants were required to handle the ladder, and another had to climb up the rungs to pull the rest of the collapsed length up high enough to reach the hooks in the saddle. Kade, already out of his seat, helped hook the ladder in place, and then he gestured for me to go first.

Feeling foolish for just sitting there watching the ladder operation instead of working on my buckles, I fumbled with them as quickly as I could, but haste and self-consciousness slowed me down enough that another healer got out of her saddle and laughingly helped me out. Hopefully none of the dragons overhead that *weren't* part of my escort noticed a silly healer among the elites who needed an unusual amount of assistance.

Kade once again helped me get going on the top rungs of the ladder before letting me go. I descended as quickly as I thought was safe, and by the time I'd reached the bottom, my cheeks were cooling.

"So," a handsome, dark-skinned, gold-uniformed drakón Peacegrowth said, coming up to me with a smile, "you're my newest assistant, are you?"

"Er," I said brilliantly, freezing up. Did he honestly think....

He laughed. *Don't you worry, Heir Sarah. I know who you are. But this is part of the act. We're still being watched, remember?*

Right. Of course.

"Yes," I said, nodding with what hopefully looked like confidence. "I am."

"Excellent," he said, gesturing ahead. "I am Edrik, the head healer of the Crown entourage to the Moonfair. Let me help you get settled."

I followed Edrik off the landing pad and through the elaborately carved arch into the mountain.

He paused in the shadow of the inner threshold, safely out of sight of the dragons in the sky behind us, and gestured grandly to the bustling court inside.

"Welcome, Heir Sarah Lind, to the King's Wing of Olsdak Hold."

I gaped once again. I had assumed from the court's size and grandeur that it was the central hub of the Hold.

It must have been hundreds of feet wide, with a tiered fountain sporting spewing dragon heads in the center. The floor was inlaid with a scale-style patchwork of normal stone tiles and glossy sapphire ones that reminded me suspiciously of *actual* scales. All the many archways leading from the central court were draped with gauzy blue curtains that were tied back just enough to not get obnoxious but still be allowed to undulate mesmerizingly in the gusts of wind coming from the landing pad and from the simple passage of people hurrying about. More gauze strung in wide, rippling streamers from every corner to meet in the center just behind a bright, glowing crystal chandelier, creating the overall impression of looking up at a sun from underwater. Large pots of lush tropical plants with enormous flowers sat in every nook, filling the fresh air with heady sweetness. Carved stone benches inlaid with more glossy sapphire material were everywhere, with velvety seats and plump, inviting cushions.

"This...is just a single *wing*?" I breathed.

"You should see the Lady's Wing," Edrik said with a chuckle as he led me across the court. "It's smaller, but even more elaborate. The Starkissed like to show off for others, but everyone knows they save the best for their own."

"I have a hard time imagining that," I said frankly as I gawked.

"Trust me," he said with a crooked smile. "But I have no complaints about the facilities. The healer's suite here is superb."

He gestured toward some other arch. "If you ever need healing, go find one of us. We are setting up in that direction."

"Should I be help—"

"Flame, no," Edrik said with a chuckle. "That is kind of you to offer, Heir Sarah, but as long as you are within the King's Wing, there's no need to keep up the pretense of being a healer. No one will be permitted inside that isn't already aware of who you are and hasn't sworn a blood oath to protect you."

I swallowed. A *blood* oath? I hadn't asked for that level of extremity. Of course...I hadn't asked for any of this.

"Speaking of suites," he said as he led me through a different arch. "This hall is full of the personal suites for the most important Crown guests. Leftwing Eskala will be in there."

He pointed to one of the first sets of elaborate doors, inlaid once again with sapphire. One of the double doors was open and attendants were rushing in and out to get ready for her.

"I'm surprised she didn't get here before me," I said.

"It's traditional for a leader of a flight to be one of the last to go through a sungate," Edrik explained. "To direct the passage through and ensure all her people get to safety before her."

Ah. That explained a bit of what Kor had meant by the highest ranking going last—not out of a show of importance (or at least not for the good ones) but rather as a show of service and protection. I liked that.

Edrik continued. "And, even if she's through by now, she'll have to greet the Lady Starkissed at the main landing circle and go through all that ceremony before making her way here. You're lucky to be such a 'lowly assistant' to have skipped all those ashes and gone straight to the Royal landing."

I felt intense relief at my near miss. Though the sun was still bright and high outside at Olsdak, I was at the end of what had been a very long, full, exhausting day, and I was desperately craving some quiet and solitude before a deep slumber.

Edrik pointed to another set of doors, these even larger and more ornate. "The Heir's Suite. Heir Koriben will stay there, of course, once he arrives tomorrow."

"Do you know exactly when?" I asked, trying to hide my eagerness as I activated my watch. "In how many hours—deken, I mean?"

He smiled broadly at me, so I was certain I hadn't fooled him. "Oh, he'll get here at first light, I imagine. Even if he wished to come sooner, he has to wait for day here for the sungate here to become active again. So...let me see...that would be about seventeen deken."

I couldn't help a sigh. So long.... More than a full revolution of my watch, which was now at only a couple Ythra hours of sunlight remaining.

"An interesting device you have there," Edrik commented curiously.

"Thanks. I can't...tell the time like you people can. So an...*artificer*—" I hoped I remembered the right word in Drona. "—made me this a couple days ago."

"Hmm," Edrik said thoughtfully. "I wonder.... Something that precise and convenient might be useful in my practice...."

"Her name is Alya," I said quickly, eager to recommend her. "She's a Strongshield in the First Flight of Goldek Gate."

I was rather impressed with myself that I'd remembered that much detail, let alone in Drona.

"She said she was going to file a patent, then release the design to the public. I'm sure she would be happy to send you the schematics then."

"I'm no artificer," Edrick chuckled as we stopped in front of the final set of doors, the ones at the end of the hall, which were wide open. "But I'm sure I can commission one. So, thank you for that information. But here we are: your rooms."

"*My* rooms?" I said, peering inside.

It was like a miniature version of the central court, complete with a smaller fountain—except even more opulence, gauze, and plushness. I started to think that my "special" room back in my hold wasn't so over the top, after all.

Edrick smiled broadly. "The King specifically requested that you be given his suite in his absence. And these would be some of your attendants now."

My head was spinning. The *King's* suite? *Some* of?

Two dark brown young women in gold uniforms with blue trim—one blue-haired drakón and one black-haired amón—approached me with welcoming smiles.

"Heir Sarah Lind," the young amón said as they both put their hands over their hearts. "It is with great delight that we welcome you to the King's Suite of Olsdak Hold. I am Vadya, and I will be the head of your staff during your stay with us."

Staff, I thought, feeling faint. *I have staff.*

Given how much I just wanted to be *alone* right now, that wasn't a good thing.

I plastered on as sincere and thankful a smile as I could manage. "Wonderful. Thank you both for...um...."

They both laughed.

"That's good enough for us," the drakón said with a wink as she hooked her arm in mine to lead me inside. She waved back at the healer flirtatiously. "Thanks, Edrik! See you at dinner!"

"See you, Fenra," Edrik said with a grin. His smile softened at my look over my shoulder of minor panic. "Don't worry. You're in good hands with these sisters. Mischief makers though they are."

"Ah, Edrik," Vadya said with a pout as she slowly closed the doors. "You wound us. When have we *ever* caused any mischief?"

"And been caught?" Edrik said dryly. "Never. That's precisely the point."

The only answer he got was their burst of laughter as Vadya closed the door in his face.

"You're going to have to make him pay for that one tonight," Vadya told her sister with a wink. Now that Edrik had pointed it out, I saw the clear resemblance between the two of them that Fenra's drakón height and coloring had momentarily concealed.

Fenra folded her arms and smirked. "And why should I? I think it was perhaps the highest compliment he's ever paid me. In fact, I'm jealous that he included *you* in it."

"You're together, I'm assuming?" I said. Then, in case that didn't translate well, I added. "A couple, I mean."

Fenra laughed and threw back her luxurious curls of blue hair to show her right ear, which displayed an emerald earring. "Betrothed, actually. Just last week."

I was suddenly *very* interested.

Trying not to show it, I asked casually, "Congratulations! So...since you know I'm knew here, perhaps you can explain this to me. Earrings indicate an engagement?"

That would explain why I had seen so many dramá by now wearing earrings, even though they often seemed to clash with their demeanors or uniforms. And why none of my drakón wore any.

"One does, yes," Fenra said, pulling her hair back even further to show her other ear, which was bare.

Ah. That also explained why Edrik had been wearing only one sapphire. I couldn't help but notice, because of his short hair, but I'd thought little of it at the time given all the many other distractions around me.

The drakón let her hair fall back. "He'll give me the other one as part of our heartbinding, just as I will to him."

"Um.... Heartbinding. Is that a wedding?"

"'Wedding'?" Vadya curiously repeated the word in English.

"The ceremony that ends a betrothal and makes it a marriage, a permanent union."

"Oh, yes, that," Fenra said with a chuckle. "Heartbinding, yes."

"Why do you call it that?" I asked intently.

They blinked and looked at each other, then back at me. "Because it binds our hearts together."

Right. Obviously. How silly of me to ask.

I felt there was a bit more to it than that, but I was drooping at this point, and I doubted I could press this much further while pretending merely idle curiosity.

Vadya, being the proper majordomo that she was, noticed.

"Ah, Sarah, don't let us addith chat your ear off. From what Kor told us, I assume that you'll be wanting some quiet and rest now?"

I nearly sagged with relief, not even caring that Kor had been revealing things about me to complete strangers. "Goodness, yes."

"Would you prefer to bathe now or in the morning?"

I smiled ruefully. "I think I'd fall asleep if I took a bath now. So...later?"

"That's just fine," she said, putting an arm around me to lead me on. So, it wasn't just Ben and Kor—dramá really were touchy people.

As we passed one arch, she pointed. "The bathing room is that way, should you wish to use it when none of us are around to direct you. But someone should be awake and ready to assist you at all times. We're aware that you can be a bit more...active at night."

"There's no need for anyone to stay up for me," I protested.

"Oh, there is," Fenra said firmly. "We're not just here to wait on you, Sarah. We're also the innermost layer in your defense."

"Oh," I said with a blink.

"It's not easy to become a Royal attendant," Vadya said with a casual wink, obviously trying to lighten the mood. "We had to be trained in everything from serving tables to mending broken bones to spearing assailants. Very exciting, never a dull moment, eh Fenra?"

"It's why we did it," Fenra said, flashing her perfect drakón teeth in a feral smile. "You can't imagine how excited we were to be given this assignment—the first of our very own. Other than Eskala, there hasn't been a female member of the Crown to serve since the Queen's death, and Eskala doesn't see nearly enough action."

As the two led me into a lush bedroom, Vadya groaned. "We were being groomed to serve Ben's consort, but of course, he took his sweet time *finding* one. We thought we'd *never* get anyone but Eskala."

"But now that's all changing, thanks to you," Fenra said with a significant wink.

My cheeks grew warm. "We're not...."

Goodness gracious, had half the Realms known how Ben felt before *I* did? Something told me the answer was yes. Of all the bits of gossip Kor kept reporting, he'd left *this* tidbit out....

Probably for good reason. Ben might have dug himself a hole from sheer embarrassment and never come out. And I might have been there right along with him.

Both Starkissed sisters looked at me with eyes too wide with innocence.

"Oh, we were talking just about you gracing us with your Royal presence, of course," Vadya said. "Nothing of more...significance than that."

Right, I thought dryly. *And I'm a drakón.*

Sure enough, even though I fell asleep almost as soon as my head hit my plush, silky pillow, I woke up in the dark to feel my blood buzzing. I didn't need to look at my watch to know that it was night, although I did anyway to count the white-pie segments that remained before dawn.

When Ben would come.

Nine, I thought with a long sigh as I let my hand fall limply back to the bed. I had only slept through Olsdak's afternoon and evening and into the first part of the night.

I'd been hoping to kill more time than that. The remaining nine hours seemed like an eternity—practically a day itself.

My quick call with Ben before bed to let him know I had arrived had only made me miss him more. And it wasn't like either of us had enough energy at the time to really chat. He was relieved to see I was alright, and I was nearly just as relieved to see him and know that he was safe for the night in a Battleblood hold—probably the most secure place for him to be in the Six Realms. But after exchanging only the basic details about our trips, he could see that I was drooping and ordered me to bed, and I hadn't summoned the energy to argue before he had ended the call.

Now, as I lay in the dark, I wished I'd had.

Well, there was nothing for it. I wasn't going to mope for nine hours in that *ocean* of a King-sized (with a capital K) bed. I'd opted to sleep on the edge, which meant that I could just roll out of it now, like normal—instead of crawling for a ridiculous length first, as I would have had to do if I'd slept in the center. It was even higher than I was used to, so that I had to slide off carefully before my feet touched the floor.

Again, my "special" bed didn't seem quite so excessive anymore.

I understood a bit why the King had made the gesture of giving me his suite, and I was touched and honored and all that—but really. Next time, I was going to sleep on one of those fancy couches or something. Probably even the plush rug underfoot would be comfy enough.

Without knowing what else to do with myself, I went in search of that bath.

As I'd been warned, a gold-uniformed, dark-haired amón attendant sat in the central area and stood immediately when I came out.

"Heir Sarah," she said hurriedly, quickly hiding her book behind her with a blush. "How may I help you?"

"First off, what's your name?" I said with a comforting smile. Her own awkwardness put me strangely at ease. And if I *had* to have "staff," then by golly, I was going to learn their names and treat them like people.

"Kathis," she replied uncertainly.

"Kathis. Nice to meet you," I said, approaching her. "Second off, good book?"

She nodded slowly, blushing more deeply. "Sorry, but—"

I waved her off. "No apologies. I'm *glad* to see that if you had to be stuck with the night shift with me, you are at least able to spend it on something you enjoy. I like to read myself."

"You...do?" she said with a blink. As if it hadn't occurred to her that Royals had hobbies.

Well, given how busy Ben usually was...maybe that wasn't such a surprise.

"I wasn't always an Heir, you know." I smiled crookedly. "Still am not, technically."

She just gave me a dubious look.

"What?" I said, putting my hands on my hips. "Surely you've heard that I haven't been invested yet. Nor...am I sure I want to be."

"Why *wouldn't* you?" she blurted out. Then obviously thought better of it, because next she stammered, "Sorry, Heir—"

I sighed. "No need to say sorry."

Was *this*...what I was like?

Honestly...it was kind of annoying.

I cocked my head and looked at her. I was still having a hard time gauging dramá ages, but amón were easier, and I was almost certain that Kathis looked my age or younger. Unusually young, from what I'd seen among Eskala's entourage.

"How long have you served, Kathis?"

Her blush returned. "Technically...this is my first day. I just graduated from the training program, and they pulled me in as an emergency measure."

That explained a few things. And raised a few more questions.

I frowned. "And they gave you the night watch? Alone?"

"Oh, I'm not alone," she said hurriedly. "There are guards outside your suite, and others keeping watch on the wall wards besides, and some of the other attendants are playing gamma through there."

She pointed at one of the smaller arches, through which I could hear the faintest echo of voices, now that I was listening for them.

I lowered my shoulders in relief. "Good."

"But, Heir Sarah, if you don't mind me asking...." She couldn't seem to help her curiosity, as unusually shy as she was for a dramá. That's when I noted from her blue trim that she was yet another Starkissed. "Why *wouldn't* you want to become...you know...."

I smiled thinly at her. "If you had served one of your leaders longer, you would know. They strike me as being good people, and good people never *want* to be in positions of power."

She stared. Then smiled slightly. "But then...by that logic, wouldn't that make you a good fit for the role?"

I blinked back at her. "Um...."

She laughed. "Maybe you should think about that a bit."

A knock sounded at the door. Kathis excused herself quickly and went to answer it. She spoke in a low murmur with someone on the other side, then closed the door and came back to me.

"Leftwing Eskala heard you were awake, so she is asking if you would like to come speak with her."

It was phrased as a request, but I had no intent of denying it. But I did start in surprise. "Eskala? How did she hear that?"

Kathis just gave me a bland, polite look that she had no doubt been trained to give when the ones she served asked stupid questions.

I groaned. "I'm being watched. Aren't I?"

Even now, somehow I was under magical surveillance. No matter how well-meaning the reasons, that was going to get old. Fast.

"Yes," Kathis said simply. She was very good at this bland politeness part.

The surveillance must have been another reason they felt comfortable posting a greenie outside my door. She was just there to make sure I had what I needed.

In the event I needed anything, suddenly, in the middle of the night, like a crazy person.

Speaking of whom....

"Why is *she* even awake right now?" I said grumpily. "I'm Moontouched, and on a different time zone besides. What's her excuse?"

Kathis was comfortable enough around me by now to roll her eyes. "Oh, it's much too early for *Eskala* to be in bed. She hardly ever sleeps. We all don't know how she does it, but she does."

"Figures," I said with a sigh. "Alright, where is she?"

"I'll take you to her," Kathis said quickly.

"There's no need—"

She just gave me that bland look again.

"Fine," I huffed, walking to the doors.

As she hurried to open a door for me, I muttered, "And you wonder why I don't want to be Heir."

She laughed quietly as I passed her through the opening.

As she had said, there were two guards—one Battleblood, one Strongshield, both drakón—standing outside my door. They saluted simultaneously as I stepped out and gave Kathis a friendly nod as she followed. She nodded back with a smile, and with much greater confidence than before, she led me down the hall to Eskala's suite. The set of guards there had no doubt been expecting us, because after another quick salute, one of them immediately opened the door for us.

We walked into another central room. An authoritative-looking young man sitting at a desk stood up quickly. "Ah, Heir Sarah. Leftwing Eskala is expecting you. Right this way."

He led me into a side room that was a bookish, reclusive professor's dream. Walls of books, stacks of papers everywhere, a cozy fireplace with a side table and armchairs, and an enormous desk, behind which sat the leftwing of the King—barely visible over the stacks of papers, books, and tablets around her.

She looked up immediately, even though she had to blink blearily to refocus her eyes. When she saw me, she stood. "Ah, Sarah dear. Thank you so much for coming. No, no, dear—"

When I had made for the chair in front of her desk, she stepped out from behind her desk and, with her arm around me, began leading me to the fire.

"Let's chat here, shall we? Much cozier. A pot of tsha, Deth?"

"Of course," he said with a smile as he closed the door behind him.

"Korinth told me you had developed a fondness for it," Eskala explained as we sat. "I would have had it ready for you, but I didn't expect you to come quite so soon. You didn't need to rush for my sake, dear."

I blinked at her. "I figured if *the King's* leftwing wanted to speak with me in the middle of the night, it had to be important."

"Ah," Eskala said, crossing her legs, propping her elbow on her armrest, and resting the side of her face in her fingers comfortably as she examined me. "I see I should have mentioned that all I wanted was to have a little chat with you, and this seemed like the best time."

"What...did you want to chat about?" I asked.

"Why, you, of course, my dear," she said with a chuckle.

I stared at her for a long moment. "Don't take this the wrong way, but...why? You're a busy woman. The fact that you're up in the middle of the night *literally* neck-deep in paperwork attests to that."

She sighed. "It's true. I *am* busy, so you have a right to ask, though it pains me that you have to. But, dear Sarah, this is in fact work for me. A large part of my duty is to know the ones I serve, and for the time being, you are among that number. Seeing how little I know now about you, and how long it might be before I have a chance like this again, I could not be spending my time better."

"I don't know," I said dryly. "*Korinth* seems to have told you plenty."

Eskala smiled thinly. "He's a good boy—"

At my snort, she laughed. "He truly is, you know. And he is terribly fond of you."

I rolled my eyes. "Oh, really?"

She shook her head indulgently at me. "Surely by now you have figured out that Korinth often displays a veneer that has very little to do with what he is actually feeling inside."

"Yes," I said, shifting uncomfortably. "That's exactly why there could be *anything* under that mask."

"You'll learn to pick up on the signs of his true feelings, I'm certain," she said comfortably. "But, as I was saying, Korinth has been...informative, but there is nothing that can replace meeting with a person for yourself. And he still has much to learn. Thinking all he has to do is observe and trick, he has asked for so few of the details that truly matter but that people are generally all too eager to share."

"Like what?" I said with a raised eyebrow.

Her smile faded and pale blue eyes became serious. "We'll wait until Deth—ah! Impeccable timing, as always."

Just then, the young man had opened the door and come in carrying a steaming tea tray smelling of the pleasantly pungent tsha Ben liked.

"It was a good thing I had thought myself to put a pot on," he said with a smile.

"Thank you, Deth," Eskala said warmly as he set the tray down. "You're invaluable. Now be a dear and see that I'm not disturbed except by urgent business for at least a deken or so, will you?"

"Of course." He nodded and left.

"A deken, huh?" I said, taking the teacup she offered me. Somehow it didn't surprise me she had *teacups*, whereas before, all I had used with Ben were mugs.

"At least," Eskala said with a sigh and a smile as she inhaled the aroma of her own tsha. "I'm hoping you and my duties will give me longer, but we shall see."

"That's some kind of 'little chat,'" I said dryly. Inside, I was trying to hide my nervousness.

Her face softened. "No need to fret, dear. I truly just wish to understand you better. Starting with just a few questions. I promise."

I shifted, then sighed. "Alright. Go ahead."

Do your worst, I thought.

She smiled, eyes serious. "What do you dream about, Sarah?"

I blinked at her. "Excuse me?"

"Not at night—or in your sleep, anyway. I mean, what do you *dream* about, during the day? What do you long for?"

My cheeks grew warm, and Eskala—far too observant—noticed. Her smile became kind. "And I don't mean Koriben either, though we can talk about him later, if you like."

"How—no, actually," I said flatly, setting my teacup down. "If I'm going to sit through an interrogation, then I want answers too. And I want this one now. Why do *you* care how I feel about Ben or how he feels about me? Or rather, why *don't* you care? Aren't you supposed to be *discouraging* me from...'dreaming' about the Golden Heir?"

Her smile thinned. "Now, why in Flame's name would I do that?"

"I don't know!" I cried. "I don't know how this all works! But I do know Ben is practically a prince. Doesn't he have to consider...I don't know, lineage, or rank, or—"

"My dear," Eskala said, smile fading completely. "He has. We all have. That is precisely the point. You are the declared Heir to the White Crown. Should you accept what your Tree offers you, you will become the first Queen of Ice, just as Koriben will one day become the King of Flame. The will of our respective Trees in this is abundantly clear, and I cannot tell you how much it relieves me—and even more so, King Kavarian—that the two of you have found your own happiness in it."

It was a very good thing I had set the teacup down. Because if it had still been in my fingers, I would have dropped it. I could feel the echo of the imaginary shatter and slosh of liquid now.

"*What?*" I wheezed.

Eskala sighed. "I thought for certain Korinth would have mentioned something about this by now."

I was near shouting now. "You can't *honestly* tell me that Ben and I are...."

I couldn't even say it.

Eskala raised an eyebrow. "Do you *not* wish to marry him?"

"I...." I stiffened. "That's beside the point."

"Is it?" Eskala said idly, raising her teacup to her lips for a sip. "Do you wish to marry him or not?"

I glared at her. "I...don't know."

Liar, one part of me whispered.

Shut up, the other said.

"Really," Eskala murmured, setting the teacup down. "Very well."

I blinked. "What?"

She shrugged. "That will do as an answer for now. But I suggest you find the answer by the time you reach your Tree, because it will determine the one you give Her."

I went cold. "This has nothing to do with that decision."

"Actually, my dear, it has *everything* to do with that decision," Eskala said, switching her crossed legs. "It is one and the same. There must be a Queen of Ice. The Queen of Ice *must* marry the King of Flame. It's up to you whether that Queen is *you*...or another."

I swallowed, though the lump in my throat didn't leave. "What do you mean? What makes you think that we...that they...."

Eskala smiled thinly. "Simply put, because that is what the Tree of Flame told King Kavarian must be."

I waited. And when nothing else came, I said flatly, "And that's it?"

"That is it. That we *know*, at least. We have speculated why aplenty, and perhaps no one has come closer than Korinth himself—which is all the more remarkable given he is not even aware of the Tree's mandate. He would never forgive me if I spoiled the explanation for him, though, so I will refrain."

"Of course," I said, leaning back with a huff. "That's it though? That's what you're going on? The Tree of Flame said that Ben has to marry the Queen of Ice?"

"That is reason enough. I understand you have grown up without the knowledge of a Tree, then let me just summarize our entire history for you: When we obey the Tree, the greatest guide and protector the Creators have given us, we survive. In fact, we thrive. But when we do not...."

I put a hand to my forehead. "Alright. Just let me get this straight. You, Kor, and even the King are all convinced that the *survival* of all the worlds...depends on me marrying Ben?"

Her lips twitched. "And quite a few other things besides, but we aren't discussing them now. To answer your question simply...yes."

"OK," I said, folding my arms. "Say I was willing. You still have one massive problem: *Ben* isn't."

Her lips twitched again, pulling further this time. But she attempted to straighten her expression as she took another sip. "Is he not? Well, that wasn't the impression I got from his farewell to you, but I'll admit, I could be mistaken."

I flushed. "He...is working through some things. Kor said so."

"Oh, that is certainly true," Eskala agreed. "I am aware of all that Korinth might have told you, and a bit more besides, and I agree that the obstacles in his mind are not trifling ones. But your statement pertained more to his heart, and I think Koriben knows that very well. His only uncertainty in that regard appears to be about your own."

"So you think I *should* just tell him how I feel?" I said, feeling a bit of relief.

She paused, pursing her lips. Took a sip. Set down her teacup. Then looked at me. "It is up to you, of course."

I huffed. "That's the answer adults give when they disagree and are expecting you to 'make the right decision' in the end."

She smiled briefly, then sighed. "You yourself said that Koriben...has some difficulties. As much as all of us who love and care for him have tried to help him...he was born to walk a hard path. A path he must walk for all our sakes, but all the harder for that. And he has made it all the lonelier by thinking some things about himself that simply are not true."

"He thinks he's a monster," I said quietly.

Eskala cocked her head. "That would be bad enough, but I am afraid it goes a little deeper than that."

"How?"

"He does not think he is worthy of love."

I blinked. "What...is the difference?"

"Not much, but there is a subtle enough one that one must not mistake them: A person who only thinks they are a monster needs only be convinced of their goodness. There is no way to convince someone that they are worthy of love."

I sat, stunned by that revelation.

The King's words echoed in my mind. *Are you unworthy, Sarah?*

Eskala had paused for a moment, then, watching me carefully, continued. "They must first decide that for themselves. Only when they are ready to reach for you can you reach back."

I stared at her, feeling a sharp pang of betrayal. "What...did the King tell you?"

"Nothing," she said, eyes meeting mine with perfect honesty. "This is merely a conversation we have had about his son, whom I love as my own, many a time. But if there is any similarity between what I just said and something you discussed with the King.... Well, I've already seen for myself that the two of you are similar in some significant ways."

Her lips twitched. "Not *too* similar, mind you. But enough that...perhaps you are precisely what the other needs, both in your similarities...and in your differences. You complement each other remarkably."

I had no answer to that. Though I felt relief that the King had kept our conversation private, I was disturbed at how close Ben and I were in this.

There is no way to convince someone that they are worthy of love.

Are you unworthy, Sarah?

Reach.

Eskala let me sit in silence for a minute as she stared into the fire and sipped her tea. My cup sat neglected on the table. It was probably cold by now. But numbly, I reached for it and picked it up anyway.

As if that was the signal she needed, Eskala looked back at me and smiled, in a way that made her eyes crinkle—the only sign of age I had seen on her timeless face. "So, Sarah. We come back full circle to my first question. What do you dream about?"

I sipped at the mildly spicy liquid, inhaling its faint, yet still pungent aroma as I stared into the fire. At one point, I might have answered that question with the answer people usually expected: what college I wanted to go to, what I wanted to major in, what job I wanted, where I wanted to live, what car I wanted to drive.

But all those things now seemed...meaningless to me.

They had lost their pull.

If they had ever had a true one at all.

I looked back at her, blinking the flames from my eyes. "I...don't know. I've changed so much since I came here. And since then...I haven't had time to dream."

"That is a wise answer," she said with a soft smile. She set her teacup down with a satisfied *clink* on the tray. "A self-aware one, for self-awareness is the beginning of wisdom. And to hear that makes me a very relieved leftwing."

My lips pulled into a weary smile. "You sound like Kor when you say that."

She tilted her head toward me, eyes bright. "Well, he learned at least something from me, after all."

"You'd think he would have turned out...differently, then. You're a...very different sort of leftwing."

"How so?" she asked, clasping her hands over her top knee. "I agree with you, but I am curious to hear which word you would use to describe the difference between us."

I thought for a moment. "You're...nice."

No, that wasn't right. I knew it the moment the word left my mouth.

She seemed to tell, but still she corrected me with a small smile. "I think you mean I am *kind*. I am not nice. A leftwing cannot afford to be. We must bear some of the heaviest burdens and venture into the greatest shadows to serve the Realms we love so dear."

She sighed. "Please do not be so hard on Korinth. Each *good* leftwing finds their own way to reconcile that love and that cruelty. Korinth has found his own, and that is by showing a warped reflection of what everyone else thinks he is back at them, and he partakes in his seemingly frivolous delights to numb himself. You could say that in his most trying moments, he becomes supremely...Starkissed. But since I am not Starkissed myself...I am not able to conceal or forget the pain at what I do so easily."

"How do you do it, then?" I asked quietly.

She smiled thinly and fingered the orange trim on her collar. "In a supremely Brightflare way: by always working. *Always* working. Even when I sleep—which, you may have heard, I do as little as possible—I am dreaming of solutions to the day's ills. It doesn't entirely ease my pain for all that I have done, and yet, I cannot stop."

"That's...surely not...."

"Healthy?" she said, eyes bright with amusement. "No. But nor is Korinth's deception or Koriben's refusal to be loved. Our jobs do not lend themselves to *health*, Sarah. You have to have a will of iron and wisdom born of hard experience, as our beloved King does, to not bend under the weight of them."

"But if even *you* haven't been able to bear it...what chance do I have?"

Her amusement faded. "I say I cannot stop working, but...to be honest, I have never truly tried. I have never wanted to. Though it is a lonely life, it is the one I have chosen, and it...suits me. I never dreamed of a mate or children, and the only friends I have ever needed are the ones I serve with, like Kavarian. Honestly, I am uncertain what I will do with myself when Korinth rightfully supplants me."

She chuckled suddenly. "Part of me hopes he will make me *his* leftwing, then."

I blinked. "That can happen?"

"It has before." Her smile faded. "Particularly...if the leftwing had to come suddenly to the post—young and unprepared."

She shook herself, as if casting off a dark shadow, and said kindly, "In any case, I hope for different things for you and Koriben. I think...the Ice and Flame have much happiness in store for you, if that is what you decide you want for yourself. They, too, are not 'nice.' But...neither are They cruel."

"Sure," I said flatly. "Not cruel for arranging my marriage."

Eskala raised an eyebrow. "They never said it had to be you. Or even that it had to be Koriben. Both of you could walk away from the call and do whatever you please, and They will not stop you. Has that occurred to you?"

"*No,*" I said immediately. "Ben would never."

If Ben did that...

He would cease to be Ben.

"You might be surprised," Eskala said dryly. "Deny your birthright, force him to marry someone besides you...and we all might just discover the limit of his obedience to the Tree."

I stared at her in horror. "No. No, you don't know what you're saying. The Realms *need* Ben...."

I trailed off at the look she was giving me. The hard smile and knowing eyes.

"Oh, they do. But you know who else the Realms need? All *seven* of them?"

I swallowed. I repeated in a whisper, "You don't know what you're saying."

Her face softened. She rose and pulled me to my feet, keeping my hands for a moment. "As much as I have gained from our talk, Sarah, I think it is time I gave you something you have not had time for thus far."

"What?" I asked, too numb to see the obvious coming.

She put her hands on my shoulders and stood on her tiptoes to kiss my forehead. "To dream, dear. To dream."

Chapter Thirty-Three

STAR

Koriben

I hate the Moonfair, I moaned.

Even now, at the crack of dawn, there were enough revelers and vendors in the maze of halls to slow my progress toward the King's Wing significantly, not to mention friends and classmates determined to greet me and try to extract some juicy gossip.

Unfortunately for them, my patience had already been worn thin by all the ceremony I had to endure after landing; the only satisfaction I got from that experience was seeing the Olsdak governor and fair organizers blink sleepily when they arrived at the landing circle and glare at me for dragging them out of bed at this deken, all the way through the welcoming. As if they didn't know that I couldn't care less if they took a page out of Lady Winthra's book: *she* didn't even bother getting up.

Maybe this would make them think twice before inviting me next year. If...I was even available. Which, Flame Above and Below, I hoped I wasn't. For many important reasons...but being excluded from participation in the Moonfair pageant was on the list.

As I hurried through the halls, I brushed the well-meaning friends off with a smile and the less well-meaning with a nod and hurried on when I could, or exchanged only the basic greetings when I couldn't. But the longer the time went on, the more my smiles became forced and my nods curt. When we hit a blockage in the hallway caused by an overturned cart, I wanted to scream, but I forced myself to bend over and help the vendor pick up her wares instead, and glared at my wings until they did the same.

She's probably not even awake yet, Yvera complained.

I snorted. Olsdak was half a day off from Sarah's hold. If Sarah were asleep, it would be because she had been up the whole night and gone to bed again.

But I knew she wasn't asleep. I could *see* her in there, somewhere, like a spot of light in my mind and not in my eyes. And that light was moving about. Had been for at least as long as we had been in Olsdak.

Was it...bad that I had watched her like that? The entire time we had been separated, every time I thought of her—which had seemed like every other moment—I had looked. Though I had wondered if I shouldn't. Or at least...if I shouldn't quite so often.

But it wasn't like I could see anything revealing—just light, just a star in the darkness of my mind where I felt all my other gates. The further away I had been, the harder it had been to even discern movement; when we had been realms apart, she had appeared to stand completely still. But I had drawn a surprising amount of comfort from seeing her star in my night's sky all the same. Every time I felt fit to burst from it all, I could look and breathe just from knowing she was there, that she was alive, and that if I absolutely *had* to...I could try to reach her.

We hadn't tried me surging to her yet, much less from a distance, so I should give her fair warning before I did. And I should *definitely* not try it if she were just stirring and getting ready for the day.

Although, Flame help me, every delay tempted me more.

"Ben!"

My footsteps sped automatically, before my brain caught up and I recognized the voice. When I did, I stopped and turned to wait for the first time.

The tall, green-haired, olive-skinned drakón I'd expected to see pushed her way through the crowd with a bright smile on her face and pulled me into a hug. I hugged Svyer tightly back, even though something smelled off about her. A new perfume?

She pulled away before I could think about it further. Besides, her specialization in healing was with medicinal plants. She was always experimenting with some new healing concoction, balm, or aroma.

"Svyer!" I greeted in delight. "I didn't know you were coming!"

She laughed. "Well, when I heard *you* were, how could I resist checking in o—"

She caught onto my pointed look and Kor's cough just in time. "—ooon *you*," she finished brightly. "You know. My busiest cousin. The cousin who is too busy jumping around the Six Realms doing super important things to *answer my calls.*"

I flushed. She always seemed to call at the worst times, like when Sarah and I were in mortal danger. Or talking. Or I was showering. Or sleeping. Or.... Yeah, that accounted for all my time these past handful of days since I'd spoken to her. Now, the part that I knew I was at fault for was not thinking of calling her back in the few spare moments I'd had to breathe.

"Sorry," I said sheepishly, offering no excuse.

She rolled her green eyes as she slung her arm around me. "You're lucky I'm related to you, so I have to love you anyway."

"You're my best, most favorite cousin," I said solemnly. With her this close, that strange smell once again tugged at my nostrils, but I ignored it for her sake.

She smirked. "That's not saying much, and you know it."

"True," I said with a crooked smile.

The closest branches of my family tree were simple: Avva had been an only child. Avvi had only one sibling, who had only Svyer. And so, for first cousins at least...Svyer was it for me.

"But," I declared. "If I *had* to have only one cousin, you're the best, most patient, most *forgiving* one I could ask for."

"That'll do," she said, slipping away. Only to mock punch me on the arm. "For now."

She nodded to Yvera in a friendly greeting. "Yv, good to see you."

Yvera shrugged. She'd never particularly liked Svyer, but she'd never *hated* her, and for Yvera, that meant they were as good of friends as any. And Svyer, to her credit, understood that.

However, Svyer's smile slipped when she had to face Kor. Her nod to him was surprisingly sober. Almost...bitter, for her.

Huh.

Not that I was one to talk about having a fireball to throw at Kor right now. But....

Svyer turned back to me, smile returning. "Heading to the King's Wing? Mind if I tag along? You know. To say hi to some *friends.*"

"Of course," I said, clapping her on the back. "Your 'friends' would be upset with me if you didn't."

As hard as it would be to give up yet more chances to get Sarah alone before the evening festivities, I couldn't begrudge her some time with the first friend she had made in the Six Realms. Especially time with a female...who wasn't Yvera.

We had been near the King's Wing already, so only a few more dek of walking finally brought us to the large arch and gate that led to that hold within the hold. The guards knew me and my wings on sight and hailed me, but I approved when they asked me to blood verify anyway.

In roughly the center of the arch, just before the gate, was an archival pedestal with a crystalline cone that ended in a hollow tip as sharp as a needle. It was a bit like the device used in blood registrations: the crystal tip took a pinprick of blood, then magic searched for a match in the records of permitted people stored in the archival and tested for consumption at the same time. If there was a match and no consumption, then the crystal glowed pure with their soulcolor; a match with consumption would show a dark column in the center. If there was no match but the blood was clear, the crystal would glow white. (Huh. We were going to have to fix that for Sarah.) Finally, if there was no match and the blood contained consumption, the crystal would flare completely black.

The test was a costly measure in magic, setup, and maintenance, and thus usually only used in the highest of security situations, but I was glad to see that Eskala was taking it.

I pricked my finger, and the crystal immediately glowed pure gold. A guard sanitized the tip, then Yvera did the same and got pure violet. Kor winced as he pricked his, which was silly; it was just a drop of blood, and we'd done this hundreds of times before, after all. Pure sapphire.

Svyer stepped forward last, hesitating. "Ben, I'm not sure I'm on...."

"Go ahead just for the consumption test, then I'll see what I can do to get you in."

While she did that, a guard pulled me aside—an apologetic Strongshield. "Heir Koriben, I'm sorry to say it, but Eskala was adamant: no one not already on the registry was to be allowed into the King's Wing without swearing a blood oath of no harm to our *special guest*."

I grimaced. While Svyer wouldn't have a problem with the oath on principle, it was extreme to ask such a thing just for a visit. Especially when she was my cousin. And, well, Svyer. Who wouldn't hurt a fly, even if it landed on her prized potted magdela. On the *other* hand...I wasn't about to let all Eskala's precautions go to waste by bringing Sarah outside the King's Wing to Svyer.

"What is it, Ben?" Svyer asked.

I sighed as I looked at her. Silently, I said, *They say you have to swear a blood oath of no harm to Sarah. Eskala's orders.*

"I'll do it," she said immediately, out loud.

"Svyer," I said, pained. "You really don't have to do this. I'll...think of something."

Although what, I had no idea. Eskala wasn't one to be easily dissuaded, and in this case, I didn't want to try. I had asked for the strictest protections for Sarah, and I couldn't be asking for exceptions now—not even for my cousin.

You think I want harm to come to her? Svyer said impatiently. *I didn't come all this way to get stopped by a blood oath to do what I'm already going to do.*

I sighed again, then nodded to her. Then looked at the Strongshield guard. "She'll do it."

The guard hesitated a moment. *The oath...reveals the guest's identity.*

Ah, I saw the problem—in her mind, at least. In order to have any real effect, Svyer had to know *who* she was swearing not to harm.

Svyer already knows Sarah's name, and has met her, I answered. *And guesses at something of what she is. But you can just use Sarah's name in the oath without having to disclose anything more.*

The guard nodded in relief, then turned to Svyer. "If you will just step in here with me, please."

She led Svyer into a side guardroom, and I followed, with Kor and Yvera lingering outside—Kor's expression unreadable, Yvera's impatient. Inside the mostly empty guardroom, a small brazier was already sitting on a pedestal for this very purpose.

The guard gestured for Svyer to begin, since the one swearing the oath had to light the fire. If Svyer had not been drakón, the guard would have given her a match.

Svyer lit the coals in the brazier with a wave of her hand. Then, drawing the knife at her waist, she sliced a line across her right palm and raised that hand over the brazier to allow the blood to drip into the flames, which hissed with each drop. I felt the presence of the Tree grow in the small room; nothing opened the gateways of Her power more than the swearing of a solemn oath. Particularly with blood.

Svyer hesitated one moment, as if struggling with something. Which was odd, considering what I knew of her and her stated willingness from before. I nearly opened my mouth to ask what was wrong.

But in that moment, she met the guard's eyes and nodded to show she was ready.

Then she repeated after the guard, word by word. "I, Svyer Peacegrowth, of my own free will, do swear by my blood and the Flame to never intend or bring harm upon Sarah Lind, unless the Tree should permit. Thus I vow."

The final caveat was usually included in such oaths as a failsafe in case the object (Sarah, in this case) should ever become unworthy of protection or un-justly try to harm Svyer, in which case the Tree would free Svyer of her oath.

Otherwise...Svyer was now bound by her blood to never harm Sarah until the day Svyer died. And perhaps beyond.

Svyer clenched her hand into a fist, seemingly with more pain or effort than should have been warranted from just that simple cut. A final few drops fell hissing into the flames, and they surged upward to harmlessly enclose Svyer's hand and seal the oath into her blood.

Then the fire fell back down and died altogether, not even leaving the coals glowing.

When Svyer's hand opened, the cut was gone, without even a scar remaining—the final proof of the Tree's acceptance of her oath.

"Very good, thank you," the guard said gratefully. "Heir Koriben, with all of that in order, would you like me to add Svyer Peacegrowth to the registry?"

"Yes, please. I have no qualms about giving her access."

"I will do so. Svyer Peacegrowth, you may now enter," the guard said, gesturing out the room and to the gate, with Kor standing in view just beside it. "Flame welcome you."

"Thank...you," Svyer said, but there was a distance to her voice and a glazed look to her eyes.

"Svyer?" I said in concern, putting a hand on her back. I knew this wasn't the first blood oath she had taken. After all, I had been there at her presentation before the Tree and witnessed the oaths of the drakón she had sworn when she had become.

At my touch, she snapped out of her daze with a shake of her head. "Fine, I'm...fine. Just...tired."

She smiled at me and strode forward. "Come on. Let's go see our mutual friend."

I trailed behind her, troubled, but unable to name why.

But I was quickly distracted from darker thoughts, because as soon as we passed through the wicket gate and into the King's Wing proper, my star came rushing toward me.

"Ben!" she cried, uncharacteristically heedless of all the stares and smiles she collected as she ran across the bustling central court to me.

I laughed joyously as she jumped into my arms, and I lifted her up for a proper hug.

"Missed me?" I asked in satisfaction.

"Of course I did," she huffed, but the pique in her voice didn't stop her from snuggling deliciously into me and wrapping her arms around my neck. "Didn't *you* miss *me*?"

Sobering, I whispered in her ear, "More than I can say."

Seeing her star in the distant cosmos had kept my lungs moving. But for the first time since I had held her like this on the mesa yesterday, I felt like I could truly *breathe* again.

"Well," she said. "Good."

Her words were enticingly breathless, in a way that made me so *badly* want to turn her head to meet mine and take the rest of her breath away. I might have lost the battle, promises be iced, but—

Yvera poked me in the back. I knew it was her because of the pointed nail.

Then she said sharply, *If you have to be all moony over her, can't you go do it somewhere else?*

Right. Somewhere else. I should do that. Sarah would want that, anyway. Oh, and yeah—promises. Those things. Right.

With a monumental effort of will, I lowered Sarah to the ground, although I couldn't help but keep a hand on her back. For an excuse, I used it to turn her.

"Look who came all this way to see you," I said with a grin, anticipating her delight.

I wasn't disappointed, except by the loss of Sarah's touch as she gasped and ran for my cousin. It was a good thing I knew they were just friends, or I might have been jealous.

Alright...I still was. Just a little bit. I was only mortal.

"Svyer!" Sarah cried, wrapping her arms around the much taller young woman.

Svyer laughed and leaned down to return the embrace. "Sarah! It's so good to see you! And to see you've somehow survived whatever scrapes Ben has been getting you into."

"Hey," I said irritably. "I'm right here."

Svyer grinned over Sarah's head at me. "Well, you certainly don't need to be. I'm sure you have important Heir stuff to attend to while Sarah and I catch up."

I was about to open my mouth to protest—I had just gotten Sarah back, and I wasn't about to give her up yet—when Sarah let go of Svyer and turned to me, cheeks heating.

"Actually, Ben.... Would you mind giving us some time?"

Privately, she said to me, *I have some...female questions.*

I didn't understand what she meant by that for one whole second. Then Sarah placed a hand on her abdomen and grimaced.

I blinked. And inwardly groaned.

That was all? Her moons?

Then again, I wasn't female, obviously, and combine that fact with Sarah's self-consciousness and obsessive need for privacy, I had better give her that time alone with the one she *did* feel comfortable talking to.

As sharp as my disappointment was. And as potent as my unjustified flare of jealousy.

"Alright," I said with a sigh, running a hand through my hair.

"We should report to Eskala, in any case," Kor said as he came to my side.

"Right," I said, forcing myself to turn and hopefully not make it look as painful as it felt. "Eskala. See you later, Sarah."

"See you!" Sarah called after me.

Thank you, she sent. *Really. I wouldn't ask this, especially not so soon after you got back, but I really do need to talk to just her for a bit. Come find us as soon as you can.*

I understand, I sent back, a bit mollified. *Take the time you need.*

I could admit to myself that I was being greedy. Just because Sarah was now *my* star, around which my whole life and being seemed to be beginning to revolve....

Didn't mean I was hers.

CHAPTER THIRTY-FOUR

TRUST

SARAH

JUST BEFORE KOR TURNED to follow Ben, he met my eyes.

Remember what I told you, he said.

Then he fell into his place at Ben's left side as they made their way across the circle toward Eskala's suite.

I remember, I grumbled, but only to myself. I was still treasuring the connection I had with Ben too much to try branching out to speaking with other people. Plus, I had this superstitious feeling that if I started speaking to Kor in my mind, it would form an echo of the same connection between the two of us—and that was something I adamantly didn't want.

Kor's reminder referred to a few moments that he had managed to get with me yesterday while Ben was busy packing his own things, in which he went on and on about how I shouldn't reveal anything about myself or our quest or a bunch of other things to anyone I might talk to at the Moonfair—even someone I might already like and trust.

"I get it, Kor," I had told him impatiently, interrupting his no doubt well-prepared lecture. "I'm not an idiot."

"I'm not saying you are," Kor soothed. "But I'm just trying to prepare you for the discomfort of saying no to someone you like, such as Svyer. Svyer is a great example. She's Ben's cousin and your friend. That doesn't mean she needs to be burdened with all this information, even if she thinks she wants to be. We *protect* her by not giving her secrets that could bring her harm."

"I know," I snapped. "I figured that out on my own, thanks."

"Wait, what?" Kor said, startled. "But, when she was asking you about your location, on the scale—"

"Of course you heard that," I said, rolling my eyes. "*That's* why you interrupted us. Kor, I'd already decided I wasn't going to tell her anything. For exactly the reasons you described. And I still won't. No matter how many times she asks or why. I won't put that kind of burden on her. It's not hers to bear."

Kor blinked. "Oh."

And then, if he had had anything more to say, he had left it at that, because we could hear Ben talking to Yvera and getting closer.

I had thought then that he'd mentioned Svyer specifically because she was one of the few people I knew in the Six Realms that didn't practically know everything already.

But now that I thought about it...had Kor known she would come? Or guessed?

It wasn't a wild guess, if you thought about it. So many people came to the Moonfair. Why not Svyer, especially if she'd heard Ben would be there?

Svyer interrupted my thoughts with a hand on my shoulder. "So," she said cheerfully. "Want to find a nice place to chat? If I remember right, there's a private garden accessible from the landing pad. If Eskala's got you cooped up in here, I'm sure you could use some sunshine."

True enough, and I might have jumped at the chance for some sun, fresh air, and escape from watchful eyes...except I felt another warning cramp clench my abdomen.

"Actually, mind coming with me to my room?" I said as casually as I could. "There's something I want to ask you about the things you got me."

She shrugged. "Sure."

I tried to walk at a pace that was fast enough to avoid the incoming disaster and slow enough to not make the cramps worse. Whatever pace I set, I figured it would be slow enough compared with Svyer's stride to seem nonchalant.

When we passed the last suite before mine, Svyer started in surprise and looked ahead to the only remaining one at the end of the hall. And whistled.

"They've put you in the *King's* suite? *Nice*."

I grimaced. "I guess. It was kind of the King to offer it to me, but it's a bit...much."

I waved to my guards and thanked them as they let me in, then waved to the couple of attendants in the main room before heading straight to my bedroom.

"Ah, come on," Svyer whispered with a wink. "You've got to get used to being treated like royalty sometime."

I started. Trying to be casual, I waved her into my room before me and then closed the door behind me. "What do you mean by that?"

"Oh, don't give me that," Svyer said with a chuckle, folding her arms. "I *saw* you and Ben just now, you know. If he hasn't asked you to be his consort yet, he's going to pretty torching soon."

As a testament to how desensitized I was becoming to everyone's assumption I was going to marry Ben (and that Ben was even remotely there yet himself), I let out a breath of relief.

So Svyer hadn't guessed about me. Or if she had, she was hiding it well.

Above and beyond protecting Svyer, I was surprisingly relieved simply because I didn't *want* her to know yet. She was the first person in the Six Realms who had befriended me, and she'd done it simply because she was a good person, back before she even knew I was Earthren, let alone suspected I was Moontouched. I knew she was too good to stop being my friend if I became a Queen...but wouldn't things inevitably change?

I wasn't ready for that change yet. If...I would ever be.

"So?" Svyer asked pointedly.

"So?" I said blankly. I'd begun rummaging through the many drawers built into the wall, where my overly helpful attendants had already stashed my belongings before I even went to bed last night. I couldn't even find what they had done with the bags Svyer had originally put them in.

"Sooo, *has* he?" Svyer said, grinning broadly as she leaned against the wall next to me. "Asked you? You're not wearing his earring, but that could just be you two trying to keep things quiet for 'important reasons.'"

"Do all drakón move this fast to marriage?" I demanded, my consternation momentarily distracting me from the urgency of the cramps.

Svyer snorted. "Flame no. And by drakón, I assume you meant dramá—all of us, drakón and amón."

"Yes, sorry," I said distractedly. "It blurs in my head, but I'm getting there."

"Then to answer you again, no. Some take weeks or days, some take years. But this is *Ben*, Sarah. He's the Heir. And...well, he's Ben."

"Apparently, no more explanation than that should be needed," I said dryly.

Svyer grinned. "If you haven't learned what I mean by that by now, then Flame help you."

"I need *your* help right now," I said urgently, feeling the first trickle. "What did you give me for *periods*?"

She blinked. "Periods? Times?"

I took a deep breath. "I mean...monthly bleeding."

"Ooooh," Svyer gasped. "Your *moons*. So sorry. Here, they should be with your normal underwear."

She began searching with me and quickly found my underwear drawer. Then pulled out one of the dark red panties that I hadn't even touched yet, because...dark red? Why? Being practically shorts, they had even more coverage than the normal underwear, so it wasn't like they were lingerie. Not that...I had a use for that sort of thing, either.

Svyer showed me why by demonstrating the thickness of the bottom lining with her thumb and pointer finger.

"See? They're filled with agun fiber, which is highly absorbent and antibacterial. They should do just fine."

"Great," I said quickly, snatching the underwear from her and darting behind the dressing divider. "Don't mind me. Just need to change real quick."

"What did you use before?" Svyer asked curiously.

"Er...linings that we would stick to the normal underwear, then throw away."

I wasn't even going to *try* to describe tampons to her.

"Oh." I could hear the frown in Svyer's voice. "That sounds...wasteful."

"It was," I agreed with a sigh.

And more uncomfortable, too. These panties were even softer and more luxurious than the normal ones, and I loved how they came down my legs like shorts. Truly leakproof. *Amazing.*

I let out a breath of relief as I slipped my pants back on. Even though, as I picked up my old pair of underwear, I grimaced at the stain I hadn't been able to avoid.

"Any ideas on how I can get this out?" I asked Svyer as I came out.

"Oh, don't worry about it," Svyer said dismissively as she took the panties and tossed them into a bin set into an alcove. "They should be able to get that out, no problem."

"I'm not going to make someone *else* get that out!" I said, aghast. I went to retrieve the panties, but Svyer held me back with a laugh.

"Sarah, it's no big deal. You're not supposed to be worrying about your own laundry right now. If you're worried about putting a burden on them, then trust me: you'll make it a much bigger deal to them if *you* try to wash it yourself in your bath or something rather than just letting them handle it in the normal way of things."

"But...." I said, cheeks flaming. I was having a hard time articulating just why this bothered me so much. "It's my *blood*."

Svyer sobered. "That is a concern, yes. But that's why you throw your clothes in there as soon as you take them off."

She pointed to the bin. "It's enchanted to remove any connection between you and the bits of you left on your clothing. Let it sit there in that bin for a few dek at least, and it will nullify even your bloodstain."

"Oh," I said, blinking. I hadn't even thought of *that* concern.

"Trust these people, Sarah," Svyer said gently, putting her hands on my shoulders. "Even just trying to get in here, I saw the lengths they were going to to protect and care for you. They know how to do that. Let them."

"I trust them," I said quickly. "I'm just...uncomfortable with making anyone else clean up my menstrual blood."

"Why?" Svyer asked in surprise. "They might think it an honor."

I stared at her. "What?"

Svyer sighed. "As a healer, I have to first specify that the fluid isn't *just* blood, but there is some. And the Tree Herself declares that blood is sacred. It's the only blood that's naturally shed for the good of all, making it the purest, most powerful kind. Women's blood."

I just continued to stare. She shook her head at me, then put her arm around me and led me to a couch.

"Come on. Are you hurting? Let me have a look at you."

She put her hands on my shoulders, and while her warm, soothing power sunk into me and dispelled the cramps in my abdomen, I thought about what she said.

It's the only blood that's naturally shed for the good of all.

Could the blood I could feel trickling even now...be sacred? Not just mine, of course, but every woman's? Even throwing theology and the loaded word *sacred* aside, was menstrual blood anything to be ashamed of?

No, I realized in a daze. *It isn't.*

It was something I should...honor.

Maybe expecting anyone else to find it an honor to clean up was a stretch. But then again, if I treated the blood of all women with such honor...why couldn't someone else do the same to mine? Even in so mundane a way as cleaning up for each other—like washing each other's war bandages. All of us equally honoring the sacrifice we all made for the survival of all.

How had it taken me this long to realize that? Mom had never trained me to be ashamed, but then, she didn't have to. My society had done that. She would have had to fight quite the uphill battle to make me *proud*.

And I still wasn't there, but maybe I'd begun.

Still, I knew not to take this new epiphany too far. If I were doing my own laundry, I would clean up for myself. But neither should I be ashamed of letting someone else do it for me for a day.

It's just a day, I reminded myself.

This time. But if I made a certain choice....

Well, Ben had picked the chore he liked doing for himself when he could: cooking. Maybe mine could be laundry.

I winced and took that back. I didn't want it to be laundry.

"There," Svyer said with satisfaction. "Better?"

"So much," I said gratefully. The cramps were entirely gone, and the bloating was more regular. It had come on unusually hard and fast this morning. Just when I was waiting in the central court for Ben, in fact. I was just debating on whether to run to a healer to ask for a pad or back to my room to look for one when he had walked in.

And then...I'd been momentarily distracted.

"Svyer, your timing is impeccable, seriously."

Something flickered in her eyes, but she smiled too quickly for me to catch what. She plopped down next to me.

"I'm happy to help. But really, any of your attendants or even Ben could have helped you find that underwear, and Ben could have taken away the pain."

My cheeks heated again. "*Ben?*"

"What?" she asked. "He's been doing a surprisingly good job of keeping you in tip-top shape so far. I hardly had to do anything. I never knew he had such a healer inside of him. I'm going to have to apologize for ever doubting him."

Little did Svyer realize just how much Ben really was the reason I was so healthy right now—and how much might be unconscious on his part. Then again, maybe I was developing super-healing independently; we still didn't know, and might never unless this connection between us broke or we stayed far apart long enough to test. Neither of which scenario I was eager to experience.

But all of that wasn't anything I could discuss with Svyer. So, I focused on my mortification as a distraction.

"I couldn't talk to *Ben* about this."

"Why not?" Svyer said in puzzlement.

"Because...he's a guy!"

"Sooo?" Svyer said. "He's not ignorant. He took the same biology and anatomy classes that I did in secondary, *and* he had a very diligent Peace-growth mother teach him more. He knows how this works for females. And, let me tell you, he's realized you are female."

"Still, guys don't...."

Then I realized that was my shame speaking again. The voice...of *my* culture, which told me not only to be ashamed for being a woman among women, but to especially be ashamed of being a woman among men.

I had just assumed that the moment Ben realized what was going on, he would willingly dump me on Svyer and run. But when I replayed that scene in my mind, particularly when he understood....

His eyes were sad. Sad that I didn't feel comfortable letting him help me right now with something that was no worse than a headache or stubbed toe...and in fact, was something much better, something much more important.

He might have actually...wanted to help. And far from doing him a favor...I may have hurt him by not even asking.

I sat there, processing the second stunning revelation I'd received in a handful of minutes.

"So," Svyer said casually. "You never actually said if Ben has asked you."

"Oh." I shook my head, returning to the present. Only to have my cheeks heat again. "He hasn't, not even close."

"Ashes," Svyer chuckled. "I just *saw* 'close,' when you two were just saying *hello*."

I griped, "I don't know why everyone keeps assuming there's more going on between us than there actually is."

"I don't know. Maybe because we have eyes. If that's what you two do in *public*, then whew." Svyer fanned her face teasingly.

"Actually, no," I said, cheeks on fire now. "What you saw is all there's ever been."

Svyer stilled. Then turned fully to face me and leaned in. "Wait, what? Surely he's at least kissed—"

"For the last time, no," I cried. "He's not there yet, alright? If he's ever going to be."

Svyer processed that for one second, then said, "Ashdust. He's *there*."

She leaned back, looking almost angry. "I don't know what his problem is right now, but trust me, Sarah. I grew up with him. He's there."

Something finally clicked in my brain. All the little things I already knew about Ben, the things he had taught me yesterday to defend myself, and the things Svyer had told me just now.

"Svyer," I said hesitantly. "I'm new, so I don't know how this stuff works for...dramá. Is there something I'm supposed to...*do* first, before kissing? Do I need to give him explicit permission? Or something?"

Svyer paused. Then hit herself on the forehead. "That's it. It must be. *Ben*...."

She sighed and looked at me. "You haven't done anything wrong, Sarah. Not from what I've seen. We don't *have* to be explicit...but permission is important. And for someone as inexperienced about this as Ben is...explicit permission is probably required. He just doesn't trust himself to judge, the poor guy. And it would go against everything he stands for to kiss you without being *sure*."

"That..." I said slowly. "...makes quite a lot of things make quite a lot more sense, actually."

"Sorry," Svyer said with a grimace. "It shouldn't have been this hard for him, honest."

"No, no," I said quickly. "I really like that about him. That's a good thing. In fact...it leads me to one final question I have that I really only feel comfortable asking you."

Svyer cocked her head. "What's that?"

"Ben has been *nothing* but completely respectful," I said slowly. "So I'm asking this not because of him but because he makes me hopeful about dramá in general. How common is it for women in your culture to be...forced?"

Svyer froze. "If you hadn't just told me that Ben hadn't...."

"He hasn't!" I said rapidly. "At all! Like I said, *nothing but respect*. I'm asking this because I'm *hopeful* of what that means for everyone. But I feel like I need to know this to fully understand where he's coming from right now."

Svyer took a deep breath. "It...happens. I won't lie to you about that. But it is rare, Sarah. It's a crime we treat more seriously than murder. The Tree is *female*, after all. So, any accusation remotely of the sort—whether the survivor is male or female, adult or child—is taken straight to the Tree, who can see into their hearts and know the truth. Judgment on the guilty is left to the Tree...and She is not merciful when it comes to such things. For the truly guilty, castration is among the least of Her punishments. Everyone knows that. So, any iced idiot with half their brain functioning thinks twice about doing such a thing."

I let out a breath. "So, when Ben was teaching me self-defense techniques yesterday to use against drunks who might make me uncomfortable...."

Svyer smiled thinly. "I can't say that Ben's fears didn't go all the way, because it's Ben, and he's not just overprotective—he's had to deal with the worst monsters in the Six Realms, consumed or dramá, for a job. But the greatest chance would still just be you being made *uncomfortable*, and that's quite a big enough deal in his mind."

I chuckled. "He also probably had Kor in mind."

Svyer stilled. "Kor...?"

Oops, I silently groaned. That was a can of worms I shouldn't have opened.

"Kor's been respectful, too," I said quickly. "Ben's just jealous...I think."

Svyer's face was still unusually sober, almost grim, even though I thought with the change in topic she would have lightened up by now. "Why would Ben be jealous of Kor?"

I hesitated. Even beside all the things this touched on that I wasn't supposed to talk about with Svyer, I belatedly remembered Kor's interest in her. I couldn't see how he would have made much progress with her in the past handful of days, but if he had, if Svyer was interested in return, would this cause her pain?

Svyer's face softened. "*Please*, Sarah. I know you can't tell me much about what is going on for you right now. But please tell me what you can. Especially about Kor's behavior toward you."

I sighed. "He's just been a bit...flirty, that's all. But that's Kor."

Svyer frowned, eyes troubled. "Flirty. Enough to make Ben, who knows that tendency well...jealous."

"It's nothing, Svyer," I said. "Trust me."

"With Kor, it's never 'nothing,'" she said flatly. "It means he wants something from you, Sarah. Torch it."

She stood, unable to sit still.

"Svyer," I said faintly. "Trust me, I don't have any interest in Kor. There's no need to be worried—"

I meant worried that I would try to take him from her, but she interrupted me with a hard laugh.

"No need? Why do you think I'm *here*, Sarah? Because I'm torched worried about you! *And* about Ben. Because as long as both of you are near *that man*, there is a cause for *deep* worry. Why won't anyone see that?"

I felt a chill. "What do you mean?"

She took a deep breath. Then she cast a quick glare at the walls before looking back at me. *I mean that Kor is not to be trusted.*

I swallowed. "Why?" I whispered.

Her eyes were harder than I had ever seen them. *Because he isn't what he seems. He pretends to be Ben's friend. He claims to be serving only for the good of the people. Lies. That man would do anything for power. He betrayed his own brother for it. What's keeping him from betraying his own King?*

I shook my head, too full of horror to respond.

Please, Sarah, Svyer begged. *He's plotting something. You have to see that. He needs Ben because he can't become King himself. But if he makes Ben King...then Kor holds all the power he can ever hope to hold. Or...at least all he could hope for before you came along. His plans can change, and maybe they now have. Maybe, just maybe, he thinks he can become a King after all. Or...at least a consort to a Queen.*

I inhaled sharply. She knew. Or suspected. "How...."

The same way I know about Kor, Svyer said sadly. *From the person who knows him best. Sol—*

A knock sounded at my door.

Moving robotically, I moved to open it, hoping my face was frozen in a somewhat neutral position.

Yet who should be standing outside my door...but Kor.

CHAPTER THIRTY-FIVE

STEAM

KORIBEN

YOU SHOULDN'T HAVE SENT Kor *to get her,* Yvera said, leaning against the wall outside my suite, where we waited. *You really are a dimtorch about this.*

I didn't exactly hear you *volunteering,* I snapped.

While all three of us were speaking with Eskala, she had suggested we take Sarah and Svyer on a walk up the path carved into the mountainside to the private Royal garden, saying what a shame it was that Sarah had been cooped up inside for so long. I was all for the plan, but Eskala had asked me to linger for a private word, so Kor had volunteered to go get Sarah, saying that he could also disguise her while he was at it. I couldn't think of anything to protest his willingness and logic, so I'd let him.

Now I'd just gotten out from my word with Eskala, and apparently Sarah, Svyer, and Kor still hadn't come out of Sarah's rooms.

He's probably charming them both into falling in love with him—at the same time, Yvera said in disgust. *Just for the challenge of it.*

Probably not true. But also...probably close enough to being true that I had a hard time keeping my fists unclenched.

Bored, Yvera asked, *What did Eskala want to talk to you about?*

Avva, of course. He...was getting worse. Actually starting to *look* weak—stumble, hold on to things—especially in the evenings. On top of the worry and pain of a son, I had the worry of an Heir. A Monarch should be kind and careful, using their power and strength with sound judgment...but they must never look physically weak. We were the people's bulwark, their sword, their shield. When we buckled...people didn't just worry. They panicked.

Eskala thought they had kept anyone who shouldn't see him that way from doing so. But there was only so long she and her people could shield him. She didn't say more than that, but I knew what she was debating in her brilliant mind. Did she let me continue pursuing the cure the Trees promised Sarah could give us? Or did she order me back to Crownhold to start...preparing?

It was the same old question from this entire year. Except now with far higher stakes for both options. Eskala no doubt knew what my answer would be, which was why she didn't ask for it. And which was why she still, for today, let me pursue the cure. She didn't want to lose her greatest friend; she still held out hope that we could save him. So, she wasn't *quite* ready to drag me forcefully back to Crownhold. But I had no doubt that if the scales in her mind finally tipped...she would.

I didn't answer Yvera, and she didn't ask again.

I seemed a bit monstrous, in that light: idly waiting to go on a simple, pleasurable walk in the sunlight with the girl who made me feel alive in a way I never had before while, worlds away, my father was slowly dying because of a bargain he had made with the Tree for my very existence.

But Sarah didn't know that. And Sarah *shouldn't* know that, not yet. Not while there still wasn't anything she could do about it more than what we were already doing.

We had to get to the Tree of Ice, so Sarah could be invested. Sarah already knew that much, was already giving her *all* to do that much. Only after we'd reached that insurmountable summit should I ask her for what only she could give Avva.

In the meantime, I should do whatever it took to give her strength and happiness. Even if that meant feeling like a monster while I held inside both the fear for Avva and my own inevitable pleasure at being with her—ice and fire that caused a steam that scalded me from the inside out.

At long last, the door to Sarah's suite opened, and Kor stepped out, looking very satisfied with himself. Svyer followed, much more subdued.

Then Kor waved grandly. "May I present...Sera Peacegrowth."

I saw what he meant as soon as Sarah stepped out.

Her hair and eyes...were now the same shade as Svyer's. Combining that rich emerald green with her warm, light brown skin, she looked like an exotic plant. A beautiful one, true, but...it just seemed *wrong*. I was briefly tempted to tell Kor to change her back.

"Hmph," Yvera said, still leaning against the wall. "I suppose it's good enough to fool fly-bys. But it won't fool anyone up close. She's still too short to be drakón."

"It's a good thing no one will get up close that doesn't already know who she is," Kor said with a raised eyebrow.

"What do *you* think, Ben?" Svyer asked pointedly.

There seemed to be a right answer here, but for the life of me, I didn't know what it was. So, I decided careful honesty was best.

"I think it looks strange, but I think that's just because I like the way she normally looks. Kor's right: it will do the trick for a walk up to the garden. Then she can change back as soon as we come inside again."

Svyer gave Sarah an *I-told-you-so* smirk. I did not know if that meant I had passed, but at least Sarah smiled back.

As we began walking, Kor said, "Well, we'll just have to come up with a different disguise for tonight, then."

"What?" I said in alarm. "Why?"

"Sarah needs to go out at least for a bit, Ben," Kor said, giving me a sidelong look.

She needs to feel for the gate, remember? If she couldn't feel it from here last night....

Torch it. He was right. Again.

"As much as I can't believe I'm agreeing with Kor on this," Svyer said with a sigh. "I...do. You can't take Sarah to the Moonfair and not let her *see* any of it, Ben."

"I am actually not that big on parties," Sarah volunteered. "For what it's worth."

Kor gave her a look, probably with the same message that he sent me, because her mouth formed an O.

"Besides," Svyer said teasingly, winking at me. "Don't you want Sarah to be at the pageant?"

When the two pieces finally clicked in my brain, I nearly stumbled from horror. Really, I should have made the connection much sooner, but I always carefully blocked out the details of the pageant whenever I could as a self-defense mechanism. I hadn't even *thought* of what it might mean to have *Sarah* there....

"No," I said in a choked voice. "No, that's exactly what I *don't* want."

"Why?" Svyer asked in surprise.

My cheeks were flaming now. "Because...because I don't! That's the *last* place she should be!"

"Ben, I won't laugh," Sarah said, walking faster to catch up to me.

"That's not the part I'm worried about!"

I'm worried you'll kill me first, then *laugh as you dance on my ashes.*

"But I want to see it," Sarah said, chin sticking out. For someone who refused to think she was meant to be a Queen, she sure could pull out an adorably imperious air when she wanted to.

"Trust me—you don't," I told her, not letting her dainty chin distract me. Too much. "Ask Svyer about the details *when I'm not there*, and you'll see what I mean. You won't want to go then."

"Ah, now, Ben," Kor said with a wicked grin as he came up on my other side. "You're assuming that—"

I narrowed my eyes at him and said dangerously, "I told you: give her the details *when I'm not there*. End of discussion."

And I thought that would be the end of it. Sarah would find out what the pageant entailed, she would avoid it like the plague, I would get through it, the end. My life, spared.

How wrong I was.

SARAH LOVED THE WALK, so even though it wasn't time alone with her, it served its purpose. She was fascinated by the stairs, carved straight into the rock of the mountainside, with the raw stone left on the exterior side to form a natural balustrade. But of course the Starkissed couldn't simply carve stairs. No, they had to decorate the walls on either side with engravings, inlaid scales, and gemstones, and when I told her that the latter glowed at night, her eyes had gone wide with delight.

She loved the view even more. Though she wasn't as winded as she might have been once, she would frequently stop just to take it all in: the blue sky, the blue water, the dark mountain slope and white sand below. To my surprise, I caught her frequently watching the drakón dance in the warm currents overhead, and something in her eyes looked...wistful. I remembered my foolish promise to myself to one day show her how truly *glorious* flying could be. I still intended to keep that promise...but today was not that day.

Given the narrow width of the stairs, we had naturally fallen into single file. I let Sarah go first so she could set the pace, and then I came right behind her. Though I'd prepared an argument that I needed to be closest to her to protect her, no one, not even Kor, seemed interested in taking that spot from me.

Though I almost wished I wasn't so close when Svyer, who was right behind me, asked me if I was planning to take Sarah down to the beach sometime.

"Er, no," I said quickly, trying desperately to keep my cheeks from flaming. "Even if it were safe, I don't think Sarah would like that."

"Why don't you ask *her*?" Svyer said pointedly.

"I think Ben is right," Sarah said calmly, not looking back from her slow climb up the latest switchback of the stairs.

"Why?" Svyer said in surprise. "Beaches are fun."

I focused very hard on looking at each step I was taking next. And *not* on Sarah, as difficult as that was with her right in front of me.

"Well, from what I can tell," Sarah said thoughtfully, casting a look down at the closest strip of sand, "you dramá seem to think it's the perfect time to be nude."

Flame help me, I thought. *Please don't let her look back at me now.*

"It is, though," Svyer insisted. "Besides just being able to soak up the sun better, why would you want to wear anything that will get sandy and wet?"

Just. Keep. Thinking. About. Steps.

"I don't get energy from the sun, Svyer," Sarah reminded her. "And I know it might be hard to believe with my darker skin, but I can still burn."

"Oh," Svyer said sheepishly. "Right. Well, *you* don't have to get undressed. But surely you could still have some fun with us."

"Maybe another time," Sarah said kindly. Though it didn't sound like she was really interested.

I let out a slow, long breath of relief. Mixed with equal parts disappointment, which I savagely suppressed.

Still, maybe, sometime in the far, distant future, if I found her a *private* beach, with just the two of us, with lots of shade....

It...was time to focus on the steps again. I had to be at least somewhat cooled down by the time we reached the garden, after all.

Which we did, all too soon after that. If Sarah saw anything amiss in me, she didn't show it.

I didn't think she did, though. She was too focused on soaking in the garden. She wandered the paths, dabbled her fingers in the fishpond and laughed when some of the bravest inhabitants came to nibble, walked through the trellis while running her hands over the leaves, smelled the giant blossoms, and ooo'ed in delight when she scattered a flight of day glowflies. And all the while, she didn't seem to care that I trailed behind her, just as entranced by her as she was by the garden. I had never seen her so determinedly...*happy*.

She needed this, I realized with a pang. That much cut through even my intoxication with her.

Something about this, she had desperately needed. Maybe it was the escape, or the piece of nature, or having nothing to do for a half-deken but whatever...she wanted to do. Or all of it. All I knew was that I couldn't spoil the moment by asking what that thing was, but I would have to figure it out, and soon. Because if I claimed to care about her at all, if I was going to dare try to be the one to be at her side for the rest of her life...I was going to have to give this to her again.

Besides...I didn't think I could ever feel a greater happiness than to make her this happy.

Fire and ice. Oh, how they both burned inside me.

Chapter Thirty-Six

APPEARANCES

Sarah

I MUST HAVE BEEN visibly drooping again by the time we got back from the walk, because Ben kindly suggested I go take a nap. When I protested, not wanting to waste this time with him on *more* sleep, he pointed out that as the sun climbed, they were reaching their highest point...and I was reaching my lowest.

And man, when he said that, I could feel it; after being up half the night, combined with the emotional rollercoaster my morning had been *and* the start of my period, I was practically swaying on my feet. Kor finally added with a wink that it was going to be a late night for me anyway, so I might as well be as rested as possible.

I finally gave in, and everyone but Ben went their separate ways, Svyer saying something about going out to enjoy the festivities, Kor something vague about work, and Yvera nothing at all.

Ben walked me to my room. In the moment, I assumed he was worried that I might not even make it that far if he didn't. Only after I collapsed into my bed did my exhaustion-fogged brain register the way he had lingered at my doorstep. But all I had given him was a hug and a mumble of thanks.

I groaned. But whatever he had been hoping for, it was too late to give it to him now. I would just have to make it up to him....

Then I was out.

When I woke up, it was with the slowness and mental fog that told me I had been out for hours. It must have been after noon at least, because as I lay there, slowly regaining functionality, I could feel my power waxing—still faint, but getting stronger instead of weaker.

Only now, in the stillness, did I finally have the space to process what Svyer had told me about Kor.

But I didn't know what to think about it. At all.

One half of me wanted to reject her suspicions outright as being too horrible and simply *wrong* to contemplate. Besides, my pragmatic side reasoned, she hadn't given me any evidence—just gut feelings and conjecture.

Because she didn't have time to, another part whispered.

That half of me thought of all the reasons Kor made *me* uneasy: His deceptiveness. His machinations. His unparalleled arrogance in thinking he was the only one who saw what had to be done to save the worlds.

But...could he really be plotting to *kill* the *King*?

He betrayed his own brother for power.

Power...or perhaps, as he saw it, the chance to save the worlds.

The darkest part of me whispered, *If that's what he thinks it will take....*

I shook my head. No. *No.* Kor wouldn't go that far. No matter his frustrations, he wouldn't commit *regicide*. He wouldn't do that to Ben. He wouldn't.

But whether that was my emotions or my intuition speaking...I simply didn't know.

I kept thinking as I crawled slowly out of bed. What I needed was more information. Preferably from an objective source, and that didn't seem to be Svyer. Whoever she had gotten her information from, she seemed to be too emotional about Kor himself for me to accept her secondhand knowledge at face value.

Just as I came to that conclusion, my eye caught my own reflection in the giant mirror attached to a wall in the bedroom.

And then I got a glimmer of an idea.

I approached the mirror slowly, as if moving toward a dangerous beast. And as I caught my own eye in the mirror and saw the silver glow overtaking the brown in my eyes....

I just might have been.

I touched the surface of the mirror, ignoring the guilty pang I felt at the fingerprints I was no doubt leaving that someone would have to clean. Then I took a deep breath. And summoned my power.

It rose from the darkness inside my belly, curling up and out like frosted ferns breaking through the soil.

I sent it an apologetic feeling for rousing it at this time of day but assured it that this was important, and it was perhaps the only moment in which I would be alone for a while to do this.

I need information about Kor, I said. *I need to know if he can be trusted.*

The power rose through my torso, through my fingers...and into the mirror. It spread across the surface rapidly, freezing the glass in its wake.

In hindsight, a mirror might not have even been necessary for this, since the ice coating formed its own reflective surface. But oh well. No one had given me an instruction manual for this stuff, for goodness's sake, so I was going to have to figure these things out as I went along.

When the ice was thick and spread enough, it stopped showing my own reflection, and another view slowly replaced it.

I recognized the room at once as being Eskala's study in her suite just down the hall. And sure enough, Eskala sat in one of the chairs by the fire, papers scattered over her lap, one of which she was studying. And who should be standing in front of the fire, with his back to me...but Kor.

Whatever the mentor and mentee had been discussing before, they seemed to be at a lull in their conversation now. Kor held a glass goblet elegantly between his fingers, filled with a dark liquid I was certain wasn't tsha. He swirled the liquid idly in his hand, but his focus seemed to be on the flames.

He took a sip, then after swallowing, broke the silence. "Any sign of our...special guest?"

"No," Eskala said immediately, though she didn't look away from her paper. "Not so much as a whiff."

Kor snorted before taking another sip. "Funny. Because I can almost smell his stench now."

Eskala lowered her paper and raised an eyebrow. "Are you sure that's not just your emotions speaking, Korinth?"

Kor turned enough so that I could see his expression, a smirk pulling at his lips. I didn't know if the darkness in his eyes was from the lighting and flickering flames or....

"Dear Eskala. When have you ever known me to do such a foolish thing as let my flameheart rule my head?"

"There's a first time for everything. And if it ever did, it would be about this."

"You wound me," Kor said with a pout. Which faded even as he turned back to the flames. "No, Eskala. My heart is fully iced over, and I am thinking *only* with my head. I knew him better than anyone. Still do, I think. He is here, somewhere. He wouldn't be able to resist a chance as good as this."

"Even if what you suspect about him is true?"

Kor snorted again. "Especially then. After Ben's challenge, it would be too perfect. Don't you see?"

"Have you told Koriben yet?" Eskala asked quietly.

"No," Kor said grimly. "For the same reasons as before. Ben has enough problems. This one is mine."

"Not if he goes for Sarah, it isn't. Or Koriben himself."

I felt a terrible chill that almost broke my concentration. I had to send a steady stream of power to maintain this spell, and that shockwave nearly ended it.

"Do you really think Ben can handle *one* more mental burden right now?" Kor demanded, eyes flashing as he looked at her. "Especially this one? He's already close to the breaking point—again. And already is paranoid enough about Sarah's safety. We tell him about this, and he might just *preemptively* go berserk."

"You don't know that for certain," Eskala said, her own eyes hard. "And if you do not warn him now, and something goes badly because of it...."

Kor looked away and took another drink. "That's my job to prevent. And my call to make. He's my Heir. I'm the one who decides what he can and can't handle."

"So it is—to a point. And for the moment, the King is deferring to your judgment. But you're playing a dangerous game, Korinth."

Kor's lips pulled into a thin smile as he looked sidelong at his mentor—eyes dark. "Don't we always, Eskala?"

The image faded, returning to my own reflection as my power ran out.

"No, no, *no*," I whispered frantically, even now mindful of listening ears.

But still the power would not come, and the ice on the mirror faded to nothing.

"No!" I cried softly, pounding the wall on each side of the mirror in frustration.

That had been the exact *opposite* of helpful. I had asked to know if Kor could be trusted, but all I had gotten were more questions and—above all—fears.

This time for Ben himself.

Kor thought someone was here, at the Moonfair, someone who meant Ben harm. Someone dangerous enough to have Eskala worried. I would have said Kor was worried, too—but didn't he say himself that his heart was locked out of this? He was coolly toying with Ben's safety, and for what? Revenge? And why? Arrogance?

All I had gotten was more proof that Kor always thought he knew what was best for everyone. Even at their own peril.

If that were the case, then....

A knock at my door.

That had better *not be Kor*, I thought with gritted teeth as I went to answer it.

To my surprise, I found Vadya and Fenra standing outside, looking about as excited as children on Christmas morning.

"Hello?" I said slowly.

"Oh, good, you're awake!" Vadya said brightly. "That makes things easier."

She hooked her arm around my waist and began whisking me in the direction of the bathroom.

I felt a sinking feeling in my stomach that had nothing to do with what I had just seen. "Makes *what* easier?"

The sisters squealed as one, "Getting you ready for the Moonfair!"

We entered the bathroom, and when I saw the veritable female army ready to tackle me there....

OK, it was just three more attendants. But all three wore Starkissed stripes and looked just about fit to bursting with wickedness as my current captors. And with the bathtub already full, covered in sweet smelling bubbles, and steaming, and with the assortment of beatification weaponry spread about....

My heart sunk into my stomach, disappearing into the nether where my power had gone.

I...am a dead woman.

Alright.

I had to admit: It wasn't as bad as I had expected. It helped that they did everything humanly possible in every moment to make me comfortable—*except* letting me bathe myself. But when one of the drakón started giving me a shoulder massage supplemented with healing energy and then did the same to my scalp while shampooing my hair....

Well, I dare anyone to not melt into a puddle of bliss.

In that way, they kept me floating through a surprisingly compliant, hypnotized daze through the whole process. Honestly, if I had drunk anything beforehand, I would have thought for certain that they had drugged me; I wasn't ruling out the incense or scented candles as having just that effect. But somehow, I didn't care. I mean...I couldn't have gotten out of this anyway, so I might as well be high during it, right?

Even when Svyer arrived near the tail end and laughed at me, I didn't come down from my cloud.

Instead, I just blinked as I saw Svyer come up behind me in the mirror in front of me, smiled dazedly, and said, "Oh, hi Svyer."

By then, I was wrapped in a warm, fluffy robe worthy of the cloud I was on, sitting in a chair in front of a mirror, and they were working on my face and hair. They had already bathed, oiled, de-haired (using this waxy substance that didn't hurt at *all*—or maybe that was just the drugs), rinsed, re-oiled, perfumed, and manicured and pedicured me.

"Hi, *Sarah*," Svyer said with a smirk. "If that's really you in there still."

"I think so," I said dopily to her in the mirror. "I'm just *really* relaxed. Isn't that great?"

"It's certainly better than I was expecting to find," she answered, smirk deepening as she put her hand on her hip.

As one of the attendants passed, Svyer mock-whispered to her, "You all certainly know your stuff."

With wide-eyed innocence, the attendant answered, "We live to serve."

"Anything I can do to help?" Svyer asked in a normal tone as she approached my chair.

My jaw dropped as I finally took her fully in. "Svyer...you look amazing!"

The olive-skinned Amazonian looked about ready to walk down a red carpet. Her luscious emerald locks were piled up in an elaborate ponytail updo, and she had on a Grecian-style emerald dress with wide open sleeves, tied at the waist with a gold belt.

"Why thank you," Svyer said with a grin as she peered over my shoulder at me in the mirror. "As much good as that does my vanity, I know *I'm* not the star of tonight."

"Who's that?" I asked, blinking stupidly.

Svyer just gave me a look that said, *Just how* much *did they drug you?*

"Oh, no," I said, cheeks heating. "I'm just going to be...um...busy. With stuff. I'm not here for the party."

"Right," Svyer said, one hand on the counter, the other on her hip. "They're going through all this work...for something other than the opening night of the Moonfair."

The drugs must have been wearing off, because my cheeks were getting even warmer, and the depth of what I had just undergone and what the attendants were still doing was finally sinking in. "Oh, this? This is...just part of the disguise."

"Speaking of which," Kor drawled as he strode in. "I'm here with the rest of it."

Yup, the drugs were wearing off.

"Kor!" I gasped, yanking my bathrobe further across my chest and causing my makeup artist to tsk at me for the suddenness of my movement. I ignored her.

Who had let *him* in?! And could I fire them?

Probably not.... Right now, all I had was an empty title.

"*Do you mind*?" I snarled.

"Mind what, darling Sarah?" he said with a smirk. "You're covered, aren't you?"

"Kor," Svyer said in a warning tone as she straightened and looked back at him.

"Oh, don't get your tails in a knot. I'm only here to drop off Sarah's disguise...which requires a bit of explanation."

In the mirror, I saw him unfurl the cloth that had been over his arm.

I stared. And though I couldn't see Svyer's expression with her head turned away from my mirror, I saw her go still.

Now, I was new. But I was pretty sure that what I was seeing was significant.

"It's...blue," I said flatly.

Deep blue. A blue eerily similar to....

"Kor," Svyer said, her voice now dangerous. Her fingers dug into the back of my chair.

"The disguise, you see, is actually *me*," he said. "There's no way we can effectively conceal who and what she is...so we might as well hide her in plain sight. Next to me."

"You're kidding," I snapped.

He met my eyes in the mirror. "Oh, we're not."

And it was true. If he had been smirking, then I could have dismissed him more easily. What made me nervous was that he was being serious.

Then something about what he'd said hit me. "We?"

"I'm here, Sarah, dear," Eskala's voice said. She came up to me, since she had been too short to appear over my chair in the mirror. "Despite Korinth's dramatics, we do think this is the best method of concealing you while giving you the access you need to Olsdak to search for...what you came here to find."

At the pause, her eyes had rested momentarily on Svyer with a wary look.

"And," Eskala continued with a thin smile. "If you wish, reveal yourself at just the right time and in just the right way."

"What do you mean?" I asked with a start.

She sighed. "As much as we have tried to conceal your presence in the Six Realms for as long as we can to allow you the time to make your decision, we cannot, in good faith to our people, do that for much longer. Nor should you want us to. Whatever you decide, by hiding yourself much longer, you will make it more difficult for either yourself or your successor to win their hearts. We must think of the after as well as the now. And now is the perfect moment to introduce yourself without admitting that is what you are doing."

"What are you talking about?" I demanded.

"This dress," Kor said, holding it up high so that I could see as much of it in the mirror as possible, "is made with the very latest magical crystal-cloth and spellweaving innovations. As such, it has a unique and special feature. When magically activated..."

"...it will change to this," Eskala finished as she laid a paper in front of me, with a detailed painting of a dress.

A...completely different dress.

I gaped, picked up the paper and looked between the two dresses again and again.

Hiding me in plain sight, indeed.

"What does Ben think of this?" Svyer demanded.

"We haven't discussed this with him," Eskala said, face set. "For very good reasons."

"Because there's no way he would allow this!" Svyer snapped.

"Yes, and even if forced, he would simply ruin the best moment for her to use it. But that isn't Ben's decision to make. It's Sarah's...and the King's. And *he* has already sanctioned this plan. In fact, he helped us form it."

I glanced at Eskala, eyes widening, heart pounding. "The King...thinks I should do this?"

She took my hand, face softening. "Only if you want to, dear. It's still your choice. But after nearly a century of rule...Kavarian is aware of how important simple gestures like this are to win the hearts of the people you rule. Because if you do not rule by baring your soul for them...you rule by wielding your fist. It's a hard, hard thing to do, to rule with vulnerability. But the alternative is even harder. And far crueler."

I took deep, steadying breaths as I stared at the dress in the mirror.

"You don't have to make your decision now," Eskala said gently. "You can simply wear this as it is. But if you decide to, then when you reach the proper moment...you can take it."

I gulped.

I thought the King had seriously overestimated my courage. There was no way I could pull something like that off, even if forced to. Doing it would invite every single person within eyesight—and tonight, there would be many, so many—to stare at me. To see me—for who I was.

I couldn't do *that*....

Could I?

Chapter Thirty-Seven

WANT

Koriben

"You ready for tonight?" Yvera teased, elbowing me.

"No," I said, giving her a dangerous look.

We were once again standing and waiting in the hall outside my suite for Sarah to come out. I had already been through my torturous—I mean, "well-meaning"—preparations and stood stiff and uncomfortable in my Starkissed-mandated finery. Yvera, of course, wore her scale plate. She was my bodyguard, after all. She was the lone person excused from Starkissed ministrations tonight.

Besides, I didn't think I had ever seen Yvera in a dress, nor ever would.

Kor must have still been getting ready himself, because he was nowhere in sight. Neither was Svyer, which was odd, since she'd mentioned before she left that she would come back in time to go with us to the feast. Besides, surely she knew I would need all the moral support I could get right now.

"Ah, come on," Yvera said, smirking. "It's just a bit of theatrics. Surely you've been around Kor enough by now to pull it off."

"I could say the same thing about you," I said darkly.

Yvera's lips pulled into a feral grin. "Admit it: if *I* had been Heir, they would have stopped inviting me by now."

I had no doubt of that. She would have set the whole pageant on fire, drugged the entire cast with dreamhaze, or smashed the Moonstar into a million pieces. And sparked a civil war in the process.

"So it's your own torched fault that you're so nice about it," she concluded.

"Yes," I said dryly. "My own fault that I am determined to keep the peace with our most magically powerful clan for so small a price as acting out their little charade every year."

Don't get me wrong—I wasn't a saint. Every year, civil war was a more tantalizing option.

"From what I've heard, your dad never made so much fuss when he was Heir."

"Because he kept hoping Avvi would show up," I snapped. "And he only had to do it *two years* before he finally convinced her to marry him."

"Well," Yvera said, examining her nails. "Then I don't know what the difference is for you, this year."

I gritted my teeth. "The difference for me is that Sarah isn't—"

Just then, Sarah's door opened. Svyer came first, which explained where she'd been. Then...Kor.

Before I could get worked up about that, Sarah came last.

My flameheart stopped. Completely.

Whoever had done her hair had been an artist, showing off its dark lusciousness to perfection with folds upon folds of glowing, diamond-studded curls and braids that framed her heart-shaped face at the sides but spilled down in waves behind her. Her skin glistened with silver sparkles down her neck, in the lines of her collarbone, and down the sides of her face and cheekbones. Her lashes seemed impossibly long, and her eyelids were a smoky enigma. Her full lips had been coated in a dark red that both blended completely with the look and drew my eye for far too long.

Most remarkable of all, there seemed to be something different about her that went deeper than the makeup or the hair or the dress, something harder to describe. Her chin was lifted, high and strong. Her gaze was sharp and direct. Her movements were graceful and precise. And when she finally found my eyes, her lips pulled into a small smile that was confident and...inviting.

I was so stunned by *her* that it took seconds, many seconds, longer than it should have for the significance of the color she was wearing to finally seep through, even though I'd felt the first stirrings of dread deep within from the moment I'd seen Kor.

But when Kor draped her arm over his....

It hit me like a blow to the stomach.

"Sarah," I said numbly. I was a bit surprised my voice wasn't breathless from the combination of hot longing and icy jealousy inside me. "You're...going with Kor."

"His idea," she said, losing some of that intoxicating confidence for a moment as her eyes dropped from mine. "Said he was part of the disguise."

"Well, obviously, she can't go with you, Ben," Kor said innocently. "Even *if* you could have someone accompany you. But no one is going to be looking for Sarah with me. And this way, all the guards that will accompany us will look like they're guarding me."

It made sense. Too much sense. Too much torched....

Svyer approached me and put a comforting hand on my arm. *It's going to be alright, Ben. This honestly wasn't her idea.*

It didn't matter. She could have said no. The woman that had stepped out of that room would have had the confidence to say no...if she had truly wanted to.

I turned and walked away. Not even caring if any of the others followed.

I...had a torched job to do.

I PERFORMED MY PART at the feast perhaps better than I had ever before—mostly because I was too numb to feel my usual self-consciousness. I took my place at the high table next to the Lady Starkissed and the Olsdak governor, endured the speeches, raised my glass politely when I was supposed to (if with only a slight delay each time), and stood and delivered my own speech (which Kor had written for me and given me to memorize that afternoon) with unusual composure. I was, for the first time, their perfect showpiece.

Turns out it's not hard to be if *everything* you do is a show.

I tried my absolute hardest to not let my gaze drift to Sarah and Kor, seated at one of the slightly lower tables that were on either side of the high table. And, mostly, I managed, probably so that anyone watching thought nothing of it.

But Flame help me....

I could always *see* her, in my mind's eye, seemingly shining brighter than ever. And seeing her...but not being the one beside her...was slowly killing me.

My only comfort, such as it was, was that every time I looked, Sarah seemed miserable. Not in a way that anyone who didn't know her would notice, but the light that had been there in the garden, and when she had stepped out of her room, had gone out. And none of Kor's best efforts at being a charming escort seemed to rekindle it.

But even that comfort was hollow—monstrous. Sarah should be happy. I should *want* her to be happy. I should *want* her to be enjoying this evening, as much of it as she could while she could. With any luck, this would be our last night in Olsdak, and I would be dragging her on to face ever greater danger with each passing day.

She deserved to be happy. She deserved to have what she wanted.

Even...

...if that was Kor.

I wrestled the entire time with myself, feeling like I were fighting inner demons twice my size and strength. But, once the feast had progressed far enough that guests at the high tables began moving about and leaving, I knew I had to make things right, before Kor could slip away with her to do their search.

Are you...alright? I asked her silently.

Because I was discreetly watching—leaning back in my chair, holding my wine glass, and looking vaguely in her direction as if contemplating the troubles of the Realms—I saw her start and glance quickly at me.

No, she said with surprising frankness. *Are...you?*

I've...been better, I said carefully. A lot better.

You don't look it, she said doubtfully.

That made me blink. I took a sip of my wine to hide my surprise. *What do I look like?*

Regal, she said, without hesitation. *I don't know if I've ever seen you look more like a king.*

Oh, I said in surprise. It was all I could think to say.

Well...becoming as kingly as my father was easier than I had expected. All I had to do was quench my flameheart.

After a pause, she said shyly, *You...look good in black.*

I couldn't help a quick glance down at my mandated apparel, the same sort of thing the Starkissed insisted on every year, albeit with whatever twist their tailors came up with. Black was the main color, always, and so that was the color of the trousers; dyed, knee-high leather boots; and high-collared shirt. They'd worked in the gold this year with a metallic weave of a golden draká twisting around my vest and a black cape with gold lining only barely attached at the centers of my shoulders—no doubt meant to evoke wings.

I had felt more than ridiculous when they put me in it, as usual. But Sarah...liked it? Thought I looked...regal?

Was she really supposed to be...complimenting me right now?

I didn't know what to say, and so silence fell between us for a few moments. She broke it this time, her voice heartrendingly soft. *Am I...forgiven?*

I started. *You have nothing to be forgiven for.*

Even my flameheart knew that. My suffering was all my own doing.

Don't give me that, Sarah snapped. Then her voice saddened. *I hurt you. I saw that, but only after it was too late. I didn't realize how much this would mean to you, when it means so little to me. I'm...I'm sorry.*

The fact that she was wearing Kor's colors...sitting with him at the opening Moonfair feast...meant *little* to her?

Of course, I groaned to myself. *I...am an idiot.*

Sarah wouldn't have understood what Kor had meant by the offer. He would have been persuasive, just talking about it being a disguise, downplaying any other significance. She really had no idea how this would look to me or everyone else here.

That doesn't matter, I told myself with clenched teeth, wrestling desperately with my hope before it could choke me.

Just because she was Earthren and didn't realize the significance of her actions did *not* mean she didn't at least prefer Kor over...anyone else.

I took deep, calming breaths, desperately glad that my seatmates had already left me to mingle. Even Kor was nudging and murmuring to Sarah, no doubt telling her that now was the time for them to leave. But Sarah was frowning and shaking her head subtly at him, always returning her gaze to me.

Waiting, I realized, for my answer.

I summoned every ounce of willpower I had to answer her with gentleness. As a brother, or a friend might. *Sarah...you deserve whatever you want. And if that's....*

Flame help me.

I couldn't say it.

For Flame's sake, Sarah snapped. *I don't want torching Kor. I never have, and I never will.*

At first, I was stunned just by hearing the epithets in my language mingling with the words of her own.

And then the meaning, and the vehement honesty undergirding them, finally sunk in.

It was like a boulder, half fire, half ice, had been slowly crushing my chest and putting out my flameheart, and suddenly it was...gone.

Instead, I had to wrestle to contain the hope that was rising up underneath instead.

Then why don't you tell him no?

Because...because...because I don't know! But I promise, the next time he tries anything, I'll tell him to torch it. I swear, Ben. This...whatever this is, it ends now.

People were approaching Kor, some relatives of his, curious looks on their faces—no doubt interested in meeting this strange girl who had shown up with him. Kor seemed to be communicating that urgently to her, because she finally listened to him, and when she looked back at me, her face was regretful.

Gotta go.

Kor pulled her to her feet and began subtly but swiftly guiding her through the crowds, and their guards—both the armored ones and the ones dressed as revelers—followed.

We can talk more about this later, Sarah said quickly. *Just...for now, know that I'm sorry, and this stuff with Kor won't happen again. I promise.*

I watched her until she was out of sight, and then I watched her star far longer than I should have after that.

She didn't need to make such promises to me. But she did. She hadn't needed to be miserable at the thought of hurting me, but she had. She shouldn't have complimented me, but she did.

Belatedly, I remembered her smile after she came out of her room and first met my eyes. How those warm browns had turned to silver for just a moment, and her dark red lips had curled in invitation.

Just for me.

She didn't want Kor.

But perhaps...she might want me.

CHAPTER THIRTY-EIGHT

JINX

SARAH

"So, WHERE ARE WE searching first?" I said brusquely. With my apology to Ben given and his forgiveness pending, I was all about getting this back down to business. And getting somewhere where I could jerk my arm out of Kor's.

But for the moment, he kept it firmly clamped down on his arm with his free hand, all the while smiling and nodding casually to everyone we passed in the corridors outside the feast hall.

"It's only just sunset. You sure you don't want to take a tour through the Moonmarket?" Kor said innocently. "Or the conservatory? It's breathtaking this time of...."

My glare finally silenced him. He sighed.

Sarah, try just a bit harder to pretend you are at least tolerating *my presence. Or people are going to suspect you are with me for ulterior reasons.*

I plastered a sweet smile on my face, comforting myself that it would make the words I spoke through my teeth all the more disconcerting.

Now that we were finally out of earshot of our tablemates, I hissed, "You *knew* this little escort business would upset Ben so much, didn't you?"

Kor snorted. "Of course I did. I'm not an idiot. Even though he is."

"Why? What does it mean?"

What did you persuade me to do to him? I thought with gritted teeth. But still, now more than ever, I refused to communicate silently to him.

He smirked at me. *Some beautiful young woman, wearing my colors and going with me, as high-ranking as I am, to the Moonfair? Why, dear Sarah...that's just one small step shy of an engagement. You have no idea the gossip we've just started.*

He seemed to contemplate that last bit with relish.

I stared at him.

Then breathed, "I am going...to kill you."

"But don't you see?" Kor said innocently out loud.

Then silently added, *That's what makes the disguise so perfect. Everyone knows the Moontouched Earthren is associated with Ben. So who this exotic, lovely stranger is that is tied so closely to me, they have no idea. I've just made you an entirely separate puzzle in their minds.*

I smiled pleasantly as we passed a couple of Starkissed who did, indeed, openly stare with curiosity. But no suspicion.

Keeping my smile, I muttered to Kor, "I don't torching care what the logic is. You knew it would hurt Ben."

I thought, *And you did it anyway—without explanation, in a way that was bound to make him assume the worst. For....*

"For his own good," Kor said, smile fading. "You know why, Sarah."

"No, no I don't. This line, you never should have crossed," I said flatly, glad we were getting far enough away from the crowds that only our guards were to be seen for the moment. "You will stop using me as a weapon against Ben *now*. In fact, you will stop hurting and endangering him 'for his own good' altogether. Or so help me, Kor...."

His face and eyes were completely serious now. "Or what?"

I set my face to flint. "I will tell him that there's a danger to him that you're hiding from him."

Kor's eyes widened, and he inhaled sharply.

Then his eyes narrowed. "What...did Svyer tell you?"

I clenched my jaw. "I don't know how much of it is true. She clearly has some beef with you that I frankly tried hard not to let color my perception of you. But you're not helping your case, Kor."

There had been no one around except the guards for a minute or two now, and even they were keeping a respectful distance to let us sort out our little—gracious, from their stiff, professional looks, you'd think we were having a lovers' spat.

Kor must have felt confident enough that trend would continue, because he stopped me and grabbed me by the shoulders. "What did she tell you, Sarah?"

The endangerment to Ben part hadn't even come from my conversation with Svyer. But I wasn't about to tell Kor that I apparently had the ability to eavesdrop on him.

I looked him in the eye. "She said you would do anything for power. That you betrayed your own brother for it."

Kor stilled. His hands dropped. For the first time, he looked...utterly defenseless.

"Interesting," he whispered.

"Is that true?" I demanded.

His lips twitched in a humorless smile, as brief as a snowflake. "True enough. Yes. *Everyone* knows that."

I just stared at him, not knowing what to say next. He hadn't denied it. And apparently what I'd thought of as a deep, dark secret was common knowledge.

So...what happened now?

The shutters over his vulnerability slowly closed. "What else did she say? I highly doubt she slandered my name with just the truth."

"Er...."

I was doubting myself and Svyer's objectivity again. Besides, even if the rest of it *were* true, confessing even vague knowledge of his plotting to his face wasn't exactly the smartest idea. Particularly with so few people around.

Even with all those guards.... Kor might just be dangerous enough to take them on.

And he was standing awfully close.

Kor's face softened, his voice becoming gentle, persuasive. "Sarah, I know it is hard, that it feels like you are betraying a friend by telling me, but this is more important than you know. If she is trying to turn you against me.... I need to know what she said to you. *Everything* she said to you. For her own good."

Big mistake.

I hardened again. "There you go again, thinking you know best. You know you can't always—"

I cut off as I felt it grow—a pull.

"Sarah?" Kor said urgently.

I looked down the hall. It wasn't the direction we had come from; it was ahead. But just to be sure....

"Kor, where is Ben supposed to be right now?"

"Mingling with the feasters, then making his way through the Moon-market to the pageant location to get ready," he said impatiently. "Why?"

I pointed. "In that direction?"

"No," Kor said slowly, pointing back the way we had come. "That way."

"Well," I said simply, keeping my finger up. "That's a promising start to the evening. I may have just found our moongate."

OF COURSE IT COULDN'T have been *that* easy. After following the pull's direction as best as we could, we still were searching for a long, frustrating half-deken.

A very uncomfortable half-deken for me and for our guards when any-one passed by, because, for an excuse as to why Kor and I were wandering scarcely populated corridors alone together, Kor would usually give them something to gossip about later.

His methods seemed to depend on the range of interest of the passerby, with the least interested just seeing him whispering sweet nothings in my ear to the most curious woman getting a glimpse of him pressing me into a nook for a very convincing fake make-out session, complete with his body fully against mine and his hands and lips at my throat.

After that person left, I shoved Kor away and glared daggers at him. "Never. Do. That. Again."

"It was completely necessary, trust me," Kor said. "That was my second-great-aunt. If I hadn't been extremely occupied, she would have stopped to interrogate us about the date for the heartbinding, and not taken no for an answer until we gave her one. Now you tell me: which would *you* have rather endured?"

He had me there. Torch him.

Of course, I wouldn't have had to choose between fake make-outs or great-aunt interrogations if it weren't for his fully conscious decision to get us into this mess.

If I didn't know better, I would have said he was *enjoying* this. It almost made me think there was something to Svyer's last, wildest accusation about him plotting to become my consort.

"I...hate you," I said flatly, and stormed off to try another direction. And our long-suffering guards followed.

I didn't know which guard reactions were the worst: the one who looked as if he would rather have been given *any* other assignment tonight, the two who had completely bland looks, or the three who were openly amused.

"You know," I said at one point, looking sidelong at Kor. "There's an easy solution to our puzzle. I could just surge to the gate."

"You could," Kor said grimly. "And if we get desperate, we can try that. But it's not ideal."

"Why?" I demanded.

"Think, Sarah. That wouldn't tell us where the gate *is*. And to get back to us, you would have to go through it again, and who knows what might be lying in wait for you on the other side."

"Oh. Right."

"At the very least, we would hardly be better off than we started, because you most likely wouldn't be able to describe to us where you are or how to get to you."

"Right," I said with a sigh.

Why did he always have to be so dang right?

About...not-people things.

At long last, at one dead end, my hands brushed something that began to glow, and the more I rubbed the wall over, as if wiping away nonexistent dust, the more lines glowed white, until finally a small door with a white tree was revealed.

"Yes," I breathed, and I pressed my hand into the door.

It swung open, revealing a small, dark corridor.

I was about to step inside when Kor held out an arm to bar my way.

"Let me go first," he said grimly. Then, without waiting for permission, he began walking cautiously down the corridor.

I shrugged. At this point, I was more than happy to let him spring any traps that might be waiting for us. In fact, I was hoping that my future-telling Moontouched ancestors had left a special surprise just for him.

No such luck. We walked down the corridor without incident and came into a plain, square room, and at the far end of it...

...was the gate, white lines glowing in the stone, with a white tree on its surface.

"Yes!" I cried, pumping my fist.

"That's a *gate*?" I heard one of the guards behind us murmur as they filed into the room behind Kor and me.

"It is indeed." Kor answered the rhetorical question with a wide, triumphant grin, his eyes never leaving the moongate.

Except to look at me, sharing in this moment.

And for that moment, just that moment, I trusted him. And forgave him. After seeing that same relief and joy that I felt in his own eyes....

How could I not?

I approached the doors and put my hands on them. They took my power from me and, once I backed up, opened slowly, revealing the curtain of ice and the Inner Rim of my hold beyond.

"We did it," I breathed.

And with surprisingly little danger and drama, too, I thought in bemusement.

Of course, even in my thoughts....

I had to jinx us.

"We did indeed," Kor said lightly. "And just in time, too."

I looked at him in surprise. "What do you mean?"

He smirked. "You wanted to see Ben in the pageant, right?"

"Yeees?" I said, but suddenly, seeing the way he was looking at me...I was no longer so sure.

He hooked his arm in mine and winked. "Then close those doors of yours, and let's go."

Chapter Thirty-Nine

M⚭NDAUGHTER

Sarah

I EXPECTED THE PAGEANT to be in some kind of central square. But Kor led me to an imposing stone façade, all marble pillars and fantastic carvings, where people were slowly filing in through various doors along the first level.

Of course, Kor skipped the lines and went straight to the front, where Yvera waited, looking none too patient.

"Finally," she grumbled. "The torched thing is about to start, Kor."

"Sorry for the delay, dear rightwing, but we had a quite unexpected early success," Kor said, smiling brilliantly.

Yvera stared at him, then at me. "You're kidding."

"Nope!" I said, grinning widely. "We did it!"

Right now, I was at peace with the entire worlds. In this moment, I could have hugged even Yvera.

But I restrained myself. Barely.

"Well," Yvera said with a slow smile. "That's going to make Ben happy."

She smirked behind her. "When he's free for us to talk to him, that is."

"Speaking of which, Yv, you'd better get Sarah into position," Kor said, pushing me at her.

"Alright, alright," Yvera grumbled, waving at me to follow her as she turned. "But you owe me for this, Kor. Big time."

"He owes you for what?" I asked as I hurried to follow her.

"For taking over hatchsitting you," Yvera muttered.

She took us to the head of a particular line, and when the usher at the door looked at her and me curiously, Yvera just snapped, "Crown business," and marched right in.

Sorry, I mouthed at him as I rushed after her.

She led me through a richly carpeted and decorated hall and down a few flights of stairs. Something nagged at me about the trickle of other attendees who were also making their way down, until I realized that all of us were young women, and all of us were being waved along by the ushers to the lowest level, past the doors at every landing.

Did theaters have segregated seating here? Seemed rather odd, when so many other things about dramá culture appeared, at least on the surface, to be equitable between the sexes—and so unapologetic about bodies and interests in each other's.

We all eventually spilled out into an open area. Upon looking around, I discovered it was the ground level of a massive theater—quite nearly the size of a stadium cut cleanly in half. Also like a stadium, this floor was without seats, even though everyone else on the upper levels at least had benches, and in the balconies, comfy chairs. It was like we were in the mosh pit at a concert, but that struck me as absurd. Surely it wasn't *that* kind of event. And besides, all the girls were dressed to the nines, were as collectively perfumed as a florist's shop, and were standing around in huddles and giggling, like belles at some kind of dimly lit ball.

"Come on," Yvera grunted, making her way through the crowds of young women toward the back.

"Yv," I said slowly as I followed, examining all the young ladies around me, and then at the completely unsegregated mix of genders and ages above.

"You wanted to be here," Yvera snapped over her shoulder. "So come on. Kor said we need to find a place near the center, but at the very back, so Ben doesn't spot you too soon."

Too soon?

Just as we reached our position against the curved concrete barrier, the horrible realization of what all of us on the ground floor had in common finally hit me: all of us were female...and around Ben's age, give or take five years...and, judging from the complete lack of earrings...single.

Suddenly, all the pieces clicked. Ben's excruciating discomfort with this whole ordeal. His reluctance to have me here. Kor's *eagerness* for me to be here.

Kor's "forgetfulness" in describing either the plot of the play...or the fact that Ben might not have a co-star.

Yet.

Just then, all the lights went out, and all conversation ceased.

For a single moment, the only sound I could hear was my rapidly beating heart.

How could I have stage fright...*when I wasn't even on the stage?*

Yet, a voice whispered.

Lights began dancing on the giant paper screen spanning the upper half of the entire stage. They came from seemingly nowhere—no spotlight, no projector. Besides, even without that clue, I could feel the stirrings of power that told me the light show was entirely and literally...magical.

Starkissed, the most magically powerful and dramatic of all the clans...knew how to create a spectacle.

But it was a breathtaking one that soon had even my jaw dropping and forgetting where I was and what could be coming.

Galaxies spun across that canvas as a beautiful, haunting music started filling the theater, seemingly coming from nowhere and everywhere at once. Shooting stars streaked, suns were born and explosively died, worlds were formed and destroyed. The glory of it went on for at least a minute as we all stood or sat there enraptured.

A single solar system finally settled into view: a massive sun taking up the left third of the screen, and a planet with broad swaths of desert that I was beginning to recognize, with two moons orbiting it.

Then, a deep, beautiful female voice murmured. Just as the music did, the voice seemed to come from everywhere at once.

Once, many, many years ago, there were two moons over Ythra.

The focus zoomed in on the planet and its moons.

But despite their combined light, and the light of Kaldrir, darkness threatened.

Shadows began creeping over the planet's equator, reaching beyond where they should be, into the sun's light.

The perspective drew rapidly in. Here, the realism faded to vague, swirling impressions of a desert landscape and sketches of figures on it, their movements violent and forceful. Black-clad live actors came onto the stage and began fighting, showing a battle of some kind that was only marginally illuminated by the light from the screen.

For the first time since its invasion and the swearing of the Covenants, the Devourer returned.

I inhaled sharply. And it was *not* the dramatic gasp of mock horror that the audience was giving out.

My fear was real.

Especially when I saw that vague, hulking shadow rise on the right side of the screen, pressing on its actors on the stage below.

The Golden King and Heir fought with all their might.

One black-clad actor whose form I recognized emerged from the dark, orchestrated chaos. Despite the scant illumination, his height and the occasional gold glimmers of his uncovered hair, his clothing, and his cloak lining made him unmistakable.

At least this part Ben seemed somewhat comfortable with: he had something vaguely recognizable as a sword in his hand and was trading stiff blows with a shadowy, all-black, cloaked and masked "monster."

But despite the best they could give, the Devourer was winning.

The hulking shadow on the screen moved forward, and as it did, its army below did as well, and Ben and his warriors gave ground.

When the night came, the moons above wept in despair for how little they could do to help the Tree's children.

The sky above the desert darkened, and the moons appeared. The hulking shadow moved forward even more, and warriors around Ben were collapsing left and right, letting out gurgling cries and thrashing in dramatic death throes. Meanwhile, Ben just kept stolidly fighting on.

The smallest and youngest moon felt keenly for the brave Heir, so she begged the Creators for the ability to help him. And They heard her cry.

I felt a tremor of trepidation.

For one night... They gave her mortality.

The smallest moon became even smaller and began sinking. Not *beyond* the horizon of the desert...but onto it.

And sent her down...to walk among us.

Just before the moon touched the ground in the small space between the fighting sides...she became vaguely human. Female.

In the real-life parallel, on the stage below, a white orb of light appeared between Ben and his monster, fully illuminating them both for the first time.

Ben looked properly grim. The monster's expression wasn't visible behind its grotesque black mask, but it recoiled as if in pain or fear.

Though she was mortal, with all her power concentrated in her small form, the moon sent out a burst of light that gave the defenders strength and drove back the darkness.

Indeed, a white flash filled the whole theater, momentarily blinding me.

Her selfless act of heroism saved our Realms that night...but cost her mortal life.

On the screen, the white female figure collapsed into a golden one. On the stage, Ben awkwardly caught a suddenly convenient young woman in a dark, flowing dress and kneeled down with her in his arms, while all other actors departed, leaving them alone.

I felt a wash of relief and jealousy at the same time. Maybe I'd read way too much into things and audience participation wouldn't be required, after all. But man.... Did that actress *have* to splay herself *all* over him, so dramatically?

The Heir, having fallen in love with her the moment he saw her, wept over her.

Ben...just kneeled there. Even with only his shadowy form visible, he somehow managed to look distinctly uncomfortable, and he held the limp girl and her contrarily clingy arms as far from him as was possible. I suddenly felt much better.

He begged the Creators to restore her, but They could not. Her moonform had perished, and vanished even as he held her.

The on-screen version of the moon girl disappeared into a bunch of white sparkles. The onstage actress was carefully pulled away, back into the darkness, by other black-clad fellows until she was out of sight. Ben's shoulders visibly sunk with relief.

Then the screen went black, the theater went dark, and the music fell silent for one long moment, as if that were the end.

Then the narrator's voice spoke in the darkness.

But...the Creators, moved by the moon's heroism and the Heir's love, said that there was one thing They could do.

On the screen, the white figure appeared again, floating in the center.

They took her spirit and, in concert with the Tree, gave it new form in the birth of one of Her children.

The figure became a white blur, going into the body of a vaguely sketched infant, who suddenly moved and squalled soundlessly. Then the screen went black again.

They told the Heir that if he was patient, and searched diligently, then he would one day find her.

I felt a sudden chill.

A light appeared on the stage. This time, not a bodyless orb, but a glowing crystalline sphere about the size of an orange, with hundreds of facets. It was carried by the black-dressed woman, but perhaps by some magic, the crystal didn't illuminate any part of her but her hands and only enough of the rest of her to recognize a skirt.

Whereas it illuminated Ben just fine, showing him slowly stand and look at the light coming toward him. He didn't look nearly as awed or hopeful as he was supposed to. In fact...he looked like he was trying very hard not to be sick.

So that he would know who she was when he found her, they gave him the Moonstar.

The woman handed him the glowing crystal, which he took stoically with both hands, and she swiftly retreated.

They told him to wait until eighteen years from the day of the battle. Then on that night, when the lone remaining moon rose, he was to throw the Moonstar to the heavens and follow where it went. The one the Moonstar fell on, They said, would be his beloved, and from that moment on, they would be one.

My heart went into full-blown panic mode, and an entire kaleidoscope of butterflies exploded into being in my stomach.

Because, of course, Ben took a visible, deep breath...and threw the crystal up into the air.

It didn't come back down—not like any normal flung object should. It just hovered there for one eternal second in the otherwise absolute darkness of the theater.

Then it began to slowly float down. Toward all the young women waiting on the ground.

No, no, no, nooo....

Surely it wouldn't come for me, right? I was all the way in the back, and pressing myself as far up against the stone barrier as I could for good measure. Surely this was some kind of lottery thing. Random chance. And chances were good that it would find somebody else before it got to me. Right?

Right?

But it just kept floating, back and back and back, down and down, making the young women part in its wake....

Kor, I thought savagely. *If you have rigged this, I am going to kill you. For real this time.*

To my horror, he replied with a laughing inner voice, which meant I hadn't just thought the words. I'd sent them.

I'm flattered that you think I could interfere with the Moonstar, dear Sarah. But I must inform you that this is all on you. It seeks...connection.

Connection.

Authentic...connection, Ben had said, when he was describing the pageant for the first time. The Starkissed, romantics that they were, were obsessed with finding someone he could feel an authentic connection to.

Could...or *already did.*

And so the crystal floated all the way back...to hover in front of me.

I looked up from it in absolute horror...to see an aisle of disappointed, confused, and curious young women. And, beyond and above them all, frozen on the stage, Ben.

Who looked just as horrified as I felt.

Everything was still for another breathless moment.

Yvera interrupted my stupor of terror with a snap. *You're supposed to take it, you dimtorch.*

Not knowing what else to do, hoping it would end this moment, I reached out and took the floating crystal. It suddenly became heavy in my hands, and I nearly dropped it.

Nobody moved. No lights came on, no one spoke.

Nothing happened to end this.

Go on, Yvera growled. *You walk to him, he walks to you.*

I sent her one look of pure terror, but her eyes were merciless flints as she looked back at me. *Do you want him or not?*

What kind of relevance did that question have *now*?

As if I'd given her the truth, she said coldly, *Well, then. Go get him.*

Seeing no other choice, I looked back at Ben...and slowly put one foot in front of the other. And Ben, matching the pace of my footsteps...began making his way to me. First crossing the stage, then walking, step by slow step, down the stairs to the ground floor.

You're already in the spotlight, Kor whispered. *So why not really make them stare?*

I gritted my teeth. *I don't know what you're talking about.*

Your dress? Ring a gong?

My...dress.

Kor had planned...this entire night. Up to this very moment.

I was truly going to kill him. If I didn't die from mortification first.

But...if I was going to die anyway....

Eskala's voice, just a memory this time, echoed in my mind. *It's a hard, hard thing to do, to rule with vulnerability. But the alternative is even harder. And far crueler.*

If I was going to die for them anyway...it might as well be while giving them hope.

I touched the magic lying latent in the dress...and let it awake.

As I began to glow, the young women around me gasped and drew back hastily, forming an even wider bubble in my aisle. And they weren't the only ones. Gasps and murmurs broke out across the theater. Even Ben froze for a moment in alarm as my dark blue dress...

...changed to pure, *glowing* white, making me shine like a spotlight in that dark theater. The heavy folds of the skirt broke apart into gauzy, effervescent layers that billowed mystically around me as I moved, and I felt air touch my sweaty back as the back panel split apart and peeled away. From the tugs now at my shoulders, I assumed more wisps of my dress were now floating behind me like gossamer fairy wings. From the halo of light I was now seeing around my head, it seemed even the gems that studded my hair were now glowing brightly.

I could not have looked more the part of the moon girl if I had wanted, tried out, and rehearsed for it.

And now one word was on everyone's lips, being repeated over and over. *Moontouched. Moontouched. Moontouched.*

This was what Eskala had meant. This was the moment she and the King had asked of me, to do my duty by the people. To compromise my need for more time for my choice with the people's need for hope. I had just told them who I was...without so much as saying the word.

Hiding in plain sight.

Ben resumed walking toward me and went a tad faster to make up for the lost time. The horror hadn't left his expression entirely, but it now warred with awe, and the awe was stronger.

Ben...was in awe of me.

Maybe...*just* maybe...this was just the *teensiest* bit worth it, for that.

We met in the center of that space. And, oh, look at that, there was a silver *star* inlaid in the floor there, marking the spot. And a pedestal just to the side, with the perfect-sized indent for the orb. Thinking I could figure this one out, I placed the orb carefully into the slot.

Then Ben and I stood on either side of the star, for a moment just staring at each other. It seemed we both were beyond blushing at this point.

What...happens now? I asked him.

He slowly got down on one knee, so his head was just below mine.

What do you think? he said faintly, reaching up to cup my cheek.

Right. Of course. This was a romance. What else? I truly wasn't thinking straight.

And now, for yet another reason.

I think...we kiss? Even my mental voice sounded breathless.

He nodded almost imperceptibly, his eyes searching. Pleading.

Is that...alright?

I nodded back. But when he still hesitated, I couldn't take it anymore. The pull from him became too much.

I threw my arms around him, digging my fingers at *long last* into that golden hair, and pressed my lips to his.

He only froze for one half of a second. Then he inhaled sharply and crushed my body to his, one hand capturing my bare back, the other my head, his fingers threading through my hair, heedless of the pins that went flying and curls that went tumbling. He moaned against my lips and wrapped his arms even tighter. We explored each other's mouths with abandon, completely and utterly forgetting the world around us in the exquisite release, in the feel, in the taste.

One of my only conscious thoughts was, *Funny—I thought his beard would be scratchy.*

But it wasn't. *His*, at least, was soft. And I found I loved the added sensation—a hundred more brushes of him against me than skin alone could have given.

The pull from him *thrummed* between us, binding me to him more closely than ever before. I felt as if I could sink into him, become a part of him.

I almost tried.

Then I felt a tugging. And a voice breaking through the fever in my mind. *Alright, that's enough, you two.*

Preservative instinct honed after days of fearing that voice catching me in this very sort of act made me freeze.

Then the roaring and clapping finally broke through, too. I blinked my eyes open and saw dazedly that all the lights had come on, and everyone around us was cheering as they tried to peer around the guards circling us. And Yvera was beside us, trying hard to pry us apart without looking like she was trying too hard.

"Ben," I mumbled against his lips.

"What?" he said, capturing my mouth again. He hadn't even opened his eyes yet.

Ben!

That finally made him blink and pull back. That was all Yvera needed to push him the rest of the way and to his feet.

Ben, she said to him as she did, but she included me in the message. *People are coming down. We can't hold them back much longer. They're going to swarm Sarah.*

He blinked rapidly, shaking his head. *Right. Right.*

Then, finally coming to, he threw his arm around me and hurried me toward a side exit, where other members of the guard waited and ushered us swiftly through before closing the door behind us.

Kor ran up to us, panting. "Sarah, can you feel the gate from here?"

I hesitated. If he had asked me a few minutes before, I would have said no. But with the pull from Ben still humming so strongly, I was able to feel another pull as I hadn't before—as if the increased strength of my tie to him strengthened all the others.

I nodded. "I can."

"Surge to it, now," Kor said.

"What?" Ben cried.

"Ben, we *have* to get her out of here. My plan was a bit more successful than even I anticipated." Kor looked back at me. "If you can, do it."

I hugged Ben quickly. "I'll be safe, I promise," I told him. "I'm going straight to the gate and in. And I won't come out until you give the all-clear."

His only reply was to curl his fingers at the back of my neck, duck down, and press his lips fiercely and briefly to mine.

"Go," he said grimly when he pulled apart.

I fixed the feel of his lips, the sight of him standing there, so regal and strong, eyes blazing as he met mine, and then I *reached* and *pulled*.

I didn't even doubt I had enough for this. After not just one but two kisses from Ben like that....

I knew I could do anything.

EPILOGUE

KAVARIAN SUNFILLED, THE DRAKÓN King of the Six Realms, was dying.

And to the young man walking through a nearby tropical copse much later that dark night, that was a glorious thing.

As he contemplated that beautiful truth, at what a deliciously perilous state the Realms were in, he breathed in the fresh sea air that wafted over him, luxuriating in it. It was the air of his birth, but his humanity was too far gone for that to move him now. No, to him, this was the air of his victory...and his vengeance.

And, at last, he had managed to slip away to make the final preparations.

When he finally stepped into the clearing he had previously chosen, his short, midnight-blue curls glistened in the moonlight. He turned his clean-shaven face upward for a moment, feeling the moon, that bright ruler of the night, reluctantly cast her light on him, forced to witness his dark works in silence.

It reminded him soothingly of the young woman that had so narrowly escaped his grasp. For now.

The ever-ravenous darkness inside him seethed, still furious at the necessary change in plans.

Soon, the young man promised it. *Soon, she will be ours. But for now, this is for the better.*

As he had had to tell it so many times that interminable day to placate it.

Now, he focused his thoughts on pleasanter things: setting up the trap that would catch their substitute (and his secretly preferred) prey. It was always so satisfying to bring a well-laid plan to fruition.

He raised his hands grandly, like a conductor about to lead an orchestra. Dark, black power rose inside him, more power than anyone who knew him knew he had. He could make that black power—and his black irises—appear in their former midnight-blue colors when he wished, but why bother with such tedious concealments now, with only the moon as his witness?

He wanted that moon to see this.

He began subtly. After all, he did not want to set off any of the many wards and protections that he knew very well were nearby to catch any trace, if they could, of this kind of magic. And so, he was forced to begin with layer upon subtle layer around him of concealments, which he had secretly refined over the years to defeat them all. First, wards to hide his power. Then to camouflage what he was about to create here from discovery.

At last, after dek upon dek of precautions, he could begin the best part.

He raised his hands again, sending his power deep within the soil, using it as a probe to find the pieces he needed. Then he used it to violently yank each boulder from the earth. They emerged like heathenishly buried corpses (ones not cremated as the dramá considered proper) bursting explosively from their graves. He would fix those deep holes later, but for now, tearing up that clearing like this was far too much fun. The power the darkness gave him made works like these mere child's play.

Even at night. Or rather, *especially* at night.

Balefully, the moon looked on, helpless to stop him as he turned the boulders in the air, setting them down one by one: the two squatter ones for the legs, the longer and flatter one for the top. The resulting construction was crude but satisfyingly so. Still, he made a few adjustments to stabilize that surface. It wouldn't do for his victim to *wobble* while strapped to it, now, would it? That would be quite unprofessional, not to mention potentially distracting the victim from the terror and despair he should be feeling just before his end.

Once the structure was completed to the young man's satisfaction, he began filling it with the darkness inside him, dedicating the altar for its black purpose. The ever-hungry darkness surged into it with pleasure, salivating for the Blood it would drink from it on the morrow.

At last, the young man approached the altar and stroked it.

Soon, Koriben Sunfilled, he thought with relish. *Soon, you will die, as you should have died years ago. But now, your Blood will give us power, and your death will sow chaos in the Realms. Who knows? It might even hasten your beloved father's demise. Then your precious Moontouched queenling will be mine.*

Then you will be King, the darkness whispered to him. *Of not just the Six Realms. Of everything.*

Yes, the young man agreed serenely.

As satisfying as the idea was of finally claiming all that was his, when he was frank with himself, he admitted he craved yet one thing more: vengeance. His blackened heart had always thirsted for power, but now his very blood burned with the desire—no, the *need*—to have his revenge at last against the one who had taken everything from him six years ago.

And that was why this was such a special night.

Enjoy your victory—while it lasts, he thought with savage satisfaction at his true enemy. *For tomorrow, I take it all. Tomorrow, I take everything from you. Everything you have fought and bled for, everything you have cherished, will come crashing down around you.*

And it would be the beginning of the end for the young woman he knew his enemy was coming to love. That was, perhaps, the most satisfying part of it all. How hilariously tragic, how inevitably doomed that love was, even without the dark young man's interference—as his enemy would know well. If anything, that longing despair now would make his enemy's agony all the greater as the young man finally claimed her.

The young man turned his face up to the void that was his birthright, closed his darkly glittering eyes....

And smirked.

Soon.

ABOUT THE AUTHOR

Leah E. Welker graduated from Brigham Young University (Provo) in 2016 with a degree in English language and a minor in editing. She then edited for seven years and pivoted to writing in 2023. She is based in the DC area, where she lives with family and her rescue Australian shepherd, Wes.

You can connect with her at

   https://www.leahewelker.com

Subscribe to her newsletter for updates, cover reveals, dog pics, and more:

   https://www.leahewelker.com/follow